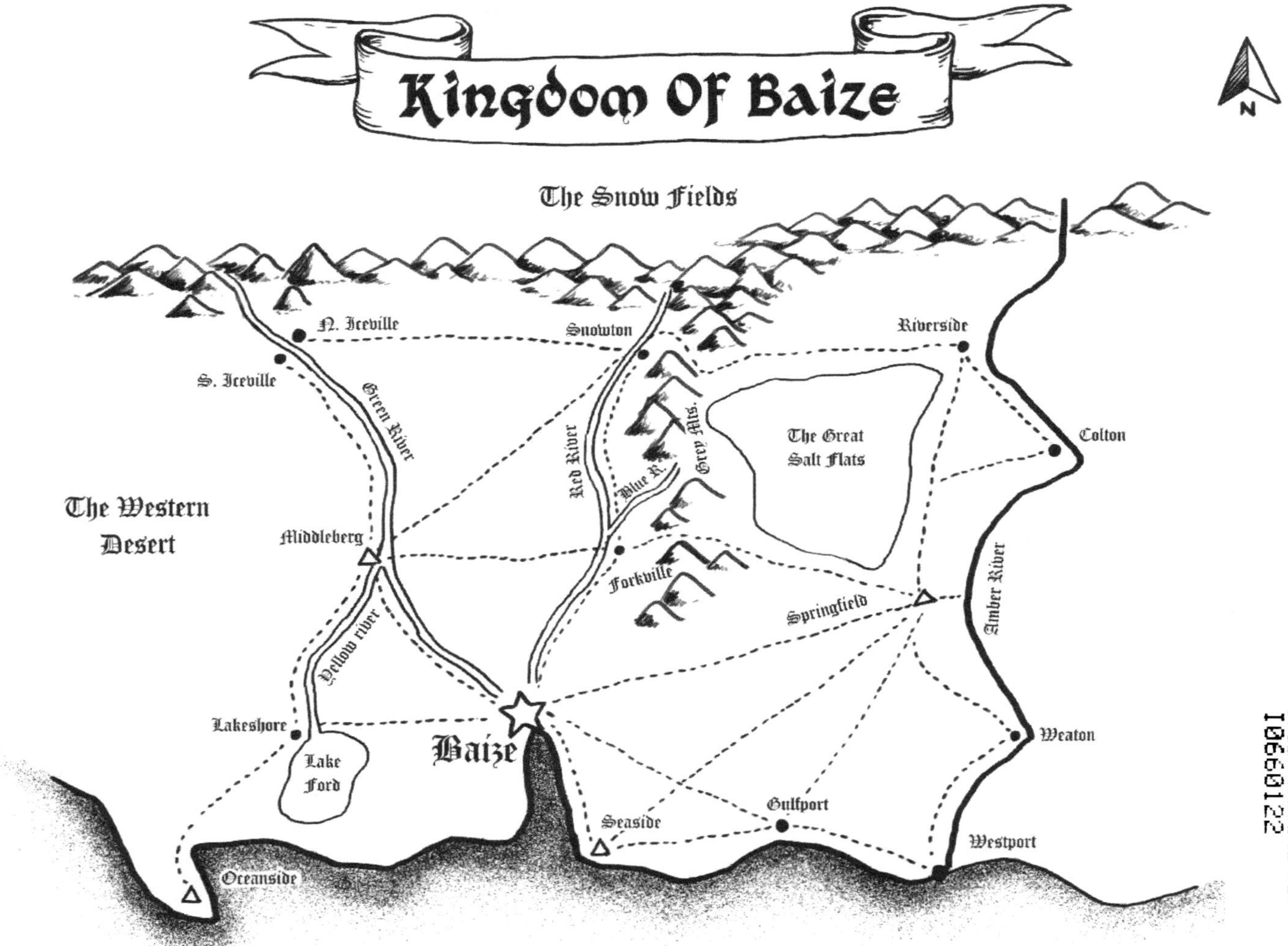
Kingdom Of Baize
N
The Snow Fields
N. Iceville
S. Iceville
Snowton
Riverside
Colton
Green River
Red River
Blue R.
Grey Mts.
The Great
Salt Flats
The Western
Desert
Middleberg
Forkville
Springfield
Amber River
Yellow river
Lakeshore
Lake
Ford
Baize
Weaton
Gulfport
Seaside
Westport
Oceanside

I0660122

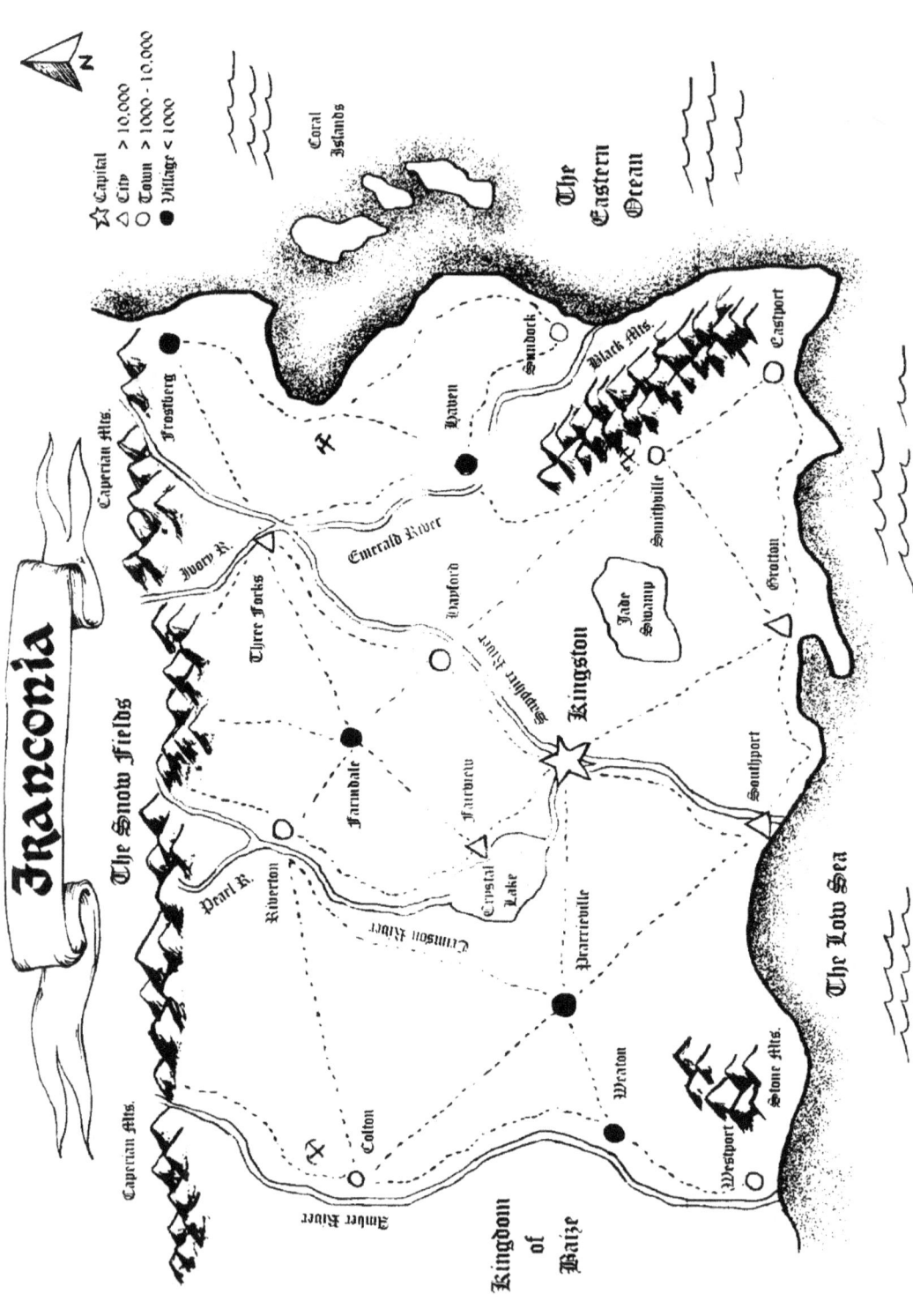

The Valor of Sorcerers

By
Robert Jones

CHARACTERS

Wizards

Mage Edward Francis, *Arms Mage, Royal Expeditionary Force (REF)*
Donovan Francis, *student, Franconian Wizards Academy*
Wizard Victor, *Court Wizard of Franconia*
Wizard Noland, *Headmaster, Franconian Wizards Academy*
Wizard Stuart, *Gatekeeper, Franconian Wizards Academy*
Wizard Toffin, *Serums Instructor, Franconian Wizards Academy*
Wizard Loren, *History and Enhancements Instructor, Franconian Wizards Academy*
Wizard Mira, *Seemings Instructor, Franconian Wizards Academy*
Wizard Dylan, *Forces Instructor, Franconian Wizards Academy*
Wizard Louis, *Court Wizard of Baize*
Wizard James, *Chief of Army Wizardry, Baizian Army*
Wizard Lake, *Chief of Naval Wizardry, Franconian Navy*
Mage Daniel, *Battle Mage, 2nd Franconian Regiment*
Mage Faith, *Southport Regional Mage*
Mage Kathy, *Assistant Court Wizard of Baize*
Mage Elianna, *Headmistress, Middleberg School of Magic, Baize*
Sorcerer Andrew, *Mentor, Franconian Wizards Academy*
Sorcerer Terry, *Mentor, Franconian Wizards Academy*
Sorcerer Curtis, *First Franconian Regiment*

Soldiers

Field Marshall Guzman, *Commander, Franconian Army*
General Diaz, *Commander, Baizian Army*
Admiral Cross, *Admiral of the Fleets, Franconian Royal Navy*
Admiral Vandall, *Commander, Baizian Navy*

Major Gerald, *Commander, REF*
Captain Matthews, *Captain HMS VALOR*
Specialist Dirk, *Assassin, 1st Company, REF*
Specialist Lance, *Assassin, 2nd Company, REF*
Healer Bone, *Healer, 2nd Company, REF*

Civilians

King Henry XI, *King of Franconia*
King Donald, *King of Baize*
Jasmine Onyx, *Franconian Minister of Internal Security*
James, *Owner, Prestige Arms*
Beverly Perrucci, *Sorcerer Andrew's mother*
Bruce, a *recluse who lives near Southport*

Dragons

Ard, *Great Dragon, Gek's grandfather*
Gek, *Great Dragon, Azure's mate*
Cobalt, *Sea Dragon, Gek's Father*
Azure, *Sea Dragon, Gek's mate*
Teal, *Sea Dragon, Chief of the Sea Dragons*
Bliz, Frost, *Snow Dragons*
Jasper, Amber, *Stone Dragons*

TABLE OF CONTENTS

Dedication

For Linda, with love

Acknowledgement

Jesh Ann for the cover design and portraits

Rizky Nugraha for the maps and illustration

About the Author

Robert Jones served in the United States Army for 23 years before retiring. He currently works for the Federal Government. This is his second novel and is the sequel to The Honor of Dragons. He lives in Northern Virginia with his wife and two children.

Foreword

Battle Mage Edward has returned. Now Edward, Wizard Noland, the Headmaster of the Franconian Wizards Academy, and Donovan have to piece together the mystery of who in the Kingdom of Franconia is protecting the dragons and why.

Gek, the Great Dragon, and his Sea Dragon mate, Azure, have just learned that Dragons can transform themselves into humans with magic. Now, they must seek out other Dragon 'Changed Ones' and enlist their help in the coming war with the humans.

Donovan is studying hard and making good progress at the Wizards Academy, but he is unaware that several of his classmates, and even some of his magical instructors, are actually dragon 'Changed Ones,' intent on doing him harm.

King Henry has finally accepted that dragons are not mythical, but he suspects that the neighboring King of Baize has sent the dragons against him in an attempt to conquer Franconia. Donald, the King of Baize, is confused by Henry's aggressive posture and has his own troubles to worry about. The dragons intend to provoke a war between the two human kingdoms, then attack when both are weakened by the struggle. This should be interesting.

Donovan Francis

Chapter One:
LEVEL TWO

Donovan flinched as the fireball raced to engulf him. He quickly poured all his remaining strength into his protective shield that had already been battered and nearly failed him twice. He wiped his brow, clearing his sweat-stained blonde hair from his eyes, and braced himself to repel the approaching fireball. He was exhausted; the Level Two testing had been going on for hours, and he was nearly spent. Donovan's knees wobbled, and a gray fog seemed to roll in, giving him tunnel vision. Realizing that he was on the verge of passing out, the young magician had to reduce the strength of his shield, hoping that he had enough stamina left to survive the attack and still remain conscious.

The testing had begun that morning; first with the History test. Wizard Loren, the auburn-haired, elderly Wizard who taught History and Enhancements, had given him a nearly blank map of the Kingdom of Franconia and asked Donovan to fill in the prominent terrain features, the mountains, rivers, and the Jade Swamp. Then came the population centers, the cities, and the towns that made up the Kingdom. Next, he had to list the Regional Mages that were assigned to the cities and towns. Lastly, he had to outline the Magical Order of Battle for the Royal Guard and Royal Navy, listing each military unit and what level of magician (Wizard, Mage, or Sorcerer) was assigned to each. Wizard Loren informed Donovan that he had two hours to complete his test, and then she turned the oversized hourglass and left the classroom.

While demanding, the History Test had not been particularly difficult for Donovan. His father, Edward, had been a Battle Mage, and his family had traveled extensively during his almost 18 winters of life. His father had been killed a few months ago in a battle with a dragon, and his mother had died under suspicious circumstances a few years earlier, so Donovan was alone except for an elderly aunt and uncle who lived in the southern coastal city of Southport.

After the History Test had come the Serums Exam. The portly Wizard Toffin, with his wild brown hair and ridiculous purple waistcoat, had simply arrived in the Serums classroom and told Donovan that he had precisely 90 minutes to produce three Serums: a sleep Serum, a Serum to produce nausea and a healing Serum that could cure nausea. Normally, concocting any of these Serums was relatively easy; the difficulty was that they each took about 45 minutes to make, so he had to make them simultaneously, which was a much more demanding task. The Serums completed and tested (on himself), Donovan moved to the Enhancements field behind the Wizards Academy stables for his Seemings Examination.

The Seemings Exam was administered by Wizard Mira, a very attractive woman who loved to play pranks on her students with her mastery of illusions, called *Seemings*. The Level Two

Seemings Test, involved the construction of a Seeming of a stationary object (to pass the test to advance to Level Three, the pupil had to produce a moving Seeming). Wizard Mira's instructions were short and to the point: "Donovan, dear, would you please produce a Seeming for me of the magnolia tree in the courtyard?"

While the mature, flowering magnolia tree stood in the center of the Wizards Academy courtyard, and students passed it every day on their way to classes, it was currently out of sight, behind the Academy buildings, so Donovan would have to create an image of it from memory. This was a much more demanding task than Donovan had expected; most Seemings were fairly simple—a rock, a desk, or even a Seeming to make an object invisible. This was by far the most complex Seeming that Donovan had ever attempted. Still, when he was done, he felt that he'd done a respectable job. While Seemings required almost no energy from the magician casting them, the mental strain to produce a Seeming as complex as this was significant. When his Seeming of the Magnolia tree was complete, Wizard Mira had simply smiled, brushed back her long blonde hair, and walked away.

The next test was Forces, which was administered by Wizard Dylan, a thin, middle-aged man with red hair. It started with a version of the hide-and-seek game that all Level One magicians played every evening. Each of Donovan's meager possessions had a Tracer spell on it. The hide-and-seek game was played by all Level One students each evening after dinner. They would take an object from a classmate and hide it (usually inside a Seeming). Once hidden, it was the seeker's task to locate and retrieve the object. To begin his Forces Test, Wizard Dylan asked Donovan to fetch his staff, which Donovan assumed was still in the wardrobe in his room. Donovan hurried across the courtyard to the Level One dormitory only to find his door open and his staff missing. Believing this to be a very poorly timed prank by a classmate, Donovan cast a Tracer spell and began searching for his staff. There were multiple residual echoes of his staff's signature around the Academy, indicating that the staff had been moved to several different places, left in place for a brief period of time, and then moved again.

Rather than rush about the Academy grounds willy-nilly, Donovan sat on the bench beneath the magnolia tree, cleared his mind, and tried to sense the location of the strongest echo of his staff. Surprisingly, he seemed to be sitting on it. After a brief moment of confusion, Donovan ran his hands over the bench, and one of the slats vanished in a flash of light, dispersing the Seeming that had been concealing his staff. He quickly returned to the Forces training area to find Wizard Dylan chatting with Wizard Noland, the Headmaster of the Academy. Wizard Noland was a mountain of a man, easily six and a half feet tall, with a broad chest and arms like a blacksmith's. He was dark-skinned, and his head was shaved bald.

"So soon? I'm impressed, Donovan. It usually takes students much longer to solve that little puzzle, and they usually arrive sweating and out of breath from running about the grounds. Well done!" said Wizard Dylan.

"It was only a simple Tracer spell," grumbled Wizard Noland. "Let's not appoint him High Wizard just yet, shall we?" Without another word, Wizard Noland strode briskly off toward his cottage.

The rest of the Forces Exam was more physically demanding. Donovan had to use the Fire spell to ignite various objects at increasing distances and then extinguish the flames immediately on command. Donovan was thankful that as the distance increased, the objects became increasingly easier to ignite. After Fire and Water came the test of the Dig spell, and Donovan was asked to magically dig holes of various sizes and depths in the rocky soil. After the Dig spell, came the test of his command of the Wind spell; Donovan had to use wind to blow a child's ball through an obstacle course of steel hoops set around the field, erected at different heights above the ground.

Donovan had no problem with the heating portion of the Temperature spell; after all, students had to heat their own shower water each morning, but as expected, Donovan was unable to use magic to cool the water (or any other substance). Donovan was deeply embarrassed by this shortcoming. The Temperature spell was one of the most basic in a magician's arsenal, but Donovan had a mental block that was keeping him from being able to execute the cooling side of the spell. This fact was known by all six Wizards of the Academy faculty, and each had tried to help Donovan overcome his block, but nothing had worked. Donovan knew that in order to pass the test to be promoted to Level Two, he had to demonstrate mastery of at least 12 of the 14 Level One spells, so all was not lost, but there was little room left for error.

When the Forces Test was complete, Donovan headed back over to the Enhancements area for the last of his trials. As he rounded the Academy stables, it began to rain heavily. Not wishing to arrive soaking wet, Donovan cast a large weather shield over himself and proceeded to his last test. As expected, Wizard Loren was waiting for him under an immense weather shield of her own. When Donovan was within ten feet of the Wizard, the rain magically stopped. Wizard Loren closed the distance between them and carefully inspected Donovan's clothes. "Very good. It appears that you cast the weather shield quickly and effectively. So, let us proceed, shall we?" asked Wizard Loren with a smile.

Donovan felt relieved to be nearly finished with this incredibly difficult test. He'd been overly confident in the days leading up to the testing, but this had been much harder than he'd anticipated. He was glad that Wizard Loren, the kindly older woman that he considered his favorite teacher, was responsible for the final phase of his testing.

The first enhancement test was Sight, and it was a simple eye test—well, simple for a magician, maybe. All Donovan had to do was read aloud the notice posted in the Lecture Hall window.

From a quarter of a mile away, Donovan could barely see the window with the naked eye, much less the notice. A quick Sight enhancement spell, successfully executed, and the notice was clear as day. Next came hearing. Wizard Loren asked Donovan to listen carefully and tell her what was going to be served for lunch in the Level One dormitory today. This proved a bit more difficult as there were other noises to filter out: the noise from the stables, the other students as they moved about the Academy grounds, and even the birds seemed to intrude on Donovan's eavesdropping. Once he was finally able to isolate the dormitory kitchen from all the other sounds, it was several minutes before he was able to hear what they were preparing for lunch.

"Lunch today is fried chicken with fried potatoes," Donovan finally answered. Wizard Loren only nodded and proceeded to walk towards the Lecture Hall. Donovan followed closely. Once inside, they proceeded upstairs to the infirmary, where Donovan had to demonstrate his mastery of three Healing spells used to treat minor injuries. While the spells were relatively simple, Healing spells sapped strength from magicians, and performing three in quick succession left Donovan weary. With the last Healing spell complete, Wizard Loren moved quickly down the stairs and across the compound into the Forces Training area. She moved so fast that Donovan had to jog to keep up, and he wondered why they were in such a hurry.

As soon as he crossed the threshold of the Forces Training area, Wizard Loren hurled a fist-sized stone at Donovan. Acting instinctively, Donovan quickly erected a shield, barely getting it in place before the stone bounced harmlessly away. For the next twenty minutes or so, Donovan withstood a furious onslaught of projectiles from Wizard Loren. She started with rocks, which gradually increased in size and speed, then sticks, sand, water, nails, horseshoes, and seemingly anything that was lying around loose in the area. The projectiles came from all sides, even from the top. While physically draining, there wasn't much thought required—just maintain the shield— don't let it fail. Then came the fireball.

Unsure if his weakened shield was sufficient to stop the fire, Donovan shielded his eyes with his right arm as the fireball sped toward him. Incredibly, the fire passed right through his shield without slowing, and Donovan cowered before the flames. When the inferno reached him, it vanished in a flash of light. The fireball had been a Seeming, which, not being real, was unaffected by shields.

"That was a dirty trick," rasped Donovan, rising from his knees and preparing to re-form his shields.

"No, my dear boy," replied Wizard Loren. "That was the final element of your Level Two test. It is designed to see if you can ration your strength. Had you passed out, you would have failed. However, it seems as if you realized the danger just in time. Congratulations."

Sorcerer Andrew, Donovan's assigned Mentor, appeared at his elbow, offering a water bottle. "Here. You need to drink something. I know you're exhausted," said Andrew proudly.

Andrew was about three years older than Donovan and had wavy brown hair.

"Where have you been all day?" asked Donovan, a little crossly.

"I've been at your side since you left your dormitory this morning," said Andrew smugly. "If you hadn't been so preoccupied with the testing, you probably would've sensed me under my Concealment shield."

"Why didn't you say anything?" asked Donovan.

"Mentors are not allowed to assist their wards in any way during testing," answered Wizard Loren. "Mentors are only present so that if a student fails their test, the Mentors know what to work on before the students are tested again."

"I see," said Donovan wearily. "Does this mean I passed?"

In answer to his question, Wizard Noland and the other Wizards of the Academy appeared, standing next to Wizard Loren. Wizard Noland unfurled a roll of parchment and read formally,

"Level One Donovan Francis, pending completion of your final task, you are hereby promoted to Level Two and will report to the appropriate instruction on Firstday morning. Congratulations."

With that, Wizard Noland departed as the other faculty members gathered around Donovan to offer their congratulations and wish him well. Once they had departed, Donovan turned to Sorcerer Andrew and asked. "So now what?"

Andrew grinned. "First, you go to lunch and inform your Level One classmates that you'll be advancing to Level Two. That also means saying goodbye to Evan and paying him any wages due. You will not be seeing him much after today."

Evan was the kitchen boy who had provided wake-up services for Donovan during his six months at the Academy. While most students looked down on the Academy cooks, stable boys, and other servants because they were former students who had failed to advance and had had the spark of magic removed from them, Donovan had taken pity on Evan and had hired him to ensure that he awoke on time each day. Evan returned the favor by warning Donovan about various initiation rituals at the Academy and what to watch out for in different classes. His help had been invaluable, and Donovan was sad to see the relationship end.

Andrew surprised him by entering the Level One dormitory and getting in the lunch line with him, since Mentors normally ate in their own dormitory. Donovan asked what was different about today. Andrew smiled, "The kitchen staff knows when a student is going to be tested for advancement, so they prepare a special lunch for the occasion. If the student fails, it's a small consolation; if they pass, it's a celebration. Mentors only attend celebrations," he said with a wink.

As soon as Andrew entered the kitchen, the other Level One students knew immediately that Donovan had passed his test, and they all came over to congratulate him. Lunch was the best meal he had ever eaten at the Academy.

As he was clearing his plate, Evan approached and said that he was sad to see Donovan go so soon but happy to know that he had done well. Donovan paid Evan a copper for the last week's wages and asked Evan if he knew anyone in the Level Two dormitory who could help him the way Evan had. After considering it for a moment, Evan said that he would recommend Jacob for the job.

"How will I know Jacob when I see him?" asked Donovan.

"He lost his left hand in a training accident as a Level Two," said Evan sadly. "Without it, he couldn't pass the test for advancement."

"I see," said Donovan. "I will certainly take your recommendation. If you ever need anything, I'll still be around."

"Thank you, Donovan. Good luck with your final task," said Evan as he scurried back into the kitchen, wiping his eyes as he went.

"What did he mean by that?" asked Donovan. Andrew smiled.

"The first day you arrived, I told you what your final task as a Level One would be. Have you forgotten?"

Donovan thought for a while; then he remembered Andrew saying that the last thing he would do as a Level One was remove his name from the wooden plaque on his door. As they walked down the hall to his room, Donovan considered how to accomplish this feat. Arriving at his room, Donovan found that all his personal belongings had already been removed and that the sheets, pillow, and blanket were neatly folded and placed in the center of the bed, just as they had been when he arrived at the Academy.

Andrew plopped down in the armless chair, looking very smug, while Donovan considered which spell he could use to wipe his name off the door plate. This wasn't an Enhancement exercise, and he didn't think burning his name off the door was the answer. "I suppose I could use a very shallow Dig spell," Donovan mused, thinking out loud. Andrew yawned.

Sensing that the Dig spell wasn't the answer, Donovan racked his brain for a useful spell. *Healing? Was the wood plaque 'injured'?* When nothing else came to mind, Donovan tried a spell designed to heal cuts and abrasions. Nothing happened. Frustrated, Donovan sat on the bed to think. As he was considering his predicament, Lisa, the youngest of the Level Ones passed by his door and waved shyly. Lisa was a good kid and extremely talented at casting Seemings for someone so young.

Suddenly Donovan had an idea, he rose, walked to the door and slapped his hand on the wooden plaque. The Seeming of his name vanished in a flash of light as Andrew rose from the chair and remarked, "Well, it took you long enough. Let's go find your new room."

Ard

Chapter Two:
THE CHANGED ONES

Their business concluded, the members of the Dragon Council quickly dispersed, each heading home to inform their Clans of the human threat and the audacious plan to deal with it. The Snow Dragons, Frost, and Bliz departed first, quickly flying north, back to the Snow Fields. The Stone Dragons were next, slowly moving west, across the Amber River, their gray scales almost invisible against the night sky.

The Fire Dragons, who would make the opening moves in the offensive against the humans, spent a few minutes in quiet conversation with Victor, the head of their Clan, who had magically taken human form and infiltrated the human ranks, rising to the position of Court Wizard of Franconia. In human form, Victor appeared as a very tall man with flaming red hair and dark eyes. He wore the red robes of the Court Wizard of Franconia. When Victor had finished giving them their instructions, the other Fire Dragons hastily departed before sunrise.

After Victor had issued his orders to his Clan, he walked smoothly over to Ard, the ancient gold, Great Dragon. "I had already agreed to your conditions, old one," Victor said angrily. "The Binding spell was unnecessary and insulting."

Before agreeing to go to war with the humans, Ard had made the other members of the Dragon Council agree to abide by the ancient agreement not to eat humans, and he added a condition that any offspring of Wizard Amanda, a Dragon-Friend of old, would be spared in the coming conflict. Ard had cast a Binding spell on the members of the Dragon Council to ensure that they would hold to these conditions. "Since you broke our last agreement, I decided that it was both necessary and appropriate," said Ard. "At our last council meeting, the Fire and Stone Dragons agreed that the land east of the river was ours and that you and your Clans would remain on the west side. Yet you crossed the river in human form and set us on a path to war with the humans without consulting the other Clans."

"So I did," sneered Victor, "and it is well that I did. Otherwise, this infant and his mother could have caused the ruin of us all!"

"There is no denying that my daughter made mistakes," said Ard gravely. "However, if I heard correctly, the humans were already becoming suspicious about 'sea serpent' sightings along the coast, and our secret might not have lasted for much longer anyway."

"I had it under control," insisted Victor. "Those sightings have already been discounted by the king as the drunken ramblings of a few ignorant, superstitious sailors that had been at sea too long. It was nothing to worry about."

"And maybe it is simply that our numbers have increased sufficiently so that it is no longer possible to hide our existence any longer and that the time for hiding is over," growled Ard.

Despite his rising temper, Victor paused to consider Ard's words. *Maybe the Old Dragon was right; perhaps it was no longer feasible to keep the existence of Dragons a secret. At least a more conciliatory approach might be in order.*

"You may be right," Victor conceded. "Perhaps the time for secrecy is over, or at least nearly over. So, what can the Great Dragon Clan contribute to our cause?"

Ard fell silent, worried about the consequences of telling Victor that, to his knowledge, he and Gek were the last of the Great Dragons. Finally, he replied, "After the 'Great Betrayal,' when so many of our kind were poisoned by the humans, the few surviving Great Dragons scattered far and wide. I honestly do not know where the rest of my Clan may be or what our numbers are today."

"You two are the last of the Great Dragons?" asked Victor, alarmed.

"I did not say that," said Ard cautiously. "I said that I have lost contact with the others of my Clan. There may be other Great Dragons to the south or in the far west; some may have even changed into human form without informing me. I do not get around as much as I did in my youth."

Gek knew that Ard was shading the truth very heavily. To their knowledge, there were no other Great Dragons in the world. The two of them were the last of their Clan. However, Gek had just learned about a Dragon's ability to magically take human form, so there were hopefully some Great Dragons who, like the Fire Dragon, Victor, had changed shape and gone to live among the humans. It was an unsettling thought either way.

"Incredible," said Victor, shaking his head. "I had no idea. Very well, then, my charge to you is to seek out the rest of your Clan, if there are any others, and inform them of our plans to provoke a war between the humans of Franconia and those in Baize. Once we are ready, the Fire and Stone Dragon Clans will begin the effort. The Sea Dragons will also help by attacking Franconian merchant ships that trade with Baize. We will meet here again in council on the first full moon of autumn, four months hence, to discuss our progress and the plans for our attack on the humans."

"If I am still conducting my search, Gek will represent the Great Dragons at that meeting," said Ard.

"If he must. Just know that his words will not carry much weight if he is indeed the last of his Clan and a half-breed at that!" snarled Victor.

"Shall we speak of your parentage, Victor? I am sure I see the grey tint of a Stone Dragon in your scales," said Ard.

"Then your eyesight is failing along with the rest of you," said Victor. "Just make sure that the Great Dragons have a representative here at the appointed time who can speak to your plans of how you can help with our war against the humans." With that, Victor removed his robe, changed back into Dragon form, and flew off into the night.

Gek walked over to Ard and said, "Ard! I am so glad to see you! This is my mate, Azure, and my father, Cobalt. I believe you already know Teal, the Chief of the Sea Dragons."

"Hello, Teal, it is good to see you again," said Ard to the Blue-green Sea Dragon. "I am glad to meet you, Azure. Hello Cobalt, it has been a long time."

"Thank you for taking care of my son," said Cobalt, "I was sorry to learn about Liza."

"Yes," said Ard sadly. "I wish I could have gotten to them sooner. Anyway, I believe it is time to teach these young ones the spell of change."

"Do you think that wise?" asked Teal. "Under normal circumstances, they are both decades too young to learn such a spell."

"I know," said Ard, "but these are hardly normal circumstances. Besides, who else but Gek can go in search of any Great Dragons who have made the change? They would not expose themselves to a Dragon of another Clan."

"You are right, but I am still unsure of the wisdom of this action," said Cobalt.

"What other choice do we have?" asked Ard. The other Dragons thought silently for a few moments, then reluctantly nodded their agreement.

"All right Gek," said Ard, "the spell of changing is 'MORPHIUS,' and the gesture is clapping your hands together. Recite the spell, please, without the gesture."

"MORPHIUS," said Gek.

"Very good. Now, once you add the gesture, think of turning into a human."

"What does a human look like? I have never seen one before," said Gek.

"Actually, you have seen two," said Ard. "The one you wanted to eat the first day we met and just now when you saw Victor in his human form."

"Oh, right," said Gek. "OK, I am ready."

"Proceed, and be ready for a shock," said Ard. "This spell takes a lot of energy from the Dragon that conjures it."

"MORPHIOUS," said Gek, clapping the talons on his forelegs together. Instantly, a tall, blonde-haired boy about 20 winters old appeared where Gek had been standing. The boy toppled forward, but Ard was ready to catch him and keep him from falling hard on the rocky ground.

"Sorry. I forgot to warn you, you need to learn how to walk on just two feet as a human."

Gek shook his head violently, trying to clear it. He staggered over and sat down on a large rock, shivering as if he were cold. "Boy, this is weird," he said. "I miss my wings and my tail! My skin feels naked without my scales. How do I look?"

"Almost good enough to eat," joked Teal, baring his teeth. Gek recoiled at the joke.

"Now, Gek," said Ard, "as a human, you have all of their frailties. You cannot breathe fire or fly, and your skin can be easily punctured. On the plus side, most humans only eat three meals a day, so you will not be hungry all of the time. Behind that tree, you will find some human clothes I brought for you."

"How did you manage to acquire human clothing?" asked Cobalt.

"I was sleeping by a pond one day during my journey here, and a couple of young humans disrobed and laid their clothing on me while they went for a swim in the pond. I simply walked off with them," said Ard mischievously.

"Clever," said Teal. "So, you have an outfit for Azure as well?"

"Well, I have some clothes that belonged to a human female," replied Ard. "But having never met Azure, they may not be a perfect fit."

Gek emerged from behind the tree wearing what looked like a burlap sack with a belt. "Is this really what humans wear? It is itchy and too loose," complained Gek.

"Be glad I found you anything at all," said Ard. "Otherwise, you would have to walk around naked until you acquired some human clothes. The idea is not to draw attention to yourself. Those clothes certainly accomplish that. Also, here is a small bag with some metal discs in it. I believe it is what the humans call 'money.' You will need it to purchase food, shelter, and clothing. There are two silver discs and several brown ones. I have no idea how much each is worth or how you may acquire more, so use it sparingly."

"All right, Azure," said Teal, "it is your turn. Do you remember the spell?"

"Yes, father," replied Azure, the aqua-blue Sea Dragon. "Is the same spell used to return yourself to your true form?"

"An excellent question," said Ard. "Yes. It is the same spell. This is a spell of *change*. Be sure that you do not think of being a bird when you cast the spell, or you will become a bird, or a dog, or a tree, or whatever you are thinking of, and *never* be able to change back to your true form. Do you understand the danger?"

"I could turn myself into a rock?" asked Gek, startled.

"Verily. That is why this spell is so dangerous and why it is not normally taught to young Dragons," said Cobalt.

"Will it work on other humans? Can I turn a human into a rock?" asked Gek.

"Maybe. I have never tried. But I do know that you can turn one inanimate object into another – say, a rock into a tree," said Ard.

"Fantastic!" said Gek.

"Dangerous!" said Ard. "If a human magic-user sees you perform magic, you will be arrested and sent to their wizards academy, where you will be unable to escape until released after several years. Assuming you can pass all of the human's ridiculous tests."

"Could I not simply return to Dragon form and fly away?" asked Gek.

"No. It has been tried. Nor can you burn through the invisible boundary that encircles the school. That has also been tried before," said Ard.

"You seem to know a lot about this," said Teal. "Have you been to this wizards academy yourself?"

"No, I sent one of the Great Dragon Changed Ones into the school long ago to learn what he could. I got intermittent reports from him, until he was unable to pass their test to become a sorcerer. The cruel humans put him to sleep and removed the spark of magic from him. When next I saw him, he was a common laborer, working with a group of humans trying to build a road through the huge swamp east of the mountains," said Ard sadly.

"I thought you said that the sleep spell would not work on a Dragon!" exclaimed Gek.

"Apparently, it does when we are in human form," said Ard. "Anyway, I tried to return Draco to his Dragon form, but without the spark, the spell would not work. He died a human a short time later."

"How sad," said Azure. "Have any Dragons passed the tests at this wizards academy?"

"Yes, several, and there are some at the academy now," said Ard.

"So, we may not be the last of the Great Dragons!" said Gek, excitedly.

"Perhaps not," said Ard, "but the others are locked in the academy, and I do not know when they will be released or if they will be able to pass the tests. Or if they will choose to help us once they are released."

"What does that mean?" asked Azure.

"It means that some of the 'Changed Ones' may decide that they prefer being humans to Dragons. They might enjoy not being hungry all the time, not having to spend every day searching for prey, or worrying about being discovered and attacked. Some of the Changed Ones have even taken human mates and had children with them. This is a problem that Victor, clever as he is, has not foreseen."

"With this in mind, I advise each of you to return to Dragon form at least once each cycle of the moon. Do it at night and make sure you are not seen," said Teal.

"Yes, father," said Azure. "Let me try the spell now."

"MORPHIOUS," she said, clapping her talons together. A human girl of about 25 appeared. She also had blonde hair but with aqua blue highlights. She had a shapely figure.

"You look gorgeous!" said Gek. As Azure quickly headed behind the tree to find her clothes. A few minutes later, she emerged wearing a tight-fitting pale green blouse and a too-short tan skirt.

"I will need to find some better fitting clothes the first chance we get," said Azure. "These are almost too tight to walk in."

"I think you look great!" said Gek.

"Thank you, Gek," said Azure. "But my eyes are up here!" she said, pointing to her eyes.

"Ah—modesty," said Ard, "how very human." Teal and Cobalt both roared with laughter.

Mage Edward

Chapter Three:

Sir Edward's Return

"Ya know, you dang near scared the life outta' Healer Bone when you sat up in that coffin," said Major Gerald, the newly-promoted commander of the Royal Expeditionary Force. Major Gerald was tall for a soldier, over six feet, with iron-gray hair and a stocky build. "The Healer told me that he nearly jumped overboard in fright," said Major Gerald.

"Sorry about that, Major," said Sir Edward, scratching his newly-grown beard. Edward was short for a Mage, just over five feet tall, about fifty winters old, with thinning gray hair. "When I woke up in the coffin, I was really thirsty. I tried to keep the noise down so as not to attract unwanted attention. I knew that my 'resurrection' was going to startle whoever was around, so I cast a silence spell around us. Good thing, too, or the Healer's scream would have woken everyone on the barge."

"Too bad it wasn't Dirk or Lance. That woulda' served 'em right for sneakin' up on me all those times." Senior Specialists Dirk and Lance were the two assassins assigned to the Royal Expeditionary Force. They both had magically spelled, camouflaging cloaks that made them almost invisible, and they liked nothing better than sneaking up on their commander and startling him.

Edward laughed. "It certainly would have. However, I think your plan for getting the dragon's head to the King was brilliant, and you didn't need to send both of your Specialists to escort my coffin downriver on a barge."

After killing a large, fire-breathing golden dragon in the foothills North of the town of Farmdale, the soldiers of the Expeditionary Force cut off the dragon's head to present to King Henry XI, who believed that dragons were mythical. Sir Edward, the Battle Mage that accompanied the expedition, had been gravely wounded in the battle with the dragon and was presumed dead. His coffin was placed in a wagon and transported by barge down the Sapphire River towards Kingston for burial. Edward had awakened from his self-induced healing coma, on the third day on the river and startled Healer Bone with his miraculous recovery.

"Anyway, after explaining that I was *not* dead, just in a deep, healing sleep, I slipped overboard and made my way back upriver to Hayford, where I procured a horse and headed back to the site where we discovered the dragon," explained Edward.

"So, explain to me how yer not dead," said Gerald.

"After I was knocked into that tree, I immediately cast a Healing spell on myself and then drank the Healing Serum that I had in my water bottle. A Battle Mage always fills his water bottle with Healing Serum before going into a fight," explained Edward. "The Compulsion spell I cast on Donovan, which compelled him to seek enrollment at the Wizards Academy, drained me of my remaining power and knocked me unconscious for almost two weeks. The coffin also had a Healing spell cast on it to aid my recovery. Without it, I might still be asleep."

"Or burned alive," said Major Gerald. "Your funeral was quite spectacular."

"Wizard Noland would have recognized a healing coma before that happened. As it was, he found my message on the coffin when it arrived and placed the body of some unfortunate sailor inside before transporting the coffin to my funeral."

"Why did ya go back to Farmdale?" asked Major Gerald.

"I wanted to make a closer examination of the dragon and her lair."

"Her?" asked Gerald.

"Her," confirmed Sir Edward. "It was a female dragon we killed. To be more specific, a *mother dragon*, protecting her baby."

"What?" exclaimed Gerald. "We missed finding a little one?"

"Yes, I found a hidden compartment at the back of the dragon's cave. It was very cleverly constructed, so I wouldn't be too angry that your soldiers didn't find it. I assume they searched the cave?"

"Yes. I sent Lieutenant Fletcher and a couple of men in. They said it was empty," said Major Gerald, angrily.

"It was by the time I got there," said Edward, "but I found small dragon footprints coming out of the cave, then heading east, along with the tracks of a much larger dragon."

"There were three of 'em?" asked Major Gerald. "How come we only saw one?"

"I suspect that the baby dragon was hiding in the cave, and the older one flew in after the battle. I saw no footprints arriving, only leaving."

"I guess we were lucky to arrive when we did."

"Indeed, Major," said Edward. "A day or two later, and we would have had to fight two dragons, not just one. I don't think the baby dragon could fly; otherwise, why would it walk away after the battle?"

"I don't know. Did you learn anything else about the dragon?"

"A great deal, actually. While dragon scales are tough, they are not fire-proof. A strong enough magician can blow a hole through them at close range. By examining the scorch marks around the battlefield, I determined that the dragon fire comes from a gelatine-like substance that they ignite as they spit toward their target. It also appears that they do not eat fruits or vegetables, only meat, and not people."

"Lieutenant Fletcher reported the same thing about not eating people. He found no human bones in the cave," said Gerald.

"A few other points; I believe the dragon was guarding her young. Once I tethered her, she didn't try to escape; she just kept circling and attacking. I expected the dragon to try to flee, but there was no strain on my tether."

"Anything else?" asked Gerald.

"Well, this is pure speculation, but it almost seemed like the dragon could hear and understand our speech," said Edward.

"Are you serious?"

"Well, it sure seemed like the beast heard me when I yelled to you that I would be the bait and try to draw her in. Then she deliberately attacked Donovan to draw my shield away so she could get a clean shot at me. I can't believe that was just happenstance."

"Dragons may be able to understand human speech. That's a frightenin' idea," said Major Gerald.

"It certainly is," said Edward. "After learning all I could at the battle site, I tracked the baby dragon and the older one as far as the Ivory River, where it seems the baby learned how to fly because there were no more tracks after that."

"What were you hopin' to accomplish? Ya didn't plan on takin' on two dragons by yourself, did ya?"

"I really just wanted to see where they were going and if there were more dragons around that we ought to be aware of," said Edward. "Still, if it came to it, I could probably have killed the baby dragon easily, and the other one is either ill or ancient."

"Why do ya' say that?" asked Gerald.

"Take a look at this dragon scale I found," said Edward, handing over a thin, brittle dragon scale that was partially covered with moss. "This must have fallen off the older dragon while they walked. Other than camouflage, it's not much protection for a dragon."

"You may be right, but you were still takin' a big risk."

"Not my first, and certainly not my last," said Mage Edward. "After I lost their trail, I headed back to Farmdale, then made my way to Fairview and eventually Kingston. I cast an illusion to disguise myself. I don't want anyone to know that I'm still alive. Being dead has its advantages, you know."

"What about Donovan? Shouldn't ya tell him at least?

"You ask hard questions, Commander, and yes, I need to let Donovan know that I'm alive. The problem is that he's confined to the Wizards Academy except on Endday afternoons when he's allowed out, but he is always accompanied by his Mentor. I need to get a message to Wizard Noland, the Headmaster of the Academy. I just can't think of a way to contact him without alerting everyone else," said Edward. The Battle Mage and the Major sat in quiet thought for a while, each sipping his ale. Battle

Mage Edward was glad to have a chance to just sit in safety and talk to a friend for a while. It had been a long time since he was afforded this luxury.

Finally, Major Gerald said, "I could slip Wizard Noland a note at the council meeting tomorrow. Wizard Victor is presenting the findings of his investigation of the plot to delay our mission, and I understand that Wizard Noland asked to attend."

"That's a great idea. Thank you. I still can't imagine why the King would put Victor in charge of the investigation. Especially since I suspect him of being behind it all."

"Maybe the King is tryin' to smoke him out," said Gerald. "Have you discovered anythin'? I assume you've been nosing around."

"I know that Victor 'discovered' that Sorcerer Snow in the Fairview Regional Mage's Office was involved. He's probably the magician who broke into the dungeon and stole your fake dragon heads. Sorcerer Snow apparently died while being questioned," said Edward. "Next, the magician who followed us from Kingston was most likely Sorcerer Zak. He's missing from the Kingston Regional Mage's Office. Lastly, Trader Rodgers from Fairview had a swimming 'accident' and drowned in Chrystal Lake. I understand he was behind the attempt to sink the ship that transported the Royal Expeditionary Force from Fairview to Kingston."

"WOOOEEE," whistled Major Gerald. "Two sorcerers and a wealthy trader! That's quite a conspiracy. What about the sinking of the *Big Jim*? Did you learn anything about that?"

"No. I've been quite busy tracking dragons and whatnot. Especially since I'm dead, you know. Besides, we want the man who killed the Sorcerers and the trader. They were obviously expendable."

"Yer right, as usual. So, how do I get this note to Wizard Noland?"

"I would suggest that you walk up behind him and drop the note on the floor, then say, 'Wizard Noland, I believe you dropped this.' No need to be secretive. Just make sure no one sees that you're the one who dropped the note," advised Edward.

"Got it. Let me get you a piece of parchment."

Edward hastily penned a note for Major Gerald to deliver to his friend. It said:

Serum Supplies

Dill Seed
Oleander
Nightshade
Hemlock
Oregano
Mint Leaves
Eggs

Eggplant

Nutmeg

Daffodil

Dandelion

Anise

Yarrow

Ajwain

Lemon Grass

Onion Powder

Niter

Erigon

"I don't understand," said Gerald.

"He will," replied Edward.

Chapter Four:

CONCEALMENTS

It was a short walk from the Level One dormitory to the one housing the Level Two magicians. Andrew led Donovan up to the second floor and down the hallway on the left. Unlike the Level One dormitory, this building had rooms on both sides of the hallway. The first floor had the same central kitchen and dining area arrangement, but it was only about twice the size of the one in the dorm from which Donovan was moving. Andrew went to the third door on the left, which already had Donovan's name on the door plate.

"Here you are. We try to keep an empty room between each occupied one for additional privacy," said Andrew. "Other than that, the dormitories are set up pretty much the same way: kitchen and dining area on the first floor in the center of the building, men's rooms to the left, women's to the right, shower rooms at the end of each hall. Not that it will help much, but I made sure that Phillip was housed on the first floor." Phillip had been Donovan's nemesis during their time as Level Ones.

"Thanks," said Donovan. "I'd almost forgotten about him. What else is different, now that I'm a Level Two?"

"Well, as I told you, your room is bigger and has better furnishings; since your room is on the west side of the building, it will be warmer, but the sun won't wake you in the morning. I heard you ask Evan about someone to help you with wake-up calls, so that shouldn't be a problem."

As they entered the room, Donovan noticed that there was a double bed, instead of a twin; the room had an area rug that covered the entire floor, the wardrobe was twice the size of his old one, with shelves on one side, and there was a leather sitting chair, a bedside table with drawers, and a work desk and chair. "This is much nicer," said Donovan.

"Yes," said Andrew, "and that's because you'll be here much longer. Before I forget, here is your new class schedule."

<u>Level Two Class Schedule</u>

First Period – Seemings – (Firstday & Midweek)
                     Martial Arts – (Twosday & Foursday)

Second Period – History (Firstday & Midweek)
                     Enhancements (Twosday & Foursday)

Luncheon
Third Period – Forces
Fourth Period – Serums
Mentor Testing – Endday mornings

"It looks very similar to my old schedule, but I only have Seemings class twice a week?" asked Donovan.

"Correct," replied Andrew, "you have four new Serums to learn: Paralysis, Stamina, Truth, and Healing for major wounds. They're much more complicated to make, and while we don't test Healing major wound Serums on students, you will be drinking your own Paralysis, Stamina, and Truth Serums. Truth Serums can be problematic, but if you confess to anything too embarrassing, like being in love with Wizard Mira, I can cast a Secrecy spell on Wizard Toffin and order him to keep your secret."

"So, how many spells do I have to master to advance to Level Three?" asked Donovan.

"In addition to remembering all of the Level One spells and your four new Serums, you need to learn the enhancement spells of Smell, Concealment, Healing (serious wounds), Stamina, Sensing, and Strength. Your Force Spells are Tether, Reduce, Enlarge, Adhere, Sleep, and Remove. You already know about producing Seemings that move, and there is also a written examination about current events," recited Andrew.

"Wow. That's quite a list," said Donovan.

"I told you when you arrived that it normally takes a Level Two magician between two and four years to learn all he needs to know to become a Level Three."

"So, does this mean no more playing hide-and-seek?" Level One magicians normally spend their evenings hiding other students' belongings, then finding their own through the use of a Tracer spell.

"Not at all," said Andrew. "In fact, that's the first spell I have to teach you before we head into town."

"Which spell is that?"

"How to cast a Concealment shield, and how to sense one. Did it ever occur to you that you never saw many Level Twos or Threes in the evenings while you were playing hide-and-seek? It's because they were playing the advanced version of the game," said Andrew.

"I guess I thought they were all in their rooms studying or something. I did see a few of them out and about, but you're right, it wasn't many. So, what's a Concealment spell?"

"Just what it sounds like – it's a spell to conceal yourself from sight. Now, you need to know that it will not make you silent – that's a different spell, and it will not protect you from the weather. You're not a Mage, so you won't be able to cast and hold two spells at once, so most students play inside when it rains. Let's head to the Forces Training area so I can teach you the spell," said Andrew.

The Forces Training area was a dry, sandy area behind the Academy stables. When they arrived, Andrew said, "Now, the incantation is *'OBSCUROUS,'* and the gesture is holding your right hand in front of your eyes, palm inward, and making a downward motion, like so." Andrew demonstrated the gesture. "Got it?"

"I think so," said Donovan. "How long will the spell last?"

"As long as you can hold it. I can hold mine for a couple of hours at a time, but there's rarely a time you would need it for more than an hour. Now, this spell requires considerably more power than any spell you've learned so far, so be ready for the drain. Do you have your water bottle with you?"

"Of course. Can I take a drink while holding a Concealment shield?"

"Yes, but remember to keep *quiet*, or your partner will hear you."

"Partner? I don't understand," said Donovan.

"To play the game, you partner up with another Level Two. It would be too confusing to have 20-odd concealed students running around, trying to find one another. So, you pair off and set the parameters of the game each evening. How long will one of you search before giving up? What are the boundaries, that sort of thing. As a new Level Two, I would suggest starting out with an inside venue, like the Serums or History classrooms, then eventually moving to one of the outdoor training areas. As our newest Level Two, I would suggest you pair up with either Troy or Kelly. They're still relatively new to the game, or the three of you could play together."

"Now for the Sensing spell. The word is *'SENSUS,'* and the gesture is holding your right hand straight out, palm outward, fingers spread, like so." Andrew demonstrated the gesture. It looked like he was trying to find something in the dark. "With the Sensing spell, you can detect a concealed person by a slight distortion in the air around them. It's particularly noticeable if they're moving," said Andrew. "Are you ready to try the Concealment spell?"

Donovan braced himself, positioned his hand in front of his eyes, and said *"OBSCUROUS"* as he lowered his hand. The energy drain hit him immediately, and Andrew was right; it was the most draining spell he had learned yet.

"Can you see me?" Donovan asked.

"No, but I can hear you," said Andrew, as he used a Wind spell to hurl a small stone at Donovan. "Tag, you're it," said Andrew smugly.

"OUCH!" said Donovan, dropping his Concealment shield. "No, fair, you never said anything about stones."

"It was just a pebble," said Andrew. "And now that you're 'It,' it's your turn to try to find me. Once you think you know where I am, toss a pebble at me and say, 'Tag.' Now close your eyes for ten counts, then try to find me. Ready? Here we go."

Andrew vanished from sight. Donovan closed his eyes and counted to ten; then he looked around. Not seeing any footprints in the sandy soil, he thought that Andrew had probably remained in place. Forgetting about the Sensing spell, Donovan remembered that he had the ability to sense people, so he cleared his mind and tried to determine where Andrew was hiding. He found him, perched on a large rock within stepping distance. Scooping up a pebble with wind, he tossed it at the rock and said, "Tag, you're it."

The pebble bounced off Andrew's shoulder and fell to the ground. "How in blazes did you find me?" he asked. "I've done that move dozens of times, and everyone else assumed that I stayed in place because they didn't see any footprints."

Donovan grinned. "Oh, did I neglect to mention that I can sense people? Apparently, even when they're concealed."

"No, you damn well didn't," said Andrew somewhat crossly. "Wait, I didn't see you cast the Sensing spell, no incantation, and no gesture. How did you do that?"

"I just cleared my mind and thought about it. I've never used a gesture or said anything before. It's something I discovered I could do on my trip down the Sapphire River from Hayford," said Donovan. "I haven't thought about it since then."

"Wait. You did this on water? Without an incantation or gesture? That shouldn't be possible!" Andrew paced around, clearly agitated. "I need to talk to the Headmaster about this," he mumbled. "In the meantime, please don't tell anyone else about this ability. You're going to spoil hide-and-seek for your classmates. At least the 'Seek' part."

Donovan came over and sat on the rock next to Andrew. "Why is this such a big deal?" he asked. "I'll bet lots of the other students can do it."

"No, they can't. Even I can't perform a Sensing spell without the incantation and gesture. The Sensing spell you are using is one of the hardest to master; that's why we start you out playing hide-and-seek as soon as you reach Level Two.

"Let's try again. This time, close your eyes and count to thirty. I'll move away and conceal myself. Use the spell to try to locate me. I will not leave the Forces Training area. Ready? Go."

Donovan closed his eyes and began counting. This wasn't going to work. Even with his eyes closed, he could sense that Andrew was moving down the tree line on the right side of the Forces Training area. After reaching a count of thirty, Donovan cast the Sensing spell, but since he already knew where to look, he wasn't sure that it was any more effective than without the incantation and gesture. Donovan scooped up a small stone, dropped the Sensing spell, and cast a Concealment spell around himself. He then walked quietly to within two feet of where Andrew was standing, tossed the stone at him, and said, "Tag, You're It." Donovan laughed to see Andrew jump so high.

"You didn't use the Sensing spell," scolded Andrew. "I know you can't hold two spells at once."

Donovan shrugged. "Even with my eyes closed, I could sense where you went. I tried the Sensing spell, but it just pointed me to where I already knew you were."

Andrew took a drink from his water bottle and sat down on a fallen tree.

"So now what?" asked Donovan.

"Let's move to the advanced lesson. You sit here and give me about ten minutes. Don't try to sense where I'm going when I leave. Practice making fire or something. After ten minutes come find me, and please don't use a Concealment shield, just walk around like a normal first-day Level Two."

Donovan nodded his assent, and Andrew headed off towards the Academy center courtyard, where he disappeared behind the stables. Donovan retrieved a pot from the wooden box under a tree at the edge of the Forces area and, for the next ten minutes, tried to make the spell for cooling water work. He had no problem heating water, but for some reason, he just couldn't make it cold. This was a source of great embarrassment for Donovan, since the cooling spell was one that all of the other Level One students mastered easily. The Wizards at the Academy believed that Donovan had a mental block because a magician had used a similar spell to freeze his mother to death.

After at least ten minutes had passed, Donovan returned the pot to the box, still frustrated by the cooling spell, and tried to sense where Andrew was. It was a little like using the Tracer spell; Donovan walked into the courtyard and felt that Andrew was off to his left and fairly close. After a brief pause, Donovan walked up to the Headmaster's cottage and knocked on the door. Jerry, the Headmaster's door warden, answered immediately.

"Hello, Jerry. I'm looking for—"

"Yes, sir, come right in. They're expecting you."

Donovan entered the Headmaster's cottage for only the second time ever, the first being the day he came to the Wizards Academy. Wizard Noland, the hulking, dark-skinned wizard, rose from the sofa in his parlor and said, "Come in, Donovan. Sorcerer Andrew has been expecting you. I had my doubts about this ability you supposedly have."

Donovan entered silently, unsure what to say.

"Andrew tells me that you can sense people under a Concealment shield without the incantation or the gesture of the spell. Since you're standing in my parlor, I guess it's true. How long have you had this ability?"

Donovan explained about his trip down the Sapphire River with Corporal (now Sergeant) Kindred, how they played a non-magical version of hide-and-seek along the river bank, and later, how Donovan was able to sense the Sorcerer and two of his three accomplices lying in wait on the riverbank, hoping to sink their boat. "But I missed detecting their rear sentry. If Senior Specialist Lance hadn't found him, we might all be dead," said Donovan.

"How far away were they when you sensed them?" asked Wizard Noland.

"I guess about half a mile. They were around a curve in the river, so it might have been closer." Andrew whistled, earning him a stern look from Wizard Noland.

"Interesting and quite remarkable for an untrained magician, on water no less. Tell me, Donovan, can you sense specific people or just people in general? How did you find Andrew just now?"

"I'm not sure, sir. It was kind of like looking for things I have a Tracer spell on. I just have a feeling when I get closer or farther away. I also remembered that Andrew said he needed to speak to you," said Donovan.

"I see. Can you tell me where Wizard Stuart is right now?"

Donovan closed his eyes and concentrated on Wizard Stuart, the Academy's Gatekeeper. He expected to find him in the Gatehouse or teaching Martial Arts class in the Enhancements Training area, but he wasn't there. Donovan expanded his search to the entire Wizards Academy grounds but could not detect Wizard Stuart anywhere. "I'm sorry, sir. I can't seem to sense him anywhere on the Academy grounds."

Wizard Noland scratched his shaved head and said, "That's probably because I sent him into Kingston to pick up some supplies for Wizard Toffin. Interesting. What you're doing is called a Seeing spell. It's the same spell your father used to locate the dragon all the way off in Farmdale. We normally only teach it to Sorcerers or Mages, and even then, the vast majority of them are unable to master it. Maybe it's hereditary. In the meantime, I still want you to play the hide-and-seek game each evening with the other Level Twos. Use the time to perfect your concealment skills, and try to at least make it look hard for you to find your classmates. I don't want you to discourage them by finding them too quickly. Do you understand what I'm saying?"

"Yes, sir. Seem to be less than I am," said Donovan.

"Exactly! Now, why don't you two head into town and celebrate your promotion."

"So how will we recognize other "Changed Ones'?" asked Gek. Gek, Ard, Teal, and Azure were seated on a rock ledge along the face of the quarry. Azure was self-consciously tugging at her skirt, trying to pull it lower on her thighs.

"Well, that is the problem," said Ard sadly. "You see, Fire Dragons always have red hair, but so do many humans; Snow Dragons have White hair, which is less common, but not unheard of; Sea Dragons have Blonde hair with blue or green highlights like Azure's."

"Does that not stand out?" asked Azure.

"Only a little," said Teal reassuringly, "over the years, we have promoted these highlights as a fashion statement among the humans, and it has caught on better than we hoped, which also makes it harder to identify a Sea Dragon Changed One now."

Ard continued, "Great Dragons all have blonde hair like Gek's, and Stone Dragons all have grey or black hair – also common among humans. Dragons are usually taller than most humans. Stone Dragons cannot swim, even in human form. Snow Dragons prefer the colder climates in the north, while Fire Dragons prefer the hotter temperatures in the south. The Fire and Stone Dragons should *only* be living on the west side of the Amber River. Sea Dragons eat fish exclusively, so they generally settle along the coast of the sea or in towns near rivers or lakes. Dragons cannot grow facial hair, so no human with a mustache or beard is a Dragon. Lastly, Dragons only eat meat. If you see a tall, red-haired man eating an apple, he is *not* a Dragon."

"That is really not much to go on," said Gek. "Is there no other way to identify a 'Changed One'?"

"Well, Changed Ones *smell* different than humans," said Cobalt, "but you cannot go around smelling every human you meet. It would arouse suspicion."

"Besides, many of the Changed Ones have taken to wearing human perfume to mask their scent," said Teal.

"You make this search sound impossible," said Azure.

"Not impossible, just very difficult. Consider, there are also Changed Ones who have produced human offspring. How likely are they to join this battle? Some may even fight *against* us," said Ard.

"So where do we start?" asked Gek.

"I will send Sea Dragons along the coast to search. I know where some of our Changed Ones settled, and they may know others," said Teal.

"The Snow Dragons will search the north, but I doubt they will find any Changed Ones. There are no human towns in the Snow Fields and only a few small settlements nearby. You two will have to search the middle of the country. I would start in the human town of Smithville and the mountains to the east of the town, then move to Hayford, then Farmdale, then Riverton, which will put you close enough to make it back here in time," said Ard. "You will have to fly from town to town since walking in human form will take far too long."

"One last thing," said Ard, "remember to take off your human clothes before you change back into your true form, as you saw Victor do, or you will destroy the garments and have to go naked until you find replacements."

Wizard Victor

Chapter Five:

INVESTIGATIONS

"So, Victor," asked the King crossly, "What has your investigation revealed so far?"

Victor, the scarlet-robed court Wizard, shifted his feet nervously and replied, "Sire, I have tried to be most diligent and thorough in my investigation of what befell the Royal Expeditionary Force recently—" "Not that 'recently,'" interrupted the King, "You've been 'investigating' for months now! You'd better have something to show for all this effort! I grow tired of waiting for answers!" The various Ministers of the kingdom, who were seated around the audience chamber, murmured their agreement. They, too, were tired of waiting for an answer and of Victor's interrogations, which normally involved the use of Truth Serum.

"Well, Sire, I did have a great many people to question, and I had to travel to Fairview and also investigate the loss of our ships on the Sapphire River—" "I know what you had to investigate!" shouted the King. "What did you find?"

"Sire, the magician who followed the Royal Expeditionary Force out of Kingston, was Sorcerer Zak, who was assigned to the Kingston Regional Mage's Office," said Victor quickly. "His associate was a known thief who was being investigated by the Kingston Enforcers for the burglary of several local businesses, as Constable Ronald can confirm!"

"Constable Ronald, can you enlighten us?" asked the King. The Constable was a dark-skinned, middle-aged man with greying hair and a slight build, unusual for someone in his line of work. "Well, Sire, there were a number of break-ins a few months ago, and we were searching for a known thief, Matthew Jennings, of Southport, who was rumored to be operating in Kingston. We were never able to apprehend him, but since the Royal Expeditionary Force set out earlier this year, there have been fewer break-ins, and Mr. Jennings is nowhere to be found. It could have been him, but without a body to identify..." the Constable shrugged.

"Very well," grumbled the King, "but why would a Sorcerer and a thief be following my Expeditionary Force, Victor?" "Sire, I suspect a foreign hand in all of this," said Victor solemnly. "My investigation seems to point to the Kingdom of Baize. I suspect that Sorcerer Zak was in their employ, and he recruited the thief to help him shadow the Royal Expeditionary Force and report on their movements."

"To what end?" asked the King, more curious than angry now.

"The movement of military forces, particularly the Royal Expeditionary Force, is always of interest to neighboring kingdoms, even seemingly non-threatening ones," replied Victor.

"But why would he take poison rather than be captured?"

"Because, as a Sorcerer, he knew that under questioning, the use of a Truth Serum would have compelled him to divulge all he knew. He must have been a *very* dedicated and loyal agent of Baize. Frankly," sneered Victor, "I am surprised and disappointed that his treachery was not detected by Regional Mage Cassandra, who was his direct supervisor."

"A very good question. Well, Cassandra, what do you have to say for yourself?" asked the King, redirecting his glare to the Kingston Regional Mage.

"Sire," began Cassandra, "I have already been questioned, *under Truth Serum*, by Wizard Victor, and I swear to you that there were no indications that Zak was anything but a loyal, hard-working Sorcerer, who performed all of his assigned duties admirably!"

"Then perhaps you were not looking close enough!" said a scowling Victor. "One does not go from being a '*loyal, hard-working Sorcerer*' to a traitor overnight! There must have been signs." The diminutive brunette Mage seemed to shrink under Victor's onslaught.

"May I ask the Regional Mage a couple of questions?" asked Wizard Noland from his seat in the gallery.

"Of course, Wizard Noland," said the King differentially. Victor scowled.

"Cassandra, as I recall, Sorcerer Zak came from the port city of Sundock, did he not?" "Yes, Wizard Noland," replied

Cassandra. "And how long had he worked for you?" asked Noland gently.

"About two years. He came to us straight out of the Academy," said Cassandra. "Did he ever take a leave of absence, or was he away from his duties for any length of time?" "No sir, as I recall, he was an orphan, and as I said earlier, he was most diligent and attentive to his duties," said Cassandra firmly. "I see. Did you notice anything odd about his behavior while he was working for you?" asked Noland.

"Well, not odd, really, but he only ate fish. In the two years I knew him, he never ate meat, bread, fruits, or vegetables— only fish. We sometimes teased him about it." "And what did he say?" asked Noland. "He said that in Sundock, where he was raised, all they ate was fish and that anything else upset his stomach." "Interesting, but hardly a sign of treason," observed Noland. "Anything else?"

"A couple of months ago, he had blue and green highlights dyed into his hair. I told him it was an odd look for a Sorcerer," Cassandra confided. "Did he have an explanation?" asked Noland. "He said he did it to impress a maiden he was pursuing. But I guess it didn't have the desired effect because he dyed his hair back to blonde a week later."

"I have no further questions for Mage Cassandra," said Noland.

"And what have you deduced from your odd questions, Noland?" demanded Wizard Victor.

"Well, Mage Cassandra has confirmed my recollection that Sorcerer Zak came from Sundock, that he had no family, and that he never traveled to the Kingdom of Baize. I would have expected a '*dedicated agent,*' willing to kill himself, to have a closer connection to Baize. Maybe the family was in their territory, or there was some other interest, but he apparently had none. I would say that it's unlikely that Sorcerer Zak was a spy for the Kingdom of Baize," said Noland coldly. "Perhaps he was bribed!" said Victor desperately. Noland laughed. "You know perfectly well that it's impossible to bribe a magician, Victor."

"Why is that?" asked the King.

"Your majesty, what could you offer a Sorcerer that he could not produce himself with magic?" replied Noland.

"Gold, women, power?" Victor said, interrupting.

Not wanting to reveal that magicians could magically replicate gold and silver currency, Wizard Noland asked, "Cassandra, were there any indications that Sorcerer Zak had wealth? Did he spend lavishly or live above his means?" "No, Wizard Noland," Cassandra replied. "He had a modest apartment in the city, and I never observed him to spend beyond his means. You know that's something we watch for." "Indeed," confirmed Noland.

"What about women and power?" insisted Victor.

"Victor, you should remember that every Level Three magician is taught how to make a Love Serum. While the ingredients are difficult to come by, with a little preparation, Zak could have enticed any maiden he wanted without resorting to dyeing his hair. As for power, what power could a Sorcerer obtain from conspiring with Baize? They have no power in Franconia," said Noland coldly.

"I agree," said the King. "So, while you may have identified who followed my Expeditionary Force, you have failed to discover *why*. What did you determine about the attack on the Expeditionary Force outside Fairview?"

"Sire, the attack was made by a gang of brigands who had been robbing merchants and travelers along the road for several weeks before the incident with the Expeditionary Force. They simply chose the wrong camp to attack," said Victor desperately. "Have there been any other attacks in the area since they tangled with the Expeditionary Force?" asked the King. "No sire, Major Gerald seems to have effectively destroyed the brigands and removed that threat," said Victor.

"Well, at least that's some good news. What about the plot to poison Major Stone?" "Sire, I personally questioned the captive that was apprehended, and using Truth Serum, I determined that he was a petty thief who was paid by an unknown party to eliminate Major Stone. The thief had no idea who hired him, and the choice of poison was completely his own. The thief did not know that the officers of the Royal Expeditionary Force would be dining with the Major that night," stated Victor.

"Why would someone want Major Stone dead?" asked the King. "My inquiries indicate that Major Stone has been most diligent at enforcing the tax laws in Fairview, Your Majesty," said Victor. "Some of the merchants I interviewed felt that the Major was over-diligent and unreasonable in his enforcement. While I was unable to determine exactly who was behind the plot, I am convinced that it was a wealthy trader who simply wanted Major Stone out of the way in order to increase his or her profits."

"And the fire in the Royal Stables?" asked the King testily.

"Just an unfortunate accident, Sire. A young stable boy had too much ale with dinner and fell asleep in the stable. He accidentally kicked over his lantern during the night. Fortunately, a passerby saw the flames almost immediately, and the fire was extinguished with minimal damage and no loss of life," explained Victor.

"An accident, Victor?" asked the King.

"Yes, Your Majesty. Not everything is a conspiracy. Accidents do happen."

"And what about the guards at the gate that attempted to delay the Royal Expeditionary Force?" asked Major Gerald, forgetting his place for a moment. "Yes, what about them?" asked the King.

"Simple soldiers, doing their jobs, Sire. It was most abusive for Mage Edward to spell them to sleep without cause," explained Victor.

"And the brick wagon with the adhesive spell?" asked the King. "Surely, you're not going to tell me that was an accident." "Of course not, Sire," said Victor hurriedly. "The brick wagon and the later spelling of Major Gerald's guards and the theft of the chests with the false Dragon heads was done by Sorcerer Snow of the Fairview Regional Mage's office."

"You're certain?" asked the King. "Why would he do such a thing?"

"Quite certain, Your Majesty," replied Victor. "He admitted his guilt during questioning. Apparently, Sorcerer Snow was an agent of Baize. He was instructed to delay the Royal Expeditionary Force for as long as possible and attempt to prevent us from realizing that Dragons are, in fact, real. He further informed me that the Dragon Sir Gerald fought north of Farmdale and was sent here by King Donald of Baize to stir up trouble in Franconia."

"Incredible," said the King. "I suppose Sorcerer Snow was also responsible for the attempted sinking of the ship that the Royal Expeditionary Force returned to Kingston on?" "Just so, your highness," replied Victor. "Sorcerer Snow also confessed to casting a Compulsion spell on Trader Rodgers of Fairview, who secretly paid Captain Bell to smuggle the crates with the accelerants aboard the HMS UNSINKABLE. I would have interviewed Trader Rodgers, but he drowned while swimming in Chrystal Lake before I arrived in Fairview. I suspect Sorcerer Snow was covering his tracks."

"Your Majesty," interrupted Wizard Noland, "if possible, I would like the opportunity to question Sorcerer Snow personally."

"Unfortunately, that will not be possible, Noland. You see, Sorcerer Snow died while being questioned. Apparently, the strain of attempting to deceive me, after having ingested Truth Serum, was too much for his heart." "How very convenient," said Wizard Noland.

"You doubt me, Noland," challenged Victor. "Not at all," said Noland. "I have no reason to doubt that Sorcerer Snow was involved. As I remember, he was always a disagreeable student while at the Academy. But my questions would have been the same: What would he gain by cooperating with Baize? And how could King Donald have 'sent' a Dragon into Franconia?"

"Hmm," said Victor in a more conciliatory tone, "perhaps Sorcerer Snow meant that the Kingdom of Baize *drove* the Dragon out of their country, through force of arms or with magic, and they did not wish to be blamed for any destruction he caused in Franconia. As to Sorcerer Snow's motivation, I have no idea. Perhaps he wanted to be promoted to Regional Mage as a reward."

"I suppose it is possible," Noland conceded, "but he still would have had to pass the test to become a Mage and receive the assignment from the King. It's a shame he cannot be questioned further."

"Moving on," said the King impatiently, "what did you discover about the attacks on shipping on the Sapphire River, Victor?"

"It was river pirates, Sire. Unfortunately, there have been several more attacks in the past few months. It seems that an unidentified magician has learned a spell that can remove a section of a ship's hull beneath the waterline, causing a clipper ship to take on water. When the ship grounds on the shoreline, pirates attack, kill the crew, and carry off the cargo." "And what, specifically, are you doing about this, Victor?" asked the King.

"Sire, I have alerted all of the shipping companies to increase the number of guards on their ships and be on the lookout for these pirates," said Victor. "As you know, detecting and apprehending rogue magicians is the responsibility of the Regional Mage. So, Mage Cassandra, we come back to you. What are *you* doing to find these criminals?" The King looked expectantly at his Regional Mage.

"Sire, there is only myself and three Sorcerers, well, two now with Zak gone, to search the capitol for unidentified magicians. Kingston has a population of approximately 50,000 citizens. If our calculations that two in every thousand people have the spark of magic are correct, that means there could be as many as a hundred unknown magic-users in Kingston. Finding the responsible rogue magician will be extremely difficult. Also, this criminal magic-user may be from Hayford or farther upriver in Three Forks!" said Cassandra.

"Then what are we going to do?" exclaimed the King. "Sire, if I may make a suggestion," said Wizard Noland, "I would temporarily assign some magical support to the shipping companies. Use a few Sorcerers from the Regional Mage's Offices or even the Royal Navy to help guard the ships down the river. The shipping companies would undoubtedly pay the crown for the use of your magical assets."

"What an excellent idea, Wizard Noland! Are you sure that you don't want the job as Court Wizard?" asked the King. "Your Majesty, I'm honored by your offer, but I believe that I can best serve the crown by training the best possible Sorcerers for your use," said Noland humbly.

"As you wish. Victor, do you have anything else to report?" "Not at this time, Sire. I will, of course, continue looking into this matter as part of my regular duties," said Victor, clearly shaken by the King's offer to Wizard Noland.

"Very well, this meeting is adjourned. Ministers, please consult with Wizard Victor, the Regional Mages, and Marshall Guzman to determine how much magical support we can provide to the shipping companies on the Sapphire River and how much we should charge them for the protection. I expect to make a profit on this! Dismissed."

As the ministers filed out of the audience chamber, Major Gerald approached Wizard Noland and, stooping down, said,

"Excuse me, Wizard Noland, I believe you dropped this."
Gerald extended the scrap of parchment with Edward's message
on it. Noland took the parchment, glanced at it for a moment,
and said, "Thank you, Major. I would have missed that." Noland
quickly put the parchment in the pocket of his robes and hastily
departed the castle.

Victor returned to his rooms, relieved to have placated the
King, at least for the time being, but worried at the implication
that he could be replaced by Wizard Noland at any time. "So,
Victor," the mysterious voice said, "you managed to save your
skin with the king. What did the Dragon Council decide?"

Victor told his superior of the plan the Dragon Council
agreed to: that the Fire and Stone Dragons would soon launch
limited attacks on the towns of Riverside and Weaton, which sat
along the Amber River, the border between Franconia and the
Kingdom of Baize. The intent was to provoke a border war
between the human armies and magicians; then, once the
humans were weakened, the Dragons would attack and destroy
them. He said that several Dragons that could master the spell of
Change would transform into human form and begin infiltrating
both countries, in preparation for the final assault. Then he
grudgingly admitted to the agreement with Ard, that Dragons
would hold to their ancient promise not to eat people and to

search for and spare any offspring of the human Wizard Amanda.

"I agree that we should abide by our ancient vow not to eat humans, but this search for Amanda's family troubles me somehow. Did they all agree?" asked the disembodied voice. "Unfortunately, yes, and Ard cast a Binding spell on us to ensure that we keep to our word," admitted Victor. "Then I suggest that you make haste in researching Amanda's genealogy to determine our risk in this matter. Do you know what happens if you break a Binding spell, Victor?" "No, what?" asked Victor, confused. "You die. Immediately. No pardons, no appeals, just instant death for anyone who was bound by the oath."

"I will consult the Archives at once," said a now-worried Victor. "That would be for the best," said the voice. "It is fortunate that Sorcerer Snow was not a descendent of Amanda, or you would have died the moment you killed him." Victor ran for the Archives.

Chapter Six:

HIGHER EDUCATION

It smelled awful. No, *awful* was not a strong enough word. It smelled nauseating. Donovan gagged on the stench and hastily shouted, "*CODA!*" Standing nearby, Wizard Loren smiled and said, "I see that your first attempt at the Smell enhancement was a resounding success, but there was no need to shout the release command."

"I didn't want there to be any question of enunciation," gasped Donovan, still trying to clear the stench from his nostrils. "What was that, Wizard Loren?" "That was the Academy's septic tank, dear boy. Specifically, the bottom of the septic tank. I apologize, but it is always the first scent Level Two magicians attempt with their first Smell enhancement. To clear your nose, try smelling what the Level Twos will be having for lunch."

Donovan muttered "*ODIOUS*" and made a 'waving' gesture towards his nose with his right hand. He immediately detected the scent of beef stew and bread fresh out of the oven. "Better?" asked Loren. "Much better," said Donovan. "I'm glad they weren't cooking fish for lunch today." "You still think we do these lessons by chance, do you? The Level Twos *always* have beef stew for lunch on the day of their first Smell enhancement class. It is one of the easiest meals to identify, and most students find it pleasing, after their first experience with the Smell enhancement spell."

The other twenty-three Level Two students smiled at Donovan's discomfort. This was the morning of his second day of classes as a Level Two magician. There were thirteen boys in Level Two, ranging in age from 11 to 19 winters old, and ten girls between the ages of 13 and 19. Donovan knew Phillip, Troy, and Kelly from their time together as Level One magicians. Phillip had been Donovan's nemesis, always trying to push him into a fight or embarrass him during a lesson. After only two days as a Level Two, Donovan thought that Phillip seemed much more agreeable and humble than he had previously. It was probably just as Sorcerer Andrew had predicted; Phillip had probably tried to bully a younger Level Two and been put in his place by a more capable, if younger, magician.

Donovan's first class with Wizard Loren as a Level Two had been History, everyone's least favorite class. The first class was a discussion about the Regional Mage's Offices, their duties and responsibilities, and how they go about their tasks of detecting previously unknown magicians and facilitating their enrollment at the Wizards Academy. Donovan knew that almost half of his classmates had been brought in by the Regional Mages, so he was not surprised by the animosity some students voiced about their experience with the process.

Phillip, of course, had the biggest beef with the Regional Mages. "I was grabbed off the street in Southport, taken home, and told to pack a bag. No discussion, no time to say goodbye to my friends, just a quick minute to hug my parents, and off we went in a box wagon, like I was some kind of criminal. I haven't seen either of my parents since!"

"I understand," said Wizard Loren, "your story is much the same as all of the other magicians that our Regional Mages find. What magic were you doing that drew their attention?" "My parents were— are, poor. My father unloads cargo on the docks of Southport, and my mother works mending sails for some of the cargo ships. I was just replicating some copper coins—not golds or silvers—COPPERS! Then I got grabbed by a Sorcerer who would just not listen to reason and shipped off here. Plus, my family was fined ten golds for my crimes! I don't know how they survived!" raged Phillip.

"Yes," said Loren, "that is exactly how most of the unidentified magicians in Franconia are found out— counterfeiting. Now, since you obviously did not know, the Wizards Academy pays all fines owed to the crown by the families of magicians brought here. So, your family did not suffer any financial burden because of your actions. The hope is that once you pass the tests and become a Sorcerer, you will justify the Academy's investment in you. Next, from your Level One History class, how many unidentified magicians did we say were probably 'at large' in Franconia?"

"I think it was about a hundred, Wizard Loren," said Phillip. "Exactly!" exclaimed Loren. "Can you just imagine how much counterfeit currency could be created and put into circulation by a hundred unknown magicians? Unlike you, most 'rogue magicians,' as we call them, replicate *gold*, not copper! That could amount to thousands of golds over several years! Our economy would be ruined! Why, with that much counterfeit coin in the market, an ale would cost almost a silver, instead of a copper!" "I suppose," grumbled Phillip.

"Plus, all of the fires and other accidents caused by untrained magicians. It is really a public safety issue as well. I know that many of you were brought here against your will, but hopefully, by now, you all understand that it really was for your own good and the welfare of the kingdom. Well, there is the bell for your next class, off to Serums with you."

In the Level Two Serums class, Wizard Toffin began explaining how to brew a Healing Serum for broken bones. "What do we need first?" he asked. "Water," said the class. "Precisely! Please draw two beakers of water, then gather five eucalyptus leaves, one tava root, three dried blueberries, one measure of yarrow root, and two measures of crushed bone marrow from the pantry." As the lesson continued, Wizard Toffin explained how to combine, sift, separate, and boil the various ingredients, as well as how to incorporate some of the Level One Healing spells into the Serum to complete it. This was much more complicated than the basic Level One Serums that Donovan was used to preparing, as it involved both spells and ingredients. When the Serums were finished, Wizard Toffin examined each vial closely for color and smell.

"This Serum should smell a bit like the eucalyptus leaves that we added to make it," Wizard Toffin said. "From experience, I can tell you that it does not *taste* very good, but in an emergency, it can heal broken bones almost as soon as they are broken. We here at the Academy recommend that all Battle Mages and Sorcerers drink some of this Serum before going into battle and that they fill their water bottles with it, just in case. If ingested immediately after an injury, this Serum can keep the magician in the fight, when they otherwise might be gravely injured."

Donovan thought back. Hadn't his father taken a drink from his water bottle right before the end? Was it possible? Could he have taken a Healing Serum? As the class departed, headed for lunch, Donovan lingered behind.

"Excuse me, Wizard Toffin, I have a question." "Yes, Donovan, what can I help you with?" asked the portly Wizard. "You said that Battle Mages often put Healing Serum in their water bottles before combat. Could such a Serum heal a broken back?" "You're wondering about your father, aren't you? We've all considered the possibility when we heard about Mage Edward's fight with the dragon. The problem is, we don't know the extent of his injuries. As I understand it, the dragon struck him with its tail, hurling him into a tree. Broken ribs from the tail strike, coupled with a broken back from the collision with the tree, plus internal injuries? I doubt that even the Level Three Healing Serum, for potentially mortal wounds, which you will eventually learn, could repair so much damage. I'm sorry, but the human body can only take so much. I wish I could give you hope, but I'm afraid those injuries were beyond repair by any Serum."

"I understand. It was just a thought. Thank you, Wizard Toffin." The kindly Wizard patted Donovan on the shoulder as he left the Serums classroom. Donovan lingered for a moment, then headed to the dormitory and lunch.

The Level Two kitchen was larger, there was more seating (of course), and the food was better than the Level One facility that Donovan had just come from. Donovan sat at the table with Troy, Kelly, and Phillip and asked how they were doing with the more difficult spells and Serums taught to Level Two magicians. They all said that it was definitely more challenging, but they thought they could master it eventually. When the serving girl came over, Donovan asked where he could find Jacob. "I'll send him right over, Sir," she said. "Please call me Donovan. Thank you—" "Janet," said the serving girl, blushing. "Thank you, Janet."

A few minutes later, a tall, brown-haired boy who was missing his left hand approached the table. "You asked to see me, Sir?" "Yes, Jacob. Evan, a friend of mine in the Level One dormitory, recommended that I hire you for my morning wake-up calls. Are you available?" asked Donovan. "Of course, Sir! I'd be happy to wake you up in the mornings! Thank you!" "Please call me Donovan. Thank you for helping me." "My pleasure. Hello Phillip." Phillip actually smiled and acknowledged Jacob before he headed back to the kitchen.

"Evan recommended Jacob for the job?" asked Phillip. "He did," replied Donovan. "Does that surprise you?" "Very much so," said Phillip. "You see, Jacob is my brother."

Early on Endday morning, Wizard Noland told Stuart that he was going into town to pick up some Serum supplies for Wizard Toffin and that he would be back before lunch. Heading into town, Wizard Noland walked into the town square and then entered the Apothecary, where he purchased several items used in various Serums. As he exited the shop, he cast a Concealment shield over himself and proceeded to Edward's house a few blocks away. As he approached the house, he sensed someone inside and that the door was unlocked. He cast a Seeming as he opened the door, so that to anyone watching, it would appear that the door remained closed. Inside, standing in the parlor, was Edward.

"Michael, my dear friend," said Edward as he came forward to embrace the Headmaster, "it's so good to see you again." "And you," said Wizard Noland. "Although I've known the reports of your demise were premature ever since I unloaded an empty casket off that barge in the harbor. I was very pleased to receive your coded message from Major Gerald. We haven't used the Serum Ingredients cipher in years. Where have you been, and why all the secrecy?"

"Well, after the battle with the dragon, I was severely injured. Fortunately, I drank the strongest Healing Serum I could make before Tethering the beast and had additional Serum in my water bottle. Even so, my Healing spell and stasis box were barely enough to heal my injuries. I'm afraid that the Compulsion spell I placed on Donovan was too much for me, and I barely remained conscious long enough to tell him farewell." "You always did overestimate your own strength," said Wizard Noland. "It's a wonder that you ever passed the Level Two Exam."

"You remember that, eh? Yes, that was a close one. Anyway, once I regained consciousness on the barge, I knew that I had to immediately return to the battle site to examine the carcass before it was too mauled by the local wildlife."

"And what did you discover?" asked Noland.

"The dragon was a female, and she was protecting her child, which was cleverly hidden in the cave and was not discovered during the hasty search by the soldiers after the battle. I learned that dragon scales are not really fireproof and that a magician can penetrate them with a Force spell." "All very insightful, but why maintain the belief that you were killed?" asked Noland.

"First, someone put a great deal of effort into preventing us from finding this dragon, and more importantly, I believe that the dragons can speak and understand human speech," confided Edward.

"Incredible!" exclaimed Noland. "How did you come to that conclusion?" "Well, during the battle, I shouted to Captain Gerald that I was going to act as bait, to lure the dragon in, so they could engage it with their crossbows. I swear the dragon heard me, understood my plan, and attacked Donovan to draw my protection to him, so she could strike me." "Hardly conclusive," said Noland. "That could have just been a coincidence."

"Perhaps, but it got me to thinking. Before I left Kingston, I searched my wife's family records and found a reference to the 'Dragon War.' The records stated that the conflict was taking such a toll on both sides that the humans and dragons agreed to a treaty whereby the dragons agreed not to eat people in exchange for a tribute of 20,000 cattle every two years. The humans agreed, and a Binding spell was cast to ensure both sides kept their part of the bargain." "So, what happened?" asked Noland. "The humans poisoned the cattle; when the dragons ate them, most of them died," said Edward. "Treacherous but effective," mused Noland. "So?"

"So how could we have made a treaty with dragons if they didn't speak our language? It would be like signing an agreement with a dog! Dragons *must* be able to speak! More than that, they must be magical, otherwise a Binding spell would be useless!" exclaimed Edward.

"You're absolutely correct. This changes everything," mused Noland. "We are in grave danger."

"That's why I kept up the ruse of being dead, so I can operate in the shadows and maybe catch our enemies by surprise," whispered Edward. "What about Donovan?" asked Noland. "He was devastated by your loss and deserves to know the truth."

"I agree, but it must be handled carefully. I'm sure my enemies have been watching him closely. How is he doing?" asked Edward. "He is remarkable. I think he's the most talented Level Two the Academy has seen in centuries," said Noland. "Level Two?" exclaimed Edward. "But he's only been here about six months!" "Indeed. It's the fastest that anyone has ever advanced to Level Two. Moreover, he is kind to the younger students and the Academy servants, who like and respect him very much. Wizard Stuart has already promoted him to Level Three in martial arts because he is so far beyond his classmates in riding and staff work. You trained him well."

"Hardly. I didn't think he paid much attention when we sparred. I guess he retained some of what I taught him after all," said Edward. "More than some," said Noland, "did you know that he can sense people without the incantation or gesture? He's going to ruin Level Two hide-and-seek for his classmates."

"You astound me! I had no idea he had that talent. You know how rare that is. So how can we inform him about me without the whole Academy knowing?" asked Edward. "Well, we're coming up during the rainy season when the Level Twos are employed to maintain the King's highways. How about I bring him over here during his first work shift? That should be in about a week. Say next Foursday?"

"That would be wonderful. Thank you, my friend."

Victor wiped his bleary eyes and sighed. He had been searching the Archives for days, trying to trace the lineage of Wizard Amanda. Early on, he had found an ancient scroll that was a record of all the Wizards, Mages, and Sorcerers in the kingdom. He supposed that it was useful to know how many magicians there were and who the king could call on for support. He found a Wizard Amanda Kniskern on the rolls and had been attempting to trace her family tree to determine if she had any descendants that the Dragons needed to be concerned about. If one of them were harmed by a Dragon, even accidentally, all of the Dragons subject to Ard's Binding spell (including himself) could die instantly.

Victor was having difficulty tracing the Kniskern family tree. They had not been one of the leading families of Franconia or even wealthy traders that there might be records of. No, it seemed the only thing of significance about the Kniskerns was that once upon a time, a member of their family had passed the test to become a Wizard. Maybe the Wizards Academy had records of past Wizards and their families. At least there was someone he could task to investigate without going himself. A visit from the Court Wizard would not go unnoticed and might raise annoying questions. He would have to speak to Loren. In the meantime, he would have his minions make inquiries to see if anyone knew anything about the Kniskern lineage. The Dragons could certainly not begin their attacks until this problem was dealt with. One unfortunate scrape on a middling Sorcerer or common barmaid who shared the Kniskern bloodline could wipe out the entire Dragon Council. Curse Ard!

Wizard Noland

Chapter Seven:
FAMILY REUNIONS

Azure and Gek went behind their respective trees and disrobed. Gek peeked around his tree and found Azure doing the same. "Just making sure you are all right," said Gek sheepishly. "Sure you were!" smiled Azure. Once disrobed, both Dragons cast the Change spell and resumed their true forms as Dragons. They placed Azure's human clothes inside Gek's, since his outfit was really just a burlap bag with holes in it. Gek then had to revert to human form in order to use his rope belt to secure the burlap bundle (Dragon talons are not designed for such a task). Azure watched in admiration while Gek hurried to be finished and change from a naked human back into a gold Dragon. "Stop smiling," said Gek, good-naturedly. "Next time, you get to secure the bundle." "Deal," said Azure.

Since it was nearly dawn and too dangerous to fly all the way across Franconia (a three-night flight), the five Dragons elected to spend the day sleeping in the abandoned quarry and set out at nightfall. Before turning in for the day, they decided that Gek, Azure, Teal, and Cobalt would head for the eastern coast with stops on the west side of what the humans called Chrystal Lake, then on to the south side of the large swamp in eastern Franconia. Teal and Cobalt would then head for the eastern coast and the human city of Eastport, where Teal believed that some of the Sea Dragons Changed Ones lived. Gek and Azure would find a base in the mountains northeast of Smithville and begin their search there. The Dragons used the Dig spell to carve out shallow caves in the rock face and settled down to sleep.

That evening, as they prepared to depart, Ard had some last-minute advice. "Remember, some of the Changed Ones will *not* want to go back to living as Dragons. You must proceed with caution. If you tell them our plan and they are unwilling to help, they may expose you to the humans or even attack you. I would say that any of them who have human mates or children will be most unlikely allies." "Then you are not coming with us?" asked Gek. "You know that I cannot fly that far and return in time for the next Dragon Council meeting. I will remain in this area, and if I feel up to it, I may change into human form. I will visit the nearby town of Colton to see if I can find any Changed Ones," said Ard.

After saying their goodbyes to Ard, the four Dragons headed off towards Chrystal Lake. They landed on the west side of the lake and found shelter in the woods along the shore. Teal, Cobalt, and Azure dove into the lake and returned with fish for dinner. The fish were much smaller than those in the Eastern Ocean, but there was an abundance of them, and the Dragons ate their fill. As the sun rose, the Dragons observed several ships traversing the lake; some were obviously fishing boats, while others were transporting cargo or passengers between the towns along the waterways. That night, they flew south, giving the human city of Fairview a wide berth. Once the lights of the city faded from view, they turned northeast and headed for the great swamp. They landed on a raised mound inside the southern border of the swamp.

"This place smells bad," complained Gek. "Do we have to stay here?" "Just for tonight," replied Teal. "I know it stinks in here, but the smell and the water will keep the humans away. Tomorrow night, you and Azure will head for the mountains north of Smithville, while Cobalt and I will head for the city on the southern coast. Cobalt and I will work our way up the coast, while you two search Smithville, Hayford, Farmdale, Riverton, and finally Colton before returning to the quarry for the Dragon Council meeting on the first full moon of autumn. That means you can spend less than one cycle of the moon searching each town."

The Dragons settled in for a damp, smelly day in the swamp. Around dusk, they were awakened by a scream from Azure and a roar from Gek, followed by a thrashing and splashing in the water nearby. Teal and Cobalt rushed over to Azure, "Are you all right? What happened?" they asked. Just then, Gek emerged from the muddy water with a large, slimy lizard creature in his mouth. Gek spat its carcass on the ground and said, "This lizard thing tried to make a meal of Azure! I tried to flame it, but it would not burn! We ended up wrestling around in the shallow water until I got a good grip on it. What is that thing?" asked a winded Gek.

"I believe it is called an alligator," replied Teal. "I have not seen one in many years. They live in swamps and ponds, I believe." "Then it is not some form of Sea Dragon?" asked Gek. "No. A distant cousin perhaps," replied Cobalt. "I would not have thought that one would attack a Dragon. Are you sure you are all right, Az?" "I think so," said a clearly shaken Azure. "It grabbed onto my tail with its mouth and tried to drag me into the water. Fortunately, my scales protected me, but I am a bit bruised. That thing had quite a bite!"

"Well," said Cobalt, "it looks like Gek has provided supper for us tonight." "Do you think there are any more of these things around?" asked Azure. "Undoubtedly, but they probably saw what happened. Alligators are slow-witted creatures, but I doubt any of them will be stupid enough to attack a Dragon again any time soon," said Teal. "So, what does alligator taste like?" asked Gek. "Chicken," replied Cobalt, "but without the feathers."

It was raining hard as the Level Twos approached the Forces Training area for their third-period Martial Arts class. "No staffs today," said Wizard Stuart. "Instead of your Martial Arts and Forces training today, you Level Twos will be doing some service projects for the crown." There were disappointed murmurs from the assembled students. "None of that now! You all need to remember that the crown pays all of your expenses while you are at the Academy. Repairing some roads and bridges is the least we can do to repay the King for his generosity," said

Stuart. "Now, each of you follow your Mentor; he or she has your assignments for this afternoon. Donovan, since this is your first time doing this, Sorcerer Andrew will take you out and show you what needs to be done. Next time, you will join one of the other groups. Class dismissed to your Mentors."

Donovan walked over to Andrew and asked, "So what's the task for today? The others didn't seem very excited about it." "That's because of the rain. Remember, we don't use Weather shields outside the Academy grounds, so go put your staff in your room and grab a cloak. It's going to be a wet afternoon for both of us."

Donovan hurried back to his room and put his staff in the wardrobe, retrieving his travel cloak. Thinking back, he realized that he hadn't worn it since enrolling in the Academy over six months ago. When he emerged from the dormitory, Andrew was waiting for him. "So, what's our assignment?" asked Donovan. "During the spring rains, many of the roads around Kingston flood due to clogged storm sewers or washed-out culverts. We clear the blockages with either Wind, Dig, Reduce, or Remove spells, depending on the situation. Since you don't know the Remove spell yet, let's hope one or more of the other spells in combination will do the trick," said Andrew.

Andrew produced a map of Kingston, scanned it, and said, "Wow. It looks like the storm drain near your house is clogged. We'd better head right over, or your house could flood." Donovan and Andrew hurried from the Academy entrance to the

82

street in front of Donovan's home. As expected, the storm drain along the road was clogged with twigs and other debris. "So, what do we do?" asked Donovan. "Try using a Wind spell to blow the debris out of the drain and into the vacant lot across the street. Not too much, though, or you'll end up knocking down that tree and making a bigger mess," advised Andrew.

Donovan focused on creating a strong (but not too strong) gust of wind, centered on the rubbish and yard waste that was clogging the storm drain, and murmured softly *"GUSTO"* and made a backhanded wave with his left hand towards the offending clog. A strong gust of wind swiftly picked up the debris and blew most of it into the vacant lot across the street. The remaining twigs and dirt were swept into the drain by the rushing water, and the backed-up water soon resumed its normal course and entered the drain and away from the street.

"Well done," said Wizard Noland from the doorway of Donovan's house. "Perhaps a bit stronger than necessary, but it certainly was effective." "Thank you, sir," said a surprised Donovan. This was, after all, the first time he had received any praise whatsoever from the Headmaster. "Wizard Noland," said Andrew. "Is everything alright?"

"Absolutely," said Noland. "Now, I must ask you both to come in and prepare for a shock, but first, let me conjure a Seeming to conceal our entrance." Once the Seeming of the closed door was in place, the three magicians entered the foyer of the house. Before they went any further, Wizard Noland addressed them sternly. "Neither one of you is to disclose what you're about to learn to anyone without my *personal* approval. Is that clear?" Both Andrew and Donovan nodded their agreement. "I will not be so discourteous as to cast a Secrecy spell on either of you, but you must keep this confidence from everyone but the four of us. Understood?" "The *four* of us?" asked Donovan, confused. "Hello, son," said Edward, emerging from the parlor.

Victor was having no luck at all. The Kniskerns were apparently an inconsequential family with no notoriety whatsoever. Not a single mention in any of the "Who's Who in Franconia" journals in two centuries, no trade patents, not even any real estate transactions that he could find. It was maddening! Victor was almost ready to forget the whole thing and conclude that Wizard Amanda had no offspring, but the consequences if he were wrong would be catastrophic. "Have you found anything yet, Victor?" asked the mysterious, cloaked, and hooded figure standing in the doorway of the Archives.

Victor jumped, startled. When he regained his wits, he replied, "No. Nothing. I found a Wizard Amanda Kniskern in the old rolls of Franconian Magicians, but nothing about their family history. I cannot find any record of descendants or anything about the Kniskerns at all. They appear to be nobodies!" exclaimed Victor. "Where have you looked?" asked the concealed figure. "I have read all of the "Who's Who in Franconia" articles for the last two hundred years, looked at hundreds of patents for inventions, examined thousands of real estate transactions, even reviewed all of the tax records for the past century, but nothing! Maybe we should just give it up and take our chances."

"I doubt that the other members of the Dragon Council would agree. Personally, since *I* am not bound by the spell, I have no objection." Victor waited in silence. He had just learned something valuable; his secretive master was *not* one of the Dragons who had been at the Council meeting. Interesting. "I will offer two thoughts on the matter. First, perhaps the Kniskerns were *not from* Kingston, so their records might be elsewhere, even in Baize. Second, I would recommend examining the marriage records. If Amanda Kniskern or her offspring had daughters, they would have taken their husbands' last name upon their marriage."

"Of course," whispered Victor. "Why did I not think of that?" Victor turned towards the doorway, but the hooded figure was already gone.

"Dad!" shouted Donovan, rushing into his father's arms. "Hello, son," said Edward. "I'm so sorry to have kept this secret from you for so long." "It was a Healing Serum, right?" speculated Donovan. "In your water bottle, and a Healing spell too, probably," said Donovan. "Yes, son. Exactly right. Only my Healing Serum was much more powerful than anything you've been taught yet. I'm sure that Jeffery, I mean Wizard Toffin, has told you that Battle Mages always drink a Healing Serum before battle and carry some in their water bottles, just in case." "He did," said Donovan, "but when I asked him about it, he said that your injuries were probably too severe for any Serum to heal."

"And he was probably correct. But the 'coffin' I brought along is called a 'stasis box.' It was imbued with a Healing spell that helped heal me as well. That's one reason that Battle Mages take them on quests." "Why didn't you tell me?" asked Donovan reproachfully. "Because I wasn't sure it would work, son. As you recall, I was in pretty bad shape. Wizard Toffin is correct that some injuries are too severe, even for the strongest Serums, and I must admit, my Serum was prepared more for burns than broken bones."

"You're just lucky that we didn't bury you as Major Gerald suggested," said Donovan, jokingly. "When I awoke, I would have realized what happened and dug or blasted my way out," said Edward. "That is one of your final lessons at the Academy—'Never assume an enemy is dead unless their head is separated from their body.' More than one enemy made that assumption to their detriment when a 'dead' magician struck them down. Anyway, enough talk of death. How are you, son?"

"Older and wiser, I hope," said Donovan, "and before you say 'I-told-you-so,' I admit, you were right, I have the spark." Edward laughed. "Finally!"

"Now, down to business," said Noland. "Donovan, Andrew, you are not to let anyone know that Edward is alive." "But why?" asked Donovan. "Son, this conspiracy goes way beyond someone just wanting to keep the existence of dragons a secret," said Edward. "What was your impression of the dragon we fought?"

"Well, it seemed like it heard and understood what you said near the end, right before it attacked me," said Donovan. "I thought so too," said Edward. "Now let me tell you what I discovered when I returned to the battle site after waking up on the barge," Edward told Donovan and Andrew about the baby dragon and the older one that he tracked across northern Franconia. He also related the story of the ancient Treaty and the poisoning of the dragons two hundred years ago.

"Yes. Wizard Loren told me about that," said Donovan. "SHE WHAT?" raged Wizard Nolan. "Wizard Loren came to me a couple of months ago and told me that she found an ancient scroll, hidden behind a Seeming in the Academy archives, that described the Dragon Wars and how a treaty was agreed to that dragons would not eat people, and we would provide 20,000 head of cattle every two years. Then we poisoned the cattle, which killed most of the dragons. You mean she didn't tell you?" asked Donovan.

"No, she damn well didn't!" said Noland angrily. "She must be part of the plot." "Not Wizard Loren," said Donovan desperately, "she's always been so nice to me!" "How so?" asked Edward. "Well, when I first enrolled at the Academy, she invited me over for tea, right after the funeral. She said that she wanted to document our quest for the Academy records."

"Tell me about the tea," said Noland. "It was just tea! Come to think of it, it did seem overly sweet, but I thought that was just the way she liked it," said Donovan. "What happened after tea?" asked Edward. "I was really sleepy, so I went straight to bed. I figured it was just the strain of the day—you know, Martial Arts practice, then a funeral," said Donovan. "It sounds like Truth Serum," said Edward. "Donovan, try to remember, what did Wizard Loren ask you about?" "She asked me what I thought about all the incidents on our way to Farmdale and about the attack on us as we tried to get the dragon's head to the King, then about you—if I was sure that you were really dead."

"She was trying to determine how much of the conspiracy we'd already uncovered—and if I was truly dead," said Edward. "Son, what's your impression of Wizard Loren?" "She's my favorite teacher," said Donovan, "she's always been kind to me and helpful. There is one odd thing, though: she doesn't use contractions." "I don't understand," said Noland. "Just like that," said Donovan, "you said 'don't,' she would have said 'I do not understand.' I've never heard her use 'can't,' 'won't,' 'don't,' 'didn't,' 'I'm,' 'they're,' or any other contraction. I thought it was just a dialect thing."

"I must admit, I've never noticed it before," mused Noland. "That's a keen observation, Donovan." "But what does it mean?" asked Edward. "I have no idea. Donovan, please start keeping track of anyone else at the Academy who doesn't use contractions. It might be significant," said Noland. "You too, Andrew."

"Sir, why am I here?" asked Andrew. "You didn't need to take me into your confidence like this." Noland looked at Edward. "Well, Andrew," said Edward, "It's because you're family." "I don't understand," said Andrew. "You are my late wife's older sister's son," explained Edward. "Your mother and father live in Southport, right?" Andrew nodded. "And you ran away from home because you thought you had the spark and wanted to enroll at the Wizards Academy." "How did you know that? My parents didn't want anything to do with magic. My mother said that her little sister married a magician and was killed because of it. When I left, they disowned me!"

"I know," said Edward gently, "your aunt was my wife, and your mother and father were not wrong in what they told you. It was because of me that she was killed." "Someone froze her in midsummer," whispered Andrew. "Yes," said Edward, "and you realize that only a powerful Wizard could do such a thing." "We think that's why Donovan is blocked from using the *THERMO REDUCTUS* spell to cool things," said Andrew.

"No," said Edward, "that may be part of it, but the block is because of me." "What?" said Donovan. "Son, I think the block is because you've never forgiven me for your mother's death." "I'm so sorry, father. I know it wasn't your fault," cried Donovan, embracing his father.

"There it is," said Edward through his tears. "That should be the last of that block."

Chapter Eight:
INSIGHTS

Victor finally felt like he was making some progress tracing the Kniskern family tree. While there were no records of how Wizard Amanda died, it seemed that she might have had a son, Robert Kniskern, who married and had children. By following the marriage records and the death records of Kingston, Victor had been able to trace four generations of Amanda's progeny. He was almost there; let's see—the last surviving male Kniskern, Raymond Kniskern, had two daughters, Beverly and Joyce. Beverly had moved to Southport and married Joseph Perrucci. There was no indication that they had any children, and Joyce—Blast it all! Joyce had married Edward Francis, and they had one son, Donovan!

"Any progress, Victor?" asked a voice from the shadows. Victor started; he was getting weary of his master sneaking up on him. "Yes! I think I have it! Wizard Amanda's only remaining offspring are a woman in Southport named Beverly Perrucci and, believe it or not, that meddling boy, Donovan Francis." "The Battle Mage's son?" asked the voice. "Just so," said Victor. "Now, I suppose I shall have to cancel my plans for his accidental death at the Wizards Academy." "Only if you want to survive this conflict," said the voice. "Wait!" said Victor, "the Binding spell that Ard cast was that Amanda's descendants 'must be spared.' Does that mean spared from death or *injury*? If Donovan were to lose a hand or his eyesight in training…" "You would need to ask Ard, since it was his Binding spell. *I* would not be too quick to assume it is only Donovan's death you need to fear. At least you seem to have solved one mystery. When will the attacks occur?" asked the shadows.

"We will coordinate the raids during the next meeting of the Dragon Council, which is scheduled for the first full moon of autumn." "Very well," said the voice, "in the meantime, I suggest that you ensure that nothing unfortunate happens to Level Two Donovan Francis or the woman in Southport. The injury or death of either could mean your doom."

"Before we head back to the Academy, I remind you two that your Mentor/student relationship has not changed, that *no one* can learn of your relationship, or that Edward is alive," stressed Wizard Noland. Both Andrew and Donovan nodded their understanding. "Now, off with you, I need to have a word with Edward."

Andrew and Donovan left the house, heading back to the Academy through the still heavy rain. "At least we'll be soaked when we arrive," said Andrew. "If we returned bone dry, people might suspect that we hadn't spent the afternoon in the rain." They trudged through the downpour, back to the Academy's entrance. Wizard Stuart opened the door as they approached. "Well, you two are back at last! I was almost ready to send out a search party!" said Stuart cheerfully. "How did it go?" "The drain is clear," Andrew replied crossly, "but Donovan needs to learn that the Dig spell is not the right one for cleaning storm drains. He made quite a mess of it that *I* had to help repair. We would have been back sooner if he had chosen a Wind spell," groused Andrew.

"Many Level Twos make that same mistake their first time," said Stuart kindly. "I am sure that he will not make the same mistake again." "I hope not," said Andrew, "or it's going to be a long Spring." Stuart laughed. "Hurry along to supper now; the bell rang a while ago." As Donovan and Andrew headed towards their respective dormitories, Donovan muttered quietly, "No contractions." Andrew nodded solemnly.

Back at Edward's house, Noland and Edward were considering what to do next. "What are you going to do about Wizard Loren?" asked Edward. "I'll begin by telling her that Donovan told Andrew about the scroll she showed him about the Dragon War and that Andrew mentioned it to me. We'll see what her explanation is." "What I can't figure out is, '*What does she gain by helping the dragons?*'" said Edward. "It just doesn't make sense."

"I agree," mused Noland. "What do you know about her?" asked Edward. "Not as much as I should, obviously. She was already an instructor at the Academy when I was appointed as

Headmaster. I think she came from Three Forks." "Was she a 'walk-in' or a 'drag-in'?" asked Edward. "No idea," replied Noland. "I guess I could ask Stuart; he's been at the Academy the longest." "I'd hold off on that for now," advised Edward. "We don't know how deep this conspiracy runs, and if some of them got into the Academy—" "Then Stuart was probably the one who let them in," finished Noland.

"There is one other possibility, one that I hesitate to mention," said Edward. "You've always brought up troubling ideas, even as a Level One, as I recall," said Noland. "What now?" "We know that dragons are magical creatures, otherwise the Binding spell wouldn't work on them," said Edward. "Agreed," said Noland worriedly. "What if dragons can *perform* magic?" speculated Edward.

"Are you suggesting that dragons can cast spells?" asked Noland incredulously. "It would explain a great deal," said Edward. "If dragons can cast spells, and if they know the Change spell—" "You're saying that dragons may be disguised as humans and walking amongst us," said Noland darkly. "It would explain much," said Edward. "But proving it could be difficult." "I think Wizard Loren needs some Truth Serum," said Noland. "Eventually," agreed Edward. "Let's wait and see what Donovan and Andrew discover. If dragons can't use contractions—" "Then we may be able to identify the lot of them," finished Noland. "Hopefully," said Edward. "But how long have they been among us, and what's their agenda? They could have attacked us at any time." "The very question I intend to eventually ask Loren," said Wizard Noland.

They left at dusk, Gek and Azure flying northeast, towards the mountains near Smithville, while Teal and Cobalt flew southeast, towards the human city of Eastport. "Remember to try and blend in," said Teal. "I would advise you to get some other clothes for Azure as soon as possible, since she is likely to attract unwanted attention from the human men wearing what she has now. Remember, you have less than one cycle of the moon in each town; find any Changed Ones that you can, and determine if they will be willing to help us against the humans when the time comes. We will meet you back in the quarry on the Amber River on the first full moon of autumn."

Gek and Azure flew towards the mountains in the distance. It was a relatively short flight, and they arrived well before midnight. "We need to find a secure place to stay," said Azure. "I do not think we should stay in the town overnight." "You are probably right, but flying back and forth each night is going to increase our risk of discovery. We will just have to play it by ear. Maybe if we find some Changed Ones, we can stay with them," Gek said hopefully. After a brief search, they found an abandoned coal mine on the Smithville side of the mountains and settled in. They decided to leave before dawn and fly as close to the town as was safe before transforming into humans. The mine was dark, dusty, and smelled funny. Gek and Azure curled up together and fell asleep.

When they woke, it was after mid-day. "We overslept!" they said together. "I guess we should just transform here and walk into town. Hopefully, it is not too far," said Gek. He transformed and unwrapped the bundle that was their human clothes. "Stop staring at me," he grumbled. Azure chuckled, scooped up her clothes, and headed deeper into the mine to transform. Gek pulled on the burlap tunic and wrapped the rope around his waist as a belt. A few minutes later, Azure emerged wearing the too-tight top and the too-short skirt.

"On second thought," said Gek, "maybe we should just stay here for a while and get used to these new bodies." "Nice try, handsome," said Azure. "Just walk me to town and stop leering." Gek smiled wickedly, then turned and fell flat on his face. Azure laughed. "Walking on two legs is going to take some getting used to," said Gek, wiping the coal dust from his face. "We should practice walking in here for a while until we get the hang of it." Azure agreed, and for the next hour or so, they staggered around the mine shaft, bracing themselves against the walls and timbers for support. Eventually, they learned to balance on two legs, without a tail as a counter-weight. Gek noticed deep bruises on the back of Azure's upper thighs. "Is that from the alligator?" he asked. "I think so," said Azure. "I need something to cover it, or the humans are going to notice." "Not just the humans," smiled Gek. Azure twisted, as if trying to slap Gek with her nonexistent tail. Gek understood her intent and laughed. "All right, let us look around. There might be something the humans left behind that will work."

After searching several shafts and side tunnels, they found an old, ragged, faded green tarp that the miners had left in the mine. Gek disrobed and quickly transformed back into a Dragon, and with Azure's help, they managed to fashion the tarp into an open-sided tunic that covered Azure from her shoulders to her knees. They used half of Gek's belt to secure the garment. "This is much better," said Azure. "I will not attract as much attention now." As they approached the mine entrance, they noticed that it was nearly dusk. "We are not off to a very good start," observed Azure. "Well, we have learned how to walk on two legs and found you some new clothes," said Gek. "I do not think that is a bad first day. Shall we sleep as humans or Dragons?" "Dragons, silly," demurred Azure. "It would be much too uncomfortable to sleep on the floor as humans."

They rose well before dawn the next day, gathered their human clothes, and flew towards the town. They landed in a wooded area just on the outskirts of the town and transformed into humans. As they walked around the town, the first thing they noticed was the smell. Smithville smelled of coal, ash, and sweat. Most of the buildings were forges, warehouses, smithies, or family dwellings. All of the roads were dirt or gravel. There were two Supply Stores in what passed for the market square, one inn, and three or four taverns, none of which were open for business yet. "I guess breakfast will have to wait a bit," said Gek.

"Can we at least find some water so I can wash up?" asked Azure. "I think I saw a fountain in the square," replied Gek. "We might as well start there."

They found the two-spout fountain in the middle of the town square. Azure hastily washed her hands and face and was rinsing off her arms when a voice behind her said, "It won't do no good." Azure turned to find an elderly woman carrying a bucket, approaching the fountain. "Excuse me?" said Azure. "Cleanin' up in the mornin' won't do no good," said the woman. "Once the foundries and smithies get goin' the air's gonna be full o' coal dust, smoke, and ash. No use washin' up until right before bed. Don't nobody wanna sleep with grit all over em'."

"I suppose you are right," said Azure. "My name is Azure, and this is my friend, um, Jed." "Pleased ta meet cha,'" said the old woman with a toothy grin. "My name's Annie. Where you folks from?" "We just came into town from Eastport," said Gek, mentioning the closest human town he knew. "We are on our way north, to visit family."

"Eastport, eh? That's a bit of a walk." "Yes," said Azure. "Is there anyplace where we can get something to eat?" "Well, the ironworks will be openin' a bit after dawn, too dangerous to work iron in the dark, ya know." "I have never worked in a forge before," said Gek. "My family were fishermen." "I expect so, bein' from Eastport. I reckon most folks down there fish for a livin.' You asked about food. Most o' the taverns'll be openin' soon. If you got coin, they got eats," said Annie.

"We have a little," said Azure. "Well, then I recommend the Farmer's Dog, right over there, across the square. Good food, reasonable prices. They treat travelers right. Not as rough as some o' the other taverns that cater to the locals." "I appreciate the advice," said Gek. "Can I help you carry the water?"

"Why, that's uncommon friendly of you. I really appreciate it. These old bones aren't meant for carryin' much anymore," said Annie gratefully. Gek filled the bucket from the fountain and asked where she was headed. "Why, over ta the Farmer's Dog, o' course," said Annie with a sly grin. Won't be no tea for ya'll without this water." Gek laughed.

"What's with the blue hair?" Annie asked Azure as they proceeded across the square. "Oh, it is just how some of the young people are wearing it in Eastport these days. Have you seen anyone around here with it?" asked Azure hopefully. Annie thought for a moment. "No. I can't say as I have. Cept', I recall old Alice had a blue streak in her hair before she went grey a few years back."

Azure

Chapter Nine:

THE SMELL TEST

Gek and Azure followed Annie into the Farmer's Dog tavern. It was dimly lit, with only ten or twelve tables towards the back of the building for customers. The bar area was near the doorway, and there were perhaps twenty barstools arrayed along the counter. The kitchen was through a double door between the bar and the seating area. "I'll be right out with some tea as soon as I get this water boiling," said Annie. "What would you like to eat?"

"What do you have?" asked Gek, hungry as usual. "Eggs, bacon, sausage, fried potatoes, maybe some leftover porridge," said Annie. "Any fish?" asked Azure. "Fish for breakfast? You're an odd duck! Then again, you did say you was from Eastport. JAKE!" Annie yelled, "We got any of that whitefish leftover from yesterday?" A voice from the kitchen confirmed that there was a bit of fish still in the icebox. "I will have the fish," said Azure. "And I would like some bacon and sausage, please," said Gek. "How much will that be?"

"A copper each for the tea and three each for the food," said Annie. "Will that be a problem?" Gek dumped the metal discs out of his money pouch onto the table, looking at the coins. Annie scooped up one of the two silver discs and said, "Be right back with your change, Jed."

Breakfast was an adventure of sorts. Neither dragon had ever eaten *cooked* meat or fish. It didn't taste bad, just *different*. Gek said that the tea tasted like hot swamp water, earning him a scowl from Azure. When they had finished eating, they asked Annie where they could find Alice. "She's got a small house on the edge of town," said Annie. "Just turn right when you go out my door and follow the road to the end of the street. Her house has a blue door and green shutters on the windows." They thanked her and headed out the door and down the street. The townsfolk were up an about now, and smoke was rising from the foundries and the blacksmith shops. Teams of horses were pulling wagons loaded with iron bars and headed down the road to Eastport or Grotton.

Gek and Azure found Alice's house without difficulty and knocked on the door. An elderly, grey-haired woman cracked open the door and peeked out. She took one look at Azure and said, "Get in here, you two! Quick, before somebody sees!"

Gek and Azure entered quickly, and Alice shut and locked the door, then pulled the curtains closed. She lit a candle from the sideboard and placed it on the coffee table in the parlor. "Sit down, sit down," Alice chided. Gek and Azure sat on the small sofa, and Alice sat in an armchair opposite them. "Now, tell me child, what is a nice Sea Dragon like you doing in a place like this?"

"That makes thirteen," said Donovan quietly. "Four Level Twos; six Level Threes; one Mentor, plus Loren and Stuart. Plus, I can't get to any Level Ones anymore. Maybe I could ask Evan—" "NO!" said Andrew emphatically. "Do not involve Evan in any way. He would give us away." "Evan is my friend," said Donovan. "I said, 'No.'" repeated Andrew. "Donovan, you don't understand; Evan's higher brain functions were destroyed when the Wizards removed his spark. It's all he can do to deliver food and drinks to the Level One students, wash dishes, and provide the occasional wake-up call to the Level Ones who pay him for that service like you did. Someone probably even had to remind him to wake you up every morning. He is incapable of figuring out which, if any, of the six Level Ones don't use contractions and report back to you. He would give himself away and probably end up dead! Besides, a Level One is not a threat to us." "Unless they're a dragon," said Donovan.

They were standing at the edge of the Forces Training area, almost at the barrier, speaking in hushed tones. "Donovan, this is all speculation. We don't even know if dragons can cast the Change spell or if not using contractions is what sets them apart from humans," said Andrew. "Besides, you need to focus more on your Level Two spells and less on who is or isn't using contractions." "But—" "No 'buts' Donovan. Leave finding the dragons to the Wizards!" "I couldn't have said it better myself," said Wizard Noland, appearing beside them. Both Andrew and Donovan jumped in surprise. "Wizard Noland," explained Donovan, "I was just—" "I heard every word, Donovan and your Mentor is right. I appreciate your diligence, but you need to refocus yourself on your studies. Some of your instructors have commented to me that you don't seem as attentive to your studies as you were as a Level One. That is unacceptable." "I'm sorry, Sir. I'm just concerned," said Donovan. "As am I, Donovan," said Wizard Noland. "Now, I have your list of thirteen names, and there is one Level One that I'm keeping an eye on. You concentrate on your lessons." "Yes, sir," said Donovan. "I did have another thought, if you're interested." "What is it?" asked Noland. "I was wondering if a dragon, who was disguised as a human, smelled different," said Donovan. "Smelled different. Hmm, I hadn't thought of that. Why do you ask?" "It's just that, during our Smell enhancement lesson, I may have used the enhancement to smell some of my classmates, and four of them smelled different than everyone else."

"Different, how?" asked Wizard Noland. "It's hard to describe, but when I cut off the dragon's head, it smelled bad. This smells like that, just weaker, if you know what I mean," explained Donovan. "Donovan, if you survive to become a Sorcerer, you may be an exceptional one," said Noland. "I never thought of using the Smell enhancement to try and root out our visitors. I will inform your father also. Andrew, when you have time, see if you can detect a different smell from any of the Mentors or students." "Yes, Sir," said Andrew.

"A final word of caution, Andrew: the next time you two discuss this, please cast a Silence spell around you. Using a Listening spell, I heard you both from my office."

"Sire, I have received troubling news from our spies in Franconia," said Wizard Louis, the tall, red-haired Court Wizard of the Kingdom of Baize. "What is young King Henry doing this time?" asked King Donald, wearily. King Donald was old, almost sixty, with thinning grey hair and a stooped posture. "Henry has sent a significant number of spies into your Kingdom, Sire. We have recently captured five new agents, in addition to the ones we already knew about," said Louis.

"What do you mean, 'the ones we already knew about'?" asked the King. Louis smoothed his crimson robes and said, "Sire, Franconia currently has about a dozen spies inside the kingdom. These are agents that are known to us. Rather than arrest and interrogate them, we simply watch them and see where they live and which of our citizens they are in contact with. At times, we feed disinformation to these agents, in order to deceive the Franconians about our capabilities and intentions."

"I see," said the King. "So what is so troubling about these new spies?" "They are apparently concentrating their efforts on learning about the defenses of our towns and cities along the

Amber River, our border with Franconia. The known spies are mainly after commercial or economic information: will the price of salt increase? How many trading ships are we building? Have we raised taxes lately? That sort of thing. These new spies are after more military-type information."

"I see. You think Henry is planning an invasion?" asked the King. "I think he is at least considering it, Sire." "What about our spies in Franconia? Do they have any explanation for this increase in intelligence gathering by Franconia?" Louis frowned, dramatically, "Sire, our agents have unconfirmed reports that the Franconians are blaming us for the supposed Dragon that recently attacked their people around the town of Farmdale."

"That's preposterous! How could we make a dragon attack Franconia?" asked Donald. "We could not, Sire, but King Henry appears to be receiving bad advice from his military leaders. He is very young, after all." "I suppose," said the King. "What have you done with the agents that you captured?" "They are being held for questioning under Truth Serum, Your Majesty. Once the interrogations are complete, I will, of course, inform you of the information we obtain," replied Louis.

"Whatever you do, don't kill them. We may need them for a prisoner exchange at some point if our relations with Franconia continue to sour. Has there been any reaction from Franconia regarding the arrest of their agents?" "None, Sire. However, that is not unusual. These matters involving captured spies are generally handled quietly so as not to alarm the public."

"I understand," said the King, "what do you recommend we do, Louis?" "Your Majesty, I have several recommendations: first, I believe we should send additional agents into Franconia and instruct them to gather military information, rather than the economic data they usually seek; second, it might be prudent to move additional forces to our border cities and towns, not many— we don't want to provoke Franconia, but enough to deter them from any rash actions; lastly, we should quietly conduct our own investigation into this supposed Dragon attack on Farmdale; it may be a 'false flag' operation, designed to stir up animosity towards us as a pretense to an invasion."

"I approve of the additional agents. Which forces do you propose moving?" "That is a question for Wizard James, Sire. My knowledge of military matters is somewhat limited," said Louis. "Well, James?" Wizard James, the middle-aged Chief of Military Wizardry in Baize, considered the question for several seconds, then said, "Sire, as you know, we have a Regiment of four Battalions in the city of Springfield; we could send a Battalion to Weaton, and another to our garrison at Colton."

"What about Riverside?" asked the King. "Sire, Riverside is a small town, surrounded by the Amber River, the Great Salt Flats, the Snow Fields, and the Grey Mountains; militarily, it has no real significance. If Franconia attacked it, we would have ample time to muster our forces to repel them." "What about

Westport?" asked Louis. "I would send additional Navy ships to provide security for Westport. We can get them there faster without straining the Army's resources," said Wizard James.

"Very well," said the King. "Louis, James, please see to all these deployments, especially the additional spies. I do not want to act without accurate and complete information. The last thing we need right now is a war with Franconia."

"Of course, Your Majesty," said Louis smoothly, "What about the investigation into the supposed Dragon?" "I want you to focus on getting me actionable information. That is your number one priority. Have your Assistant—Kathy? Yes, assign the task of investigating the dragon attack to Mage Kathy. She's been itching to do something other than financial audits."

"As you command, Sire," said Wizard Louis.

Alice looked at Gek and sniffed. "You do not smell right. There is a hint of Sea Dragon there, but something else too." She paused, considering. "A Great Dragon! I am honored! I have not seen a Great Dragon in decades!"

"I am Azure, daughter of Teal, Chief of the Sea Dragons," said Azure. "And this is Gek, Son of Cobalt, a Sea Dragon, and Liza, a Great Dragon. He is the grandson of Ard." "How is old Ard?" asked Alice. "I have not seen him since he visited the

Coral Islands, almost two centuries ago." "Ard was well when we left him about a week ago. He complains that 'everything hurts' and he is getting old," said Gek. Alice laughed. "Ard was old two hundred years ago," said Alice, smiling. "So, what can I do for a Great Dragon and his mate?"

"We are searching for Changed Ones," said Gek. "Are there any others, besides you in Smithville?" "There used to be," said Alice sadly. "Now, there is only me." "What happened?" asked Azure. "Most of us that settled here were Sea Dragons," said Alice. "Oh, every now and then, a Great Dragon would wander through town, but few settled here. It is the smoke, you see. The dust, smoke, and ash get *everywhere* once the furnaces are lit and the smithies begin working hot iron. We were used to the fresh sea air; the smoke was intolerable to most of the others."

"Why did you stay?" asked Gek. "I fell in love with a handsome human blacksmith," said Alice, "I was young, and my human form was shapely. Some of the men in town tried to take advantage, but my Thomas protected me and drove them away. We were inseparable after that." "What happened to him?" asked Azure, gently. "Oh, he died. About fifteen years ago. Old age, you see. That is one of the problems that comes with mating with a human. While we are *transformed* into human likeness, we still retain our 'dragon-ness' if you know what I mean. Our tastes in food and our long lifespan. All of the Changed Ones have experienced such."

"I never considered that," said Gek. "So, why do you seek the Changed Ones?" asked Alice. Gek considered his answer before replying. "The head of the Dragon Council has decided that it is time for us to come out of hiding and resume our rightful place." "You plan to make war on the humans?" asked Alice. "Yes," said Gek. "A human magic-user killed my mother a short while ago, and I mean to take my vengeance."

"Your mother was the Great Dragon killed north of Farmdale?" asked Alice. "You know about that?" asked Gek. "Yes. Smithville may be a small town, but such news travels fast. Besides, that was months ago." "So, will you help us?" asked Azure.

"What could I do?" asked Alice. "I am old. I cannot breathe fire. Now that my Thomas is gone, I bear no love for the humans in this town, but since *the incident,* they have left me alone and tolerated my presence in their community. Annie is my friend."

"The Incident?" asked Gek, "what was that?" "After my Thomas died, I let my guard down, and the blue highlights in my hair returned. Much as your hair, dear," Alice said to Azure. "The villagers thought the blue hair marked me as a witch. They tried to burn me at the stake." "What did you do?" asked Azure, shocked. Alice chuckled. "I spelled them all to sleep. Then, while they were sleeping, I dyed my hair grey, as it is now. When they awoke, they could not remember why they were outside my door. They have left me alone since then, although I do keep my hair grey, just in case."

"Why not just leave?" asked Azure. "Like Ard, I am too old to travel far, and I do not know if the Sea Dragons would accept me back into the Clan after so many years," said Alice. "If you wish, I can talk to my father, Teal. He could order the Clan to allow your return," said Azure forcefully.

"You are kind, dear, but I think I will remain here. While I may not be able to do much, I will assist my kin when the time comes," said Alice. "Thank you, Alice. Do you know where we should go next to look for other Changed Ones?" asked Azure.

"Hmm," thought Alice. "I would try Hayford, a larger town to the northwest, then maybe Farmdale. That was always 'Great Dragon country.' But first, let me get you some better clothes, Azure. It looks like you have been rolling around in a mine. I also have some of Thomas's old clothes that might suit you better than that burlap sack, Gek." "Thank you, Alice," said Azure. "That would be much appreciated."

"How are you set for money?" asked Alice. "I do not know," said Gek, "here is what we have." Gek emptied their few coins onto the table. "Oh, no," said Alice. "That is only one silver and six coppers. A silver coin is worth ten coppers. If you had a gold coin, it would be worth ten silvers. Sixteen coppers might pay for one night in an inn or three meals for the both of you. You will need to find a job to earn enough coins to continue your search."

"What kind of job could I get in this town?" asked Gek. "Do you know the Dig spell?" asked Alice. "Yes," replied Gek, "but what good is that?" "Tomorrow, I will take you to the Mining Company. They are always looking for workers. Go into the mine and use the Dig spell when you are working alone. Dig shallow holes! Too much, and they will suspect you are a magician! After a few weeks, you will earn enough coins to complete your search," said Alice.

"What about Azure?" asked Gek. "I would not leave her unguarded." "Azure can stay with me and help with the chores around the house. It would be best if she were not seen in town again. There could be trouble. The two of you will sleep here, of course." "Thank you, Alice," said Gek. "I am glad you did not let the smell drive you out of this town."

Chapter Ten:

GESTURES

Donovan stood in the field beside himself. He looked himself over closely, searching for any flaws or mistakes. When he was satisfied, he called to Wizard Mira, "I think I've got it this time, Wizard Mira!" The attractive Seemings teacher approached and examined the Seeming closely. "Hmm, Yes, I think you've done a good job with this one," she said. "Now, cast it behind that rock over there," said Mira, pointing to a large rock about ten yards away.

Donovan concentrated, looking at the rock, then cast a Seeming of himself, standing behind it. The Seeming was blurry, almost transparent, and his legs were *inside* the rock. "So, you see," said Mira, "casting Seemings at a distance is much more difficult than a Seeming near you. Also, you need to judge distances better, so your Seeming does not end up inside something like a rock. You may release the Seeming." "*CODA*," said Donovan quietly, and the Seeming of himself disappeared.

"Very good," said Mira. "I want you to practice casting Seemings at a distance. They do not all have to be of yourself; pick something easier, like a box or a cauldron. Then see how far away you can cast them and still have them look real." "When would I ever need to cast a Seeming at a distance?" asked Donovan. "Well, consider your fight with the dragon. If you cast a Seeming of yourself too close to you, I imagine that the dragon could have flamed both you and the Seeming at once. Couldn't it?" "I should have thought of that," said Donovan quietly. "When will we learn to cast Seemings that move?"

"Patience, Donovan, patience," admonished Mira. "Once you master Seemings at a distance, we will move on to casting Seemings that move. Casting a moving Seeming of significant size requires more power. Most Seemings require almost no physical effort. Large, moving Seemings are much more demanding. Besides, you already know how to cast small Seemings that move." "I do?" asked Donovan, confused. "Of course, have you never thrown a Seeming of a stone at a classmate during Shields or Martial Arts practice?" asked Mira.

"No. Now that you mention it, I never have. Level One Lisa cast one at me once, and Wizard Stuart used a Seeming of a staff against me when we sparred for the first time. I'd forgotten about it," said Donovan thoughtfully. "If Stuart had to use a Seeming against you, then you must be exceptionally good with a staff," said Mira. "I suppose so. He advanced me to the Level Three class in Martial Arts," said Donovan.

"I know," said Mira. "For now, concentrate on Seemings at a distance."

Donovan felt that the Level Two training (so far) was not much more difficult than the spells and enhancements he had mastered as a Level One magician. The main challenge was remembering all the different incantations and gestures. More than once, he'd performed the wrong gesture with an incantation, and just as Wizard Loren had explained, the spell hadn't worked. Some of the gestures were intuitive, waving your hand towards your nose for the Smell enhancement, flexing your right bicep for the Strength enhancement, and the 'grabbing' motion of the Tether spell, while the gestures for some, like the spell for heating and cooling things (putting your hand on your chest), didn't make much sense. There were always chuckles among the students when someone made the wrong gesture for a spell, and it didn't work.

The fact that Donovan had overcome his block for the cooling spell had been a topic of great excitement at the Academy, for about a day. Then everyone forgot about it, and things got back to what had passed as 'normal' at Wizards Academy. Wizard Loren had been especially interested in how Donovan had overcome his block.

"Well, ma'am," explained Donovan, "Wizard Noland was helping me one evening after dinner, and we talked about what happened to my mother, her being frozen to death by a magician, and how that was likely causing my block. Wizard Nolan suggested that it might be because I had never forgiven my father for my mother's death." "Yes, that could certainly explain it. After all, there is healing in forgiveness," said Loren.

"It just never occurred to me to forgive my dead father," said Donovan. "I mean, it's a little late now. Anyway, once I said the words, 'I forgive you, father,' I felt something inside me change, and the block was gone." "Well," said Loren, "I am so very glad that your block is gone. Wizard Noland is a wise man."

"Your Majesty, I have reports that the Kingdom of Baize is moving forces from their garrison in Springfield south towards Weaton," said Victor. "Why would they do that?" asked the King. "I can think of no reason other than a precursor to an invasion of Franconia, Sire," said Victor. "From Weaton, they could march south and attack Westport or proceed east through Prarrieville and then on to either Southport or even Kingston."

"Jasmine, what do you know of this?" The King asked the head of the Royal Watchers, his agency of spies. "I am afraid that Wizard Victor is correct, Your Majesty. My agents have also reported the movement of armsmen, both infantry and cavalry, out of Springfield. I should know by tomorrow whether they turn east towards our town of Weaton on the Amber River or continue on the road south to the Baizian city of Gulfport on their coast." "Why would they move troops now?" asked the King. "It might just be the normal rotation of troops that occurs in late spring or early summer, or as Victor implies, they could be planning to attack Weaton," said Jasmine Onyx, the Minister of Franconian Internal Security.

"Have we done anything to provoke them?" asked the King. "Well," replied Jasmine, "As you commanded, I have increased the number of our agents in Baize lately, and a few of them have not reported in for several weeks. They may have been captured and detained, but there have been no official protests or accusations of spying from Baize."

"What do you recommend, Victor?' asked the King. "Weaton only has a single infantry company, the 15th, stationed there. The closest reinforcing force we have nearby is the 10th Battalion in Westport, Sire. I would recommend sending one Company of infantry and a Squadron of cavalry from the 10th to 'conduct maneuvers' between Westport and Weaton, so they will be close at hand if needed," said Victor.

"What about magical support?" asked the King. "Sire, because of their location on the border, the 15th Company in Weaton has a Sorcerer assigned to it, and there is the Regional Sorcerer also. I think two Sorcerers should be enough. If the Baizian's intent is to draw forces away from Westport, the 10th Battalion's Battle Mage and his Sorcerer assistant will be needed there. If you think it wise, we could move the Second Regiment from Kingston to Prarrieville, to block any advance on Kingston. You recall that Prarrieville only has one battalion, the 11th stationed in the town, and only a single Sorcerer."

"What do you think, Marshall Guzman?" the King asked his military commander. Marshall Guzman shifted uncomfortably. If there was no invasion, moving troops around would cost money, something the King was loathe to part with. On the other hand, if there was an invasion, and he failed to act, it could mean his head. "Sire, I think Wizard Victor's suggestion about the field exercises for the two Companies in Westport is appropriate, but I think moving a single Battalion from the Second Regiment, say, First Battalion with the Regiment's Battle Mage and the Battalion's Sorcerer, to reinforce the battalion in Prarrieville would be sufficient for now. Moving the entire Second Regiment would cost a lot of coin."

"An excellent suggestion, Marshall!" declared the King. "I like a man who considers the costs of military operations! Send out those orders today, and tell the forces to make haste." "As you command, Sire," said Marshall Guzman, who hurried from the throne room to issue the orders.

"Is there anything else we should be doing, Victor, Jasmine?" asked the King. "I will alert the Forces in Weaton, Sire," said Victor, "and instruct them to increase their scouting patrols and strengthen their prepared positions along the Amber River." "And I will increase the reporting frequency of my agents in Baize, Sire," said Jasmine. "Very well," said the King. "Keep me informed." "Of course, Sire," said Victor and Jasmine in unison.

"I can't do it," said Phillip angrily. "Do what?" asked Donovan. "This Remove spell! I've tried everything, but it just won't work for me," Phillip said. "What are you trying to remove?" "This stupid rock," replied Phillip, "but it doesn't matter; no matter what I try to remove, it doesn't work!" "Blocked?" asked Donovan. "I guess so. It probably has to do with what happened to Jacob." Not wanting to pry, Donovan just waited.

"Go ahead and ask," said Phillip. "Everyone else already knows." "I didn't want to pry into your personal business," said Donovan softly. Phillip waited a moment, then said, "Jacob is two years older than me. He was also a 'drag-in. When he was caught by the Regional Mage, he took full responsibility and protected me from being brought here with him. We were both counterfeiting coins. I got caught a year later by the same damn Mage. Anyway, Jacob was performing the Remove spell, and when he performed the gesture, (flicking your right wrist, with the back of your hand toward the object being removed), his left hand was between his right hand and the object he was trying to remove. His left hand disappeared instantly, and it couldn't be healed."

"That's terrible!" said Donovan. "Didn't Wizard Dylan warn him of the danger?" "I don't know," said Phillip. "They certainly warn students now, don't they? He might have warned him. Jacob never did listen well." "So, Jacob couldn't pass the tests to be a Sorcerer," said Donovan sadly. "No," confirmed Phillip. "Some spells have to be cast with the left hand, and some, like shields, require both hands." "I'm sorry," said Donovan. "So am I," said Phillip, "and now it seems that because of that, I have a block for this spell."

"Hmm," thought Donovan. "I wonder if this is like my block." "How so?" asked Phillip. "After my mother was frozen to death by a magician in mid-summer, I never forgave my father, who was a Battle Mage, for not protecting her better. Wizard Noland suggested that I forgive my father, even though he's dead now. Once I did, my block vanished." "So, you think I need to forgive Jacob for removing his own hand?" asked Phillip doubtfully. "I don't know," said Donovan. "I think you're angry with Jacob for not succeeding here and then returning to help your parents or even being able to help you with your lessons here." "You may be right. I am angry with him," said Phillip. "Then tell him you forgive him at dinner tonight and see if it helps. Wizard Loren says that there is healing in forgiveness." "I'll give it a try, thanks," said Phillip.

"In History class, you said that you haven't seen your parents in two years?" asked Donovan. "A little longer, so?" "So, if you want, I could lend you some money, and we can arrange for them to travel here for a visit one Endday afternoon," said Donovan. "You'd do that for me? Why?" asked Phillip suspiciously. "Call it penance for making you look foolish when we sparred," said Donovan. "Besides, it's just a loan." "I would appreciate that very much!" said Phillip.

Chapter Eleven:

COUNCILS

"**D**ad, why aren't you a Wizard?" asked Donovan. Across the sitting room in Edward's home, Wizard Noland laughed out loud, and Sorcerer Andrew looked curious. "Your son asks good questions, Edward!" said Noland.

Edward ignored Noland's jab. "Well, son," answered Edward, "there are a few reasons I haven't taken the Wizard's Test yet. At first, I decided that it was better to be a strong Mage than a weak Wizard." "I don't understand," interrupted Donovan. "Right now, as a Mage, I can cast two really strong spells and hold them for hours at a time," explained Edward. "Trying to hold three spells at once is much more difficult and takes more power from the magician. Sometimes, two really strong spells are better than three weaker ones. A weak shield would not have protected us from the dragon fire."

"I keep telling you that over time, you will learn to hold three spells as strongly as you hold two spells now," said Noland. "I know, Michael," said Edward, "and I intend to take the test eventually. The second reason I hesitated was that several of my friends who took the Wizard's Test before I was posted to Prarrieville died during the testing." "What?" said Donovan, alarmed, "the test can kill you?" "Only in extremely rare cases," insisted Noland.

"It was three cases in the same year," said Edward, "and I knew all three of them. They were strong Mages and yet, none of them survived the testing. That was right after High Wizard Jones died. The timing always seemed suspicious to me." "You suspect foul play?" asked Noland. Edward sat in thought for a moment before answering. He sipped his wine and scratched his head. "I had no proof, nor any way to find any," said Edward finally, "and let's just say that I was dissatisfied with the results of the inquisitions after each."

"Why didn't you say anything to me?" asked Noland. "You had just been appointed as Headmaster of the Wizards Academy," said Edward. "I didn't want any suspicion or blame to be cast in your direction, even though you had nothing to do with their testing." "Who did conduct the tests?" asked Noland. "With no High Wizard available, the testing was conducted by the Court Wizard and two instructors from the Academy," said Edward. "Let me guess, Wizards Stuart and Loren," said Noland. "Exactly," confirmed Edward.

"Anyway, before I could investigate any further, I was assigned to the garrison in Prarrieville. Almost immediately, I noticed that weapons started coming up missing, and then Joyce was murdered. After that, I devoted myself to other matters than the Wizard's Test," said Edward darkly. "Dad—," said Donovan. "No, son, it's alright. When I was assigned as the Battle Mage for the First Regiment here in Kingston, I planned to take the Wizard's Test as soon as my duties permitted. Then

I got sent looking for a dragon, and now I'm presumed dead," finished Edward.

The silence dragged on as the four magicians sat in thought. Finally, Andrew asked, "Sir, we've identified twelve students and two faculty in the Academy that may be in league with the dragons. What are we going to do about it?" "The Mentor asks good questions," said Edward with a sly grin. "I know he does," said Noland, "and I've been giving it a lot of thought. If I slip Loren or Stuart some Truth Serum, they'll realize that they're unmasked. What happens then, if all the dragons transform and attack? The students would be trapped inside the barrier, and I don't know how we could fight fourteen dragons at once. If they killed us all, Stuart could release them into Kingston without warning or keep the Academy as a secure base!"

"I have another question," said Donovan. "I haven't learned the Change spell yet, but does it take both hands to conjure?"

"I cannot believe that so few of the Changed Ones will help us!" said Gek angrily. "Besides Alice in Smithville, the two Snow Dragons in Hayford, and the one old Sea Dragon in Riverton, none of our kin seem the least bit interested in going to war against the humans!" Gek and Azure were back in the rock quarry north of Colton, awaiting the rest of the Dragon Council. Their search for Dragons transformed into humans had found two dozen Snow and Sea Dragons, but with only a few exceptions; the Changed Ones were perfectly content with their lives as humans and had no interest in any conflict.

"Well," said Teal, "it has been over two hundred years. Living as a human that long was bound to make them passive." "Passive," snorted Gek. "Except for the two Snow Dragon brothers in Hayford, almost all of the others are cowards! I suspect that the only reason the two in Hayford agreed to join us is that their human lives are so miserable! I think they are thieves or smugglers, with no friends and a poor quality of life, even as humans.'

Azure said, "At least Alice will help." "I am not sure how much she can do," said Gek. "She cannot breathe fire, and we do not even know how big she is. She could surely cause some panic among the humans, but we found out that there is at least one magic-user in Smithville and a company of soldiers. Alice could be hurt, killed, or driven off quickly." "And the old Sea Dragon in Riverton only agreed to destroy some ships once the war starts," said Gek. "I do not blame him, though; he is almost as old as Ard."

"Maybe the Fire or Stone Dragons will be more willing to fight," said Cobalt. "The Sea Dragon Changed Ones that Teal and I found were only willing to fight the humans if they attacked our islands. Otherwise, they would prefer not to get involved either."

"Tomorrow is the full moon," said Gek, "should we go into Colton today and quickly search there?" "No need," said a gravelly voice. "Ard!" said Gek. "Well met, Gek," said the ancient Dragon. "I wish I had better news about the two Great Dragon Changed Ones I found in Colton, but they are married and have six human children. I was sure that they would not aid us, so I did not even ask. I heard a rumor of several humans that I suspect are Fire Dragons who live in Riverside on the other side of the river, but I would not violate our agreement by crossing the river."

"It is well that you did not, old one," said a Fire Dragon who landed suddenly in the quarry. "I am Rose of the Fire Dragon Clan, and I bring news to the Dragon Council. My mate and I have marshaled the Clan, and we stand ready to attack at the command of the Dragon Council." "How many Fire Dragons do you bring to battle?" asked Ard. "There are one hundred and fifty in the Clan, but fifty are either too old or too young. But one hundred Fire Dragons are gathering in the Great Salt Flats; they should be assembling now."

"A hundred Fire Dragons!" exclaimed Gek, "that sounds like an overwhelming force." "Indeed," said Rose, "but once assembled, we must attack quickly. There is little prey in the Salt Flats, and my kin will devour one another once the hunger sets in. I must rejoin my mate to keep the Clan in line. We will return tomorrow to hear the Dragon Council's plan." With that, Rose took flight, back across the river and into the night.

"That is heartening," said Ard. "I am sure the Snow Dragons will attack the human settlements near the Snow Fields, but I doubt they will come very far south. What of the Sea Dragons, Teal?" "My Clan will fight," said Teal, "but only to secure our islands. Most of the Clan are pacifists and are content with their lives as they are." "Then it will be up to Stone and Fire," said Ard. "It may not be enough."

"How can you say that?" asked Gek, "a *hundred* Fire Dragons could lay waste to the humans!" "If Rose promised a hundred, then maybe seventy will arrive, and she is right; they will fight amongst themselves if kept together for even a few days without enough food for all." "What about the Stone Dragons?" asked Gek. "Will they fight?"

"Probably," said Ard, "but they are slow and ponderous, and I do not know how far across the river their Clan settled or how dispersed they are. They are formidable in battle, but it may not be enough." "Why not?" asked Gek. "Because you all have forgotten the *plan*," said Victor, as he strolled into the quarry. "I *said* we needed to get the humans to fight each other before we attack! Once they are weakened by fighting each other, then it *will be enough.*"

"And how do you propose we get the humans to fight each other?" asked Teal. "My plan is already in motion," said Victor. "Even now, the king of Franconia is rushing soldiers to the border with Baize. Once they are there, we will provoke a series of border 'incidents' which will cause the humans to go to war with each other. I will, of course, advise the king of Franconia to attack to secure his reign. The boy is so easy to manipulate."

"What kind of 'border incidents' do you have in mind, Victor?" asked Ard. "It will start with three Fire Dragons flying from this side of the river, in daylight when they are sure to be seen, and attacking the human city of Riverside. The King of Baize will assume they were sent against them by Franconia. A few days later, three Stone Dragons will ford the river and attack Weaton under cover of night. There will also be attacks by the Sea Dragons on ships from both kingdoms."

"How will we know when to strike?" asked Azure. "*I* will know. After all, I am the Court Wizard of Franconia, a close advisor to the king. I will know their plans and their weaknesses. I will also know what their losses are in soldiers and magicians."

"When do we begin?" asked Gek, excitedly. "The attack on Riverton will occur at the next full moon," said Victor, "it will take at least that long for the Franconian soldiers to reach the border." "But the Fire Dragons are gathering to attack now!" said Gek. "No," replied Victor, "I saw Rose departing and ordered her to delay the gathering of their Clan until we are ready. They will assign their three fiercest Dragons for the attack on Riverton and have them here at the next full moon, ready for the assault."

"What of the Council meeting tomorrow?" asked Ard. "Is it still necessary?" "Yes," said Victor, "we need to inform the Dragon Council of our preparations, and I have news about

Wizard Amanda that I will share with the Council." With that, the Dragons dispersed about the quarry, each settling down for an uneasy day's sleep.

"You think we should remove their hands?" asked Wizard Noland, incredulously. "Sir," said Donovan cautiously, "it would prevent them from changing into dragon form. I would prefer it if we could just remove one hand, which would prevent the Change spell from working, but I understand that there are a lot of destructive spells that a one-handed magician can still conjure."

"He's right, Michael," agreed Edward. "Even the Kill spell can be cast with just the right hand." "Why not just kill them, then?" asked Noland. "Because we need to question them, under Truth Serum, to root them all out. Stuart might know all of the students because he admitted them, but Loren might know others in Franconia that we need to eliminate," said Edward.

"I've always liked Wizard Loren," said Donovan sadly, "I would hate to see her killed." "You realize that once we do this, eliminate the dragons in the Academy; any others in the Kingdom may attack immediately," said Noland. "Then we need to make sure we're prepared," said Edward. "I'll check with Major Gerald to see how we're coming with procuring and issuing crossbows. I have a feeling that we'll be needing them sooner rather than later."

"I agree," said Noland, "how do you propose we deal with Stuart and Loren?" "Once we're ready, call Stuart to your office and slip him some Truth Serum. Casually ask him if he is a dragon. If he says 'yes,' immediately remove his hands. Then, Compel him and find out from him which other students are dragons. Once we know them all, we'll have to deal with Loren, then any Mentors, and students from most the dangerous to the least." "How do you propose we accomplish that?" asked Noland. "It would probably be easiest on an Endday morning, during Mentor testing," offered Andrew.

"So, we have to wait for the humans to approach the border before we attack?" asked Crimson, the Fire Dragon representative. "Yes," said Victor, "we must let the humans fight each other first, while we watch and savor the spectacle." "Once their forces and magic-users are decimated, it will be time to strike hard." "But you want three of our best fighters to attack Riverside after the next full moon?" "Yes, and they need to attack from the east, from this side of the river, so the Baizians believe they were sent against them by Franconia," explained Victor.

"When do we get to attack?" asked Jasper, the Stone Dragon Clan Chief. Victor grinned, "About a week later, after the Baizian envoy has lodged his complaint with the king of Franconia about the attack on Riverside. This is so that your attack looks like retaliation." "And you think the humans will attack each other after these raids?" asked Bliz, the Snow Dragon Clan Chief. "If not, we will arrange other provocations," said Victor.

"What about the Sea Dragons?" asked Teal, "What role do we play?" Victor considered for a moment. Usually, he had no use for his water-borne cousins. "You may begin attacking ships of both countries after the next full moon. There is no need for you to wait for the land forces to approach each other," said Victor.

And what would you have us do, Victor?" asked Bliz. "I would ask your Clan to attack the cities of Iceville and Snowton in Baize and Frostberg in Franconia. They are the closest to the Snow Fields. I will send you word to attack once the humans have begun to fight against each other," replied Victor. In truth, he did not expect much from the Snow Dragons.

"And what task do you have for the Great Dragons?" asked Ard. "Both of you?" sneered Victor. "I have a special assignment for you. It involves your spell, ancient one. The one that Binds us to spare Wizard Amanda's offspring. I have found only two remaining descendants of that line. One is a woman named Beverly Perrucci, and she lives in the human city of

Southport, and the other is the son of the Mage who attacked your mother," he said, looking at Gek. "The boy, Donovan Francis, is currently at the Wizards Academy in Kingston. Because of the foolishness of this old one, if harm should come to either of these humans, the entire Dragon Council, including you, Gek, and your mate, will die, instantly. I can think of no better mission than for the Great Dragons to guard this random woman in Southport and your mother's killer."

"Are the soldiers moving?" asked the Stone Dragon Changed One. "Yes," replied Louis, the middle-aged, balding Court Wizard of Baize. "In fact, I gave orders for the entire Regiment in Springfield to depart. Two battalions are headed for Weaton, one for Colton, and the fourth is on the way to Westport." "How did you manage that?" "I simply told Wizard James that the king had a change of heart and presented him with a false set of orders, signed and sealed by the king, of course." "Excellent! Once the forces arrive at their destinations, I will report this aggression to King Henry and encourage corresponding moves by Franconian forces."

"When will the attacks begin?" "Victor has arranged for three Fire Dragons to attack the city of Riverside from the east side of the river the day after the next full moon. They will attack in daylight so they can be seen flying from Franconia. I advise you to move any of our allies out of Riverside immediately so they are not caught up in the attack. You know how some Fire Dragons are; they may kill everyone in the city unless they run out of inferno," said the Stone Dragon.

Louis ran his fingers through his thinning red hair and said, "I know of at least two members of my Clan that live in Riverside. I will send word to them. You know, it would be best if the attack did not kill *everyone* in the city. There should be some survivors left to tell the tale to the king and spread the news to the people of Baize." "An excellent suggestion. I will make sure that the attacking Dragons spare some of the residents. Is there anything else?"

"The king has ordered Mage Kathy to conduct an investigation into the Dragon attack that occurred in Franconia to see if it was real or merely a fanciful tale by drunken Franconian farmers," said Wizard Louis. "Tell me about Mage Kathy," said the Stone Dragon. "She is an accountant who knows magic," said Louis, dismissively. "She grew up here in the capitol. Her father was a middling magician, and her mother was a scribe. She has been my assistant for three years, but all I have her doing is auditing the finances of the kingdom. She travels a lot since I do not want her observing me too closely."

"What do you think she will discover?" "You know as well as I do that rumors and fantastic exaggerations must be spreading among the Franconians. She will probably hear everything from 'It was just a hoax,' to 'a 500-foot long gold

Dragon destroyed the town.' There will undoubtedly be talk of a government cover-up and secret and Dragon-slaying new weapons. I expect that Mage Kathy will have a hard time sorting fact from fiction."

"Should we arrange for her to have an accident?" asked the Stone Dragon, coldly. "I do not think so. It might serve us best if she returns with a story of Franconian-bred Dragons working at their behest," said Louis, smiling at the thought. "Very well. I will leave her to you."

Chapter Twelve:
A CALL TO ARMS

"Ya gotta be kiddin' me!" exclaimed Major Gerald. "A dragon attack? Soon? Maybe dozen's o' dragons? Sir Mage, I hope yer jokin'." "I'm afraid not, Major," said Edward. "Has this got anythin' ta do with our troops bein' moved towards the border with Baize?" "What troops? When?" asked Edward, shocked.

"The King just ordered two companies from Westport to move towards Weaton to conduct field training exercises, and the First Battalion from the Second Regiment is moving to take station in Prarrieville, 'just in case' Baize invades," said Major Gerald. "Why would the Kingdom of Baize invade us?" asked Edward, rhetorically. "We've been at peace for decades, why, they're our best trading partner." "I don't know, Sir Mage, but somethin's got the King spooked," confided Gerald. "Rumor has it, the Court Wizard wanted to move the entire Second Regiment to Prarrieville. That is, 'til Marshall Guzman talked the King out of it by mentioning the cost."

"Good for the Marshall!" said Edward. "I don't like the sound of this, especially if Victor has a hand in it." "I know you two don't get along," said Gerald. "Major, I'm going to tell you something in confidence. I think Victor is behind the attempts to stop us from finding that dragon." "That's a very serious charge, Sir Mage. Can ya prove it?" "All I have is circumstantial evidence, Major. Nothing that would convince the King. But Victor's 'investigation' into our adventure with the dragon ended up pointing to a lot of dead men and supposed "coincidences" that just happened to occur while we were in the neighborhood. I don't buy it. Not one word!" said Edward.

"I wondered about that myself. Then there was the problem with Specialist Lance," said Gerald. "What 'problem'?" asked Edward. "Well, once Lance, Corporal Kindred, and Donovan got the dragon's head to the King, Victor kept insistin' that it was a 'Great Bullion Lizard,' not a dragon. Accordin' to Corporal Kindred, Lance actually agreed with the Wizard. That is, 'til Donovan threw the dragon's head at the King's feet. That sure blew the lid off things!"

"Specialist Lance said it was a lizard? But he was right there with us! He knew better!" insisted Edward. "I know. When I asked him about it, he said that he got all confused and felt compelled to agree with the Wizard for some reason," said Gerald. "Victor must have cast a Compulsion spell on him." "A what?" "A Compulsion spell," explained Edward. "Just like the one I cast on Victor to suggest I accompany you on the mission and on Donovan to get him to go to the Wizards Academy when I thought I was dying."

"That explains a lot," said Gerald, "so wadda we do?" "Has the Marshall purchased any more crossbows from Prestige Arms?" asked Edward. "He ordered a company's worth," said Gerald, "but as I understand it, James wouldn't come down

135

enough on the price, and the King wouldn't pay five silvers for each. It's a shame, too, 'cause I understand that James hired more help and made about two hundred of 'em, expecting a big contract. He may be in a pinch."

"Damn! This sounds like Victor's work. I'll tell you what, if I give you a hundred golds, can you find a way to get it to James and purchase those two hundred crossbows?" asked Edward. "Where would you get that kind of coin, Sir Mage?" "Well, I admit that half of it is the Death Benefit the King paid to Donovan. I guess since I'm not really dead, I'm not entitled to it. The rest is almost all of my life savings," said Edward.

"You'd give that up?" "Major, I believe that we're about to be attacked by scores of dragons. Crossbows are our only hope of repelling such an attack. My gold won't do me any good if I'm *really* dead. Now, how quickly can you two get it to Fairview and get back here with the crossbows?" Edward asked to the empty air beside Sir Gerald. Both Lance and Dirk threw back the hoods of their concealment cloaks. "For a dead Mage, you're still pretty sharp," said Dirk. Major Gerald just sighed. He was used to the Specialists sneaking up on him. Edward ignored the compliment and repeated, "How fast?"

Lance thought for a moment, "If the Major approves, we can take a ship leaving Kingston tonight and be in Fairview in three or four days. Figure a day to load and three or four days back. Call it two weeks, tops." Major Gerald nodded his approval. "Just one thing, sir Mage, how do I explain two hundred new crossbows to the King?" asked Gerald. "Tell him they fell off the back of a wagon," said Edward. The three soldiers laughed.

"I will not do it!" shouted Gek. "Yes, you will!" roared Ard. "You will if you want to survive this war and protect Azure! She is under the Binding spell, too!" They had been at this for hours, ever since Victor had charged Gek with protecting Donovan Francis, the son of the Mage who had attacked his mother. "That Mage murdered my mother!" shouted Gek. "I hate him, and I hate his son!"

Ard took a calming breath and tried again. "First, the Mage did *not* kill your mother." "How can you say that? You were not even there!" said Gek. "Gek, your mother was not killed with magic. She was killed by a dozen iron arrows. Magicians do not shoot arrows! I do not deny that the Mage was involved. He probably used his magic to find you. Anyway, according to Victor, your mother killed the Mage during the battle! We do not even know if the boy was there when it happened! He was probably trapped in the wizard's school like all the other beginning magicians," said Ard reasonably.

"I do not care! He is a human magic-user, and I hate him!" "Just as he undoubtedly hates you," said Ard sadly. "What?" asked Gek. "Think about it, rationally," said Ard, "A dragon killed his father; what kind of son would not hate all Dragons after that?" "Ard is right, Gek. I do not have reason to hate humans like you do, but it is not fair to blame the son for the deeds of the father. Besides, according to Ard, if the son— Donovan? If harmed by a Dragon, we will all feel the same injury."

"Why can you not just cancel the spell, Ard?" asked Gek. "Because I do not know how," said Ard, contritely. "With the Dig spell, once you have made the hole, the spell ends. It is the same with the Sleep, Fire, and Change spells; once used, they just *end*." "What about the Concealment spell?" asked Gek. "You tell me," said Ard, crossly. "I do not know that spell. How do you stop it?" Azure said, "Well, it just ends after a while." "Well, the Binding spell does not. Maybe when I die, it will end, and maybe it will not. I admit, it is ironic that my spell to protect Wizard Amanda's progeny has ended up protecting the son of the Mage that fought your mother. Still, I do not regret the spell."

"What?" said Gek. "Gek, the Wizard Amanda saved your mother's life. She lived for another hundred years. That is many times the lifespan of a human. I am saddened by Liza's death but grateful to Amanda for her life. Eventually, the cycle of hate must end. You hate the Mage for killing your mother; Donovan hates Dragons for killing his father. Where does it end?"

"It ends when all of the humans are dead!" said Gek. "So, you are saying that humans and Dragons cannot coexist? That one of us must exterminate the other?" asked Ard. Gek nodded. "I doubt that all of the Changed Ones would agree with you. In any case, it is a moot point. You and Azure must fly to Kingston, change into human form, and protect Donovan from the firestorm that is coming. Just as I must travel to Southport and find the human, Beverly Perrucci, and protect her. Otherwise, we all die."

Mage Kathy sat at her desk, twirling her long blonde hair, pouring over a map of Franconia, and planning how she would proceed with her investigation. It was a long way from the city of Baize to Farmdale; at least two weeks from Baize to Springfield; then another week to the border town of Colton; then fifteen to twenty days from Colton to Riverton; and finally, a week from Riverton to Farmdale. Call it fifty days, and that didn't include stops in Colton and Riverton to interview people and get their take on what transpired around Farmdale. Or, she could take the sea route. A ship could have her in the Franconian city of Southport in two weeks, and from there, she could go overland or take a Franconian merchant ship directly to Kingston or even Fairview.

She eventually decided that it was much faster and safer to travel by ship. King Donald wanted information quickly, so he could make informed decisions. The overland route would take over six months to get there and back, assuming she was not delayed by bad weather, bandits, or being apprehended as a spy.

No, she needed to take a ship, probably as far as Fairview. Kathy jumped as a familiar and unwelcomed hand came to rest on her shoulder. "Wizard Louis, you startled me."

"I just came by to see how you were progressing with your plan to investigate the supposed Dragon attack in Franconia," said Wizard Louis, sliding around to lean on her desk, invading her personal space. Again. Mage Kathy had an intense dislike for the Court Wizard. She knew that he wanted a romantic involvement with her, or at least a passing one, and the Court Wizard was loathe to take the hint that she was not interested in such a relationship. Undeterred by her repeated rejections, Louis was constantly dropping not-so-subtle invitations to 'visit him in his quarters for consultations.' Invitations that Kathy ignored by pretending not to understand the offers. She suddenly decided that she did *not* want Wizard Louis to know her plans.

"Looking at the most current map we have of Franconia, it looks like it'll take me a little over six months to get to Farmdale and back. Do you think we have that long?" "Hmm," said Louis, "we might. I doubt that Franconia will move against us before then, but you might have trouble returning if they close the borders while you are on the wrong side of the river." "I'm sure I won't have any problems slipping past some sleepy border guards," said Kathy confidently.

"I expect not," said Louis. "Still, it could be a complication. Anyway, how you proceed is up to you. I just came by to see if you needed any help or advice." "I think I'll be able to manage," said Kathy. "Of course you will. But if you ever need anything, my chamber is always open to you. Day or night," said Louis, suggestively. Kathy repressed a shudder and smiled, "Thank you. I will certainly keep that in mind."

Louis sauntered off down the hallway, and Kathy resumed her study of the map. She decided that she needed to get out of the palace sooner rather than later and resolved to check the harbor immediately, then adjust her plans based on what she discovered. She had decided to pose as a historian, documenting the encounter with the dragon. She wondered if she should take someone with her to watch her back in case things became confrontational in Franconia. *No, a historian would not have a bodyguard,* she thought. Kathy would be on her own.

Chapter Thirteen:
COMPLICATIONS

They flew to the outskirts of Kingston, landing behind what appeared to be an abandoned warehouse, and changed into human form in the fading darkness. After traveling in Franconia for months searching for Changed Ones, Gek (Jed) and Azure had proper clothes, money, and a convincing back-story. They were two young lovers who had run away from wealthy but abusive parents in Fairview, and they were seeking their fortunes in the Capitol city. They took a room in the Boar's Head Inn near the center of town, paying for a week's stay in advance. The room was comfortable, with a stout bar for the door. Once inside, they barred the door and conversed in hushed tones.

"So," said Gek, "we are here. Now what?" "I love a man with a plan," said Azure, playfully. "Now, my love, we stroll around the town and see if we can find any Changed Ones who can help us. We know that Donovan is inside the wizard's school, so we need to find out where that is and how to get in." "We cannot risk getting trapped inside there for years as others have!" said Gek forcefully. "I, for one, do not want to have to remain in human form for any longer than necessary." "But how can we protect Donovan if he is in there and we are out here?" wondered Azure.

"We should just get familiar with the city for the next few

days, and maybe we will come up with an idea," said Azure with a yawn. "A very good idea," said Gek. "Come to bed. Maybe I will think of something."

Over the next two days, they explored the city of Kingston. It was a bustling metropolis full of merchants, soldiers, and beggars. They found the garrison where the soldiers were quartered and observed about a hundred men leaving the city, headed west. They did not look happy. On their third day in the city, they spotted a tall, elderly man with grey hair coming out of the Apothecary shop. He certainly *smelled* like a Changed One. Gek approached him and said, "Excuse me, sir, my sister and I are looking for the wizard's school. Can you direct us?" Wizard Stuart looked them both over closely, sniffed, and said, "Come with me quickly before you are discovered. It is not safe for you in this city."

Dirk and Lance entered Prestige Arms carrying a small chest between them. As they stepped inside, an attractive young lady greeted them. "Good morning, Sirs. My name is Maria. How may I help you?" "Is your father here?" asked Dirk. "Major Gerald, the commander of the Royal Expeditionary Force, sent us." "Just one moment, Sir," said Maria. "I'll fetch him." Maria practically ran into the back office to get her father. James emerged quickly. "You asked for me, Sir?" asked James hopefully.

"Yes," said Lance, "I understand that you have about two hundred crossbows to sell. We would like to buy them for the Guard." Astonishment and joy played across James' face. "That would be wonderful, Sir! But I thought that the King wouldn't agree to my price of five silvers each—" said James.

"He has reconsidered," said Dirk, placing the chest on the counter. "Here are one hundred golds. We'll wait while you count them. Are the crossbows packed for shipment? We need to get back to Kingston on the next ship leaving port," said Lance. "Yes, yes," said an excited James, "the crossbows are packed in ten crates out back. There are twenty crossbows, complete with draw harnesses and two hundred bolts in each crate." "Do you have a wagon to help us transport them to the harbor?" asked Dirk. "Of course," said James, "let me get them loaded. BILL! FRANK! Load those crates of crossbows on the wagon! We got a buyer! Yes, now, you idiots! Hurry up!"

Lance and Dirk smiled, "I like this guy," whispered Dirk. "Sir," said Maria, "did you say you were with the Royal Expeditionary Force?" "We are," confirmed Lance. "Do you know Donovan Francis?" asked Maria hopefully. "Of course!" said Dirk, smiling, "Donovan is a good friend of ours." "How is he doing?" asked Maria, "I was so concerned when we heard that his father was killed by the dragon."

"I saw Donovan just a few weeks ago," said Lance, "he's doing fine. He enrolled at the Wizards Academy and is already a Level Two magician." "That's wonderful! I'm so happy for him. Please tell him that Maria said "Hi" the next time you see him." "We shall certainly do so," said Dirk. Just then, James emerged from the back office, "All loaded up, gentlemen, which ship are you sailing on?" "The HMS SWIFT, under Captain Long," said Lance. "I'll have your cargo loaded and meet you on the dock with your Bill of Lading," said James. "How much is the shipping fee?" asked Dirk, reaching for his money pouch. "Sir, when you place a hundred-gold order, shipping is free," said James. "I *really* like this guy," said Dirk. As they headed back to the port, they heard the boom of thunder in the distance.

"Where are you two staying?" asked Wizard Stuart tersely, "Do not talk, just take me there! Move!" Gek and Azure led the fretful Changed One to their room and barred the door. "What is a Sea Dragon and a—a Great Dragon doing in Kingston?" asked Stuart. "There are twenty-five magic-users in this town! Any one of them could have identified you as having the spark of magic and brought you, unwillingly, to the Academy, where you would spend years before being released!"

Gek hesitated, then said, "I am G—" "No names!" said Stuart. "It is safer for you if I do not know your names. Just tell me why you are here." "We have come because, at the last meeting of the Dragon Council, Ard made all the Council members promise to find and protect any progeny of the Wizard Amanda, a Dragon-Friend of old. He cast a Binding spell on us. If anything happens to one of Amanda's descendants, everyone bound by the spell will die. Victor, of the Fire Dragons, determined that there are only two remaining descendants. One lives in Southport, and the other is called Donovan Francis, and he is said to be here, in the wizard's school. We have come to protect him."

Wizard Stuart laughed hysterically. "Protect Donovan? The son of Battle Mage Edward Francis?" "The very same," said Azure. "That boy needs no protection," said Stuart, "he is already almost ready to advance to Level Three, but I doubt those fool Wizards will promote him this soon. They will make him wait at least two more years." "But if anything happens to him in the coming conflict, everyone on the Dragon Council will die!" said Gek. "It is a chance we cannot take!"

"What 'coming conflict'?" asked Stuart. Gek and Azure explained about Victor's plan to provoke a war between the humans of Franconia and Baize, and when the two sides were weakened, the Dragon Clans would attack. "I wish Victor had included us in his plans," said Stuart. "There are fourteen Changed Ones at the Wizards Academy, all of whom were brought here against their will by Regional Mages after they were found to have the spark. Some will join us, but others probably prefer their lives as humans."

"Do you know which will support us and which will not?" asked Gek. "No, and I am not sure how to make that determination. I need to think about this and discuss it with the one Dragon I am sure is with us. In the meantime, you two need to move to…Prarrieville. It is a small town due west of here, about three hours flight. There are fewer magic-users there to detect you. Return in one week and meet me here. Then we will decide what to do about the Changed Ones at the Wizards Academy," said Stuart. "What about Donovan?" asked Gek. "I will protect Donovan," said Stuart.

"WHAT DO YOU MEAN THREE DAYS?" asked Dirk. "I mean that this storm system is expected to last at least three days, an' it's too rough to sail in," said Captain Long. "I'm sorry, but there's nothing I can do about it, and before you ask, there are no other ships heading out in this weather either." "Captain, this cargo has to be delivered to Kingston immediately!" said Lance. "You can try taking it by land, but that's at least a ten-day trip, and this weather won't help any," said the Captain. "Once this system blows over, we can be in Kingston in three, maybe three and a half days." "I guess we go by water," said Lance.

"Can one of us stay on board to guard the cargo?" asked Dirk. "As you wish, but it might get a little bumpy, even tied to the pier," said Captain Long. "That's all right. This cargo is very important to us. Is it loaded yet?" asked Dirk. "Yes," replied the Captain, "I had it loaded in the rear cargo hold and lashed down. It's not anything fragile, is it?" "No, just some weapons for the garrison in Kingston. The King would be unhappy if anything happened to them, though; *very unhappy,*" said Lance. "I understand," said Captain Long, "there's a hammock in the hold next to the crates that you can use."

"Let me grab some food from the tavern, and I'll take the first watch," said Lance. "I'll go aboard and check out the arrangements," said Dirk, "get enough food for two," he whispered. "We're not leaving this ship unguarded. Not after what happened on my last trip from Fairview to Kingston."

"Well, this certainly complicates things," said Loren. "Damn, Victor, for not telling us his plans!" "I suppose we could just kill Donovan in order to get rid of Victor," mused Stuart. "And kill off the entire Dragon Council? No, that is too high a price to pay just to get rid of Victor." They were seated in the front parlor of the Gatehouse, which doubled as Stuart's residence. The armchairs were soft and comfortable, and the fire on the hearth kept the room warm despite the driving rain outside. "So, how can we determine which of the Changed Ones here will support us and which will side with the humans?" asked Stuart.

"Truth Serum would work," said Loren, "but they would remember being questioned." "What about Truth Serum, followed by a Secrecy spell if the Changed One gives the wrong answer?" asked Stuart. "That should work," said Loren, "provided that the Secrecy spell holds. One mistake and we could be exposed. Tell me, how many Changed Ones do we have at the Academy?" Stuart thought for a moment, then said, "There are three Great Dragons, including me; four Snow Dragons, including you; three Sea Dragons; three Fire Dragons; and one Stone Dragon—fourteen in all. Besides us, there is one Mentor, six Level Threes, Four Level Twos, and one Level One. The Stone Dragon, Raymond, is due to be given his final Level Three Test next week. I do not think he is going to pass it, so he will surely join us, but we have to act quickly, before Raymond fails his test and has his spark removed."

"Give me a list of the students, and I will make twelve vials of Truth Serum this afternoon and begin questioning the students tomorrow," said Loren. "What should we do about Donovan?" asked Stuart. "Nothing right now," said Loren, "but if it becomes necessary, we may have to elect a new Dragon Council."

Ard sipped his water and watched the ships sail in and out of the port. It really was rather pleasant here in Southport. The weather was mild, and the humans were uncommonly kind to the crippled old man who just liked to sit on the bench overlooking the harbor and watch the boats. He had located Beverly Perrucci after a few brief inquiries in town. Beverly and her husband Joe were well-liked but generally ignored by the townfolk. They were not wealthy or connected, just honest, hard-working folk. Neither had ever shown any magical ability.

"Nice view, don't cha think," said a voice behind him. Ard turned and was surprised to find Beverly standing behind the bench. "Do you mind if I share the bench with you?" she asked. Recovering quickly, Ard said, "Please join me, and yes, the view is spectacular." "I often come down here in the evening to meet my husband when he gets off work. My name is Beverly," she said. "I am Alan," said Ard, "and I am pleased to meet you." They sat side by side for a time, watching the ships bob at anchor as the sun set. Eventually, a weary man headed up the pier towards them. "That'll be my husband, Joe," said Beverly. Ard and Beverly rose from the bench and greeted her husband. "Joe, this is Alan," said Beverly. The two men shook hands, and Beverly said, "How was your day, dear?" Joe replied with a grunt, "Same as always, lift and pull; lift and pull. Take a break; then start again." "That sounds very tiresome," said Ard sympathetically. "Well, it's a livin," said Joe. "I really wish that son of ours hadn't gone and run off all those years ago! We could really use his help these days."

Ard staggered, trying to recover his scattered wits. "You have a son?" he asked, fearing the answer. "Yep. But the boy was scatter-brained, kept claimin' that he had the spark! Never

150

heard such nonsense! I told him I didn't wanna hear about it anymore; that he needed to get hisself an honest job. There's plenty of 'em around, if'n your willin' to work hard. Andrew never would listen, though. He headed off to the Wizards Academy up in Kingston, and we never heard from him again." "That is a shame," whispered Ard. "I guess so," said Joe, "I been thinkin' a lot about him lately. You know, about *choices* and regrets. Things we might have done differently if we only knew better. You know what I mean?" "I do indeed," said Ard, "Well, I had best be going. I have a long way to travel tonight."

"It's been nice talking to you," said Beverly, "safe travels." Ard walked as fast as his aged legs would carry him. He had to get to Kingston and warn Gek that there was another descendant of Wizard Amanda's to protect. This was getting complicated.

Mage Kathy boarded the ship, the KBS GREYHOUND, bound for the port city of Westport. With the stiff breeze out of the north, they should make it to Westport in a little over a week, and if she could book passage on a Franconian ship, she could be in Southport about two weeks from now. The GREYHOUND was a two-masted schooner, built to sail the coastal waters around Baize. The vessel normally transported light cargo, consumer goods, some salt and spices, and a few paying passengers heading south to the city of Seaside, a tourist destination for the few Baizian citizens who could afford it.

Not wanting to attract unwanted attention, Kathy had booked the cheapest class of cabin on board, planning to remain in her room for most of the voyage if possible. She also conjured a gold wedding ring, in order to give the appearance of being a married woman. She traveled light, with only a backpack and a small satchel that held her writing journal, inks, and quills. She brought little in the way of coin, planning to replicate whatever she needed on the way. She didn't want to appear wealthy and make herself a target for thieves and cutthroats.

As she was leaving the palace, Wizard Louis appeared and gifted her an ornate dagger, with a jeweled pommel, *"just in case."* She had thanked Louis effusively, then, after determining that the dagger had a Tracer spell on it, hidden the dagger in a wagon loaded with barley that was headed to Springfield. Once she was out of sight of the palace, Kathy cast a Concealment shield and backtracked to the port where the ship was waiting at anchor.

High tide came in as the sun set, and the GREYHOUND left port, traveling quickly east. The seas were calm, for which Kathy was grateful. To hurry them along, Kathy cast a Wind spell, creating a stiff breeze out of the west. Not so much as a gale, which could imperil the ship, but enough of a wind to shave at least a day off their travel time to Westport. For the most part, the voyage was uneventful except for the young fool who thought to pay Kathy an unannounced visit in her cabin the second night at sea. Kathy spelled the brigand to sleep, then, using the Silence and Strength enhancement spells, carried him up on deck and threw him over the side. Surprisingly, his disappearance went unnoticed, or at least *uninvestigated.*

Eight days out of Baize, after a brief stop in Seaside, the ship arrived and docked on the Franconian side of the port of Westport. As Kathy prepared to disembark, she sensed a magician on the pier. He was apparently some sort of Franconian Customs inspector, checking the cargo of the various ships for contraband. Not wanting to be noticed as someone with the spark and questioned, Kathy ignited the mainsail of the ship next to hers. As the Sorcerer and several burly men raced over to put out the fire, Kathy slipped ashore and headed quickly to the shipping office to inquire about any ships headed to Southport, Kingston, or Fairview. Kathy told the shipping coordinator that she was returning to her husband in Fairview after visiting her ailing sister, who lived on the outskirts of Westport.

As luck would have it, there was a ship due in the day after tomorrow, and after discharging its cargo of wheat and cotton, it was headed back to its home port of Fairview, with just brief stops in Southport and Kingston. Kathy was amazed at her good fortune. Until the shipping agent told her the price. For the trip all the way to Fairview, the rate was three golds for the cheapest cabin. "THREE GOLDS?" asked Kathy. "Why, that's almost a year's wages!" "I'm sorry, said the shipping master, but that's what Captain Bell charges now. He's increased his prices since he and his ship, the HMS UNSINKABLE, received the King's Commendation for bringing the Royal Expeditionary Force back to Kingston after they dealt with that dragon."

Kathy was stunned. That ship's crew would be a wealth of information! Worth every copper, whatever the cost. Thinking quickly, she said, "I apologize for my outburst. I had no idea that I'd be returning home on such a famous vessel. How much is a first-class cabin? I would really like the opportunity to hear Captain Bell's tales of his adventures." The shipping master brightened significantly at the prospect of booking such an expensive passage. He informed Kathy that for a first-class cabin and a seat at the Captain's table, the price would be an additional two golds.

Sensing that she was being fleeced, Kathy said, "If that includes a room in the best Inn while I wait for the ship to arrive, you have a deal." The shipper frowned and said, "My lady, there are no fine Inns worthy of a lady like you in Westport, only sailor's digs. How about this? I have a spare room at my place, free room and board, and a safe place to wait. Westport can get a little rough some nights." "I accept your offer, sir, as long as the room has a lock and a bar for the door. My husband would not like to hear that I spent the night in another man's house without certain *assurances.*"

A deal was quickly struck, and the shipping master led Kathy upstairs. Conveniently, he lived above the shipping office in a three-bedroom apartment that was mostly empty since his wife had passed away and his son went to sea on a merchant ship. Kathy promised to bring him his payment after she unpacked some things and inquired what was for dinner. After being shown to her room, Kathy retrieved her only gold coin from a hidden compartment in her shoe and quickly replicated five more. Replacing the gold in her shoe, she unpacked her few things and made a note in her journal:

1. Traveled to Westport on the KBS GREYHOUND. The Royal Expeditionary Force (REF) returned to Kingston from Fairview on the HMS UNSINKABLE, under the command of one Captain Bell. I have been most fortunate to book passage on this same vessel and hope to learn a great deal from the Captain and his crew during our voyage back to Fairview. The ship was awarded the King's Commendation for returning the REF to Kingston after "dealing with the dragon." At least King Henry believes there was a dragon. Total cost:

   • Transport from Baize to Westport on KBS GREYHOUND – 6 Silvers (meals included)

   • Transport from Westport to Fairview on HMS UNSINKABLE – 5 Golds (meals included)

Chapter Fourteen:
PLACES EVERYONE!

"Dad, do you think dragons are really evil?" asked Donovan. "Why do you ask, son?" said Edward. "I'm just thinking about something Loren said to me. She said that maybe dragons are not really *evil*, just *hungry*, and that's why they only asked for food in order to end the last war." Edward sat in thought for a while, "She might be right, son. Of course, we suspect that she *is* a dragon, so she might have been trying to influence your opinion about dragons. On the other hand, I would say that she does have a unique perspective on the issue."

They were seated in Edward's study, having let Andrew head off into town so they could have some private time. "Could she be reasoned with?" asked Donovan. "How so?" asked Edward. "Well, at the end of the Dragon War, you said we signed a Treaty with the dragons. That implies a level of intelligence and a willingness to compromise," said Donovan. "Yes, it does," said Edward thoughtfully. "Of course, we double-crossed them and then tried to kill them all. That kind of betrayal leaves a lasting impression, I imagine."

"I wonder if any of them prefer being humans," said Donovan softly. "What?" asked Edward. "I mean, think about it: most humans are not always hungry, and they're not being hunted and feared. I'll bet some of them would rather be humans than dragons." "That's a big leap, son. Why would a dragon choose to remain in human form?" wondered Edward.

"What if they fell in love, got married, even had children?" asked Donovan. "How long does the Change spell last?" "As long as the conjurer wants it to, I suppose," said Edward. "It doesn't take any power to maintain; once it's cast, the spell is over, so it would last for years, maybe decades, even after the magician dies." "If you were a dragon who had been living as a human for years, would you want to go back?" mused Donovan. "I guess it would depend," said Edward. "If *my* parents were killed by eating poisoned cattle, at a *Peace Celebration*, I could hold a grudge for a long time."

"The Truth Serum is ready," said Loren, "I will start questioning the students today, starting with Sorcerer Terry, the only Mentor who is a Changed One." "Do you need anything from me?" asked Stuart. "Just keep anyone from disturbing me during fourth period for the next few days. I have no classes to teach, and I normally spend fourth period in my cottage. But it would not do for Wizard Noland to pay me a visit while I am questioning Changed Ones with Truth Serum," said Loren. "Indeed not," said Stuart. "Very well, I will be in or around the stables, easily able to intercept anyone coming to see you. Are you sure that the Secrecy spell will work?" " It would not if they were in Dragon form, but I am sure it will work on them in their human form," replied Loren.

They sat for a moment, sipping their wine. "Have you thought about what we will do to those who will not join us?" asked Stuart. "I guess it will depend on how many 'problems' we have. It would be hard to explain if five or six students suddenly died in training accidents." said Loren. "We could space it out over several months…" "Stuart! The next full moon is in a little over a week! That is when Victor plans to launch the Fire Dragons against Baize. Once it becomes common knowledge that there are Dragons in the land, attacking humans, even *Baizians*, the humans will begin hunting Dragons in earnest. We need to act before then. The last thing we need is for one misguided Changed One to tell Wizard Noland our secret," said Loren.

"Well," said Stuart, "the Level Twos start their lessons on boats this week. I suppose if a couple of boats sank, a student or two might drown…" "When was the last time one of the Academy boats sank?" asked Loren. "It has been a few years," admitted Stuart. "Maybe *overturned* is a better idea. There is also always a chance that a student or two will fall overboard."

"Several times?" asked Loren skeptically. "Maybe two or three boats could collide, then while multiple students are splashing around in the water, a couple of them go down, unnoticed." "I thought we taught all of our students how to swim before the 'performing magic on water' lessons," said Loren. "If

158

a couple of them are knocked unconscious before they go in, knowing how to swim will not help them," said Stuart smugly.

"I suppose that could work. Once," said Loren, "What else?" "Remember that idiot, Level Three Stone Dragon from a few years ago?" asked Stuart. "The one who tried to blackmail us?" asked Loren. Stuart nodded. "I believe you turned him into a rock during his Change spell class," said Loren with a smile. "Classic." "We might revisit that one," said Stuart, "but only if necessary. It would undoubtedly arouse suspicion." "I hope we do not have to kill too many of them," said Loren, "I have grown quite fond of some of them."

The HMS Swift docked at the Kingston pier (finally). It had taken almost two weeks to get the crossbows from Fairview. Now, the challenge was getting them into the hands of the archers who would need them. Edward and Major Gerald had already done the calculations: The 15th Company in Weaton needed eight crossbows; the two companies headed towards Weaton from Westport needed sixteen total crossbows; and the First Battalion, from the Second Regiment that was marching towards Prarrieville, needed thirty-two crossbows. They also planned to send sixteen crossbows to the two remaining companies in Westport and thirty-two to the Ninth Battalion in Colton. That left ninety-six crossbows to distribute between

Southport and the Kingston garrison. Since Kingston had two Regiments and Southport a single Regiment, they decided to divide the remaining crossbows proportionally, with thirty-two going to Southport and sixty-four remaining in Kingston.

While they were waiting in Fairview for the storm to blow over, Senior Specialist Lance had gone to see Major Stone, the commander of the Third Franconian Regiment, stationed in Fairview, and advised him strongly to purchase some crossbows for his soldiers. Lance had also asked James, the owner of Prestige Arms, to continue crossbow production, predicting a large order for them was coming from the crown soon.

"So how do we get these crossbows to the soldiers without Wizard Victor or the King hearing about it?" asked Edward. "You leave that to me," said Major Gerald. "The guard has some storage warehouses outside the garrison where we can store 'em without anyone knowin'." "How long to get these crossbows to the troops on the border?" asked Edward. "Maybe a week. Depends on the weather. The troops in Prarrieville will get 'em first; then it depends where them two companies from Westport are as to whether they get theirs before or after the delivery to the company in Weaton." "I understand," said Edward. "How will you get them there?" "The crossbows headed for the border are bein' loaded into First Company's wagon as we speak. They'll be on the road within the hour. Specialist Dirk and Healer Wells are delivering them personally." "Thank you, Major." "So, what are you going to do about Victor?" asked

Major Gerald. "When the time is right, I'm going to kill him," said Edward.

Where in blazes could those two be? wondered Ard. He had rushed north to Kingston to warn Gek and Azure that, in addition to protecting Donovan, they also had to protect a student named Andrew from any harm. Victor had been wrong when he assured the Dragon Council that there were only two surviving descendants of Wizard Amanda: Donovan Francis and Beverly Perrucci. It turns out that Beverly had a son, Andrew, who had run away from home and gone to the wizards school. Gek and Azure would have to guard the two students, while Ard would have to return to Southport to watch over Beverly. *I just need to find them in all this jumble of humanity!* Thought Ard.

After fruitlessly wandering through the city, Ard eventually settled himself on a bench across from a bakery. The aroma of freshly baked bread was pleasing, even to a dragon disguised as a human. He had only been there a short while when an elderly woman came out of the gray building next to the bakery. She looked around cautiously, then proceeded down the street. As she walked past Ard, she stopped and smelled the air. She then turned and approached. "What in the world are you doing here, ancient one?" Loren asked. Ard had also caught the scent of Dragon and was not surprised by the question. "I am looking for my grandson and his mate," said Ard, "have you seen them?"

"I have not met them personally, but I know of whom you speak," said Loren cryptically. "Why are you looking for them? They are not here." "Not here!" said Ard, "but they are supposed to be protecting someone!" "Yes, I know, but Donovan is a student in the Wizards Academy. If they had gone in to protect him, they would not be able to get out," said Loren. "So they abandoned their duty?" asked Ard. "No," said Loren, "they entrusted it to me and my *associate.*" "I see," said Ard. "Do you know where I can find them?" "I believe they went to Prarrieville, some leagues west of here, to await any news. There are fewer magic-users in Prarrieville to detect them," whispered Loren.

"That is wise," said Ard. "I suppose that I can tell you my news then. There is another human that must be protected. Victor did not discover him during his search, but I have learned that one inside the academy, named Andrew, is also a descendant of Wizard Amanda." "That is a problem," said Loren, "There are two Andrews at the Academy."

Kathy was pleased. While her room had not been luxurious, it was clean and secure, and the shipping master had been polite and unassuming. The food he provided was better than anything she had eaten in the last week, so she was content. It was also nice to see the HMS UNSINKABLE pulling into port, right on schedule. All she had to do was get down to the ship once it had off-loaded its cargo and stay out of sight until they weighed anchor.

From her window, she had watched the magical Customs inspector and his three big assistants patrolling the docks. They checked every ship coming and going. She was going to need another distraction to get on board the HMS UNSINKABLE and she doubted that another fire was the answer.

As she watched the ship being unloaded, she saw the shipping master walk up the gangplank and begin conversing with what could only be the Captain of the ship. He pointed up at his apartments, clearly telling Captain Bell about her booking passage and her current location. Captain Bell shook the shipping agent's hand and motioned for him to go quickly and return with his passenger. The shipping agent hurried across the pier and entered his office, calling upstairs, "Mistress! The ship is here, and Captain Bell says they'll be finished unloading within the glass. He wants to sail with the tide this evening and requests that you hurry down and board immediately."

Kathy already had her things packed and was ready, but now she needed to think of something to distract the magician on the dock and quickly. As she was escorted to the ship by the shipping master, Kathy removed several sections of the supports and bollards holding up a section of the pier, sending the astonished magician, his three assistants, and five sailors toppling into the water, along with several crates that they were inspecting. Without breaking stride, Kathy walked calmly onto the gangplank and asked the Captain, "Permission to come aboard, Sir?"

Wizard Louis re-read the message from Riverton. The two Fire Dragon Changed Ones indicated that they were departing the town as soon as the messenger hawk heading back to Louis was away. That was good; they should be well clear of the town before the Dragon attack in a few weeks. The two Dragons, Flame and Ember, were headed for the Fire Dragon colony in the Grey Mountains. Louis considered what else he could do to prepare for the coming conflict.

He summoned Marissa, one of the Cook's assistants. When she arrived, Louis closed the door and informed her of the planned attack. Louis asked her to inform the other Changed Ones in the city, so they would be prepared if called upon. As a servant, Marissa was able to move freely about the palace and the capitol city without exciting comments or even notice. Louis was aware of five Changed Ones in the city, three Fire Dragons, and two Stone. The Fire Dragons worked in the Blacksmith shop, while the Stone Dragons operated the town mortuary, fitting occupations, Louis thought.

While Louis knew about the Changed Ones in the city of Baize, he was less sure about any others in the kingdom. It was not uncommon for his kin to transform into human shape when the hunger got too bad. Hopefully, most of them changed back into Dragons after they had sated themselves, but Louis knew that that was not always the case. There might even be a few Changed Ones who preferred to remain as humans. That could pose a problem; while Victor's plan was to set human against human, if some of the Changed Ones sided with the humans, there could be Dragon-on-Dragon fights; and Stone Dragons were formidable enemies.

He would need to send a message to the Stone Dragon Clan Chief and find out if he knew how many Stone Dragon Changed Ones there were in the kingdom and exactly where their allegiances were. Stone Dragons were notoriously stubborn. If they got it into their heads that their life was better as humans, it might be difficult or impossible to change their minds. He would need to talk to the Stone Dragon Changed One, who was posing as a night Baker in the palace, what was his name— Gary? Yes, Gary. He might have some insights on whether he preferred his life as a human to being a Dragon.

Finding the Stone Dragon colony was not going to be easy either. Louis had never been there, but he knew that it was somewhere in the Western Desert, in an underground cave complex. Hopefully Gary could give him precise directions, or maybe go in Louis's stead. The Stone and Fire Dragons had an uneasy alliance, after all. They each kept to their side of Baize, generally divided by the Green River, but that was just an unofficial boundary.

Finished with his plotting for the day, Wizard Louis went out in search of some female companionship. There were several willing servants who were smart enough to realize that being *favored* by the Court Wizard was a quick path to advancement, and no one wanted to remain a chambermaid for her entire career.

"So, Victor, the full moon is in three days. Are your preparations complete?" asked the voice that seemed to come from the walls of his bedroom. "Completely," said Victor, "the Fire Dragons will meet me in the quarry north of Colton in three days and attack the Baizian city of Riverside the next day." "And then?" asked the ceiling. "Sea Dragons will begin attacking ships of both nations up and down the coastlines of both the Eastern Ocean and the Low Sea. I expect an angry visit from the Baizian Ambassador within a week, demanding reparations," crowed Victor. "And what will you tell the Ambassador?" "It depends," said Victor, "if he is humble and civil, I will tell him that I will look into the matter; if he is arrogant and demanding, I will kill him."

"Then what happens?" asked the door. "A few days after the visit from the Ambassador, Stone Dragons will attack Weaton," said Victor. "That will certainly enrage the king. What course of action will you recommend?" Came the voice from the window. "A ground assault on the city of Springfield, with simultaneous naval raids on the Baize port cities of Gulfport and Seaside, and maybe even a feint on their capitol of Baize," said Victor. "That should certainly get the conflict started. What role do the Dragons have in this spectacle?" asked the floor. "Why, none at all. After the first few raids, we will simply sit back and watch the humans destroy each other," said Victor smugly. "You appear to have managed this well, Victor. I am pleased."

Gek

Chapter Fifteen:

THE CURTAIN RISES

"**I** cannot believe it! Two! Only two of the Changed Ones will aid us," shouted Loren. "That idiot, Level Three Stone Dragon, Raymond, who is on the verge of being put to sleep and having his spark removed, and the Level One Sea Dragon, Susan, who, according to Wizard Toffin, cannot master a simple Level One Serum!" They were seated in the parlor of Loren's cottage, discussing the situation. "How are we going to kill ten students in three days?" asked Stuart.

"You won't," said a voice from the corner of the room. Instantly, both of Wizard Loren's hands vanished, leaving perfectly clean, healed stumps. Stuart bolted for the door but was immediately seized by an incredibly strong Tether spell. His arms were pinned to his sides, unable to cast even the simplest Level One spell. "Allow me," said Wizard Noland as he dropped his Concealment shield. "*DELERE,*" he said while flicking his right wrist towards Stuart. Stuart's hands were similarly cleanly and efficiently removed. "NO! NO! NO! NO!" cried Stuart. "My hands," screamed Loren, "What have you done?"

"Firstly, I have prevented both of you from changing back into your true forms as dragons. So, whatever happens *now*, you will face it as humans. Secondly, we have prevented you from conjuring any spells to injure anyone or escape. The only reason either one of you is still alive is so that you can be questioned," said an angry Wizard Noland. "I will never betray my Clan," said a defiant Stuart. "Nor will I," said Loren quietly. "We shall see," said Noland. "Thirst can be a powerful motivator. All either of you will be provided is water laced with Truth Serum. Eventually, you will drink. Or you will die. I understand that you can die of thirst in three days, and if I heard you correctly a moment ago, that's just about right."

Wizard Nolan led Loren to her bedroom, commanded her to lay on the bed, and then spelled her to sleep. Stuart had to be dragged forcefully to the spare bedroom, where he was similarly put to sleep with a spell. Once done, Edward dropped his Concealment shield. "We need to sterilize these rooms, remove *everything* from them. When they wake, there should be nothing but four walls, a window that won't open, and a carafe of ice-cold water laced with Truth Serum," said Edward. "No bed?" asked Noland. "They can sleep on the floor," said Edward angrily. "I don't want them finding a way to hang themselves with their bedsheets. We need to take their clothes, too." "Is that really necessary?" asked Noland. "Yes," said Edward. "They may have a vial of poison or a belladonna berry hidden in their clothing. We can't afford to let them take the easy way out. We can leave them each a nightshirt. Clothes are given in exchange for cooperation." The two returned and removed everything in both rooms, leaving only the two sleeping forms on the floors, with a carafe of Truth Serum-laced water.

"I need to summon the staff and explain what has happened and post a guard on them, but first, we need to see to the two—

what did Loren call them 'Changed Ones'?" asked Noland. "I suppose they should be spelled and their spark removed. We'll pick up a new chambermaid, and the King will get another man for his road crews." "I'd keep it quiet from the other students until we've rooted out the other 'Changed Ones.' Once they learn what happened to Loren and Stuart, they may change their allegiance," said Edward. "In the meantime, I need to go deal with Wizard Victor before he slips away." "Be careful," cautioned Noland. "Always," said Edward.

Victor strutted through the palace as if he owned the place. Servants hid whenever they heard him coming, afraid of incurring his wrath for some minor offense. As he passed the old woman mopping the floors, she swept the mop too far and touched the hem of his scarlet robe. "Fool!" shouted Victor. "Did you not see me coming?" "Of course I did," said Edward, looking up. Victor recoiled in shock, "You!" he said. "Yes, me. Goodbye, Victor." With a quick slashing motion with his right hand and the incantation *"TERMINA,"* Victor fell dead, landing on the floor in the dirty mop water. Another quick spell to Remove his neck, then Edward laid the mop next to Victor's now headless body and slipped out of the palace, smiling happily.

"All lessons are canceled for today," Noland told Edward. "I will need a new History and Enhancements teacher and a new Gate Warden. Any suggestions?" Edward thought for a moment, then said, "I would recommend Daniel, the Battle Mage from Second Regiment, here in Kingston, for Loren's position. He was injured some years ago, a broken leg, as I recall, that never really healed right. Campaigning is difficult for him, but he's a competent Mage, who I'm sure can pass the Wizards Test." "And the Gate Warden?" asked Noland. "How about Mage Faith, from the Southport Regional Mage's Office?" suggested Edward. "In keeping with tradition, if you replace Loren with a man, Stuart's replacement has to be a woman, and as I recall, Mage Faith is uncommonly good with a staff."

"What about Mage Cassandra from the Kingston Regional Mage's Office?" asked Noland. "I would have thought her to be an excellent candidate for either position." "I agree, but I plan to recommend her to the King as the new Court Wizard," said Edward. "A female Court Wizard? I'm not sure that's ever been done before," said Noland. "There's a first time for everything," said Edward.

"What should we do next?" asked Noland. "Well, we have suspicions of who the other ten 'Changed Ones' are. What say we bring them into your office, one at a time, past the window where Stuart is being held? If he sees that we already know who they are, it might break down his resistance quicker and get him talking," suggested Edward. "You think he'll talk?" asked Noland. "I think he is the more likely of the two, despite his bluster. Loren's quiet resolve may prove to be more difficult to overcome," said Edward.

"You think she would rather die than betray the dragons?" asked Noland. "We can't let her die," insisted Edward. "But you said—" "I told her a lie, my friend," said Edward. "It's always best if prisoners confess of their own free will. If not, we can always use a Compulsion spell to get her to drink the Truth Serum." "I never realized just how devious you are," said Noland with a grin. "Is there anything else we should be doing?" Edward hesitated. "Come on, my friend, out with it," said Noland. Finally, Edward said, "I think you need to accelerate the training and advancement of your students. We no longer have the luxury of time to train them to be perfect Sorcerers. I believe that even without the three imposters we have eliminated, the dragons are going to attack soon."

"So, we send out untrained Sorcerers?" asked Noland. "Not *untrained*, my friend, but perhaps *less* trained than previously. The current Mentors should be released to the military, and our best Level Threes tested and promoted to *probationary* Sorcerers, to remain here as Mentors." "Even Andrew?" "Yes," said Edward. "We can no longer afford for Donovan to be the only student with a dedicated Mentor." "You knew they were cousins?" asked Noland. "Yes," said Edward. "I knew that my wife's sister had a child, and I heard that he ran away from home at a fairly young age to apply for acceptance at the Academy. I've kept track of his progress over the years." "Why didn't you tell me?" asked Noland. "To protect both of you, my friend. I'm sure now that Victor was behind my wife's murder. He also tried to have Donovan killed twice. If he had learned that I had a nephew with the spark—" "I understand," said Noland. "So where should I send Sorcerer Andrew?" Edward thought for a while, "How are his magical skills on water?" "Excellent," replied Noland, "You think I should send him to the Navy?" "I don't think that this coming war is going to be fought on the land alone. Didn't Loren call Level One Susan a 'Sea Dragon Changed One'?"

"I cannot find Stuart anywhere," said Gek. "I wonder if something has happened to him." "Maybe he does not get to leave the school very often," suggested Azure. "Well, we can only wait one more day, then we have to head back to the quarry for the Dragon Council meeting." "I am still not sure how we can protect this human if he never comes out of the school," said Gek. "Should we go in?" asked Azure. "Absolutely not," said Gek, "I will not risk either one of us getting trapped in there."

Just then, a Town Crier walked by shouting, "COURT WIZARD MURDERED! READ ALL ABOUT IT! WIZARD

VICTOR DECAPITATED MERE STEPS FROM THE THRONE ROOM! READ ALL ABOUT IT! PALACE IN CRISIS!"

"We need to get out of here!" said Azure. "Back to the room; we will depart at nightfall," said Gek. They hurried back to the inn, entered their room, and barred the door. "It could just be a coincidence," whispered Azure, "Victor *was* very disagreeable as a Dragon. He probably made enemies as a human, too." "I do not doubt that Victor had enemies," whispered Gek, "but one of them was strong enough and clever enough, to kill him *inside* the palace. I do not like it."

Wizard Noland called all of the Wizards Academy faculty to a staff meeting in the Lecture Hall. Staff meetings were rare but not unheard of. Once all of the teachers and Mentors were assembled, Wizard Toffin said, "I wonder what's keeping Loren and Stuart." "They will not be joining us," said Wizard Noland, striding into the room, followed by Edward; the assembled faculty gasped. "Please, everyone, sit down. We have much to discuss," said Noland. The Wizards and Mentors seated themselves, almost overcome with curiosity.

"First, I am pleased to inform you that the report of Battle Mage Edward's death was premature," said Noland. "I will let the Battle Mage fill you in on events of the past few months and what brings us here today. Mage Edward?" "Thank you, Wizard Noland," said Edward formally. Over the next hour, Edward explained the efforts that were made to prevent the Royal Expeditionary Force from finding the dragon; the effects of the new crossbows during the battle, and finally, his use of Healing Serums and spells, and the use of the stasis box that saved his life. He then explained waking up on the barge headed down the Sapphire River, and his return to the site of the battle. "The dragon we killed was a female, and there were indications that she was protecting a young dragon that was not detected by the soldiers of the Royal Expeditionary Force after I was rendered unconscious," said Edward. There were murmurs amongst the assembled faculty. "I also detected the tracks of a much older dragon, who apparently arrived after the battle and departed in the company of the baby dragon."

"*More Dragons?*" "*How many could there be?*" "*What should we do?*" "*Does the King know?*" "SILENCE!" commanded Wizard Noland. The crowd quieted. "Edward, would you please continue," said Noland. Edward went on to explain his suspicion that dragons could understand human speech and what he discovered about the end of the last Dragon War. "When I shared this with Wizard Noland, we wondered if dragons, being magical creatures, could actually *cast* spells. We have determined that they can."

"*Dragons can do magic?*" "*Impossible,*" "*Inconceivable,*" "*Frightening!*" Noland raised his hand, and the crowd quieted again. "You are all correct," said Edward. "It is frightening, inconceivable, and outside of our understanding. Nevertheless, it is *true*. Moreover, dragons know the spell of Change." "What could they do with that knowledge," asked Wizard Dylan, "change a sword into a pillow?" "No," said Edward, "change a dragon into a human." The last pronouncement stunned the crowd into silence. They all sat still, afraid to ask the next question. Finally, Wizard Mira asked it, "You mean that dragons walk amongst us? That they have been spying on us for years, maybe decades?"

"Dragons do indeed walk among us," confirmed Edward, "but they are not all evil or seeking to harm us. However, there are some that thirst for revenge at what was done to their kind two centuries ago." "How can we identify them?" asked Wizard Mira. "Wizard Noland and I have discovered two ways to identify a 'Changed One,' which is the dragon's term for those who have assumed human form." "Please tell us how," said Mira. "The first way is to listen to their speech; dragons do not use contractions, like 'didn't,' 'isn't,' 'won't, 'can't,' and 'I'm.'" "And the second way?" asked Mira. "By their smell. Dragons smell different than humans. However, they have learned to mask their scent with perfume or cologne," said Noland.

"Ridiculous!" shouted Wizard Dylan. "Why on earth would a dragon want to transform into a human?" Edward looked at Mentor Terry and nodded. Terry stepped forward and said in a halting voice, "At— at first, it was just to survive," said Terry. There were gasps from the assembled staff and several cast protective shields, but Noland held out his hand and stilled the crowd. "Go on, Terry," he said gently.

"Yes, Sir. You see," Terry explained, "after most of the adult Dragons were poisoned during the 'Peace Celebration,' those of us left were young—we had trouble finding food for ourselves. Many starved. Then, a kind Wizard named Amanda found the Dragon colony and began healing us of the poison; she tended our wounds and found food for us. She was a true Dragon-Friend. It was from Amanda we learned that we could do magic. A young Dragon heard her recite the Dig spell as she prepared a grave for a Dragon that she could not save. The Dragon repeated the spell with the gesture, and it worked. Before then, we had no idea that we could perform magic like the humans did."

"How did you learn the Change spell?" asked Wizard Toffin. "Once we knew that we could do magic, we kept a close watch on Wizard Amanda, learning everything we could from her. There are some spells that a Dragon cannot cast, since it is difficult for us to stand upright in Dragon form, so any spell that uses both hands is almost impossible to cast. The Change spell is difficult, as it requires us to 'rear-up' and clap our front feet together before we fall back to earth, but, obviously, it can be done."

"Why do you remain in human form?" asked Wizard Mira. "To avoid being forever hungry," said Terry. "Since I transformed, I have seldom been hungry. I have also met human friends, it is not such a hard decision, really. I would not be here except that the Regional Mage in Weaton found me and recognized the spark. All of the Dragons here at the Academy are 'drag-ins,' as you call it." "How many dragons are there in the Academy?" asked Wizard Dylan.

"There are nine in addition to Terry," said Wizard Nolan. "What are we going to do about it?" asked Mentor Jason. Wizard Nolan gave Sorcerer Jason a firm look and said, "The nine Changed Ones remaining in the Academy have all been subjected to a Binding spell. If they attack a human or aid the hostile dragons in any way, they will die instantly." There was a collective sigh of relief from the assembled magicians.

"Now I will answer your earlier question, Jeffrey," said Wizard Nolan to Wizard Toffin, "Wizard Loren, Wizard Stuart, Level Three Raymond, and Level One Susan were all dragons intent on the destruction of the human race." There were cries of disbelief from the crowd. Wizard Noland continued, "Level Three Raymond and Level One Susan have had their spark removed. Susan will remain with us as a chambermaid, and Raymond has been transferred to the King's Road Crew." "What of Loren and Stuart?" asked Mira. "Loren and Stuart are both being held for questioning. They may know other Changed Ones in the kingdom that must be confronted." "Did you use a Binding spell on them as well?" asked Wizard Toffin. "No," said Noland, "that wouldn't work. They might have simply broken their word in order to die before betraying their Clans."

"Clans?" asked Mira. Wizard Noland looked to Terry for an explanation. "There are five species of Dragons, each in its own Clan: Great Dragons, like the one Mage Edward fought; Sea Dragons, that live in the oceans; Snow Dragons that inhabit the Snow Fields of the north; Stone Dragons that live west of the Amber River, and Fire Dragons that also normally live in the Kingdom of Baize." "What clan are you?" asked Wizard Dylan. "I am a human," said Terry forcefully, "but I was a Fire Dragon." Mentor Celeste fainted.

"Would someone please revive Celeste so we can continue?" asked Edward. Wizard Toffin produced a smelling salt from his robes and held it under Celeste's nose; she came awake immediately. "Now, in answer to your questions about Loren and Stuart, Mage Edward and I removed both of their hands, so that they can't cast any spells or transform back into dragons." "Don't you think that was a bit extreme?" asked Wizard Mira. "Not at all," Noland replied, "at the time, they were discussing how to kill the ten Changed Ones who would not support their planned attack on us."

"What happens now?" asked Wizard Mira. "Now we come to it," said Noland, "First, I have identified replacements for Loren and Stuart. Battle Mage Daniel from the Second Franconian Regiment will become the Enhancements and History instructor, effective on Firstday, and Mage Faith from the Southport Regional Mage's Office will replace Stuart as soon as she can get here from her current location. *I* will man the Gatehouse until Mage Faith's arrival. Next, at the earliest opportunity, Mages Edward, Daniel, and Faith will undergo the Wizards Test for promotion to the rank of Wizard. Furthermore, in light of the impending crisis, the twelve most prepared Level Threes will be tested and appointed as *provisional* Sorcerers. Once these appointments are made, all current Mentors will receive assignments to the armed forces of Franconia." Mentor Celeste fainted again.

"I WANT ANSWERS!" bellowed the King. "I want to know how my Court Wizard could have been murdered within the Palace! This is an intolerable breach of security! You! Captain Bark! Please tell me why I should not sack my entire Personal Guard and send you all to the road crews!" The assembled Ministers and Advisors all shrank back from the enraged King. None of them had any answers, and none wanted to incur the King's wrath. Captain Bark paled and stammered, "Please, your highness—"

"Your Majesty," said Edward, dropping his Concealment shield and stepping forward, "It's not Captain Bark's fault. When I decided to kill Wizard Victor for crimes against the Crown, none of your Personal Guard could have stopped me." The King sat back down on his throne, speechless. "Your Highness," said Edward softly, "I have evidence that Wizard Victor was directly responsible for your parent's death and that he was plotting your murder as well. Had I not acted quickly, Victor might be sitting on that throne now instead of you." The assembled crowd gasped at Edward's pronouncement. "My parents? You have proof?" asked the King. "I do, Sire," said Edward, "but perhaps a more private setting would be more appropriate for this conversation." "Of—of course," stammered the King. "We will adjourn to my private study. Jasmine, Marshall Guzman, um—" "It would be helpful to have Wizard Noland and Major Gerald present as well, Your Majesty," suggested Edward. "Yes, of course, Wizard Noland, Major Gerald, attend," said the shaken King.

Once seated in the King's private study, the King had regained his composure and his temper. "Mage Edward, you had better have a good explanation for your supposed 'death' and disappearance. I paid a fifty-gold death benefit to your son, and you'd better believe I want it back!"

"Your Majesty, once you hear my explanation, I hope you'll agree with the reasons for my absence and my actions regarding Wizard Victor," said Edward. "Well then, let's hear it," demanded the King. Edward explained about his encounter with the dragon near Farmdale, how he survived his injuries, and what he and Wizard Noland subsequently discovered about dragons and their ability to perform magic and change into human form. "You're telling me that there are dragons, disguised as humans, walking amongst us?" asked the King incredulously. "Yes, Sire," replied Edward. "I hope you have proof of this incredible claim!" said the King.

"Your Majesty, Wizard Noland and I captured and disabled two of these imposters inside the Wizards Academy as they were plotting to kill several students, who are dragons, that would not join their imminent attack on Franconia," stated Edward. "Inside the Wizards Academy? How is that possible?" asked the King, becoming increasingly agitated. "Sire, one of them was Wizard Stuart, our Gate Warden and Martial Arts instructor. He had been at the Academy for decades. That is undoubtedly how the imposters were admitted," said Noland. "Who was the other one?" asked the King. "Wizard Loren, the History and Enhancements teacher," said Noland sadly. "I have known Loren for years, and I never suspected anything, until I heard her with my own ears."

"Wait," the King said, catching up, "you're saying that Wizard Victor was a *dragon in disguise*?" "Just so, Your Highness. As soon as I realized your peril, I rushed to the palace to eliminate him," said Edward. "And you suspect that he was responsible for my parent's death?" asked the King. "Your Highness, your parent's untimely death in a carriage accident was never investigated to my satisfaction. I long suspected, but had no proof, that a magician was responsible for the carriage going over that cliff," said Edward. "And Wizard Victor was riding with the escort," mused the King.

"Circumstantial," said Jasmine, speaking for the first time. "But corroborated by Wizard Loren under Truth Serum," countered Noland. "What did you do to these other dragons you discovered who were disguised as humans?" asked the King. "I laid a Binding spell on them to never transform back into a dragon and never do anything that would cause harm to a human," said Noland. "And if they violate this *Binding spell*, did you call it? What happens then?" asked Jasmine. "If one breaks a Binding spell, one dies. Instantly," said Edward.

"I see," said the King. "What about my fifty-gold death benefit, Edward?" "Your Majesty, I'm afraid that I've already spent it," said Edward. "What!" exclaimed the King. "I used it, along with fifty golds from my personal savings, to purchase two hundred crossbows from Prestige Arms in Fairview, Sire. I understand there was a delay in their procurement. Some negotiations over the price, I believe?" asked Edward. "Yes," replied the King, considerably calmer. "Victor assured me that we could get them for three silvers each, instead of five." "I suspected as much, Sire. I know James, the proprietor, and he is an honest man and loyal. It probably costs him at least four silvers to make one crossbow; selling them for three silvers each would ruin him."

"When will these crossbows arrive?" asked Marshall Guzman. "The troops in Prarrieville should have them by now, maybe the company in Weaton as well. It may take longer to locate the two companies that are out on maneuvers. There are also crossbows enroute to Westport and Southport, and forty of them in a warehouse in Kingston, awaiting distribution." "How did you arrange that so quickly?" asked Jasmine. "I sent the gold with the Senior Specialists from the Royal Expeditionary Force three weeks ago," explained Edward. "They returned last week with the crossbows, and Major Gerald used one of his Force's wagons to rush the weapons west to our troops."

"Without my permission?" asked the King mildly. "Sire, if Victor had learned of the crossbow purchase…" said Edward. "I understand," said the King, "I have only one more question. How did you identify these disguised dragons?" "Dragons apparently don't use contractions, sire. Also, they smell different than humans. Once we knew what to look for, we were able to locate those inside the barrier that guards the Wizards Academy," said Noland.

"Are there others in Kingston?" asked the King. "Assuredly," said Edward, "we will, of course, launch a search for any other Changed Ones, beginning in the palace." "At once," ordered the King, "and I mean, as soon as you leave this room." "Of course, Sire," said Wizard Noland, "there is one other matter; I would like to recommend Mage Cassandra, the Kingston Regional Mage, to replace Victor as your Court Wizard." "A mere Mage?" asked the King. "Sire, as soon as we finish scouring the palace for Changed Ones, Mage Cassandra, Battle Mage Edward, and Battle Mage Daniel from Second Regiment will be given the Wizards Test for promotion to the rank of Wizard. Battle Mage Daniel will replace Wizard Loren as an instructor at the Academy. I have also recalled Mage Faith, the Southport Regional Mage, so that she can be tested and assigned as the Gate Warden for the Wizards Academy, replacing the traitor, Stuart." "Very well," said the King, "I wish you luck in the testing, Edward, although I doubt you will need luck." "Thank you, Your Majesty, I appreciate your confidence in me," said Edward humbly.

"Sire, while these dedicated magicians look for disguised Dragons in the palace, I need to discuss our operations in Baize with you," said Jasmine. "Of course," said the King. "You others are dismissed. Marshall Guzman, see to distributing those crossbows to our troops immediately and see about ordering more *at the same price*, mind you." While Jasmine conferred with the King, Noland and Edward searched the palace and grounds for any more Changed Ones. They found nothing.

The minute that the HMS UNSINKABLE reached the pier at Southport, Mage Kathy knew she had a problem. There was a female magician waiting on the dock, who was obviously going to be a passenger on the trip to Kingston and maybe even as far as Fairview. The journey from Westport had not proven to be as informative as Kathy hoped; the crew only knew second-hand rumors of the Royal Expeditionary Force's encounter with the dragon, not having been there themselves. All she learned was that the soldiers claimed to have fought a fifty-foot-long golden dragon that breathed fire (a sticky substance they compared to "flaming strawberry jam") and was generally impervious to swords, spears, and arrows. Axes apparently were able to penetrate dragon scales, but the wielder seldom got a chance for a second swing.

The soldiers told the crew about a new weapon called a *crossbow*, which Kathy had never heard of before. According to the sailors, the Battle Mage, who was killed in the attack, procured these new weapons from an arms dealer in Fairview. Kathy made a note to locate and visit him. In order to have more time to question the crew and Captain, Kathy had conjured a headwind out of the east, which delayed their arrival in Southport by almost a full day. But now, there was a slim, dark-haired magician on the dock, waiting to board.

Kathy retired to her cabin and shut the door. There was no use bolting it because any magician worth her salt could blast open any locked door (or just remove the hinges). It was less than a glass before the magician knocked on her door. "Come on in," said Kathy.

Mage Faith entered cautiously. She had sensed the presence of someone with the spark as soon as she stepped on board. A brief conversation with Captain Bell had revealed that there was a first-class passenger who boarded in Westport and was supposedly headed home to Fairview. Captain Bell reported that she was a most courteous, attractive, but inquisitive woman.

"So, Sorceress, what brings you to Southport?" asked Mage Faith. "Sorceress?" replied Kathy, "I assure you, Miss, I am not—" "Stop the denials," said Faith, cutting her off. "I sensed the spark of magic in you as soon as I came on board. If you are not a Sorceress, you are at least a rogue magician and one too old for enrollment at the Wizards Academy." "I see," said Kathy, "may I have your name?" "I am Mage Faith. Until recently, I was the Southport Regional Mage, responsible for finding those with the spark in Southport. I have been recalled to the Wizards Academy in Kingston in order to attempt the Wizard's Test required for assignment as an instructor at the Academy."

"I am Kathy, just Kathy, and while I do not deny that I may have the spark, I am only thirty-two. Is that too old to enter the Wizards Academy? If so, what is your policy concerning 'old, rogue magicians?" asked Kathy. "Well," confessed Faith, "the cut-off age for students enrolling in the Academy is twenty. Since you have obviously been able to control your magical abilities without causing harm to the citizens of Franconia or been caught counterfeiting coins, our policy is to require you to submit to a Binding spell, promising never to harm anyone using your magic or use your magical ability to counterfeit coins, then let you go about your business."

"Oh, my," said Kathy, "I'm afraid that is quite impossible." Faith's mood darkened, "And why is that?" "Well, as an attractive magician yourself, I'm sure that on occasion, you've had to fend off aggressive, presumptuous men with magic. I've had to do so on several occasions. Were I to submit to the Binding spell you suggest, I would be helpless against future assaults upon my person. There must be another solution."

Faith thought for a moment. She knew *exactly* what Kathy was talking about and understood her dilemma. "How about this? A Binding spell, never to *unjustly* harm another with magic." Kathy smiled and said, "That sounds reasonable. *I, Kathy Hima, solemnly promise never to unjustly harm another person with magic.*" Mage Faith drew her finger along the deck and muttered the incantation for the Binding spell. Once the spell was in place, Faith asked, "So, Kathy, where are you headed?"

Kathy spun the tale of her returning to Fairview after visiting her ailing sister in Westport. Mage Faith wasn't entirely sure that she believed her, but with the Binding spell in place, she had no qualms about allowing her to continue her journey without further questioning. "So, are you going to Fairview too?" asked Kathy. "No, I am disembarking in Kingston; as I said, I've been recalled to the Wizards Academy to be the new Gate Warden and Martial Arts instructor."

"Really? Did something happen to your predecessor?" "I'm not really sure," replied Faith, "Wizard Stuart was old when I graduated, and that was years ago. Maybe he just decided to retire." "Captain Bell and his crew have been telling me about a battle with a dragon some months ago. Have you heard anything about it?" asked Kathy.

Faith frowned, "What would Captain Bell know about that?" "Oh, apparently, the HMS UNSINKABLE transported the Royal Expeditionary Force back to Kingston from Fairview after the battle. They were awarded the King's Commendation, whatever that is, for their service. I imagine the soldiers told the crew about their adventures on the voyage. You know how soldiers like to brag." "Hmmph," said Faith, "All I know about it is that Mage Edward, a friend of mine, was killed by the dragon." "I'm so sorry. I had no idea. None of the crew mentioned that a Mage fought alongside them." "Edward was probably holding the dragon with a Tether spell to keep it from escaping. I imagine his other spell was some kind of a shield, but I can't be sure. Maybe Captain Gerald, the commander of the Royal Expeditionary Force, can tell me, if he's still in Kingston."

"What's a Tether spell?" asked Kathy, innocently. "Sorry," said Faith, "it's a spell that allows a magician to keep someone or *something* in their sight. You can't reel the person in, like a fish, but you can keep them from escaping. It's a very useful spell for capturing criminals or rogue magicians." Kathy laughed. "I'm confused, though. If the Mage was killed by the dragon, how did the soldiers manage to kill it?" "You ask good questions," said Faith. "That's the other thing I need to find out from Captain Gerald. Well, I better find my cabin. I'm sure we'll be casting off soon."

Once Mage Faith was gone, Kathy retrieved her journal and made more notations:

2. Interviewed the Captain and Crew of the HMS UNSINKABLE. They say that the REF described the dragon

as being 50-feet-long, gold in color, and impervious to conventional weapons. Dragon fire is a flaming, gelatinous substance that sticks to whatever it touches. The REF killed the dragon with a new weapon called a 'crossbow.' These 'crossbows were purchased from an arms dealer in Fairview. Must research upon arrival in Fairview. Total cost: Zero

3. Arrived in Southport and was immediately discovered as someone with the spark of magic by a Mage named Faith. Had to submit to a Binding spell never to unjustly harm another with magic, in order to remain free. Mage Faith told me that another Mage, Edward, fought the dragon with the REF but was killed during the battle. The commander of the REF is Captain Gerald. If Mage Faith can pass the Wizard's test, she will be appointed as the new Gate Warden for the Wizards Academy in Kingston. Question: What happened to the previous Gatekeeper? Mage Faith also believes there was a dragon. Total cost: Zero

Chapter Sixteen:

SWIMMING LESSONS

"**S**tuart is dead." "How? Did he kill himself?' asked Wizard Noland. "No," said Wizard Dylan, "we just didn't realize how many spells and Healing Serums he was taking each day just to keep himself alive and vibrant. I mean, he was old for a human; I have no idea how old of a dragon he was." "I understand," said Noland. "I never considered he might have been three hundred years old before he transformed. How is Loren doing?" "She is despondent. I mean, she sees no future for herself. She can't transform back into a dragon, and without hands, she is completely dependent on others for even simple tasks like dressing herself," said Dylan.

"Could we fashion her prosthetic hands, hooks or claws, something like that?" asked Noland. "I'm sure we can," said Wizard Dylan, "but could she do magic with prosthetics? For that matter, she could attack someone with a hook or a claw." "We should offer her the artificial hands, on the condition that she accept the same Binding spell we laid on the other Changed Ones," decided Noland. "I will see to it at once and let you know her decision," said Dylan.

As Wizard Dylan departed, Sorcerer Andrew knocked on the Headmaster's door. "Come in, Sorcerer Andrew. Are you ready to depart?" "Yes, sir," said Andrew. "I just came by to say farewell and ask you to open the exit for me." "Have you told Donovan you're leaving?" "Yes. Sir, are you sure it's wise to appoint Terry as his Mentor? I mean—" said Andrew. "I know exactly what you mean, Andrew, and I'm not sure it is wise, but I'm sure it will be *instructive*. Which ship have you been posted to?" asked Noland. "The HMS VALOR, sir. Her Sorcerer, Jordan, was promoted and sent to replace Mage Faith in the Southport Regional Mage's Office."

"I have heard nothing but good things about Captain Matthews and the VALOR. The ship and crew have a reputation for excellence in the fleet," said Noland. "So I understand," said Andrew, with a hint of worry in his voice, "I have big shoes to fill." "Andrew, you are the most capable Mentor at the Academy. Otherwise, I would not have held you in reserve until Donovan arrived." "Really?" asked Andrew. "I always thought it was because you had doubts about me." "Not a one, Andrew, not a single one. Now, walk with me."

They headed across the courtyard toward the Gatehouse. As they approached the Mentor's dormitory, an enormous Concealment shield was released, and all of the remaining Mentors, and the newly promoted *provisional* Sorcerers stood in formation, saluting Andrew as he departed. When they entered the Gatehouse, Wizard Noland offered a final piece of advice. "Your first task when you get on board your ship will be to ensure that there are no Changed Ones in the crew. Keep your shields up and watch your back." As they left the Gatehouse, Andrew saw his favorite horse from the Academy stables, saddled and tied to the hitching post by the door. "A final gift from the Academy. I know you favor this fellow; you can stable him in the Southport Regional Mage's stable," said Noland. "Thank you, Wizard Noland," said Andrew, choking up. Wizard Noland rose to his full height, raised his right hand toward Andrew, and said formally, "Go forth in strength, Sorcerer Andrew Perrucci, serve the Kingdom above all personal desires, and return to us when you are prepared to test for the rank of Mage." With that, Noland turned abruptly, entered the Gatehouse, and closed the door firmly.

As the full moon rose over the walls of the quarry, the assembled members of the Dragon Council shifted about nervously. All knew that Victor was dead. Gek had not been quiet about sharing the news. "What do we do now? Should we proceed with Victor's plan, or do we abandon it and return to our Clans?" "We stick to the plan," said a Stone Dragon who stepped into the quarry, seeming to emerge from the very rock. "It is true that Victor is gone, but his plan was sound. It *will* succeed if we but have the courage to act."

"Who are you to address us so?" asked Ard. "I have not seen you in Council before." "My name is of no concern to you, old one, but I am the Queen of the Stone Dragon Clan. It was I that commanded Victor, and I who will see our plan succeed!" There were murmurs among the rest of the Dragon Council but general agreement. "Now, if the Fire Dragons are ready to kill some humans, depart at sunrise and attack the human city of Riverside. Be sure to leave some survivors to spread the tale of your attack," said the Stone Dragon Queen.

"As for you three," she said, addressing Gek, Azure, and Ard, "The boy Donovan Francis remains at the wizards academy, but the Sorcerer named Andrew Perrucci has been assigned to the human navy, aboard the ship HMS VALOR, while his mother, Beverly remains in Southport. I suggest that the ancient one guard the boy Donovan, while you two travel to Southport. Ensure that none of our kin attack the VALOR, and the council will be safe from the Binding spell you foolishly cast, ancient one."

"The humans have learned ways to recognize us," continued the Stone Dragon. "How do we avoid detection?" asked Gek. "The humans have discovered that Dragons do not combine words as humans do. We say 'can not,' 'will not,' 'do not,' 'does not,' and 'we will' while humans use other words to mean the same thing. To avoid detection, guard your speech! Say nothing if possible. If you must speak, avoid using the words "not," "will," and 'are.' It takes concentration, but it can be done. Next, they have learned that we smell different, so adopt the human practice of wearing a liquid that smells like flowers, vanilla, or mint. This will mask your scent. If you keep your distance from them, your scent will be harder to detect. So far, only their magic-users know about our Changed Ones. They are afraid of panicking their citizens if knowledge of our ability to perform magic becomes known," said the Stone Dragon.

"So, you believe the plan will still work?" asked Bliz, the Snow Dragon. "I do," said the Stone Dragon. "Proceed according to the plan; Fire Dragons attack Riverside; I will inform my Clan after the Kingdom of Baize protests the attack, so they will know when to attack Weaton. We must get the humans to fight each other! Snow dragons, wait for my signal and then begin raiding villages along the edge of the Snow Fields, Sea Dragons, attack ships from both human kingdoms at the next full moon!" The Dragons nodded in agreement, but the Queen of the Stone Dragons was not the inspirational speaker that Victor was.

"I must depart now to resume my place among the humans," said the Stone Dragon Queen. "Attack without mercy, for you shall receive none from the humans."

"All right, let's get this over with," said Edward warily. Wizards Noland, Dylan, and Mira stood before him in the Forces Training area. "Very well. The test is simple. Battle Mage Edward! We three Wizards stand against you! Your task is to cast three spells, a different one for each of us. No lethal spells, please. Once cast, we will each try to break your spell. You must hold your spells for one turn of the hourglass. If any of us break your spell, you fail the test." *So simple, yet so incredibly difficult,* thought Edward. *Which spells to use?* Then, an inventive solution came to him, and he smiled. "I'm ready," said Edward. "I will turn the glass, then you will cast your three spells, and we will begin," said Wizard Noland. "Begin," he said as he turned the hourglass.

Edward faced Mira and said, *"NERVO"* as he made a grabbing motion with his right hand. A strong Tether enveloped Wizard Mira, pinning her arms to her sides, rendering her incapable of casting any kind of counter-spell. Next, he faced Wizard Dylan and said, *"LIGARE,"* and made a fist with his left hand, instantly paralyzing him. Lastly, he walked over to Wizard Noland, his biggest challenge. Wizard Noland looked at Edward with surprise as Edward placed his right hand over Noland's head and said, *"REFUGIO."*

"A Weather shield? Over *my* head? I have *never* seen that one tried before!" "How would I even break a weather shield cast by someone else? I concede the hour, my friend." Edward smiled and said *CO*—," then he stopped mid-word. "Nice try, Michael, you 'break a weather shield' by fooling the Mage into ending it himself. Sorry, you will just have to stay dry for an hour."

The paralysis spell took no effort to maintain, so for the rest of the hour, Edward concentrated on keeping the Tether around Wizard Mira tight enough to prevent her from using her hands to conjure a counter-spell to break the Tether. Mira struggled mightily at first, then ceased her efforts, seemingly resigned to not being able to break the Tether. As the sands in the hourglass ran out, Mira made one last strenuous effort to break free, but Edward had anticipated the ploy and kept the Tether tight. When the last sand slipped from the glass, Edward prepared to release his spells, when inspiration struck. He walked over to the hourglass and touched it. The Seeming vanished with a flash of light, revealing the real hourglass with a few remaining sands still to fall. "I told you he would never fall for that," said Noland to Mira. *"CODA,"* said Edward, releasing all three spells, once the last sands had fallen. "Did I miss anything?" asked Wizard Dylan, recovering. The four Wizards laughed.

The dragons attacked an hour after dawn. They flew in low, crossing the Amber River right over the bridge that separated Franconia from the Kingdom of Baize. The Franconian border guards cried out a warning to their Baizian counterparts, but it was far too late in coming. The Baizian guard post on the west side of the river was reduced to flaming embers before the frightened guards could even draw their bows to defend themselves.

Two of the Fire Dragons continued west to the town proper, while the third continued circling the burning guard post, ensuring that none of the Baizian guards survived the attack.

Being so early in the morning, most of the residents of Riverside were still in bed. Only the early-risers, most of them fishermen, who were preparing for the day's work, had any chance to flee their homes. The dragons spared no one; every house was flamed, and every business, decimated.

The dragons flew over the city, circling, watching for survivors, chasing the terrified citizens through the burning city in some sort of deadly game of Hide-and-Seek. The people cried out for their magician to help them, but the Riverside Sorcerer was one of the Dragon Changed Ones who had left on "family business" a week ago. As two of the town's Royal Couriers raced their mounts south to safety, the dragons remembered that they were supposed to ensure that some of the inhabitants were to be left alive to spread the news of the attack. They figured that two survivors were enough.

To complete the deception, the dragons returned to the Franconian side of the Amber River, again flying low enough to be easily seen by the cowering Franconian guards. The three Fire Dragons returned to the rock quarry above Colton, unscathed and very pleased with themselves.

"All right, today will be your first lesson on controlling boats and conjuring magic on water," said Mentor Terry. There were five Level Two students in the group: Donovan, Asia (a Snow

Dragon Changed One), Julie, Ahmanda, and Capri (a Sea Dragon Changed One). To say that Donovan was uneasy about having a dragon Changed One for a Mentor and being in a group with two others was an understatement. Just yesterday he had argued against it with Wizard Noland. "You want to assign one of *'them'* as my Mentor?" he had asked. "Level Two Donovan, I *am* assigning Sorcerer Terry to be your new Mentor," said Noland sternly. "Sorcerer Terry has been here ten years. He has been a Mentor for two years, and his dedication to this Academy has never come into question. When it became known that Stuart and Loren were taken, he immediately came to me and confessed. *I* did not have to seek him out. He willingly submitted to Truth Serum and the Binding spell and then gave us the names of all the other 'Changed Ones' here at the Academy. If he violates the Binding spell *in any way*, he will die, instantly, before any spell he attempts to conjure takes effect. Moreover, Terry is highly motivated to help us." "Why is that?" asked Donovan. "Because his clan will see him as a traitor and kill him on sight if they can," said Noland. "This matter is closed. If you wish to advance to Level Three, you will need Terry's help and counsel. You are dismissed."

"Donovan, are you with us?" asked Terry, the tall, red-haired Mentor. "Sorry," said Donovan, "You were saying?" "I was saying that to control your boat, you use a Wind spell. You can steer the boat from side to side, speed it up, or slow it down with wind, but you have to be cautious; too much wind and you will capsize your boat; too little and you will have no effect. There are some spells you should never use on a boat this size: Fire, obviously; Water, as you may sink the boat; Sand— we do *not* want large quantities of sand in our boat; the Enlarge or Reduce spells must be used very cautiously; and if you conjure a protective shield that is too large, your shield may accidentally knock one of your classmates overboard. Lastly, your temperature spells will not work at all on water. Can anyone guess why?"

"No one? Very well, it is because you are already *on water,*" said Terry. "For some reason, the spells to heat and cool liquids fail when used on water. Apparently, the spell attempts to heat or cool the entire body of water you are sailing on. No Wizard alive is powerful enough to heat or cool an entire river, lake, stream, or even a small pond." There were murmurs of understanding from the class. "If any of you are eventually assigned to the Royal Navy, you will have to use *science*, to heat water aboard your ship." "What is *science*?" asked Capri. "Science is what non-magical people use to perform tasks, like heating water for tea," said Terry. "Asia, if you could not use magic, how would you heat water?" Asia thought for a minute, then she said, "I would use fire, like we do in Serums class to keep our Serums hot." "Exactly!" said Terry. "Well done, and that is the difference between science and magic. Science *always* works. If you put a cauldron of water over a fire, the liquid inside will heat up, *always*. If a magician is too weak to conjure the *'THERMO INTENSIF'* spell, they can always make a fire. On board a Navy ship, Captains often forbid Sorcerers the use of the

Fire spell, because it is so dangerous on board a ship. On a ship, meals are prepared in a shielded room called a *galley*. The galley has devices used to contain the fire, in order to heat water and cook food."

"I have a question," said Donovan. "You called these vessels 'boats' but said the Navy has 'ships,' what's the difference?" "An excellent question, Donovan," said Terry. "Quite simply, a 'boat' is a smaller vessel that can fit on a 'ship.'" "I don't understand," said Julie. "Why would you ever want to put one sailing vessel onto a bigger one?" Terry smiled. "All Navy ships have smaller vessels, much like these," he said, pointing to the ten boats moored to the Academy pier, "they are called 'lifeboats' and are used to evacuate the crew if the larger ship sinks for some reason. Everyone understand? Good! Now, I understand that you all know how to swim?" The five students nodded. "I hope so," said Terry, as he conjured a strong gust of wind, blowing them all into the Crimson River.

Wizard Louis was fuming. Damn, those Fire Dragons! They were supposed to leave some of the townsfolk alive! Instead, only two terrified Couriers escaped from a town of over five hundred. Those two fool Couriers had been so frightened that they fled to Colton. Colton! The one town in all of Baize with no Messenger Hawk service. After a few days in Colton, they eventually made their way to Springfield and, a week later, were able to send a hawk to Baize. This delayed Louis's plans by almost two weeks.

When the message *finally* arrived, Louis took it directly to the King. "Sire! I have just received a report that Franconian Dragons have attacked our city of Riverside and completely destroyed it!" "When did this happen?" demanded the King. "Almost two weeks ago, Sire. The day after the full moon." "Then why are we just hearing about it now?" "Your Majesty, apparently, only two residents of Riverside survived the attack. They were Royal Couriers, stationed on the outskirts of town. They escaped the attack, but, unfortunately, they fled to Colton, where there is no Messenger Hawk service. After recovering from their shock, they immediately rode to Springfield and sent the message from there," said Louis.

"What evidence do we have that this attack was initiated by Franconia?" asked the King. Louis temporized, "Well, Sire, several people saw the dragons fly across the border from Franconia. The report indicates that they flew right over the border crossing, in plain sight of witnesses." "So, the dragons flew in from the east. That doesn't mean that Franconia sent them," said the King.

"Perhaps not," said Louis slyly, "but they certainly did not do anything to warn or assist us." "True," said the King. "What do you recommend?" "I would humbly suggest that you instruct our Ambassador to Franconia to issue a most stern warning to

King Henry. Maybe even demand reparations to rebuild the town and compensate the bereaved families."

"Draft me a message, and I will dispatch it immediately." "I took the liberty, Sire," said Louis, handing over a message.

Ambassador Bozeman,

Dragons have attacked and destroyed our city of Riverside. They came from the east. Please express our displeasure <u>in the strongest terms</u> to King Henry. In light of this attack, I am ordering that our border with Franconia be closed to all trade. Additionally, any Franconian ships in Baizian ports must depart immediately. Normal trade will resume only after these cross-border incursions cease and reparations are made to rebuild the city of Riverside.

Donald, King of Baize

"Send it," said the King.

Five students landed in the river with a splash. They all bobbed to the surface, shocked and gasping for air. Donovan and Capri began swimming to the nearby bank, while Julie, Asia, and Ahmanda were swept downriver, barely able to keep their heads above water. The current wasn't fast, but it was steady.

Once Donovan reached the shore, he helped Capri climb onto the bank and then looked for the others. "I'll Tether Ahmanda, you get Asia," said Donovan. "Right,' said Capri. The two of them cast Tether spells onto the two youngest members of their group. They could not pull them to shore because that's not how Tethers work, but holding steady, the current quickly swung the two girls to the riverbank within sight. That left Julie, who was nearly out of sight, struggling against the current. "I have an idea," said Donovan, "I'm going to jump back in. You conjure a Tether on me, and I will Tether Julie." "Got it," said Capri. Donovan dove back into the river, surfacing and swimming strongly towards Julie; when he got close enough, he sputtered *"NERVO"* and made a grabbing gesture with his right hand. As he did so, he felt Capri's Tether spell wrap around him. Donovan kicked his feet to keep his head above the water, and the current rapidly brought him safely to shore. Once on solid, if muddy ground, Julie was brought safely to the shore as well.

"BRAVO!" exclaimed Mentor Terry as he walked up to the soaking-wet students. "In all my years, I have never seen a finer example of quick thinking and teamwork! Well done, you two," he said, addressing Donovan and Capri. "As for you three," Terry said, speaking to Ahmanda, Julie, and Asia, "while you were able to keep your heads above water, I would hardly call that swimming. For the next few Endday afternoons, you will practice swimming in the river. When you can make it to either shore before rounding that bend in the river down there, you may resume going into town on Enddays." The three students groaned.

Mentor Terry addressed Donovan and Capri, "What made you think of using the Tether spell?" "Well," said Donovan, "I would've thrown a rope, but I didn't have a rope. I knew that I could hold them with a Tether, and I assumed that the current would push them to shore." "The Tether spell was all Donovan's idea," said Capri, "I was just happy to be on shore." "And the double Tether?" asked Mentor Terry. "Julie was almost out of sight. I didn't think I could throw a Tether that far, but if Capri Tethered me, and I Tethered Julie…" Terry smiled, "As I said, the finest effort I have ever seen for this lesson. Feel free to use a warm wind spell to dry yourselves; then, I believe it is time for dinner."

When they reached the dinner table Phillip asked Donovan how his first 'Magic on Water' lesson went. Donovan exploded, "Terry blew all of us into the river with no warning! It's lucky we didn't all drown!" Phillip laughed. "They always do that. It's to teach you the importance of learning how to swim. Most students *say* they know how to swim, but splashing around in a waist-deep pond isn't the same as swimming." "You can say that again," said Donovan. "So how far downstream were you when Wizard Dylan plucked you out?" asked Phillip. "We never saw Wizard Dylan, Capri, and I swam to shore and used Tether spells and the current to get the others to the riverbank." Phillip whistled. "Tethers, huh? I wish I'd thought of that. I made it to shore alright. Being from Southport, I know how to swim, but the other four students in my group ended up in a boat with Wizard Dylan, about a half-mile downstream."

"Did you see the new instructors arrive?" asked Phillip. "No," said Donovan, "I was too busy taking a bath. Who are they?" "I only know one of them, Mage Faith, from the Southport Regional Mage's Office. I hear she's very good with the staff. The other Mage came in a couple of days ago. I don't know him, but he walks with a limp," whispered Phillip. "I imagine they'll both have to take the Wizard's Test before teaching classes," said Donovan.

"You are correct, Donovan," said Mentor Terry, coming up behind them. "But, as I understand it, the Wizard's Test only takes an hour, so Wizard Faith and Wizard Daniel should be ready to begin giving instruction tomorrow." Donovan gulped. "If you are finished eating, I would like a word with you, Donovan." "Of course, Sorcerer Terry," said Donovan.

They walked through the central courtyard and into the Enhancements Training area, where they took a seat on a couple of benches. "I understand you have some misgivings about having a Changed One as a Mentor," said Terry. "I do not blame you. I, myself, have some misgivings about being a Mentor to a Dragon-killer." "I suppose I can understand that," said Donovan, "but, *technically*, I didn't kill the dragon. I just broke its wing. An archer from the Royal Expeditionary Force fired the kill-shot." "I see," said Terry, "anyway, the first thing you should know is that I had a long talk about you with Sorcerer Andrew before he left for his assignment with the Royal Navy. So, I know about your father, what happened to your mother, and what brought you to the Wizards Academy. I wanted to give you an opportunity to learn about *my* life before I came here," said Terry.

"So, what's it like, being a dragon?" asked Donovan. "I am *not* a Dragon; I am a Changed One," said Terry. "I *was* a Fire Dragon, but I can never transform again. In answer to your question, being a Dragon was *frightening.* I was born in the Grey Mountains, near the Red River in central Baize. I had four brothers and one sister. When prey became scarce, my parents ate my brothers and my sister," said Terry sadly. "That's terrible!" said Donovan. "But not uncommon," confirmed Terry. "Dragons often eat their young in order to survive. You see, Dragons only eat meat; no fruits, no vegetables. Anyway, I fled before my parents came for me. Being the oldest, I was the first to learn to fly, and it enabled me to escape." "Where did you go?" asked Donovan. "I hid on the east side of the mountains, near the Great Salt Flats. I ate small game: rabbits and squirrels, an occasional fox, but it was barely enough. I was constantly hungry and afraid."

"How did you get here?" asked Donovan softly. "One day, while I was lying in the forest, waiting for prey to wander by, I heard an older Fire Dragon teach the Change spell to her son. Once they had moved on, I tried it myself," said Terry. "It obviously worked," said Donovan. "Yes," said Terry, "but I was left standing in the woods, naked, cold, and still rather hungry."

"What did you do?" asked Donovan, now very intrigued by Terry's story. "I wandered south, for a day, until I came upon a cabin near the edge of the mountains. It was deserted, but the owner had left behind some warm clothes and a little food. The next day, I continued south to the town of Forkville. There, I found a job with a salt merchant," said Terry.

"What is a 'salt merchant?'" Donovan asked. "A trader who deals in salt, of course," replied Terry. "The Great Salt Flats make up most of the land between the Grey Mountains and the Amber River. Merchants skim off the top layer of soil, then separate the sand from the salt. It is hot, back-breaking work, but at least I was fed and provided shelter. Once we had gathered enough salt, we took it by wagon to the city of Springfield to sell it." "I bet it wasn't worth much," said Donovan. "What makes you say that?" asked Terry.

"Well, if the salt was just lying on the ground, where anyone could collect it for free, I doubt anyone would pay very much for it," said Donovan. "You are partly correct," confirmed Terry, "and that is how I was discovered. You see, my employer was a smuggler. He did not sell all of his salt in Springfield. He took it farther south, to the area just north of Weaton. Under cover of night, a boatman crossed the river, loaded the salt, and smuggled it into Weaton, where the price of salt was considerably higher. My employer asked me to accompany the shipment, arrange the sale with the buyer, and then return with the payment." "What went wrong?" asked Donovan.

"The buyer was the Weaton Regional Mage," said Terry. "He immediately detected that I had the spark, confiscated the salt, and had his assistant bring me here. That was ten years ago." "And you never thought of going back?" asked Donovan. "Oh, I may have *thought* about it once or twice, but being a human is much safer and more pleasant," said Terry. "Does that answer all your questions?" "Almost," said Donovan, "how many students have drowned over the years after being blown into the river?" Terry laughed, "None, actually, although I heard that Raymond gave it a good try." "Raymond, the Level Three Changed One?" asked Donovan. "Yes, "said Terry, "He was a Stone Dragon. Stone Dragons cannot swim, not even in human form. He sank to the bottom of the river." "How did he survive?" asked Donovan. "He just walked across the riverbed to shore. His Mentor must have been a Changed One also, or he would have been discovered. That was before I passed my Sorcerer's Test," said Terry. "How could they have gotten away with it?" wondered Donovan. "I expect Wizard Loren and Wizard Stuart helped cover it up," said Terry.

"One last question," said Donovan, "how many kinds of dragons are there?" "An excellent question. There are five types of Dragons: Great Dragons, like the one you fought in the north, are gold in color; Fire Dragons are red; Stone Dragons are grey or black; Sea Dragons are blue or green; and Snow Dragons are white or light gray. Before you ask, Capri is a Sea Dragon Changed One, which is why she can swim so well, and Asia is a

Snow Dragon Changed One, which is why she cannot swim well—yet."

Chapter Seventeen:
WEATON IS BURNING

"Your Majesty, I must protest in the strongest terms this unprovoked attack on my country!" said the Baizian Ambassador. "I have no idea what you're talking about, Ambassador," said the King, confused. "I have not issued any orders for my troops to attack you. Did you receive any such orders, Marshall Guzman?" "No, Sire, my troops have not crossed the Amber River in decades," said Marshall Guzman.

"Your Majesty, a force of dragons was seen crossing from the east side of the river and attacking the town of Riverside. The town was utterly destroyed, and we have over 500 casualties!" said the Ambassador. "Do you deny sending these beasts to attack us?" "I categorically deny it," said the King. "How could I order dragons to do anything? Everyone knows that dragons are mythical." "I beg to differ, Your Majesty. Dragons are certainly *not* mythical; in fact, *we know* that your Royal Expeditionary Force slew a dragon north of Farmdale earlier this year," said the Ambassador, growing red-faced.

"How could you know about anything happening in Franconia? Have you been spying on us?" demanded the King, becoming angry in turn. "Your Majesty, such deeds are common knowledge. Traders and merchants have been discussing the dragon for months," said the Ambassador calmly, trying to cool the temperature of the room. "And because of these rumors, you think we command dragons to do our bidding? If anything, killing a dragon should make us enemies, not allies. What do you say to that Ambassador?" asked the King.

"The fact remains that at least three red, fire-breathing dragons attacked Riverside, and they were seen coming from your side of the Amber River. If you did not send them, then it is at least your responsibility to prevent such incursions in the future," concluded the Ambassador. "And I repeat, we had nothing to do with this attack on Baize!" said the King. "Unfortunately, such an attack did occur; consequently, we are closing our borders. There will be no trade between Baize and Franconia until further notice. No Baizian ships will visit your ports, and all Franconian ships will be required to immediately depart our ports. We will re-evaluate our actions when conditions warrant," said the Ambassador officially.

"Very well. In light of your bellicose actions, I hope you will understand if I move additional forces to my cities along the border. We will not attack, but we *will* respond to any aggressions by Baize *or its allies*," said the King. "You are dismissed."

The Ambassador departed in a huff. After the door closed behind him, the King looked at his Minister of Internal Security and said, "Well, Jasmine?" "He is worried, Sire, as is his King. Worried men often make bad decisions," said Jasmine. "Yes," said the King, "but he is not wrong; dragons *are* real. Why would dragons attack Riverside?" "Perhaps they saw an opportunity. After all, Riverside is the only Baizian city north of the Great Salt Flats. With no humans around for leagues, the dragons may simply be trying to carve out a territory of their own," said Jasmine. "What do you recommend?" asked the King.

"Sire, I am no military strategist," said Jasmine coyly, "but it would seem prudent to move additional troops to Colton, from the Seventh Battalion in Riverton. What do you think, Marshall Guzman?" The King looked at the Marshall. "That would be my recommendation, Your Majesty," said the Marshall, "I would also recommend putting the Royal Navy on alert. The Baizians may become aggressive at sea as well." "An excellent idea, Marshall! Please alert the Admiralty and have all ships assume a war footing, cancel all leaves, and recall all sailors to their ships," commanded the King. "At once, your highness." The Marshall hurried out to issue his orders.

"Your Majesty," said Jasmine, "with the closing of the borders, I need to travel to Weaton in order to meet with my agents and pass along your orders." "How will you accomplish that if the borders are closed?" asked the King. "There are always smugglers and *other operatives* that can slip across closed borders, Sire," said Jasmine with a wink. "Of course," said the King, "I will leave it up to you."

"Welcome, Wizard Daniel, Wizard Faith," said Noland, "I'm so glad that you were able to pass the Wizard's Test and assume your new duties at the Academy." "I appreciate the opportunity, Wizard Noland," said Daniel. Daniel was stocky, like a weight-lifter, with jet black hair and a scar on his left cheek. "Michael, please, we're all equals now. So, before I get into your duties, there are a few things I need to tell you that are not yet common knowledge and must be kept within the magical community for the time being." Noland then told them about the existence of dragons, how they could perform magic, and that they could change into human form. Both Wizards were shocked by the news, especially about Wizards Loren and Stuart. When he told them of Victor's death, Wizard Daniel said, "I never liked Victor. I don't know how he ever passed the Wizard's Test." "I suspect that Loren and Stuart helped him," said Noland. "He paralyzed me, and when I awoke, the hour was up. I never suspected anything." "Those two fooled us all," said Faith.

"Yes," replied Noland, "now for some good news, if you haven't heard already, *Wizard* Edward was *not* killed by the dragon. He survived and is currently roaming about Kingston under concealment, looking for more Changed Ones." "Hah!" said Wizard Faith, "I knew that Edward was too skilled a Battle Mage to die from being thrown into a tree!" "Thank you for the vote of confidence, Faith," said Edward, dropping his Concealment shield. The three Wizards jumped in surprise. "Sorry about that; I guess I've been hanging around Specialists too long," said Edward. "Faith, it's good to see you again.

Daniel, how's the leg?" The Wizards shook hands and reseated themselves.

"So Edward, any luck?" asked Noland. "Not yet," said Edward. "There are just too many smells in this city to localize a dragon, unless I get really close, and that's assuming that they're not wearing anything to disguise their scent. I thought I sensed one outside the Gatehouse a few days ago, but nothing since then." "I don't suppose you can continue the search for too much longer," said Noland, "I expect the King will have a new assignment for you soon." "I'm hoping to convince him to assign me to the Royal Expeditionary Force," said Edward. "Major Gerald and I work well together, and they're usually in the thick of things, but they have no organic magical support." "Probably Victor's idea," said Daniel. "Anyway, I plan to ask, maybe with just a *bit* of Compulsion," said Edward. "Is that how you get all the plumb assignments?" asked Faith, jokingly.

"Back to the matter at hand," said Wizard Noland, "Edward and I believe that we'll be in conflict with the dragons soon, so I need you two to help me get these students ready quickly." "What do you need?" asked Daniel. "First, I'm extending each class period by one hour. We'll start breakfast at five instead of six and delay dinner until seven. I've already released everyone who has passed the Sorcerer's Test to the military or the Regional Mage's Offices, promoted the most capable Level Threes to *Provisional* Sorcerers, and assigned them as Mentors. Daniel, instead of Franconian History, I want you to concentrate on *Military* History. Teach them tactics, then cover significant

216

battles, both Army and Navy. We're going to need Sorcerers who can fight, not chase criminals or detect unauthorized magicians, at least for a while." "I understand," said Daniel.

"Faith, riding, and staff work are going to be important in the coming months. Push them *hard*," said Noland. "How hard?" asked Faith. "Don't kill anyone, but broken bones can be healed. Combat medicine is your purview, Daniel, as is performing magic on water. We'll need to assign some of the students to the Royal Navy soon." "We're going to have some unhappy students," said Faith. "Better they be unhappy and prepared, than happy and unprepared," said Edward. "Including Donovan?" asked Faith. "Especially Donovan," said Edward. "I'll inform the students about the new schedule at dinner tonight. We begin tomorrow morning," said Wizard Noland.

They walked right up out of the river, three Stone Dragons breathing fire. The border guards were caught completely unprepared and fled in terror. The customs house went up in flames first, then the guard shack. The towering flames lit up the night sky. People ran helter-skelter, screaming, "Monsters!" Most were killed outright, burned to charred hulks before they made it across the street. The dragons rampaged through the town, knocking over buildings with their tails and claws, setting fire to anything that would burn. Then suddenly, one of the dragons was knocked sideways, by a strong blast of magic as the Fifteenth Company entered the fray along with their Sorcerer.

"Use the crossbows," yelled the Sorcerer, "bring them down!" A blast of fire reached out for the Sorcerer, but he managed to conjure a shield just in time. Crossbows began firing, striking the dragons who roared in annoyance and anger, the crossbows having little other effect, seemingly unable to penetrate the hardened scales of the Stone dragons. Unfortunately, many of the bowmen were also too slow in reloading, and several were killed before they could get off a second volley. Then, the dragons took flight, and things really got out of control. The three dragons circled the town, setting buildings alight and flaming anyone foolish enough to expose themselves. Then suddenly, the dragons stopped breathing fire, as if they had run out of fire-breath.

"I got this one," shouted the Regional Mage, finally entering the fray and casting a Tether around one of the dragons as the other two flew slowly back across the river. The dragon thrashed and pulled but could not break the Tether. Without fire breath, the dragon had no choice but to fly at the Sorcerer holding him and attempt to kill him with teeth and talons. Just before he reached the Mage, he was knocked sideways again by the other Sorcerer. The dragon slammed into the ground, scattering burning timbers about. Once the dragon was on the ground, soldiers wielding spears and axes foolishly charged in, trying to penetrate the dragon's thick skin. One lucky axe-man managed to make a shallow cut on the right wing where it met the shoulder. The dragon roared in pain and, using his head, sent the axe-wielding soldier flying across the street. The dragon's tail-whip scattered the other soldiers, but that left an opening for the four remaining crossbowmen to fire another volley without hitting their comrades. At closer range, the crossbow bolts stuck into the dragon, but without causing fatal injuries.

The dragon ran for the river, but the Mage kept the Tether on him. The Sorcerer from the Fifteenth Company raced in close and, using the last of his strength, used a Blast spell to blow a hole through the dragon's forehead. Both dragon and Sorcerer collapsed to the ground.

A strange stillness settled over the burning town. Gone were the shouted voices of the soldiers and magicians and the roar of dragons. All that remained was the crackling of the flames and cries of the wounded. The Regional Mage rushed to tend to the fallen Sorcerer from the Fifteenth Company, but he was dead. He had given his life to slay the dragon.

Donovan ducked and spun to his left, narrowly avoiding the blow from Wizard Faith's staff. She was *quicker* than Stuart had been, and Stuart had been the best at the Academy. Unlike Stuart, Faith used *everything* when she sparred: Seemings, wind, sand, even water. Donovan ignored the Seeming of a stone flying at him, determined not to be distracted by another

Seeming, when the very real stone slammed into his shoulder, knocking him to the ground; then Faith's staff was on his throat. "No fair," gasped Donovan. "There is no 'fair' in combat, Donovan. You may be the best student with a staff, but you're not ready for a fight against a determined magician yet."

Donovan rose and rubbed his shoulder, "So how am I supposed to stop stones?" he asked, "I can't strike with a shield up! A weather shield can protect my eyes from sand, but it's not strong enough to stop a stone." Wizard Faith smiled wickedly, "This is really Wizard Dylan's area, but you need to learn how to cast a small shield. Think of one as big as a pumpkin, then hold it in the air in front of you and use it to *deflect*, not block, objects thrown at you."

"But I can't cast two spells at once," protested Donovan, "if I cast a small shield, I'd have to drop my weather shield." "Not my problem," said Faith with a smirk. "Besides, who says you can't cast two spells at once?" "I'm not a Mage yet," said Donovan, "heck, I'm not even a Level Three yet." "Donovan, a Mage has to be able to cast two spells at once and hold them both for three hours. Nobody said you couldn't try casting two and holding them for a few minutes while we spar," said Faith reasonably. "For that matter, who told you that you can't try to cast two spells at once?" "I guess I just assumed…" "Don't assume! For that matter, if you can cast three spells at once, who's going to stop you? Just don't use too much of your energy casting spells, or you'll pass out or worse. Are you ready to try again?"

A sneaky idea occurred to Donovan, and he said, "Let's do it." As Faith raised her staff, Donovan said, *"NERVO,"* and made a grabbing motion with his right hand as he swung his staff toward Faith with his left hand, stopping just short of her. He said *"CODA"* a moment before Faith broke his Tether. "Excellent!" said Faith. "I was hoping you'd think of that! You need a stronger Tether, though." "Isn't that cheating?" asked Donovan. "Again, THERE IS NO SUCH THING AS 'CHEATING' IN A FIGHT! At least, not unless you agreed to 'No Tethers' before you began," said Faith. "Now, let's try again. No Tethers this time."

"Has anyone ever beat you with a staff?" asked Donovan. "Only one magician," said Faith. "Wizard Noland?" asked Donovan. "No, your father," replied Faith.

"Captain Matthews, I'm Sorcerer Andrew," said Andrew, introducing himself. "Captain Horatio Matthews," said the Captain of the HMS VALOR, "You may call me 'Captain' or 'Sir.'" "Yes, Sir," replied Andrew. "So, you're my new magician," said Captain Matthews, looking him over, "ever been on a ship before?" "Not a Navy ship, Sir," said Andrew, "but I grew up here in Southport, so I've been aboard many commercial ships and smaller trading vessels." "Can you swim?" asked the Captain. "Of course, Sir. All Sorcerers are taught to swim at the Wizards Academy if they don't know how when they arrive," explained Andrew.

"Is that so?" asked Captain Matthews, "and just how do the wizards test you?" "They blow you into the middle of the Crimson River and see if you can make it to shore," said Andrew. "HAH!" said the Captain, "I approve! Well, now that you're assigned to the VALOR, let me show you to your cabin and lay out your duties for you." The Captain led Andrew down a steep staircase to the first landing. "The ship's magician is considered an officer, so you'll have a small cabin to yourself, and you'll eat in the Officer's Mess. You'll also stand a deck watch. I'll explain what that means later," said Captain Matthews.

"Yes, Sir," said Andrew, "Captain, before we go any further, is there someplace private where we can talk?" The Captain gave Andrew a long look, then said, "In my cabin, this way." The Captain led Andrew along the landing to the rear-most cabin, which spanned the breadth of the ship. The Captain took a seat behind a large desk, which Andrew noticed had clips and compartments to keep anything from being displaced by the movement of the ship. "OK, Sorcerer Andrew, talk," said the Captain, "and this had better be important." "It is, Sir." Andrew then explained that dragons were real, that they could understand human speech and perform magic, and that they could transform into human form.

"You're sure about this?" asked Captain Matthews.

222

"Positive, Sir. We uncovered two dragons masquerading as Wizards at the Academy," said Andrew. "What did you do to them?" asked the Captain. "One is dead; the other had her hands removed so that she can't perform magic. She's being questioned under Truth Serum to learn all that she knows," said Andrew. "Are there different types of dragons?" asked Captain Matthews. "Yes, Captain, as far as we've been able to determine, there are five types of dragons: Great Dragons, which are gold in color; Fire Dragons, which are red; Stone Dragons, which are black or gray; Snow Dragons, that are white or light grey, and Sea Dragons that are blue or green," said Andrew.

"I knew it!" exclaimed the Captain. "I knew that we saw a sea serpent off the Coral Islands last year! But when we reported it up the chain, I was told to lay off the rum while I was on duty!" said the Captain excitedly. "Why wouldn't they listen to me?" asked the agitated Captain. "It was probably Victor, the Court Wizard," said Andrew. "He suppressed all reports of dragons to keep their existence secret." "Why on earth would the Court Wizard do that?" asked the Captain. "Because he was a dragon," said Andrew quietly.

"Do you know how to identify these—imposters?" asked Captain Matthews. "Yes, Sir," said Andrew, "for one thing, dragons don't use contractions when they speak. They apparently can't say 'can't,' 'won't,' 'don't,' 'we'll,' you get the idea." "Dragons can't say 'can't'?" "Correct, Captain, that's how I know that you're not a dragon in disguise." "Huh," said the Captain, "anything else?" "Yes, Sir, dragons, even in human form, *smell* different than normal humans," said Andrew.

"They smell different?" asked the Captain, "how so?" "Well," said Andrew, "dragons smell kind of reptilian, if you know what I mean." "And you can smoke them out?" asked Captain Matthews. "I believe so, Sir," said Andrew. "So, before we cast off, can I smell your crew?"

Kathy stood on the pier in Fairview. Fortunately, there were no Sorcerers prowling around, looking for contraband or rogue magicians. The voyage from Kingston to Fairview had been uneventful, but Kathy had not learned anything more about the dragon attack near Farmdale. Not knowing where to go, Kathy headed for the town square. Once there, she immediately spotted the Crossroads Inn, and while it looked a little on the rough side, she decided that there was no better place to begin her inquiry.

She secured a room on the ground floor at a rate of a silver a night. She paid for a week in advance, hoping to be done and on her way to Farmdale before the week was up. She sat in her room and considered how she should proceed. She definitely needed to find the arms dealer who made crossbows, and she should interview as many of the townsfolk as it took to get a clear picture of what they knew about dragons. She decided that she could probably learn a great deal by simply sitting in the Inn's tavern and listening to the gossip that was always spewing from the customers.

One problem was that she needed a disguise. There had been far too many instances of her being accosted in taverns by drunks, soldiers, or other would-be suitors, some of whom did not like to take 'No' for an answer. While she was perfectly capable of dealing with these situations, it would not do to draw unwanted attention to herself or run into another Franconian magician looking for those with the spark.

She knew that she could cast a Seeming to make herself look old and hideous, but that might be detected by a wandering Regional Mage. She finally decided that she could probably take up a position in the adjoining stable, cast a Concealment spell and use a Hearing enhancement to listen in on conversations in the tavern. She cast her Concealment before she left her room, then maneuvered carefully around the nearly empty tavern, leaving by the open front door. She entered the stable and found a relatively comfortable place to sit up in the hayloft. At least there, she would not have to worry about anyone stumbling into her.

Kathy peered through an open knothole in the boards and got a partially obstructed view of the tavern. There were only a few customers, most having what passed for breakfast. Casting her Hearing enhancement, Kathy settled down for a long day of eavesdropping.

As night fell, Kathy considered her day well-spent. She had learned that, until recently, Fairview had been overrun with refugees from Farmdale and the surrounding countryside, who were fleeing the dragon. While many of the rumors had come second— and even third-hand, little better than hearsay, a few of the conversations Kathy had overheard had been first-hand accounts of a fearsome gold dragon that had carried off livestock, burned farms, and killed friends and neighbors. Kathy was convinced that there was indeed a dragon that had been living somewhere around the town of Farmdale.

Having decided that; there really was no need to actually travel to Farmdale. Kathy doubted that she would learn anything more than she already knew. That meant that she just needed to visit the arms dealer, and then she could be on her way home. As she was leaving the stable, she found a crumpled up and discarded newssheet in the waste paper bin. She retreated to her room and smoothed out the wrinkled paper.

The paper was several months old, but the lead story was about how persons unknown had broken into the Fairview garrison's dungeon and stolen three of the Royal Expeditionary Force's pay chests. There was a rumor that one of the chests contained a dragon's head, bound for Kingston and the King and that it would have taken a magician to pull off such a heist. *Why would a magician want to conceal the existence of dragons?* Kathy wondered. She decided that that question was outside the scope of her inquiry. Nevertheless, she pulled out her journal and made another note.

4. Arrived in Fairview. Townsfolk all confirm numerous refugees in town fleeing the area around Farmdale because of frequent dragon attacks. Heard several eye-witness accounts of the dragon and the destruction it caused. Additionally, I discovered a newssheet documenting a theft of three pay chests from the Fairview Garrison dungeon. One of the chests purported to contain a 'dragon's head' that was being taken to King Henry as proof of the dragon. Theft speculated to be the work of a magician. No need to travel to Farmdale. Total cost: Five Silvers (one week's stay – Crossroads Inn, Fairview)

Early the next morning, Kathy was in the tavern, asking the proprietor for directions to the local arms merchant. Unsurprisingly, there were three weapons manufacturers in the city: Acme Arms, Prestige Arms, and Royal Armaments. Kathy resigned herself to visiting all three if she had to. The first place she visited, Acme Arms, only produced swords, axes, and spears. They were aware of the new crossbows but supposedly had no idea where they were coming from.

As Kathy entered Prestige Arms, her hopes rose. This merchant made everything from cavalry breastplates to trebuchets (ammunition not included). As she browsed around the shop, a young woman approached her. "May I be of assistance, Ma'am?" asked Maria. "Perhaps," said Kathy, "do you know where I can find the owner?" "My father is in the back," said Maria. "Let me fetch him." Maria dashed out the back door, and James, the proprietor, followed her back into the shop a short time later.

"You asked to see me, Miss?" "Yes," said Kathy with a smile, "you're the owner?" "I am, and my name is James. What can I help you with?" "Well, I am going to be doing a lot of traveling soon, so I was wondering what you had in the way of *personal protection* for a lady traveling alone." James thought for a moment, then directed Kathy to a display case near the back of the shop. "I have a fine assortment of small daggers here that can be easily concealed," said James. Kathy frowned.

"Where would I hide something like that, I wonder?" she asked. James blushed and said, "Most of my female customers prefer the forearm sheath, but there is always the calf or thigh holster that is, perhaps, easier to reach in a pinch. Depending on your attire." Kathy laughed, flirtatiously, shaking her head. "No. I'm not an assassin, and it has been my experience that wearing a skirt that short usually attracts unwanted attention. Don't some gentlemen's canes have blades inside them?" "They do, but that's not an accessory normally carried by a lady," replied James. "Is there something like that for women, a parasol, perhaps?"

"I'm afraid I don't have anything like that. If a shorter blade would do, I do have something that might interest you. James opened a locked drawer beneath the display case and extracted an elaborately decorated folding fan." "A fan? Is the edge reinforced and sharpened?" "I have seen fans like that," said James, "but this is something different. This device will serve as a fan," said James, flicking it open, "but when closed, if you press this inlaid pearl button…" James pressed what appeared to be a decorative inlay, and a six-inch blade the width of her finger sprang from the top of the fan case.

"Yikes!" squealed Kathy. "That's incredible!" "Yes, it is," replied James, "but only good for close-in work." "Can I try it?" "Of course. Here is how you re-arm it." James pulled out a block of wood from under the counter, placed it on the display case, then put the tip of the blade on the block and pushed it back inside the handle. It locked in place with a 'click.' James gently handed the fan to Kathy. Kathy pointed the top of the fan towards the wall and pushed the button. The knife blade sprang out. "Fantastic!" she exclaimed. "How much penetrating power?"

James looked suspiciously at Kathy. "If my assailant is wearing a leather jacket, will this blade punch through or be stopped?" she asked. "Come with me," said James, leading Kathy out back to the work area. As they entered the open foundry yard, Kathy couldn't help but notice James' assistants diligently making crossbows. "Over here," said James. Kathy walked over to where James was holding a finger-width wooden slat. "Put the edge on the wood and push the button," commanded James. The blade neatly pierced the wooden slat. "It won't go through plate armor, my lady, but cloth and even chain mail shouldn't be a problem."

"How much?" asked Kathy. James bit his lower lip and then said, "One gold. I'm sorry it's so expensive, but it takes a lot of work and craftsmanship to make a spring that strong but small enough to fit in a fan." "I'll take it," said Kathy. James smiled in relief. "Now that I have the *personal protection* taken care of, what do you have for corporate protection?"

"Corporate protection? I don't understand," said James, confused. "My family will soon be shipping very expensive goods across Franconia in carriages and coaches. Those shipments will need security without attracting unwanted attention caused by outriders or additional guards. A sword or spear is not the best weapon for a coach driver. Even a bow is somewhat unwieldy." James frowned, considering. "What about a mace or a truncheon?" he asked.

"Too short-range," replied Kathy. "Let's cut to the chase," she said. "I've heard from some of the soldiers in the Royal Expeditionary Force that you made the weapons that they used to slay the dragon near Farmdale. How much for a crossbow?" James nodded, seeing the game at last, "They're not for sale." "Why not?" "I'm under contract to the crown not to sell crossbows to anyone but the Royal Guard for the next two and a half years."

"Our arrangement could be kept secret," whispered Kathy. "No, my lady. Even though he's dead, I'll not break my word to Sir Edward. I promised to only sell to the Guard for three years, and I stand by my agreements." "An honest man," said Kathy.

"Very well. I understand. When they do become available, what do you think they'll cost?" "The first model sold for a gold. At least, I sold the first one to Mage Edward for a gold, and he reimbursed me a gold each for the sixteen he replicated for the Expeditionary Force."

"He paid golds for crossbows that he replicated? If he was a Mage, then he could have made them for free! That's extraordinarily generous of this Mage—Edward, did you say?" "Yes. Edward was a good man. He died during the fight with the dragon," said James, sadly.

"If I leave you a five-silver deposit, will that reserve one of the first commercial crossbows for me?" "Five silvers is too much. Leave me one silver and your name, and you will have the first."

Kathy left Prestige Arms a gold and a silver lighter, but much happier. Crossbows *did* exist, and they could kill a dragon! She now had all the information that she needed. It was time to get back to King Donald. Tomorrow, she'd visit the port and see about booking a passage back to Westport. As Kathy entered the Inn, she heard shocking news from the Town Crier: "EXTRA! EXTRA! READ ALL ABOUT IT! BAIZIAN DRAGONS ATTACK WEATON! DOZENS KILLED! WAR WITH BAIZE IMMINENT! EXTRA! EXTRA!"

Kathy bought the extra edition newssheet and took it to her room to read. The details were sparse, really not much more than rumor and wild speculation, but the underlying story was that the Franconian town of Weaton had been attacked by three Black dragons that apparently walked across the Amber riverbed and attacked. One had been killed by a Sorcerer, but the other two had casually flown back across the river, leaving the town in flames.

Although it was late in the afternoon, Kathy grabbed her pack and satchel and hurried over to the port. She needed to secure passage immediately, before Franconia (or Baize) closed their border to traffic. Based on what she'd heard about young King Henry, she judged that she had little time. Luck was with her, and she found a small merchant ship that was sailing that evening for Southport. It was not as large and fast as the HMS UNSINKABLE, but it would do the job.

After the ship cast off, Kathy conjured a strong north wind, which propelled the small ship quickly south. She had to be careful not to overdo it and cause the sails to rip. As she stood on deck, the merchant Captain walked up to her and said, "If this gale holds, we'll be in Kingston in three days and Southport in seven. I've seldom seen such a strong tail wind. Especially this time of year." Kathy nodded, pulling her cloak close against the wind. "I need to get to Westport as soon as possible, Captain. Do you have any suggestions of how I may accomplish that?"

The young Captain smiled, "My cousin, Nathan, operates a small fleet of ships that transport cargo to and from Westport. I'm sure he could get you there for a reasonable price." "Thank you, Captain. That would be wonderful," said Kathy. "My husband will be most appreciative of my quick return." The Captain's hopes for a *closer* association with Kathy died with the 'husband' comment (as Kathy intended), and the Captain quickly excused himself to see to 'ship duties.'

Gek and Azure landed on the coast, southeast of Southport, just before dawn and changed into their human forms. "We need to find some Sea Dragons and convince them to start attacking human ships," said Azure, "except for the one Andrew is on. What was its name again?" "The VALOR," said Gek, "How will we know which ship that is?" "Humans usually put their ship's names on the back of the ship," said Azure. "Do you think all the ships will have magic-users on them?" asked Gek. "No," said Azure, "from what I remember, some ships just carry goods that the humans trade with one another, while others are warships built for fighting. I suspect that only the warships have magic-users on them, and maybe not all of them."

"It would certainly be much easier and safer for us to attack ships without magic-users," mused Gek. "Just remember, we need to attack ships from *both* countries, Franconia and Baize," said Azure. "How do we tell them apart?" asked Gek. Azure thought for a minute, then said, "Well, we have noticed that most human ships have a colored cloth tied to the top of the pole at the back of the ship. Maybe different countries use different colors, so they can identify their ships at a distance." "That makes sense," said Gek. "So, how do we tell the warships from the others?" "No idea," said Azure. "We should probably walk around the place where the ships are anchored and see if we can tell which is which."

"That sounds like a good plan," said Gek, yawning. "But it will have to wait until tomorrow; I am exhausted." "Me too," said Azure, "where should we sleep today?" "I think I saw an abandoned hut, just a little way up from the shore," said Gek. They walked about two hundred yards when they came upon a dilapidated shack, made of what looked like driftwood and mud. However, it was *not* abandoned. "Hold it right there, you two," said a gravelly voice, "What do you want around here?" Gek looked around and spied an old man, seated on a rotten tree stump beside the hut.

"We were looking for someplace to rest," said Gek. "We did not realize the house was occupied." The old man laughed. "Thought it was deserted, eh? Well, I get that a lot. What's your business down here?" Gek, thinking quickly, said, "You see, sir, my girlfriend and I went for a moonlight walk along the beach last night. I guess we went a bit too far. We are headed back to Southport, but we have been walking all night, and we were looking for a place to rest for a couple of hours."

The old man gave Gek a knowing wink and said, "I doubt you were walking *all* night, but I understand. I was young once, too, believe it or not. Well, come on in. It's not much to look at, but it keeps the rain off my head, mostly anyway. There's a room in the back you can bunk in for a while. I got to go collect my driftwood. Be gone a coupla' hours at least. If you're still here when I get back, we can have some tea and talk for a bit. Gets a mite lonely out here, ya know. My name's Bruce, by the way." "I am Jed, and this is Azure," replied Gek, "we appreciate your hospitality." "You two go rest up. I'll be back before the sand gets too hot to walk on," said Bruce as he headed towards the beach.

The back room had a dirt floor, and the walls were made of disjointed pieces of driftwood and other flotsam that Bruce had collected over the years. Beams of light showed through the gaps in the walls, but there was enough room for both of them to sleep relatively comfortably. Before he drifted off to sleep, Gek said, "Maybe we should stay a while and talk to the old man; he may be able to tell us what we need to know so that we do not need to go into the city after all." "Good idea," murmured Azure, as she drifted off to sleep.

"All right, you two. It's time to get up. You don't want to sleep the whole day away," said Bruce. Gek and Azure rubbed the sleep out of their eyes and sat up. "What time is it?" asked Gek. "It's just past noon," said Bruce. "I guess you two did walk all night, after all. You slept half the day away."

Gek and Azure rose and walked into what passed for the main room of the hut. There was a crude table made from a shipping crate and three rickety stools that had seen better days.

Bruce placed three steaming cups of tea on the table and said, "Help yourself." Gek and Azure nodded their thanks and sipped the tea cautiously. Bruce eyed the two and said, "So, what brings a Sea Dragon to Southport?"

Chapter Eighteen:
NAGGING QUESTIONS

"Sorcerers normally fight from *behind* the front lines," said Wizard Daniel. "Can anyone tell me why?" "Because our shields would get in the way of our own troops?" asked Stephen. "Partially correct," said Daniel, "if your shield is too big, it could block or deflect our archer's arrows, but mainly, we need to be able to see the battlefield to know where we can do the most good. If the enemy is about to break through on the left flank, but you are on the right flank, you'll be out of position. Normally, the magician's place is close to the force commander, so he can direct them to where they're needed. That's not cowardice; that's good military tactics."

"Don't some commanders prefer to lead from the front?" asked Kyle. "Some do," said Daniel. "Those are usually the ones that die first. Enemy archers are trained to look for and target *leaders*. If you can take out the commander, you can disorganize the opposing force and improve your side's chances of victory. If you're near your commander, there's a chance that you can provide a shield for both of you, but a magician's job is not simply to provide protection for the commander. If that's all you do, you could be the last two left standing, while the rest of your force is routed."

"Most times, a Sorcerer is given a special mission by the commander. It could be to remove the enemy commander, destroy a key bridge or a piece of siege equipment, or even eliminate an enemy magician. This is one reason we put so much emphasis on perfecting your Concealment shields and your ability to detect concealment, because the enemy commander may send his magician after *you*!" The students were quiet. The Hide-and-Seek game didn't seem so much like a game anymore.

"Ambassador, why did the Kingdom of Baize attack Weaton without provocation?" demanded the King. "Your Majesty, I assure you that King Donald gave no such order!" said the Baizian Ambassador pleadingly. "As you recall, we ourselves were attacked by dragons! At the time, you assured me that you did not control the dragons and could not command them to attack. Why do you now suppose that *we* could control them?"

"I know that you had troops on your side of the Amber River," said King Henry, "Why did they not come to our assistance during the attack?" "Sire, please be reasonable. If our soldiers had crossed the river, you might have viewed that as an invasion or thought that we were in league with the dragons, which I assure you, we are not!"

"Ambassador, your words are unconvincing. I think you need to return to Baize for your own safety. I am also recalling my ambassador from Baize for 'consultations.'" "As you command, Your Majesty, but I urge you to consider the possibility that the dragons are somehow cooperating with each other to provoke our two kingdoms into war," said the Ambassador as he hastily departed.

The King sat back on his throne, considering the Ambassador's words. "Jasmine, what do you think?" he asked. Jasmine thought for a moment, then said, "The Ambassador raises an interesting idea, Sire, but it seems inconceivable that a pack of ignorant animals could concoct such an intricate plan." "I agree," said the King, "but why would three Stone dragons attack Weaton?" "Stone Dragons, sire? I thought all Dragons were the same," said Jasmine, appearing shocked by this information.

"No. I had a report from Wizard Noland. It seems that there are five types of dragons: Fire, Stone, Snow, Sea, and what he called Great dragons. The three dragons that attacked Weaton were reportedly dark gray in color, indicating that they were Stone dragons. I received several scales from the one that they slew. The scales are distinctively different from the golden ones Major Gerald provided from the Great dragon they fought." "How interesting," said Jasmine, "but I would say that that makes the Ambassador's theory even more unlikely." "Why is that?" asked the King. "Well, it supposes that two different Clans of Dragons are cooperating. I find that highly unlikely." The King stared at his Minister of Internal Security for a long while, as if sensing that something was amiss, but ultimately dismissed his concerns as just normal anxiety over the current situation.

Azure was stunned by Bruce's question, "I—I do not know what you are talking about," she finally stammered. "Sure you do," said Bruce with a toothy smile, "you're a Sea dragon, no use denying it. I lived with one for over thirty years, so I know a Changed One when I see 'em." Looking at Gek, he said, "I'm not *exactly* sure what you are, but you're *not* a Sea dragon, at least not entirely. I figure you're a half-breed. What is it, Snow and Sea?" "Actually, Great and Sea, if you must know," replied Gek.

"Great and Sea! Of course! Don't see many Great dragons anymore," said Bruce. "Anyway, my question stands: what are you doing in Southport?" "We are looking for other Changed Ones," said Azure quickly, "and to learn what we can about the human ships that sail these waters." Bruce thought about her answer for a minute, then said, "No Changed Ones in the city proper—too much chance of being discovered by Regional Mage Faith, though I heard she'd been reassigned to Kingston. No, most of the Changed Ones moved east, years ago, out towards Grotton. Better fishin' in those waters." "I see," said Azure, pretending disappointment.

"I hate to say it," confided Bruce, "but most of the other Changed Ones I knew are most likely dead by now, unless, of course, they changed back into dragons. I'm sure dragons live a lot longer than people. Why the interest in our ships?" Gek jumped into the conversation, "The Coral Islands are becoming too crowded, so the Sea Dragon Clan is planning to move some of the families west, to the shores of the mainland. We came to scout out some potential areas for them, but we kept running across human ships. We need to know which ones might have magic-users on them, so we can avoid them."

"Hmmm," said Bruce, "I didn't know the Sea dragons were so *reproductive*, but then, all I know about Sea dragons I learned from my Celeste, and she passed away years ago." "You knew a Sea Dragon?" asked Azure. "I was married to one," said Bruce. "We met in Southport, where I was working as a tailor. Poor thing came in sopping wet, wearing rags she found in the trash. I took her in, made her some decent clothes, and even hired her as my apprentice. She was *exotic,* with those blue highlights in her hair. Eventually, we fell in love and got married. Anyway, one day, the Regional Mage came by my shop, sayin' that he sensed someone with the spark of magic nearby. I laughed and told him that if I knew how to do magic, I sure wouldn't be sewing for a livin.' He seemed to accept that and said it was probably a customer, and he'd be checkin' back periodically. Fortunately, Celeste was out buyin' cloth when the Mage came by. When I told her what happened, she said we had to leave; *immediately.*"

Bruce paused, savoring the memory, then he continued, "I figured she knew that she had the spark, and the Mage was gonna send her off to that Wizard's school up in Kingston. So, we up and sold the business, took what we could get, and headed out of town. We stayed in an inn for a couple of days but heard the Mage was lookin' for us. I guess it was kinda suspicious, leaving so soon after his visit. Anyway, we moved out here and built what we could outta driftwood and scrap lumber. Eventually, she told me that she was a Sea dragon, who changed herself into a human with magic." "And that did not scare you?" asked Gek. "By then, I was so in love with the girl it wouldn't have mattered if she was a pine tree," said Bruce. Azure laughed.

"So, how did you survive way out here?" asked Gek. "Well, she would transform into a dragon and bring back fish for us to eat. There was never much, but enough for us. Sometimes, she would sleep in that back room in dragon form. I never really asked how old she was. I mean, it's just not polite to ask a woman her age, you know. But as humans, we age as people do, and eventually, well, she just passed away in her sleep," said Bruce sadly.

"Anyway, you were asking about ships. I understand because I had just about the same conversation with Celeste when we moved out here. So, the only ships with Sorcerers or Mages on 'em belong to the Royal Navy. The Navy only has two kinds of ships: Frigates and Battleships. Frigates have three masts that look like trees with no branches. The masts hold the sails, big sheets of cloth that ships use to catch the wind to move the ship.

Frigates ride low in the water, and they're faster than Battleships. Battleships also have three masts, only they're taller. Battleships are bigger than frigates, and they have taller sides, because they're used to carry soldiers. The men who drive the ships are called 'sailors.' As I understand it, all Navy ships have at least one magician on board," explained Bruce.

"How do we tell these Navy ships from merchants or traders?" asked Azure. "Easy, said Bruce, "all Navy ships fly the flag of the Royal Navy."

What a moron! thought Wizard Louis. *Not only could the Stone Dragon Changed One, Gary, not remember where the Stone Dragon colony was, but he was not even sure he wanted to be a Dragon anymore!* All Louis had been able to get him to promise was that *if* he was threatened with exposure and death, then he would transform back into a Dragon and attack the humans. Louis just could not fathom how Gary could prefer his life as a human servant, a night baker at that, to being a powerful Stone Dragon.

With no help from Gary, Wizard Louis had to go in search of the Stone Dragon colony himself. He told King Donald that he needed to travel to Middleberg in order to look into some troubling rumors he supposedly heard about dragons congregating in the Western Desert. The King insisted that he depart at once and investigate these rumors. Louis 'borrowed' the fastest horse in the King's stable and raced towards Middleberg. As soon as he was out of the city and on the open road, Louis transformed into Fire Dragon form, killed and ate the horse, and proceeded west towards the Great Western Desert.

Each night for a week, Louis flew low over the desert, looking for the oasis that marked the entrance to the underground cavern system that was home to the Stone Dragon Clan. He was beginning to despair (and he was also very hungry) when, on the sixth night of his search, he found a small corpse of palm trees, surrounding a shallow watering hole. He landed immediately and began scouring the area, looking for the entrance to the caves. He was about to give up and move on when he fell into the entrance (literally), which was cleverly covered by an illusion of a mound of sand.

Louis fell ten feet and landed with a 'THUMP,' startling awake the Stone Dragon that was supposed to be guarding the entrance. The sleepy Stone Dragon guard asked, "Who goes there?" Louis brushed the sand off his back nonchalantly with his tail and replied, "I am Lumen, a Changed One of the Fire Dragon Clan, called *Louis* by the humans. I have come to speak with the Clan Chief of the Stone Dragons."

The bleary-eyed Stone Dragon asked Lumen to wait in the entrance while he went to see if Jasper, the Clan Chief, had time to speak with him. Louis paced back and forth across the cavern entrance, waiting for the plodding Stone Dragon to deliver his message and return. After several long minutes, the guard returned and said, "Follow me, please." The Stone Dragon led Louis down a long, winding passageway, past many side tunnels and a few open but empty chambers he could only assume to be family dwellings.

Eventually, they came to a large open cavern where there were perhaps a dozen Stone Dragons milling about idly. At the far end of the cavern, Jasper, the Stone Dragon Clan Chief, waved them over. "What brings you to the realm of the Stone Dragons, Lumen?" Jasper asked. "I need to speak to you about the war with the humans," said Louis. "Quartz, this does not concern you. Please return to your guard post and re-establish the illusion over the entrance that this *visitor* has undoubtedly dissolved." Quartz, the dragon guarding the entrance, nodded sleepily and trudged back up toward the entrance.

"You will have to forgive Quartz," said Jasper. "He is young, and we do not get many visitors. I am sure you awakened him from a deep sleep. He was put on guard as a punishment for breaking Clan rules and is not happy with his post right now. Fortunately for us, he is one of the few Stone Dragons that can conjure the magical illusion that conceals the entrance to our colony." "He was most definitely asleep," said Louis crossly. "However, the illusion that masks your entrance is most effective. I never saw it until I fell through the opening."

Jasper smiled, "It is one of the few magical spells that we know; that, the spell of Change, and the Digging spell, of course. What can we do for you, Lumen?" "I have come to ask how your preparations are progressing with regard to the conflict with the humans," said Louis.

"We have done our part by attacking the human city, which cost us one of our best fighters. Now we are *waiting*," said Jasper angrily. "Waiting for what?" asked Louis. "Waiting for the humans to begin fighting each other! That was the plan, was it not? For the first time in a century, one of our Clan has been killed by a human magic-user! His family mourns for him. The rest of the Clan wonders what the other Clans are doing to punish the humans."

"My Clan destroyed the human city of Riverside, killing over five hundred humans and burning the city to the ground! At sea, the Sea Dragons are attacking the human ships from both Franconia and Baize. I do not know what the Snow Dragons are doing, but the humans should be at war with each other very soon."

"What of the Great Dragons? What are they doing to help?" asked Jasper. "I do not know," admitted Louis. "I do not believe that there are many of them left. Have you heard of any Great Dragons on this side of the river?" Jasper thought for a moment, then said, "There used to be a family of Great Dragons that lived on the shore of the big lake, but I have not seen or heard anything about them in years."

"That is good news!" said Louis. "I feared that the Great Dragon Clan was extinct except for the ancient one, Ard, and his grandson, Gek. Anyway, the reason I have come is that I need to know how many Stone Dragon Changed Ones there may be in the kingdom." Jasper looked troubled. "I do not know," he said finally. "Too many, I suspect. Those few that live here in the colony are all that remain of my Clan who have not made the Change. There are only twenty-five of us, and many are women and children."

"So few," Louis gasped. "What happened to the others?" "Most of them changed into human form," replied Jasper. "There is not enough prey in the desert to sustain very many Stone Dragons, and, unlike our Sea Dragon kin, we cannot feed on the fish in the river or in the lake, not being able to swim. Several of my Clan have tried, but fish are too fast for a Stone Dragon walking along the bottom of the lake, and it takes a great many turtles to sate a Dragon's hunger."

"Is there no prey beyond the desert?" asked Louis. "I hope there is," said Jasper. "Many of my Clan have flown off to the west in search of a place where prey is plentiful. None have ever returned. I do not know if they found what they were seeking or died of hunger in the desert." "What about in the north, near the Snow Fields?" "Again, there may be enough prey there to sustain a pack of Stone Dragons, but if there is, none of my kin have returned to inform us of such."

"Have you gone yourself?" Jasper shook his head, "No. My eyesight is failing, and I fear that if I stray too far from the colony, I will never find it again. The desert is vast, and one sand dune or oasis looks much like another." "But you attended the Dragon Council on the other side of the Amber River!" said Louis. "Yes, but I was accompanied by Amber, who is much younger than I. Without her help, I might never have found my way back."

Louis considered the situation. He had counted on the Stone Dragons to defeat the humans once the war began without knowing how few they were in number or how scattered the Clan was. "When we eventually decide that the time is right to attack, what can the Stone Dragon Clan do?" Jasper answered immediately, "There are several human cities on this side of the Amber River. Three of my Clan decimated the human city of Weaton. We will certainly be able to cause much destruction in the Kingdom of Baize." Louis considered this and decided that it was probably all he could hope for from the slow-moving and slow-witted Stone Dragons.

"So, you have no idea how many Changed Ones may be at large?" Jasper shook his head, "There used to be over seventy Stone Dragons in my Clan, but so many have left to go north or west or Changed into human form, I have lost count. However, I would offer the opinion that any who are in human form may not be willing to help us." "Really?" "Yes. The few I have spoken to over the years have told me that their lives are much better as humans. They are not constantly hungry or spending most of their nights searching for prey. Some also prefer living above ground to life in this cavern system."

Louis was troubled by this news. Finally, he asked, "What can you tell me about the attack your Clan made on the city of Weaton?" "The three most aggressive members of the colony attacked the town by walking across the riverbed. They had set most of the city on fire and destroyed several buildings before the human magic-users appeared. One of them cast some kind of containment spell on Marble, and he was unable to escape back across the river with the other two. Basalt and Lava reported that they all had run out of inferno before they attempted to depart."

"What about these *crossbows* that are said to be such a threat to us? Did the humans have them?" "Yes," said Jasper, "but they were not fatal to us. Have you ever been stung by a wasp while in your human form?" "Once," replied Louis. "It is much like that. It stings and does not feel very good, but it is certainly not as fearsome a weapon as was reported to us during the Dragon Council. At least not to Stone Dragons. Basalt and Lava returned with many of these steel arrows embedded in their scales. We just pulled them free without further injury. Still, I would hate to get hit in the eye with one."

"Interesting," said Louis, "then how was Marble killed?" "We do not know. I suspect it was the two magic-users working together. Lava and Basalt flew out of the town, assuming that Marble was right behind them. They did not discover his disappearance until they were halfway home." Louis thought this was an incredibly stupid way for a Dragon to die, abandoned by his kin, who did not even notice he was not with them until it was too, too late, but he kept this thought to himself.

"What did your Queen say about that?" "*HER,*" said Jasper, angrily. "She calls herself our Queen and no one has ever corrected her, but she was not selected for that role. Onyx was the mate of our Clan Chief many years ago when he died mysteriously at the very young age of one hundred and fifty. She suddenly proclaimed herself 'Queen' and started giving orders. When no one objected, it seemed like a done deal." "How did her mate die?" asked Louis. "We suspect he was poisoned but had no way to prove it," said Jasper angrily. "Over time, she became increasingly demanding and authoritarian. You know how we dragons hate that. Eventually, several of the older, larger members of the Clan confronted her, and she soon departed the colony. We had no idea that she had flown to the other side of the river and changed into human form."

"Why was this not mentioned during the last Dragon Council?" asked Louis. "What would have been gained? We had already agreed to Victor's plan. We did not need to air our dirty laundry to the rest of the Dragon Council," explained Jasper. "But, she claims to be your QUEEN!" exclaimed Louis. "She can *claim* to be the Empress of all Dragons, but that will not make it so," said Jasper, reasonably. "Just know that her words are not binding on me or the rest of the Stone Dragon Clan."

Louis accepted this new information stoically. While this did not change anything, it certainly made his trip into the desert worthwhile. Louis expressed his thanks for the information and told Jasper that he was going to depart and return to Baize to continue undermining the human efforts in the struggle. They walked back up to the entrance, where they again found Quartz sleeping peacefully.

Louis asked which way it was to the city of Middleberg, since he had lost his sense of direction after being underground, and the desert looked the same in every direction. "Head towards the rising sun, and you will find it," offered Quartz sleepily. "There are almost no humans in the desert between the colony and the city, so you need not be concerned about being seen. The city sits on the Green River. If you pass the river, you have gone too far. Once you get to the river, fly north or south to find the city."

Louis nodded his thanks, thinking that maybe Quartz was not useless after all. He took flight, heading east, leaving the Stone Dragon colony behind.

"Dad, how did you beat Wizard Faith with a staff?" asked Donovan. Edward laughed. "She told you about that, did she? Well, I used Seemings," said Edward. "But Seemings are harmless," protested Donovan. "I mean, they're good as a distraction, but I wouldn't think they'd be any good against someone like Wizard Faith." "She didn't think so either," said Edward, "but I didn't use them as a distraction, but as an attack." "I don't understand," said Donovan. "What happens when you touch a Seeming?" asked Edward. "It vanishes," said Donovan. "Not exactly," said Edward. "Here, let me show you." Edward conjured a Seeming of a rock. "Go ahead, Donovan, touch it and tell me what happens."

Donovan touched the Seeming, and it vanished in a flash of light. "So?" he said. Edward sighed, "I see a more personal demonstration is necessary. All right, let's try it again." This time, Edward 'threw' the Seeming of a rock at Donovan's face. Knowing that it was just a Seeming, Donovan took no action to avoid it. When the Seeming touched his nose, it vanished in a flash of light, temporarily blinding him. "I get it!" said Donovan excitedly, "the flash is distracting or momentarily blinding." "Very good," said Edward, "just don't get so focused on conjuring Seemings that you forget your staff work. Even someone dazzled by a Seeming can hit you if you let down your guard."

"How do you counter the effect?" asked Donovan. "You can use your staff to touch the Seeming before it gets too close, you can dodge or duck your head, or you can blink your eyes when the Seeming reaches you. But if I send multiple Seemings at you in rapid succession, you can't really keep your eyes closed for too long before my staff hits you." "That's genius! I can't wait to try it on Wizard Faith the next time we spar!" Donovan said excitedly. "She knows about this tactic, so don't be too disappointed if it doesn't work as well as you expect," grinned Edward.

"So, how are your other studies going?" asked Edward. "Frankly, I think I'm ready for the Level Three Test. Serums are much easier now that I can cool them with magic. Performing magic on water is harder than I imagined, but I'm improving." "That's good," said Edward, "because we may need to accelerate training again." "Why? What's happened?" asked Donovan. "Three Fire dragons attacked the Kingdom of Baize from *our side* of the Amber River; then, a couple of weeks later, three Stone Dragons attacked and nearly destroyed Weaton," said Edward.

"Did we stop them?" asked Donovan. "Two flew back across the river, but Sorcerer Justin from the Fifteenth Company killed one of them," said Edward. "I'd like to buy that Sorcerer an ale," said Donovan. "You can't. He put all his power into the Blast spell that killed the dragon. He didn't survive," said Edward sadly. Donovan swallowed the lump in his throat and said, "Was it worth it?" "I don't know, son, the dragons had stopped breathing fire; maybe the Stone dragons only have a limited amount of fire breath. It might have been better to just let him get away. I don't think we can win this war by trading Sorcerers for dragons. I think there are more of them than there are of us."

"How can you say that? We haven't seen a dragon in centuries!" said Donovan. "Son, think about it. There were fourteen Changed Ones here at the Academy, plus three that we know about near Farmdale, then six more in the two recent attacks. Including Victor, that makes twenty-four dragons. How many more hostile Changed Ones are there in Franconia? How many dragons are in Baize? There have also been multiple reports of 'sea serpents' off the east coast for years. I suspect they are, in fact, Sea dragons."

"Are you saying we can't win?" asked Donovan. "No. What I'm saying is that I don't think we can trade magicians for dragons one-for-one without destroying ourselves. Maybe that's why they agreed to a Peace Treaty all those years ago," said Edward. "You're not suggesting that we *negotiate* with them, are you?" asked Donovan. "It may come to that," said Edward. "That's one reason we're keeping Loren alive. We may need her as an intermediary." "A what?" asked Donovan, confused. "Call it an 'Ambassador to the Dragons.' She can talk to both sides, and the dragons might not see her as a traitor and kill her on sight," explained Edward. "Have you talked to her since she lost her hands?" "I wouldn't know what to say," said Donovan softly. "She pretended to be my friend, but she was planning to kill me. How do you forgive something like that?"

"I don't know that she was planning to kill *you,* son, but she and Stuart were plotting to kill the other Changed Ones at the Academy in order to keep their secret. Maybe they thought they had to do it to protect their race. Let me ask you something; when you came here, if someone told you that dragons were planning to kill *other dragons*, would it have bothered you at all?"

Chapter Nineteen:

DECISIONS, DECISIONS

"**C**an you see 'em?" yelled the Captain. "Yes, Captain. They're about two leagues away, two points off the starboard bow!" yelled Andrew, pointing at the ship that was under attack. "How the blazes can you see that far?" asked the Captain. "It's an enhancement spell, Sir. It improves my eyesight," replied Andrew. The Captain grunted, "Well, keep it up. I hope we can get there in time. "COME TWO POINTS, STARBOARD, AND PUT ON MORE SAIL!" he bellowed at the crew. Another topsail unfurled, and the ship's speed increased, but only marginally.

"Would more wind help, Captain?" asked Andrew. "Aye, but just a bit, mind you. Don't you shred my sails like my last Sorcerer did." Andrew nodded his understanding, concentrated, then said *"GUSTO,"* and made the backhand wave with his left hand. The wind picked up, pushing the ship along at a noticeably faster pace. "That'll do, Andrew," said Captain Matthews. Andrew noted that this was the first time the Captain had called him just 'Andrew.'

As the HMS VALOR got closer to the ship under attack, they saw that it was a merchant ship, probably carrying foodstuffs for the port city of Grotton and that it was under attack by at least three Sea dragons. Two of the dragons circled the ship in the water, shooting high-pressure jets of water at the hull, just above the waterline, while the third flew overhead, attempting to get close enough to shred the ship's battered sails with its talons. Only the ship's heroic bowmen were keeping the flying dragon at bay for the moment.

As the VALOR approached, Andrew asked the Captain which dragon posed the greatest danger to the ship. "The ones trying to bore a hole in the hull," shouted the Captain. "A ship that size will have spare sails below deck!" "On it," said Andrew. Andrew cut off the Wind spell as the VALOR pulled along the port side of the merchant ship. Leaning over the starboard railing, Andrew fired a Blast spell at the dragon between the two ships, knocking it underwater. The dragon flying over the merchant ship turned to attack the VALOR, but as he neared the rear of the vessel, he suddenly broke off the attack and dove underwater, the other dragon on the starboard side submerged also.

"Watch 'em," yelled the Captain, "they may try to come up under us!" the crew raced to the railings, bows drawn, but the three dragons never resurfaced. After a few minutes, with no activity, it appeared that the dragons had fled, and the attack was over. The HMS VALOR pulled alongside the merchant ship, and the two Captains conversed. "All hail the Royal Navy!" shouted the merchant Captain; his battered crew cheered their appreciation. "Captain William Stone, at your service, Sir. We thank you for your timely arrival," said the Captain of the FS RABBIT.

"Captain Stone, why didn't you wait for the convoy?" asked Captain Matthews. "It's scheduled to leave Southport in two days!" Because of the recent dragon attacks, most merchant ships had elected to travel in convoys, escorted by one or more Royal Navy ships for protection. It didn't stop all the attacks, especially if a ship ran too far ahead of the escorts or fell too far behind. These outliers were prime targets for attack, but some of the Captains were either overconfident or their dilapidated ships simply couldn't keep up with the convoy.

"It was pure greed," admitted Captain Stone. "You see, Captain, I can *be* in Grotton in two days. When a flotilla of cargo ships arrives in a port, the price of everything drops. If you can beat the convoy to port, you make more money." "Well, it almost cost you your ship and crew," groused Captain Matthews. "I hope you learned your lesson." "Aye, Captain. That I did. Besides, after this, I'd likely have a mutiny if I tried this fool stunt again." "Understood. Can we render any further assistance?" asked Captain Matthews.

"We have spare sails below deck, but if your Sorcerer can do anything about the holes in our hull, we'd sure appreciate it. We're taking on a bit of water," said Captain Stone. "I could ask him," replied Captain Matthews with a sly grin, "but ship repairs generally come with some sort of *compensation*." "How about two casks of Fairview rum?" offered Captain Stone. "A fair bargain," said Captain Matthews, "I'll see what he can do."

Andrew overheard the conversation between the two Captains. When Captain Matthews turned to him, he said, "I can repair the hull of the RABBIT from here, sir, but it would be best if I took a longboat and got closer to the damage. Especially if any of it's below the water line." Captain Matthews smiled, "We'd have to launch a boat to retrieve the rum regardless. Take your time and do a good job of it." "Aye, Aye, Captain," said Andrew. "When you're done with the repairs, we need to talk. Something about that attack bothers me," said Captain Matthews.

Andrew boarded the longboat with two crewmen and they were lowered over the side of the VALOR. Andrew instructed the crewmen to row as close to the damaged hull of the RABBIT as they felt was safe. The oarsmen seemed to appreciate that consideration. Once in position, he used an Enlarge spell, to 'grow' the adjoining hull planks to fill any holes made by the Sea dragons. For good measure, he added an Adhesive spell to 'stick' the newly enlarged boards to their neighbors. By the time he was finished, Andrew was physically exhausted. He took a drink from his water bottle as two large casks of rum were lowered into the longboat by the crew of the RABBIT. "Those repairs should hold, Captain," said Andrew to the Captain of the cargo ship, "but I'd have them inspected by a shipwright once you reach port. This was my first repair at sea," Andrew explained. "From the inside, those repairs look good as new, and there's no water coming in. We thank you," said Captain Stone.

The longboat was pulled back onto the VALOR and the casks unloaded and stowed below. The crew looked very happy. Andrew made his way to the Captain's cabin and knocked. "Come on in, Andrew," said Captain Matthews. Andrew entered and settled heavily into the armchair opposite the Captain's desk. "Tired?" asked the Captain. "Yes, Sir. Between the chase, the fight, and the repairs, I'm a bit fatigued," confessed Andrew. "You did good work," said the Captain. "Now, did anything about that attack strike you as strange?"

Andrew thought for a moment, then said, "The dragons broke off their attack awfully quickly after we arrived. I would have expected a little more fight out of them," said Andrew. "My thoughts exactly!" said the Captain. "We know that the dragons have been avoiding Navy ships, probably because of the magicians on board. I suppose one of those Changed Ones you told me about informed the dragons that all Royal Navy ships have at least one Sorcerer assigned." "That makes sense," said Andrew, "and I understand them wanting to avoid tangling with a Sorcerer or a Mage, but how are they identifying which ships are Royal Navy and which are commercial vessels? I mean, structurally, the FS RABBIT isn't that much different from the HMS VALOR."

"Hmm," said the Captain, "that's a good point, and we need to think about it. Still, I have reports that other Royal Navy ships have been attacked by dragons. Some vigorously, despite their magicians. What makes us so special? I mean, this makes five encounters we've had where the dragons have run away from us as soon as we arrived!" "I honestly don't know, Captain. Perhaps the ship's reputation? Wizard Noland told me that the VALOR had a fine record with the fleet," speculated Andrew. "I suppose that's true," said the Captain, "so you're saying that they see our name on the hull and run away? I would have thought they'd do the opposite and send more dragons after us." "I don't know, Captain. It's just a wild guess on my part," said Andrew with a yawn.

"Well, that's a problem for another day," said the Captain cheerfully. "In the meantime, you earned us two casks of rum, and the crew will be drinking your health for the rest of this voyage. Let's go join them, shall we?" "I hate to disappoint you, Captain, but I'm so tired, I can barely keep my eyes open. Besides, Navy Regulations prohibit magicians from becoming inebriated when at sea. That's because a drunken Sorcerer once sank his own ship by removing the keel." The Captain laughed. "Well, go get some sleep then, and again, well done."

Donovan lunged forward, staff extended, but Wizard Faith easily dodged the attack, spinning to the right and using wind to hurl another stone toward Donovan's feet. Donovan jumped to avoid the rock, then sent four Seemings of birds straight at Faith's eyes. She swatted the Seemings away with her staff, then swung it low. "I see you've been talking to your father," she said. "Yes, and he warned me that Seemings might not work against you any longer," gasped Donovan, trying to catch his breath. Faith switched her grip, holding her staff at the very bottom with her right hand, swinging it like a club. It was the opportunity Donovan had been waiting for. *"REDUCTO,"* he said, pinching his right thumb and forefinger together, the gesture aimed at Faith's staff. Her staff instantly shrank to a mere hand-span in length, as Donovan placed his staff on Faith's shoulder.

"Damn! Your family is just full of surprises!" said Faith. "A Reduction spell! Who would have thought it? OK, from now on no magic when we spar, just staffs." "Agreed," said Donovan. "Actually, starting next week, I think we'll advance to the Level Three instruction of fighting with staffs on horseback." "That should be challenging," said Donovan. "I've never sparred with anyone while mounted." "It takes a *lot* of practice," said Faith, "you can't move about as freely as when you're on foot, and you have to avoid hitting your own mount with your staff. I can tell you, mounts do *not* appreciate being hit with staffs. Enough for today, you two are dismissed for Endday activities."

Sorcerer Terry and Donovan followed Wizard Faith towards the Gatehouse, then proceeded out into the town. As they wandered past the Bakery, Terry paused and sniffed the air. "You smell something?" asked Donovan, triggering a Smell enhancement of his own. The scents of Kingston were almost overpowering, from the pleasant aromas from the Bakery, to the smell of leather and glue coming from the Cobbler Shop and the smell of all the people and livestock passing by. "I thought I smelled something strange, but I cannot localize it. There are so many more scents out here than in the Academy grounds," said Terry. They walked on, barely noticing the gnarled old man sitting quietly on the bench across the street from the Bakery.

As they headed towards Donovan's house, Ard nodded to himself in satisfaction. Since Donovan was in the company of a Changed One, Ard's worries were over. He could return to the quarry above Colton, knowing that a Fire Dragon, much younger than he, was protecting Donovan from harm.

As they entered the house, Donovan found his father sitting at the dining room table, replicating a crossbow. "Dad, is that my crossbow?" Donovan asked curiously. "No, son, this is a replica of it that I made a few weeks ago. I'm trying to make enough for the entire Royal Expeditionary Force, not just the bowman. Their swordsmen are brave, but as we saw, next to useless against a dragon," said Edward. Terry cleared his throat awkwardly.

"Sorry, Dad, this is my Mentor, Sorcerer Terry," said Donovan, belatedly. Edward hastily put the crossbow away and rose to greet Terry. "Terry!" said Edward, shaking hands, "So nice to meet you at last! Wizard Noland has expressed great confidence in you."

"I appreciate the thought, Wizard Edward," said Terry. "Come on into the living room," said Edward, leading the way. "I would offer you some tea, but perhaps you'd prefer something else?" asked Edward. "Plain water would be fine," said Terry, "to a Dragon, even a Changed One, tea tastes like warm swamp water." "I never realized that; I shall keep it in mind," said Edward. "So, what brings the two of you out? Oh, it's Endday, isn't it? I've been working so hard that I lost track of the days. So, how was your sparring session with Wizard Faith today?" Donovan grinned, "You were right about her being ready for the Seemings. She just batted them away with her staff," said Donovan. "I told you not to count on that," said Edward, "so what did you do then?"

"He used a Reduction Spell on her staff and turned it into a wooden dowel," said Terry. "I have never seen such a thing done before." "Hah! Good one!" said Edward. "I'll have to remember that." "So, Wizard Faith says no more using magic when we spar, and we're going to start sparring on horseback next week," said Donovan. "Then you've passed all your Level Two Martial Arts training," said Edward. "Sparring on horseback is a Level Three class. *Advanced*, Level Three."

"Any advice for me?" asked Donovan, hopefully. "Roll up your sleeves before you start. Horses don't like anything touching their ears. Keep your strikes high; if you hit either horse, they may react in unexpected ways, like bucking you *both* off. Horses can't see Seemings, so don't bother. When fighting a real enemy, use a Dig spell under the horse's hooves. You can also Tether a horse; Fire will often spook them into flight, but it might spook your horse, too. When sparring on horseback, the goal is to knock the other rider off their horse, so jab your staff at them. Have you learned to conjure small shields yet?" asked Edward. "I can hold one for a little while," confessed Donovan. "Good," said Edward, "use the small shield to deflect your opponent's staff and jab with your own. Just be mindful that the other magician may also have a small shield to deflect your staff." "It sounds complicated," said Donovan. Edward and Terry laughed.

"Before I forget," said Donovan, "Sorcerer Terry thought he smelled something funny when we came out of the Wizards Academy this afternoon." "Was it a 'dragony' something?" asked Edward. Terry nodded. "I have smelled the same thing," mused Edward, "but it's very faint, and the Bakery smells help cover it." "What do you think is causing it?" asked Donovan. "My suspicious mind says it's a Changed One, watching the entrance to the Academy," replied Edward. "To what end, I don't know. Maybe they're looking for Loren or Stuart to come out. Did you see anyone suspicious hanging about?" "Not really, just an old man sitting on the bench across the street from the Bakery," said Terry. "Hmm. I think I've seen him there before myself. I'll check on it periodically until we're ordered out."

"Are you going somewhere?" asked Donovan. "Sooner or later, the King is going to send the Royal Expeditionary Force out to deal with the threat from the Kingdom of Baize. That's why I'm working on these crossbows so diligently," said Edward.

"Dad, how come there are no old students at the Academy?"

asked Donovan suddenly. "Edward smiled, "You mean old like me?" "No. I mean, I don't think there's a student in there who's older than twenty-two. I can't believe that the Regional Mages found all the rogue magic-users. There must be some that slip through the cracks."

"You're right," said Edward. "In fact, there must be dozens, maybe hundreds, that we don't find before they turn twenty. The Academy doesn't accept Level Ones that are older than twenty winters old." "Why not?" asked Donovan. "We tried once, but inevitably, the older students tried to bully the younger ones and ended up in the infirmary or dead," said Edward. "So now, if we find someone twenty or older with the spark, we put a Binding spell on them so they can't hurt anyone with magic or use their power to counterfeit coins, which would hurt the Kingdom. As long as they use their magic responsibly, we leave them alone. If they violate the Binding spell, they die."

"It is not working," said Gek. "What do you mean?" asked Teal, "We have destroyed many human ships and damaged dozens more!" "Yes," said Gek, "but the plan was for the humans to fight each other. That is not happening, at least not at sea." "You are right," said Cobalt, "maybe they are fighting on land, and we have not heard about it yet."

"If they were fighting on land, their ships should be fighting each other, right?" asked Azure. "I suppose so," said Teal. "We should learn more at the next Dragon Council on the next full moon. At least we have been able to avoid attacking the ship with Andrew on it. I just hope the humans do not figure out why we have been avoiding the HMS VALOR or transfer Andrew to another ship."

"Sometimes I wish Ard had never cast that Binding spell," said Gek.

"Your majesty, something must be done to respond to these attacks!" insisted Jasmine. "These dragons are obviously being sent against us by the Kingdom of Baize, while they proclaim no knowledge of them!" "But how would the King of Baize induce dragons to attack us?" asked the exasperated King. "Perhaps he promised them some of our land if they help him defeat us," said Jasmine. "If there are Changed Ones there, perhaps an agreement has been reached between the Dragons and the Baizians."

"Then why would dragons attack Riverside?" asked Wizard Edward. "I would suggest that it was a 'false flag' operation, designed to give the Kingdom of Baize an excuse to attack us that their citizens would accept," said Jasmine. "And the attacks on the ships?" asked Edward. "The reports I have seen indicate that both Franconian and Baizian ships have been attacked by Sea dragons."

"The majority of the ship attacks have been against Franconian vessels. Perhaps the Dragons mistook Baizian ships for ours. How would a Dragon know the difference?" asked Jasmine. "Why would Baize risk their own ships being attacked?" asked Marshall Guzman. "Who knows what a Sea Dragon thinks?" asked Jasmine. "I understand that a lone Sea Dragon attacked Smithville; she destroyed several forges and smithies, then leveled several private homes, seemingly at random, before fleeing towards the Eastern Ocean."

The King was silent for a while, considering the conflicting advice from his counselors. Finally, he asked, "What do you recommend, Jasmine?" "Sire, I respectfully suggest that the Royal Expeditionary Force proceed at once to the border and launch a punitive strike on the Baizian city of Springfield." "Is that wise?" asked the King. "We need to bring these attackers to heel, Sire. A limited strike on one of their cities should make our resolve clear."

"Marshall Guzman, what is your opinion?" asked the King. "Sire, if the Kingdom of Baize is indeed behind these attacks on Franconia, we must respond. The Royal Expeditionary Force is the ideal unit for such a strike. I would recommend a rapid assault with the objective of raiding the garrison's treasury and returning. Limit our actions to the Baizian military, no burning buildings or destroying civilian structures. Just a rapid action to demonstrate our capabilities and resolve."

"Wizard Edward, what is your opinion?" asked the King. "Sire, if the Baizians are behind these attacks, then I agree that we must respond. The operation Marshall Guzman suggests is limited and proportional. However, I must point out that if the Royal Expeditionary Force is attacked by multiple dragons, you could lose fifty-one soldiers and one Wizard for absolutely no gain." The King thought about that for a moment, then said, "In war, risks must be taken. Marshall Guzman, immediately dispatch the Royal Expeditionary Force. Their objective is the Baizian city of Springfield; they are to engage the Baizian military forces in the area, raid the treasury, and return as quickly as possible. I will also authorize one additional Sorcerer from the Second Regiment to accompany the force as additional magical support. The Sorcerer will be selected by Wizard Edward. I want the force to depart within the week." "By your command, Sire," said Marshall Guzman.

Louis landed about half a mile south of the city of Middleberg and transformed back into human form. He had decided to tell the city officials that his horse had stepped in a hole and broken its leg, forcing him to walk most of the way from the town of Lakeshore. When he arrived in town, he immediately went to the City Hall and demanded to speak with the Mayor.

"So, Mister Mayor, what preparations have you made to guard against dragon attacks?" Dean, the Mayor of Middleberg, explained what the city had done after the report of the attack on Riverside. "Well, we've constructed some shelters around the city for the townspeople, made of solid stone that won't burn. We've also set up a watch, with several of our soldiers assigned to scan the skies and alert us of any approaching dragons. There is also a system of bells around the city to warn the citizens of an impending attack. The Captain of the Royal Guard Company assigned to Middleberg has recalled all of his soldiers who were on leave, and we've also activated the City Militia and armed them with bows. We've also practiced several fire-drills, forming bucket brigades to put out possible fires. Being so close to the river helps."

Louis made careful notes of all the locations of the watch towers and alarm bells, as well as the shelters that the Mayor had prepared. "It seems like you have a good plan, Mayor, but I would recommend focusing the defenses on the north and east side of the city. I do not believe you have to worry about dragons attacking from the desert," advised Louis. The Mayor scratched his head and said, "Normally, I'd agree with you, Sir Wizard, but we're talking about *dragons*, not conventional forces. I reckon that dragons can fly around and attack us from any side they choose."

Louis had to admire the Mayor's intelligence. "I suppose that is true," he conceded, "but they will most likely fly in from the east, so maybe just concentrate the watch towers in that direction." The Mayor thought it over, then said, "You're probably right about that. I'll see to it." "What magical support do you have in the city?" asked Louis.

"Well, there's the two Sorcerers assigned to the fifth Company of the Royal Guard, but I think one of them has been assigned to customs duty at the docks, looking for Dream Dust smugglers. Then there's Mage Elianna, who has a gaggle of young apprentices she's trying to train. Not sure they would be much help, though; I think most of 'em are only ten or eleven years old."

"Where does Mage Elianna live?" asked Louis. "She's got this big place on the west side of town. I think it used to be a warehouse, but she's converted it into a schoolhouse for young magicians." "I see," said Louis. "I may pay her a visit to see how her students are progressing. We may need them all sooner than we hoped."

Louis took his leave and departed City Hall. He spent the rest of the afternoon wandering about the city, checking (and marking) the location of the dragon-shelters and the watch towers. As evening fell, Louis headed toward the west side of town, looking for Mage Elianna and her apprentice magicians.

He found the warehouse easily. It was large and one of the best-maintained buildings in Middleberg. Louis assumed

Elianna was using her students to help maintain the building with magic. The sign on the front gate read: *Middleberg School of Magic.* Louis went through the gate and knocked on the front door. A young woman with long dark hair answered immediately. "I am looking for Mage—" "Wizard Louis! We are honored! Welcome! Please come in. Children, this is Wizard Louis, the Court Wizard of Baize," the young Mage exclaimed.

"Sir, I am Mage Elianna. How may I serve you?" Louis was very pleased and flattered by the effusive welcome and difference shown by the young Mage. He wiped his dusty shoes on the mat and entered the building. "I have come to check on military and civilian preparedness in Middleberg because of the threat from the Dragons. I thought I would stop by and determine what magical resources the city may have to call upon if needed."

"Of course. How wise!" said Mage Elianna. "Well, to begin with, I have twelve students in training at present. Children! Line up by age and bow to the Wizard!" The dozen students arranged themselves by age; the oldest looked about sixteen, and the youngest barely ten years old. They bowed respectfully to Louis and said in unison, "Welcome, Wizard Louis. We live to serve." Louis was very much impressed. This was the first such school he had ever visited, since he felt that such inspections were beneath his station as Court Wizard.

"Mage Elianna, I need a word in private," said Louis. "Of course! Stephen, take charge of the class. Go to the far end of the building and resume our work with Concealment shields." The oldest boy, Stephen, bowed again and ushered the other students to the far end of the extensive warehouse, where they began casting Concealment shields. "You train them well in discipline, I see," said Louis. "Well, I have to. Children with the spark who have any practical use of their magic are often unruly and somewhat disrespectful when they arrive."

Louis smiled, "I understand, and I suspect I was much the same as a child. Now tell me about them." "Stephen is eighteen and is the oldest. In another year, maybe eighteen months, he'll be ready to take the Sorcerer's Test. The others are years away from being ready for that, and the present instruction I'm providing is slowing their overall development," said Elianna humbly. "Why do you say that?" asked Louis. "Because I'm concentrating on those spells and Serums that will be most useful in *war*. By that, I mean, protective and Concealment Shields, the Seeing, Strength, and Stamina Enhancements, the Blast and Kill Force spells, and Healing spells and Serums. They will eventually make good fighters, but they are far behind in learning the other spells and Serums that most magicians learn at their age. We are working hard; the children rise before dawn, prepare their own breakfast, and then begin their lessons. Other than a brief meal period at midday, we do not stop until well after dark. We have supper, then work on Serum preparation until bedtime."

Louis nodded his understanding. This Mage was far too efficient and insightful for his purposes. "I understand, but I believe your efforts are focused in the right direction. These are not normal times, and the spells you have mentioned may indeed serve these young ones better than learning the Tracer spell or some of the other spells that will not help them survive a Dragon attack. Why the Seeing Enhancement, though?" "Once they master that ability, I plan to post some of them with the city lookouts. They will be able to see dragons coming much sooner than normal people." "Of course," said Louis, "very good. So, how are they progressing?"

"They each have unique abilities; some are very good with shields but struggle with Enhancements, others can Blast a boulder to rubble but are unable to Heal. It is a challenge to instruct so many and try to get them to the same level of expertise. Additionally, I must admit, we do not have much time to work on the various Serums, and that is where their skills are weakest." Louis nodded his understanding. "The only Serums they should be working on are Healing Serums, but I agree that you seem to be concentrating on the right things." Mage Elianna looked relieved to have the Court Wizard's approval.

"I didn't mean to imply that we are not making Serums, Sir. We end each day by making a dozen vials of Healing Serum before bed. We have several hundred vials prepared already, each marked with the date, so we know when they will expire. Would you like to see?" "Of course," said Louis, shocked. Elianna led Wizard Louis to a back room where there were dozens of chests, each containing about fifty vials of Healing Serum. "I have never seen so much Healing Serum in one place in all my life," confessed Louis. Mage Elianna beamed.

"You have a great deal of Serum here," said Louis. "How do you plan to dispense it all?" "Next week, I will take some of these chests to the Royal Guard and the rest to the City Council. I believe their plan is to distribute at least one vial of Healing Serum to every soldier and at least one to every family in the city." Louis nodded. This city was run far too well for his liking. He would need to do something about it, and soon. "How have you been able to afford the ingredients for so much Serum? I thought they were quite costly." Mage Elianna smiled, "I understand that they are in other places, Sir Wizard, but most of the ingredients grow wild in the area around Middleberg. Between the damp terrain along the river and the dry soil to our west, most of the ingredients are gathered at little to no cost. The Mayor has assigned the unemployed men and many of the women in the city to gather the herbs and spices required. In fact, once this crisis is over, we may even be able to export Healing Serum and make a considerable profit on the sale. It could be a whole new industry, with considerable taxes going to the crown!"

"Amazing!" said Louis. "I had no idea. I will certainly mention your efforts to King Donald on my return to Baize." Mage Elianna smiled. "Would you join us for dinner? We have plenty, and I'm sure the children would relish the opportunity to speak with someone as important as the Court Wizard." "Alas, while I would enjoy that very much, I must return to Baize this evening. There is much to do, and I have many towns and cities to visit in the coming weeks. Before I go, could you give me a brief tour of this facility? It seems most efficient."

"I would be honored," said Elianna, "please, come this way." Mage Elianna guided Louis through the vast warehouse. There were rooms designed for practicing Force spells, a large outdoor area with a pavilion for spells that had to be performed outdoors, a Serums classroom, completely stocked with crates of ingredients, a storage area, sleeping areas for the students, privies and shower rooms, and a respectable kitchen. As they entered the kitchen, Mage Elianna introduced Asia, the cook. Elianna explained that, in addition to herself, there were four staff members who ran the school with her: a cook, a supply clerk, and two security guards who protected the school from vandals and brigands. "We have some valuable items here, you see, and we can't expect the students to study magic all day and then stand watch at night."

"Have there been break-ins?" asked Louis. "We had one; the villain stole several vials of Healing Serum. Since then, we have had to hire guards. The city constables also make several rounds of the building each night, just in case." Louis frowned, "It is unfortunate that such measures are necessary." "Yes, but if we ever start producing Healing Serum for sale, we will probably need guards to provide security for the transportation of the Serum as well. But that is a problem for later. We have enough problems now."

Before leaving the kitchen, Louis looked into the large pot on the stove. The cook was preparing beef stew for dinner. It smelled wonderful. Louis dropped three Nightshade berries into the pot when no one was looking. That should kill some of the students and sicken the rest. "You seem to have matters well in hand, Mage Elianna," said Louis as he left the kitchen. "Now I must return to Baize. I will inform the king of your diligence here."

After departing the school, Wizard Louis paid a visit to two of his agents in the city. He instructed the Fire Dragon Changed One to spell Mage Elianna's guards to sleep that night and either steal or destroy the valuable Healing Serum they had spent so much time and effort preparing. He told the Changed One exactly where the Serum was stored in the facility. He said that he did not think there would be much resistance tonight because most of the staff and students would be either dead or dying from food poisoning. He ordered the second Changed One to overwatch the theft, in case there were problems.

After giving the Changed One his orders, Louis returned to the City Hall and requisitioned amount in the name of the king. A fine steed was provided and after a brief word with the Mayor, Louis departed Middleberg, riding south towards the town of Lakeshore. He hoped to locate the family of Great Dragons that may or may not live in the area around Lake Ford, and he decided that he needed to visit the *Lakeshore School of Magic*, or its equivalent, and determine if he needed to take any action to reduce their effectiveness. The new horse met a similar fate as the one he left Baize on, and after feasting, Louis quickly flew south, looking for any signs of Dragons.

"So, it's off to battle dragons again, eh, Edward?" said Major Gerald. "And any Baizian troops and magicians we might encounter, Major. Don't forget about them," said Edward with a smile. "Of course, the Baizian Army and magicians. How could I forget about them?" said Gerald. Edward laughed, "Relax, Major. The last time you campaigned with me, you got promoted to Major! Stick with me, and you'll make Colonel in record time!"

"And if we run into a dozen dragons this time instead of just one?" asked Major Gerald. "Then I hope your men can shoot. I think I forgot to mention to the King that I made a crossbow for every member of the Royal Expeditionary Force. Your swordsmen and spearmen can learn a new skill besides hiding from dragons," said Wizard Edward. "I said before that you were a sneaky one. Some things never change," said Gerald.

"We also got permission to take an additional Sorcerer with us, and I know just the one," said Edward with a smile. "Who is that?" asked Gerald. "Sorcerer Curtis, from Third Battalion, Second Regiment," said Edward. "Why him?" asked Gerald. "Because he is scheduled to take his Mage Test in two weeks," said Edward. "I'm pretty confident that he's going to pass, so we get a Mage for the price of a Sorcerer," said Edward happily.

Kathy stood on the pier in Westport, carefully searching for the ever-present magical Customs inspector she expected to encounter any minute. She needed to get across the border and find a Baizian ship headed for the Capitol. The shipping agent had informed her (rather rudely) that there were no Baizian ships in port, and no Franconian ships were being allowed into Baizian coastal ports until further notice.

Kathy knew that if she could just get to the Baize side of the river, as the Assistant Court Wizard, she would be able to commandeer a ship if that's what it took to get her back to Baize. Louis's words about closed borders being an *inconvenience* now came back to haunt her. She walked along the boardwalk along the river on the eastern side, carefully watching for soldiers or magicians. As she neared the bridge across the Amber River that divided the two sides of the city, she saw soldiers and the Sorcerer, manning the border checkpoint. The gates on both sides of the bridge were closed and locked, and soldiers paced back and forth across the entrance. *No good*, thought Kathy. Even with a Concealment shield, she could not get past them and over the eight-rod high gate without being detected. She would have to find another way.

As she headed back down the street that bordered the river, she passed a tavern just in time to see a Franconian soldier tossed out the door by the establishment's bouncer. "And STAY out until you can pay your debts!" shouted the burly tavern bouncer. The soldier shook his head groggily and got to his feet, somewhat unsteadily. Strapped across his shoulder was a crossbow.

Kathy, thinking quickly, ran to the soldier and said, "Oh, you poor man! Here, let me help you." With Kathy's assistance, the soldier staggered over to a nearby bench. He was clearly inebriated, and slurring his words. "Thank you, Mistress. I just need a minute to get my bearings." "Is there anything I can do to help?" asked Kathy. "Not unless you can loan me a gold to pay the tavern owner. He's quick to offer credit to soldiers, but the interest he charges is usury!" proclaimed the drunken man.

"I do not have that much I can loan you," said Kathy. "At least not without some collateral." "Collateral? What's that mean?" asked the soldier. "You give me something valuable to secure the loan," Kathy explained. "Once you repay me, I will return whatever you offer as collateral." "I don't have much," said the soldier sadly. "What about that crossbow?" asked Kathy innocently. "Can't," said the soldier. "The Captain said he'd fine me a gold if'n I lost it."

Thinking quickly, Kathy said, "How about this, I will lend you two golds, with the crossbow as collateral. That way, you can repay your debt and also pay the gold to your Captain if you are unable to repay me in time." The soldier was obviously not thinking clearly because he quickly handed over the crossbow, the draw harness, and three iron bolts. Kathy quickly replicated two gold coins and placed them in the soldier's hand before spelling him to sleep.

Kathy could not believe her good fortune! She slipped into the alley and quickly used a Reduction spell to shrink her journal and the crossbow and its accessories to a size small enough to fit in her backpack. She quickly continued down the street, putting some distance between herself and the sleeping soldier. Continuing her search for a way across the river to the Baizian side, Kathy was becoming concerned.

It was maddening! She could see the other side but not reach it. Kathy walked to the very end of the pier and gazed out into the open ocean beyond. *Maybe she could swim out, then return on the Baizian side. No good.* While she could swim, she doubted that she could make it far before one of the small Franconian patrol boats caught her and hauled her back to shore. It would not do to be captured with a miniature crossbow in her backpack. As she watched, a Baizian cargo ship, the KBS DOLPHIN, released its mooring lines and prepared to cast off from the Baizian side of the port and head west.

In an act of inspired desperation, Kathy secured her backpack tightly and cast a Tether spell on the aft railing of the DOLPHIN as it turned west and began picking up speed. She was savagely jerked off the pier and into the water, being pulled behind the departing ship. Franconian guardsmen on the pier assumed that she was trying to defect and began yelling and firing arrows at her. Kathy erected a shield all around herself, which had the double effect of protecting her from the projectiles and also keeping her on top of the water, where she was battered by the wave action of the sea and the wake of the ship.

Kathy was dragged along by the DOLPHIN for several hundred yards without anyone on the ship being aware of her. Before the ship got too far from the shore, Kathy released the Tether spell but kept the ball-like shield in place. She was grateful to discover that the wave action pushed her towards the seawall on the Baizian side of the port. As she neared the wall, Kathy spotted a ladder used to launch small boats, bolted to the breakwater. When she was close enough, she took a deep breath and released her shield. She briefly submerged, then kicked to the surface and swam to the ladder.

Climbing up the ladder, Kathy noticed three young ruffians, lounging on the boardwalk. The three noticed Kathy and walked towards her, shouting offers to help her out of her soaking wet clothes and help her warm up. Kathy used a warm Wind spell to quickly dry herself, hoping the young thugs were observant enough and wise enough to leave her alone. They were not, and when they got too close, Kathy used another Wind spell to blow the three of them into the ocean.

I hope Mage Faith wouldn't consider that 'unjust,' she thought, realizing that she was going to have to be more careful in the future, lest she violate the Binding spell. Now dry and alone, Kathy hurried along the boardwalk until she came upon a Baizian Naval ship, the KBS GULFPORT, that was preparing to cast off. Kathy rushed to the gangplank before the crew could retract it and began climbing the steep ramp.

"Permission to come aboard, Captain?" she called. "Permission denied, Miss. We're a Royal Navy ship, not a commercial vessel. We don't take civilian passengers," said the Captain. Kathy completed the climb and stepped onto the deck, "That's good, Captain, because I'm the Assistant Court Wizard to King Donald, and I need to get back to Baize immediately," said Kathy.

"Baize?" sputtered the Captain. "That's impossible! We're headed on our normal patrol route to Oceanside! We can't divert to Baize! That would take us days off course." "Nevertheless, Captain, I am commandeering this vessel on official business. I have important information for the King about what is occurring in Franconia and will brook no delay."

"Before I can make any such accommodation, I'll need proof that you are who you say you are," said the Captain. "Very well," said Kathy, "hold on." Kathy conjured a near-gale force wind that jolted the ship forward, nearly rending the mainsail, while simultaneously tethering the sailor manning the big ship's helm, keeping him from falling overboard. "Enough, Sorceress! I believe you! Don't rip the sails!" Kathy reduced the force of the wind slightly and released the Tether spell.

"I apologize, Sorceress. I meant no disrespect. If you can keep the wind like this, we can easily divert to Baize and still make it to Oceanside on schedule." "Thank you, Captain, and I am Mage Kathy. Where is your ship's magician? I would speak with him." The Captain frowned, "Sorcerer Jordan was transferred to Fleet Headquarters in Seaside," said the Captain, "and his replacement has not yet been assigned." "You have no magician aboard? When did Sorcerer Jordan leave the ship?" asked Kathy, alarmed at the news.

"Jordan left about a month ago," said the Captain, "and every time I ask about a replacement, I get told 'soon.'" Kathy was disturbed by this news and wondered if the same thing was happening on other Navy ships. She decided to look into it when she got home. "I had no idea, Captain, but rest assured that I will make inquiries at the Admiralty once I return to Baize. Can I assume that that means that the magician's cabin is available for my use?" "Of course, Mage Kathy, let me show you the way." The captain led Kathy down to the vacant magician's cabin and asked if she needed anything else. "A cup of hot tea would be wonderful, Captain. Thank you. If there is anything you need in the way of magical support, please feel free to ask," said Kathy cheerfully.

The captain excused himself, and a short time later, a steward brought in a pot of hot tea along with milk and sugar. Kathy thanked the Steward and removed her journal, enlarged it, and made the final notations about her mission.

5. Met with James, the owner of Prestige Arms in Fairview. He has the contract to make crossbows for the crown. His contract requires that he not sell crossbows to anyone but the Royal Guard for three years. I put down a deposit for the first commercially available crossbow. Total cost: One Silver (Crossbow deposit)

6. News has reached Fairview of a dragon attack on the Franconian town of Weaton. Details are lacking, but the borders between Franconia and Baize have been closed. Total Cost: One Copper (Newssheet)

7. Secured transport from Fairview to Southport on the first available ship. The ship's owner has a cousin who owns a fleet of ships that transport goods from Southport to Westport. I intend to take the first ship departing Southport. Total Cost: One Gold (transport from Fairview to Southport)

8. Secured transport from Southport to Westport. There are no Franconian ships traveling to Baizian ports. Getting back across the border may be difficult. Total Cost: One Gold (transport from Southport to Westport)

9. All border crossings in Westport are closed and guarded by both soldiers and magicians. Managed to procure a crossbow from a drunken soldier and reduce it to fit in my pack. Total Cost: Two Golds (Crossbow)

10. Tethered a Baizian cargo ship and used it to escape to our side of the border. Have commandeered the KBS GULFPORT to transport me to Baize. Expect to arrive in seven or eight days. Using a wind spell to expedite the voyage. The GULFPORT's Captain informs me that his Sorcerer (Jordan) was reassigned to Fleet Headquarters in Seaside a month ago and he has not received a replacement magician. (Further investigation required) Total cost: Zero

11. Total Mission costs:

- Transport Baize to Westport — 6 Silvers (meals included)

- Transport Westport to Fairview — 5 Golds (meals included)

- Fairview Lodging — 5 Silvers

- Fairview meals (5) — 3 Silvers

- Crossbow deposit — 1 Silver

- Newssheet — 1 Copper

- Transport Fairview to Southport — 1 Gold (meals included)

- Transport Southport to Westport — 1 Gold (meals included)

- Crossbow – 2 Golds

Total Mission costs: 10 Golds, 5 Silvers, 1 Copper

There was something wrong with the stew. One sniff and Mage Elianna detected the faint smell of Nightshade. "SPOONS DOWN!" she shouted, startling the students and staff who were seated around the dining table. "Has anyone tasted the stew yet?" she asked urgently. "I had a couple of spoonfuls," said Sally, quickly growing pale. Elianna rushed to her side, pulling a vial of Healing Serum from the pocket of her robe, "Drink this quickly!" Elianna said, while casting a Healing spell over the now convulsing girl. It was too late. Sally grasped Elianna's arm and cried out before becoming still, as death took her. Mage Elianna cursed.

"Did anyone else taste the stew?" "I sampled it many times while I prepared it, Mistress," said Asia, the cook, "but I feel fine." "Here, drink some Healing Serum, just to be on the safe side." Asia quickly drank the Serum but reported no ill effects of the stew, and that her aching back felt much better after drinking the Serum.

"What happened, Mage Elianna?" asked Stephen. Still in shock at Sally's death, Elianna said, "Someone poisoned our stew. I think it's Nightshade, a deadly poison. Asia, besides yourself, who had access to the stew?" "Why, no one, Mistress. There hasn't been anyone else here, except Wizard Louis. Come to think of it, he did look into the pot of stew while he was here, but you don't suspect…"

"At the moment, Wizard Louis is my *only* suspect. He's the only stranger who's been here today, and as you pointed out, he had access to the kitchen," said Elianna angrily. "But why would the Court Wizard of Baize want to poison us?" asked Stephen. "I have no idea," said Elianna. "He seemed so pleased with our preparations for the conflict with the dragons. It just doesn't make sense!"

"What should we do?" asked Taylor, the youngest boy. "First, we dispose of this stew and anything that touched it. Everyone put your spoons and bowls into the pot. Gently! Don't splash any around!" said Elianna. The staff and students gently placed their dinnerware into the pot of stew, which Mage Elianna then vanished with a Remove spell. "Now I want everyone to go take a shower and wash yourselves thoroughly! Use hot water and lots of soap. Put your clothes in the laundry bag. I will have to dispose of them, just in case. I will provide new clothes for you when I get the chance. Asia, if you're feeling up to it, I need you to gather any kitchen utensils that came into contact with the stew and place them outside the kitchen door. Then sterilize the kitchen! I want every surface washed with bleach, including the floor."

Students and staff rushed to do her bidding. Mage Elianna

went to her room and disrobed, then quickly vanished her clothes, took a hot shower, then put on fresh garments. Her mind was racing. *What else could Louis do to harm the school? The Healing Serum!* Elianna raced to the storage room, but everything was in order. One of the security guards knocked on the door. "Is there anything I can do, ma'am? It's a terrible thing that happened."

"Yes, Owen, it is terrible to be betrayed like this. I'm concerned that an effort will be made to either destroy or steal the stock of Healing Serum we've worked so hard to make." "Would you like me to go alert the Royal Guard or the city constables and get some extra security?" Mage Elianna thought about it, then decided on a different course of action.

"No, but I do want all of these chests moved to the sleeping area, and I want them replaced with the chests full of empty vials we have for the next batches of Healing Serum. I plan to lay a trap and capture whoever comes for them. You and Randy begin moving these chests immediately."

Without another word, Owen picked up one of the chests and headed towards the sleeping area. Randy soon joined him, and within a glass, the Serum was secured in another room, having been replaced with chests full of empty vials. Elianna returned to the dining area, where the worried students were gathering after their showers. "Luke, please go and gather all of the laundry bags. Here, wear these gloves. Please place all of the bags and the gloves outside by the kitchenware. We will dispose of it directly. Luke, a boy of perhaps fourteen, raced upstairs to collect the almost empty laundry bags. He quickly deposited them outside with the kitchen utensils that the cook had designated for destruction.

Once all of the potentially contaminated items had been gathered, Mage Elianna turned the destruction into a lesson, teaching all of the remaining students the Remove spell. They returned to the dining area, and Mage Elianna addressed them, "I wish there was a better way to do this, but I am going to have to Remove Sally's body as well. I wish we could give her a magician's funeral, but I will not risk any of you becoming contaminated by her clothing or touch."

Elianna said, "Goodby, Sally. You were a good girl and would have made a fine Sorceress. I'm sorry I failed you. You will be avenged." After these words, Elianna removed Sally's body. After wiping away her tears, Elianna instructed the cook to similarly sterilize the dining table and floor, while the students went outside to place a marker for Sally.

They headed out to the outdoor training area, and Mage Elianna selected a stone block and inscribed the following words:

HERE LIES SALLY DUBOSE

AGE 12

MURDERED BY A TRAITOR

"All right, children, everyone back inside. We still have work to do tonight," said Elianna. When they were all inside, Stephen asked, "What do we do now, Mage Elianna?" "Now, we set a trap for whoever is coming to steal our Healing Serum."

The students were positioned all around the school, most of them under Concealment shields. Luke was on the roof, using a Seeing Enhancement to keep a lookout for anyone approaching. Just after midnight, he saw them, three hooded forms, moving through the shadows cast by the crescent moon.

The culprits entered the Serum storage room and began hauling the empty chests out to a pre-positioned wagon in the alley. Once all of the chests were loaded, one of the men climbed up to the driver's seat while the other two sat in the back of the wagon with the supposedly valuable cargo.

Suddenly, all three men fell asleep. When they awoke, they were tethered to chairs in separate rooms with very angry adolescent magicians guarding them. Elianna was in no mood to be gentle or merciful. After questioning the two hired henchmen, who knew nothing beyond being told that there was a forgotten cache of valuable Healing Serum stored in an abandoned warehouse that was free for the taking. Elianna killed both criminals and vanished their bodies.

The third man (the driver) was clearly the ringleader. He refused to answer any questions, other than insisting that he had never met Wizard Louis. Elianna left the interrogation room after an hour, frustrated. "This one is strong, and something about him does not smell right. I'm not sure who he's working for." "Should we just kill him?" asked Stephen. "No. We need information," said Elianna, "I'm just not sure how to get it." A glint came to Stephen's eyes, and he said, "I have an idea."

An hour later, Wizard Louis entered the interrogation room, dragging the seemingly lifeless body of Mage Elianna. "Well, you three have certainly made a mess of things," he rasped at the bound prisoner. "Give me one good reason why I should not end your miserable life right now!"

"Please, Wizard Louis! You told us that this place would be full of dead bodies, with no security! We secured the Healing Serum as you ordered but were spelled to sleep by multiple magicians! I swear I did not betray your secret! Spare me!" The Seeming of Wizard Louis dissolved, revealing Stephen and Mage Elianna sat up and smiled. "Oh, we intend to spare you. You are going to be the star witness during Wizard Louis's trial."

The Royal Guard was summoned to take control of the prisoner, and they arrived within the glass. Unfortunately, as they were transporting the bound and gagged prisoner to the dungeon, he suddenly dropped dead without a mark on him.

Wizard Louis was having no luck. If there was a family of

Great Dragons in the neighborhood, he could not find them. He had spent the last three days flying over the forest on the west side of Lake Ford with no signs of Dragons, Great or otherwise. He had almost decided to give up when, out of the clouds above him, a Great Dragon descended and asked, "Are you *trying* to be discovered, Fire Dragon?"

Louis looked over and said, "I have been looking for you, and I had almost given up hope. We need to talk!" The Great Dragon thought for a minute, then said, "Very well, follow me." Rising back up above the clouds, the Great Dragon headed east, to the other side of the lake, where he landed in a narrow valley. As Louis landed next to him, the Great Dragon made a motion towards the tree line, and a female Great Dragon and two younger Great Dragons emerged and walked over.

When all were gathered, the Great Dragon said, "I am Ig, and this is my mate, Cam, and our children, Leon and Ana." "I am Lumen," said Louis. "I learned that there might be a Great Dragon family living near the lake from Jasper, the Clan Chief of the Stone Dragons. I am so glad to meet you! The Dragon Council feared that the Great Dragon Clan was extinct except for two that we know of that live east of the Amber River, Ard and his grandson Gek."

"How is old Ard?" asked Ig. "I have not seen him in centuries! It is good to know that he is still alive! What happened to Liza, his daughter?" "She was slaughtered by the humans about a year ago after she took to raiding farms for prey and was discovered by the human magic-users." "That is sad news," said Ig. "Are there no other members of my Clan left?" "None that we are aware of," said Lumen sadly. "There may be some Great Dragon Changed Ones trapped in the human wizards' academy in Franconia, but we have had no contact with them for several years."

"What are 'Changed Ones?'" asked Leon. "They are of no concern to you," replied Ig sternly. Looking at Lumen, he asked, "Why did you seek us out? You have searched for many nights, flying below the clouds, where the humans could see you!" said Ig. "Perhaps we should speak in private," suggested Lumen. Ig nodded, and Cam and the children walked back into the concealment of the forest.

"My children have not been taught the spell of Change yet," said Ig. "Now they will wonder about 'Changed Ones' and ask incessantly. You have just caused their mother and me an inconvenience we did not need." "I apologize," said Lumen, "I forgot their youth. Anyway, with the death of Liza, the humans have discovered that Dragons exist. They are searching for us like never before. The Dragon Council has decided that it is time to confront the humans and resume our rightful place in the world."

"We have lived in this glen for decades, and the humans have never come within miles of us. I doubt that we are in any real danger from them," said Ig, confidently. "Liza and her son thought the same," said Lumen smoothly. "They did not know that the humans had invented a new weapon that fires iron arrows that can penetrate Dragon scales, at least all Dragon scales except for those of the Stone Dragons. Since you were not at the Dragon Council, your voice was not heard. Our war has begun. Fire Dragons attacked and destroyed the human city of Riverside a month ago; then Stone Dragons attacked the city of Weaton on the east side of the Amber River. Sea Dragons are attacking human ships at sea, and the Snow Dragons will soon begin their assault on the towns and cities near the Snow Fields."

Ig considered Lumen's words. Finally, he asked, "What would you have us do?" "Do you know of any other Great Dragons? We need your Clan's strength and cunning in this war," said Lumen. "There may be others," admitted Ig reluctantly, "but I have not seen them in years. Some transformed and moved into the city of Oceanside, while some remained in Dragon form and flew west to seek a place beyond the desert. I hope they found something to their liking. None of them ever returned."

Lumen considered Ig's words, then asked, "Could you go into Oceanside and seek out any Great Dragon Changed Ones? For that matter, would you or your mate be willing to seek out those dragons beyond the western desert? Jasper also said that many Stone Dragons went west to find a better place to live. One with more prey and fewer humans." Ig considered the request, and finally, he said, "I will change and go into Oceanside seeking others of my Clan. If I find any, what should I tell them?"

"Tell them that war with the humans is coming, and we need their help, but you must first determine if they will assist us. Far too many of the Changed Ones we have approached have said that they prefer their lives as humans and will not help us. Be especially wary of any Changed Ones who have taken human mates." Ig shuddered at the thought. "I would not have imagined that. Is there no one else you can send to look beyond the desert? I am loathe to abandon my mate and children, particularly if war is brewing." Lumen considered the suggestion.

"I would ask you to attend the next meeting of the Dragon Council, where we can discuss who should search the area beyond the desert. Perhaps this is a good mission for the Snow Dragons." Ig nodded, "When and where is the next meeting of the Dragon Council?" "The Council meetings are held in the abandoned rock quarry just north of the human city of Colton, on the east side of the Amber River. Do you know where that is?" Ig nodded, "Yes. It has been many, many decades since I was there, but I remember. When is the next meeting?"

"With the conflict, the council meets every month on the night of the full moon," said Lumen. "That is too soon," said Ig. "If I am to enter Oceanside and search for Changed Ones, I will need more time, at least a full cycle of the moon, maybe two. I will meet the Council on the third full moon from today." "I understand, and you are quite correct. We will await your report. In the meantime, I will return to Baize, change into my human form, and return to my duties as Wizard Louis, Court Wizard to the king."

"Please return to your home by flying directly east; you have already endangered my family with your low-flying search above the town of Lakeshore." "I apologize again," said Lumen, "and I will certainly take your advice." While this meant he would not be able to inspect the magicians' school in Lakeshore, Louis doubted that they were much of a threat to his kin. Lakeshore was a small town, after all.

Major Gerald

Chapter Twenty:

CLOAKS AND CROSSBOWS

Donovan looked up from his bubbling Truth Serum as his father walked into the classroom. "Jeffrey, I need to speak with Donovan for a moment, if that's all right," said Edward. "Of course, Edward," said the chubby Serums instructor, "Donovan, I'll keep your Serum boiling for you. Best keep your hourglass with you so you know when it'll be ready." Donovan took the hourglass from the table and followed his father outside into the courtyard.

"Son, as I expected, the Royal Expeditionary Force has been ordered to the border with Baize. We'll be leaving tomorrow, so I came by to let you know and give you some last-minute fatherly advice," said Edward. "First, while we have rooted out all the Changed Ones here at the Academy, there are undoubtedly still some in Kingston. I checked out the street in front of the Gatehouse, and the smell was gone, but so was the old man we saw. If you see him again, *get Wizard Noland,* do *NOT* approach him yourself, understood?" Donovan nodded. "Now, I will likely be gone several weeks, maybe as long as a couple of months; I'll let you know when I return. Do not believe any reports of my death unless Wizard Noland confirms it to you. Last, you will likely be taking your Level Three Test soon. You'll have to successfully perform twenty-five of the twenty-nine spells you have learned so far and all seven Serums to pass.

The current events test has been replaced by a test on military tactics. You have already passed the Martial Arts and Riding tests."

"What do I need to know about the Sorcerer's Test?" asked Donovan. Edward smiled. "You have to successfully perform thirty-four of the thirty-eight spells and all eleven Serums. You also have to demonstrate that you can hold one spell of your choosing for three days. Choose a spell or enhancement that doesn't take too much power. Personally, I used the Tracer spell and passed that part of the test easily." "The Sorcerer's Test sounds hard," said Donovan. "It's supposed to be," said Edward. "There are only thirty-eight spells *that we know of,* but you can combine them in interesting ways to create different effects or accomplish tasks in creative ways. Now, I've got to go, and your Truth Serum is almost done." Donovan noticed that the sand in the hourglass was almost gone. He gave his father a quick hug and rushed back to the classroom.

Edward headed across the courtyard to the Headmaster's cottage. The door opened as he stepped onto the doorstep. Noland met him in the entryway. "Off so soon?" asked Wizard Noland. "Yes," said Edward, "the Minister of Internal Security convinced the King that we need to launch a punitive expedition on Baize in response to these dragon attacks. There's something about her I just don't trust." "Could she be a Changed One?" asked Noland. "Possibly," said Edward, "but she chooses her words carefully, so as not to need contractions, and she always wears a heavy vanilla-scented perfume. Without more proof than that, the King would never believe the accusation."

"I'll keep an eye on her," said Noland. "Anything else?" "Yes," said Edward, "I believe that a Changed One has been watching the entrance to the Academy. His scent is very faint and is masked somewhat by the Bakery. He looks like an old man. I haven't seen him in the last few days, though, so he may have moved on." "You think he was looking for Stuart or Loren?" asked Noland. "That's the most likely explanation," confirmed Edward. "I'll keep an eye out for him," said Noland, "anything else?" "Yes," said Edward, "I'd like you to have the Level Three students work on replicating Donovan's crossbow as their Replication spell lesson. The Academy may need some before this is over." "How hard are they to replicate?" asked Noland. "It takes me about an hour, while bouncing around in the back of a wagon," said Edward. "So, very difficult," mused Noland, "it should be a good challenge for them." "The replicas don't need the silence spell on them; they just need to work," said Edward. "Once replicated, they should practice using them. I have a feeling that Crossbows will be much more useful than staffs soon. They're hard to draw, and take some practice to hit what you aim at, but if you practice near the boundary, at least you shouldn't lose any bolts." "I'll get them right on it," said Noland.

The two Wizards left the cottage and headed for the Gatehouse; as Edward left, Noland said, "Be careful, Edward. Something about this mission just doesn't smell right to me."

As the Royal Expeditionary Force headed out of Kingston, Sorcerer Curtis rode with Edward in his wagon with the Sorcerer's black horse tied to the hitching ring on the back of the wagon. "I can't tell you how happy I am to have you along with us this time, Curtis," said Edward. "I sure could have used your help on our last mission." Curtis was tall, dark-skinned, with black curly hair. He wore a red quilted jacket over burgundy pants. "I appreciate the opportunity, Wizard Edward," said Curtis, "I was definitely getting tired of sharpening and maintaining weapons in the Second Regiment's armory day after day." "I understand," laughed Edward, "I've done a lot of weapons maintenance in my time also. Now, a few things you need to know about the Royal Expeditionary Force: There are two companies, each commanded by a Captain, the Force commander is Major Gerald, and he's a good leader who came up through the ranks."

"I've always heard good things about the Royal Expeditionary Force," said Curtis, "they have a fearsome reputation." "And it's well-earned," said Edward. "Next, each company has a Senior Specialist, whose job is to take out enemy sentries, break into supposedly secure rooms, and scout out places that are too dangerous for normal troopers. They both have cloaks that have Concealment spells on them, and they like nothing better than sneaking up on unsuspecting commanders and magicians. Isn't that right, Dirk?" Edward asked the empty air beside the wagon. Dirk threw back the hood of his cloak, so just his head was visible and complained, "Sir Edward, sometimes you take all the fun out of this job. I just wanted to introduce myself to the Sorcerer." "Huh, likely story," said Edward, "I suspect you were testing him, just like you tested me on our first time out."

"I knew he was there," said Curtis, "just like I know the other one is on my side of the wagon." Lance laughed as he opened his cloak. "You choose good help, Wizard." "I hope so," said Edward, "I didn't pick Curtis by chance. Curtis, this is Senior Specialist Dirk and Senior Specialist Lance." Curtis nodded a greeting and said, "Those cloaks are quite remarkable. I could barely even sense you at this distance. Farther off, and I wouldn't have known you were there." "These cloaks are exorbitantly expensive," said Lance, "but absolutely essential for a Specialist."

"Hmm, that gives me an idea," said Edward. "Lance, Dirk, when we fought the dragon before, did she sense either of you during the battle? I assume you were cloaked." "We were indeed, Sir Edward, and no, I don't believe the dragon ever sensed either of us; at least she never blew fire in our direction." "Well, this time, I have a feeling that we're going to be facing more than one dragon, maybe a lot more. I'm going to talk to Major Gerald and see if we can imbed a Concealment spell in all the other soldier's cloaks."

"Everyone? Even that big oaf, Johanson?" asked Lance. "Even that big *soldier* Johanson," corrected Edward. "The regular soldiers will never be able to take your place as Specialists; as I just pointed out, they lack your special skills, but if we expect to sneak up on a pack of dragons, concealment cloaks could mean the difference between life and death." "What about the wagons?" asked Dirk, "Surely you can't cloak them." "Not all three of them," said Edward thoughtfully, "but we might use some kind of Seeming…"

"That's just great," grumbled Lance, "pretty soon *anyone* will be able to sneak up on the commander." Edward laughed and said, "Speaking of Major Gerald, where is he?" "I think he's up with the front of the column," said Dirk, "Do you want us to go get him for you?" "Yes, please, and without startling him too badly," said Edward. Lance and Dirk rode forward to look for Major Gerald.

Edward looked sideways at Curtis and asked, "So, I understand that you're one of us who can sense people without the incantation and gesture?" "Yes," said Curtis, "I practically ruined Level Two Hide-and-Seek when I was at the Academy." "My son, Donovan, is there now, and he has the same ability, as do I. It's fairly rare, you know." "So I've heard. Do you really think we can imbed Concealment spells into the cloaks?" "Someone figured out how to do it. I suspect that between the two of us, we can figure it out," said Edward.

Just then, Major Gerald rode up. "You wanted to see me, Sir Edward?" "Yes, Major. First, I wanted to introduce you to Sorcerer Curtis. Curtis, this is the Force commander, Major Gerald." "I'm pleased to meet you, commander," said Curtis. "Likewise," said Gerald. "I'm really glad ta have extra magical support along this time, we nearly got Edward killed on our last outing." "So I heard," said Curtis.

"This time, commander, please don't try to bury me unless my head is separated from my body," said Edward. "I guess Donovan told you about that, huh?" asked Gerald. "Yes. People are forever declaring me dead prematurely. Having to dig myself out of a grave is not as easy or as pleasant as you might imagine. I've had to do it twice now, and that's more than enough." Gerald and Curtis laughed. "Anyway, Major, the reason that I wanted to talk to you is that I have an idea that might give us a real tactical advantage on this mission."

"I'm always lookin' fer that, Sir Mage—I mean Wizard. What do ya have in mind?" "What would you think about our putting Concealment spells on every soldier's cloak?" "You mean like the ones on Dirk and Lance's?" "Maybe not exactly the same, but as close as we can make them," said Edward. "Hmm, an invisible force would certainly be a huge advantage, even when we're not fightin' dragons. What do ya need ta get started?" asked Gerald.

"I'll need your cloak, Lance," said Edward, looking at the empty space next to Major Gerald, "and one of the soldier's cloaks." Lance materialized next to Major Gerald and handed over his cloak. "I promise to return it as soon as I've got the first new one made," said Edward. Major Gerald handed over his cloak, "Here, you might as well start with mine; that way, if it doesn't work, the rest of the soldiers won't be too disappointed." Curtis took the cloak from Major Gerald and placed it in the back of the wagon with Lance's.

"Major," asked Edward, "what's our route to Springfield?" Major Gerald produced a map from his saddlebag, unrolled it, and said, "From here, it's a straight shot to Prarrieville; then, we can either turn south to Weaton or north towards Colton. Weaton's closer, but we know that they've already been attacked by dragons." "Can we cut across?" asked Edward. "I'm not sure," said Gerald. "There might be a trail that's not on my map. The troops in Prarrieville will know. It might be rough on the wagons, though." "I think I remember a trail from when I was stationed in Prarrieville. It's not as big as a road, but bigger than a game trail. Smugglers used it," said Edward. "Well, if smugglers used it, then it was probably wide enough fer a wagon. We'll just have to see when we get there," said Gerald.

"We better get started on those cloaks," suggested Curtis, "we don't know how long it's going to take to make forty-nine of them." Edward looked at Major Gerald and asked, "Can you ask Senior Healer Bone if he would drive my wagon while we work?" "Only if you promise not to scare him to death again," laughed Major Gerald as he rode off to find the Healer. "What did that mean?" asked Curtis. "Healer Bone was in the wagon, being carried by a barge down the Sapphire River, when I woke up in my stasis box. It kind of startled him," said Edward. "That's an understatement," said Healer Bone, as he climbed into the wagon. "I jumped so high, that I almost went overboard and into the river."

Edward laughed, "I hope to *never* do that to you again. Healer Bone, this is Sorcerer Curtis." "It's a pleasure to meet you, Sorcerer," said Healer Bone. "Likewise," said Curtis. "Major Gerald told you what we need?" asked Edward. "Yes, Sir," said Bone, "he said something about your trying to make specialist's cloaks for all of us, so we can sneak up on the dragons." "That's about the size of it," said Edward. "That is, if we can make it work." "You'll make it work, Sir Wizard. I'm not sure there's anything you *can't* do."

"I think it's the ensigns, Captain," said Andrew. "What?" asked Captain Matthews. "The ensigns! That's how the dragons can tell the difference between Navy ships and commercial traffic; they look for the flags!" exclaimed Andrew, pointing at the Royal Navy flag. "Hmm," said the Captain, "Yes, that might be it. So what can we do about it?" "Well," said Andrew, considering, "either we have all Franconian ships fly the Royal Navy flag, or none of us fly it." "None of us?" asked the Captain. "If every ship flies it, the dragons will not know which ships have magicians on board, and there might be fewer attacks; if no Navy ships fly it, more will be attacked, but we might kill more dragons, at least initially, until the dragons figure out what we've done," said Andrew.

"This is above my pay grade," said Captain Matthews. "This is a decision for the Fleet Admirals, maybe even the Admiral of the Navy or the King." "Maybe we could try both," suggested Andrew. "How can we do both—Oh, I see, you mean in one fleet, no one flies the colors; in the other, everyone does," said Captain Matthews. "Still, this is a decision for the higher-ups." Andrew looked worried. "What? You have that look that says there's a problem," said the Captain.

"Sir, it's just that, well..." "Out with it, Andrew!" barked the Captain. "Sir, we, the magicians at the Academy, believe that there's a spy in the palace, working with the dragons. If we tell the King..." said Andrew. "The dragons will know what we did," finished the Captain. "Anyway, it's still not our decision, and even if the dragons know *what* we did, it still doesn't help them identify Navy ships, does it?" "I guess that's true," said Andrew.

"When we dock in Grotton tomorrow, you're coming with me to talk to the Admiral and the Fleet Wizard," said the Captain. "Me?" asked Andrew. "Your idea," said the Captain, "so you get the credit or the blame."

"OBSCUROUS," said Edward, making the required gesture. The cloak on the table vanished. "You did it!" said Curtis. "Wait," said Edward. A few minutes later, the cloak reappeared. "Damn," said Curtis, "It just doesn't last." The two magicians had been trying all morning to replicate Specialist Lance's concealment cloak without success. They could make Major Gerald's cloak vanish, but the spell only lasted a short time before fading. "I'm beat," said Curtis, "you don't happen to have any Stamina Serum on you, do you?"

"THAT'S IT!" exclaimed Edward. "What, Stamina Serum?" asked Curtis. "I hope I can just use a Stamina spell," said Edward, "I didn't bring enough Stamina Serum to soak forty-nine cloaks in or the ingredients to make that much Serum. Let's see that cloak again." They laid Major Gerald's cloak back on the makeshift table and Edward said, *"OBSCUROUS ENDURO,"* while performing the gestures. The cloak vanished and did not reappear. "Brilliant!" said Curtis. "Congratulations!" Edward chuckled, "Just this morning, I told Donovan that sometimes you could combine spells in unusual ways to effect creative solutions. I should have listened to my own advice."

"Specialist Lance said these cloaks were "exorbitantly expensive," but this is a simple combination of spells. It doesn't even take that much power. Why, we can have all of the cloaks completed by this evening. I wonder what makes them so expensive?" wondered Curtis. "It's probably because of the specialized market," said Dirk, appearing in the wagon beside them. Curtis jumped in surprise. "There are only six other Specialists besides me and Lance. There is only one in each Regiment in the Franconian Army. You would have to charge a lot for each, if you could only sell a total of eight." "It's also likely that only one other magician in Franconia has thought of combining those two spells. He or she has a monopoly on the Concealment cloak market," said Edward. "What brought you by just now?" asked Curtis. "I heard Wizard Edward yell, 'THAT'S IT!' so I figured you'd been successful, and Lance wants his cloak back. He says he feels naked without it."

"Here you go, good as new," said Edward. "Now, if you could please have someone round up the other forty-eight cloaks for us, we'll get back to work."

"I need this delivered to Mage Arnold in Colton," said Minister Jasmine, handing a small, sealed scroll to the Kingston Regional Mage's Courier. "By the fastest means possible, please," she said sweetly. "It is vital that he receive this message immediately." "I can send it by Messenger Hawk," said the Courier. "It should reach him by this time tomorrow, as long as there are no storms between here and Colton, that is."

"Tomorrow will be fine," said Jasmine, "here is a silver for your trouble." "Thank you, Minister! I'll see to it immediately." The Courier practically ran down the corridor to the cages that held the hawks that magicians and Court Ministers used to convey messages quickly over long distances. Jasmine smiled, there would be a *very* special welcome awaiting the Royal Expeditionary Force when they reached the outskirts of Springfield.

Wizard Louis sat at his desk. He was not pleased. Mage Kathy had returned much faster than he anticipated, and he had barely returned to Baize before her untimely arrival. His Tracer spell had given him the impression that she was still in Springfield, and he assumed that she was trying to work up the nerve to cross the border into Franconia. Instead, she had deceived him and gone by water, reducing her travel time from six months to a little over two months. Her report also stated that there were indeed dragons, and the witch had even brought back a crossbow and presented it to the King before he could intervene.

Now, he was forced to address her report. Besides costing over ten golds, there was not much to criticize. Still, she had not spoken to any eyewitnesses about the dragon. All she really had was rumor and hearsay. If not for the damn crossbow, her report could be dismissed out of hand, and her first solo mission be declared a total failure. Something needed to be done about her. Soon.

Louis started as someone knocked on his door. "Yes, what is it?" Louis shouted. The door opened, and Mage Kathy entered, "I was just checking to see if you had any questions about my mission report, sir," said Kathy, humbly. "I have just finished reading it, and I must admit, I am disappointed," said Louis. "What do you find disappointing?" "First, you spent over ten golds and brought us back only rumor and hearsay!" said Louis. "I do not find a single interview with anyone who actually saw a dragon with their own eyes! Everything you have reported is second-hand information or wild speculation. Why did you not travel to Farmdale and speak to any farmers directly?"

"Because, from what I heard, there were no farmers who saw the dragon and lived to tell the tale," explained Kathy. "Why was no one in Kingston interviewed? Some of them might have at least been able to confirm the existence of this mythical dragon's head, that was supposedly stolen in Fairview." "Because the Franconian magicians are extremely adept at discovering people with the spark! If I had spent any time at all in Kingston, I might have been arrested as a spy!"

"You *were* a spy! And a damn ineffective one! Other than the crossbow, which we have been unable to replicate by the way, your mission seems to have been an abject failure! I expected better of you, Mage Kathy!" Kathy fumed. Wizard

Louis was being unreasonable.

"First of all, Wizard Louis, I left Baize with a single gold coin that was my own. I replicated it to pay for all my expenses! I have not filed a claim for reimbursement from the crown for so much as a copper!" said Kathy. "So, you are saying that all you wasted was time!" Kathy took a calming breath. "Wizard Louis, recent events have shown that there are indeed dragons living in the land. I believe that in my absence, you reported a dragon attack on Riverside to the King! *I* was sent to inquire whether dragons exist. If you doubt my 'second-hand' reports, then perhaps you should go interview the residents of Riverside yourself!"

"Mage Kathy, you are being insubordinate! I suggest you retire to your quarters and calm down before you say something I cannot forgive. You are dismissed. If I require further clarification from you, I will send for you." Kathy left Louis's office, shutting the door *firmly*. This was not over. Besides, she still had the reassignment of Naval magicians to investigate.

When the Royal Expeditionary Force camped for the night, Major Gerald assembled the men. "All right, listen up! The Wizard's got somethin' for ya," Edward and Curtis stepped forward, and Edward said, "You all know that we may be fighting a dragon again, maybe more than one. To help you, I've made a crossbow for every soldier, so you won't have to rely on swords and spears anymore," there were murmurs of approval from the assembled soldiers. "Sorcerer Curtis and I have also embedded a Concealment spell on the cloaks we collected from you this afternoon. With them, you'll be practically invisible. However, you will not be *silent*," said Edward, "so when we camp each night, you need to work on moving quietly under concealment with your crossbow. My hope is that we can sneak up on any dragons we come across and kill them with minimal risk to ourselves. Those of you who have never fired a crossbow before will also need to practice reloading quickly. It takes time to learn, but it could save your life. One last thing, *remember where you put your cloak*; if you lay it down somewhere and forget where you left it, you may never find it again. I recommend turning it inside out whenever you're not wearing it."

The soldiers formed a line behind the wagon to receive their cloaks and crossbows. They were very grateful to the two magicians. Major Gerald came over and said, "You two may have just made the Royal Expeditionary Force unbeatable!" "Formidable, certainly, Major," said Edward, "but the cloaks will not protect the men from dragon fire or even a stray arrow. Make sure they know that. Overconfidence kills more men than swords." "That's very true," said Gerald, "and I'll be sure to pass that along to them. Now, I expect you're both tired. Go get some sleep. We have the watch tonight."

"I don't like the idea of merchants flying the Royal Navy flag!" said Admiral Cross, "and I don't like the idea of Royal Navy ships *not* flying it!" Captain Matthews and Andrew stood before the Admiral of the Fleets and the Chief of Naval Wizardry; neither was happy with their suggestion of how the dragons were identifying and avoiding Navy ships. Andrew, thinking quickly, said, "Sirs, what if we designed a flag that is *similar* to the Royal Navy ensign, like the same color, but with a different symbol? That might fool the dragons, at least temporarily."

Wizard Lake considered Andrew's suggestion. "That might work, Admiral, and it would address both of your concerns." The Admiral grumbled, "I suppose so, but I want final approval of the design of this new Franconian flag!" "Of course," said Captain Matthews, "Sorcerer Andrew and I will get right on it and have it ready for your approval before the VALOR sails with the next convoy in three days." "Very well," said the Admiral, "Captain Matthews, I've heard how you saved the FS RABBIT from an attack by three Sea dragons and helped her with repairs. My nephew is a member of her crew, so I'm grateful." "All in the line of duty, Sir," said the Captain.

"I'd like a word with Sorcerer Andrew before he leaves," said Wizard Lake. "Of course, Sir Wizard, I'll see you later,

Andrew," said Captain Matthews as he hastily left the Admiral's office.

Wizard Lake led Andrew to his office and then asked, "So, Sorcerer Andrew, how are you finding Navy life?"

"Being from Southport, I grew up on ships, Sir," Andrew replied. "So far, my first few weeks in the Naval Forces have been exciting." "I imagine so," said the Wizard, "during your encounters with the Sea dragons, which spells do you find most effective against them?"

"So far, the only spells I've conjured have been Blast and Paralyze, Sir. Of course, I've used the Wind spell to increase our ship's speed and the Sight enhancement in order to improve my vision, when looking for dragons or when posted as a lookout." "Have you tried using the Kill spell yet?" "No, sir. I'm afraid that would take too much power. Sea dragons are *big*." "Indeed. Be careful with your Blast spell; I have a report that the Sorcerer from the Fifteenth Infantry Company in Weaton killed a dragon with one but put so much power into it that he did not survive," said Wizard Lake. Andrew gulped. "I will certainly keep that in mind, sir" "Get that ensign design to us as soon as you can," said the Wizard, "it would be good if we could test it out on your return convoy to Southport. Dismissed."

Mage Elianna arrived at the Middleberg garrison headquarters before noon the following day. In her cart was enough Healing Serum for every soldier in the Guard. Captain Alex was very grateful for their diligence in making the Serum. "I heard what happened last night," he said. "Do you have any idea who the thieves were?"

"No, Captain. We interrogated them all, but no one talked. I guess I should have spent some time teaching the children how to make Truth Serum instead of just Healing Serum. We might have learned a great deal from the ringleader. I doubt that the other two knew any more than they were told," said Elianna. She decided to keep Wizard Louis's involvement to herself until she had additional proof. Without the witness, she doubted that she would be able to convince the King of Louis's guilt.

Once the Royal Guard had their allotment of Healing Serum, Elianna headed over to City Hall to give the rest of the Serum to the Mayor and the City Council. She had decided that it was no longer wise to keep so much Serum at the Middleberg School of Magic, and it would be safer to get what she had distributed to the people of Middleberg.

Mage Elianna had no idea how to prove Wizard Louis poisoned their food or sent the brigands to steal or destroy the Truth Serum they had prepared. *It was maddening!* Without concrete proof, she would not be able to prove Louis's guilt. *I could always travel to Baize and settle this myself,* she thought, but that would leave her students alone and leaderless. *Any*

Messenger Hawk I send will undoubtedly be intercepted or destroyed, she thought.

She could take her students on a 'field trip' to the capitol, but that would leave Middleberg without any magical support they might be able to provide. She thought of hiring an assassin, but killing the Court Wizard would be nearly impossible, very expensive, and there was no guarantee that the effort would be successful. Besides, whoever she hired might sell her out, which would cause even greater problems.

Elianna wished there was someone she could confide in. *What about Mage Kathy?* she wondered. Kathy and Elianna had trained together as apprentice magicians in Baize before Elianna had been sent to Middleberg to run the school when the previous Mage had retired and moved to Oceanside. *How could she get a message to Kathy without Louis finding out?*

She finally decided that her only course of action was to send Stephen. He was the oldest and most advanced student. He had the best chance to make it to Baize, deliver her message, and return. Determined that she had to do something before other Magical Schools in Baize suffered a similar fate, Elianna sat in her office and composed a message.

Kathy,

Court Wizard Louis paid us a visit this week. After he departed, I discovered that the beef stew we had prepared for our dinner was poisoned with Nightshade. A promising young magician died as a result of the poisoning before I was able to detect it. I was able to stop the other students from consuming any stew, and they are unharmed but distressed. Wizard Louis was the only visitor we had that day, and I personally gave him a tour of the school (including the kitchen where dinner was being prepared). I have no proof that Louis poisoned the stew, but I have no other suspects.

Additionally, that night, three brigands broke into the school and attempted to steal over a hundred vials of Healing Serum I and my students had prepared for the people of Middleberg. I anticipated the break-in, and we captured the criminals. Two were lackeys with no knowledge of who hired them (I terminated them), but the third confessed to being sent by Wizard Louis, who I had informed of our efforts to produce a sizeable quantity of Healing Serum for the city.

Unfortunately, while the ringleader was being transported to the Garrison Dungeon, he suddenly dropped dead of unknown causes. I suspect another magician was involved, but I have been unable to determine who was responsible.

I need to get this information to someone reliable, and you were the first person I thought of. I cannot leave Middleberg at this critical time. The dragons may attack at any moment, and I cannot, in good conscience, abandon my eleven remaining students and leave the city with only two Sorcerers. I do not know what you can do with this information, but I needed someone to know what has happened to us, and I do not trust Messenger Hawks. This message is being delivered to you by Stephen, my most advanced student. He has brown hair and a scar on his left wrist. He is the only one I trust to deliver it to you safely.

Mage Elianna

After sealing the scroll, Elianna cast a Reduce spell, shrinking the message to the size of a small stone. She summoned Stephen and informed him that she needed him to deliver the disguised message to Mage Kathy Hima, the Assistant Court Wizard of Baize. After provisioning Stephen with enough food and water for the six-day trip, she gave him instructions on how to find Mage Kathy in the Royal Palace and warned him not to be seen by Wizard Louis or his life could be forfeit. She also advised him to take extra precautions on his way to Baize. "We know that there is at least one other magician involved. He or she killed the ringleader as he was being transported to the dungeon. I doubt the magician would follow you, but they may send word ahead by messenger hawk," cautioned Mage Elianna. "Once the message has been delivered, return here at once. I don't want you to remain in Baize for even one night. Understood?" Stephen nodded

"I hate to send you out alone on such a perilous mission, but there is no other that I can send who I trust," said Elianna. "Beware of brigands and *other hazards* on the road, and do not let your guard down until you are safely back in Middleberg. Farewell!"

They had been on the road to Prarrieville for two days and would likely reach the town tomorrow. The soldiers were in high spirits, with the new concealment cloaks and crossbows. Major Gerald rode up to Edward's wagon and noticed that Edward and Curtis were scanning the skies above them, looking worried. "Is there a problem, Wizard Edward?" he asked. "I think so, Major," replied Edward. "Do you see it, Curtis?" Edward asked. "Yes," said Curtis, "you're right, it's a Fire dragon."

"A Fire dragon! Where?" exclaimed Gerald. "Relax, Major. He's almost directly overhead, ducking in and out of the clouds, using them for cover. I think he's just following us. If he meant to attack us, he'd have done it by now," said Edward. "I don't see anything," said Gerald. "I think that's the point; he's so high in the air, we can only see him by using a Sight enhancement spell."

"So, what do you think it means?" asked Gerald. Edward sighed, "It means we're being followed again, not with a Tracer spell like last time, but by a high-flying dragon. I never would have noticed him except for a break in the clouds. Of course, I've been looking around with the Sight enhancement since we left Kingston." "Why is that?" asked Major Gerald.

"Sir, Minister Jasmine seemed a little too eager to send us, specifically us, out on a punitive expedition, with no real evidence that the King of Baize is behind these dragon attacks," said Edward. Gerald sighed, "First Victor, now the Minister of Internal Security? Couldn't you smoke her out?" "No. She's been choosing her words very carefully around me lately and wearing heavy perfume to mask her scent. Without proof, the King would never believe me. I'm not sure he's totally convinced that Victor was a dragon. Accusing Minister Jasmine, without solid evidence, would have been too much for him." "You're saying we're walking into a trap," said Gerald.

"I'm afraid so, Major. Still, Jasmine doesn't know about the extra crossbows or the concealment cloaks," said Edward thoughtfully. "So, what do you think their plan is?" asked Gerald. "If I was behind it, I'd find a good spot for an ambush on the Baize side of the Amber River and attack with multiple dragons," said Edward. "Can I see your map again?"

Major Gerald took out the map and unrolled it. "See, right here, once we ford the river, the road leading to Springfield goes through this pass. Put some dragons on either side, maybe one dragon blocking the road. That's a kill box," said Edward. "So what do we do?" asked Curtis. "Well, we sure don't go in there blind," said Edward. "Maybe there's a way to get behind them and sneak up on them. I need to think about this," said Edward, "at least we have a few days before we get there. Don't worry, I'll think of something." "I'm *so* glad you picked me to come along on this expedition," said Curtis. Major Gerald laughed, despite his concern, "Don't worry about it, Sorcerer. Wizard Edward is *sneaky*."

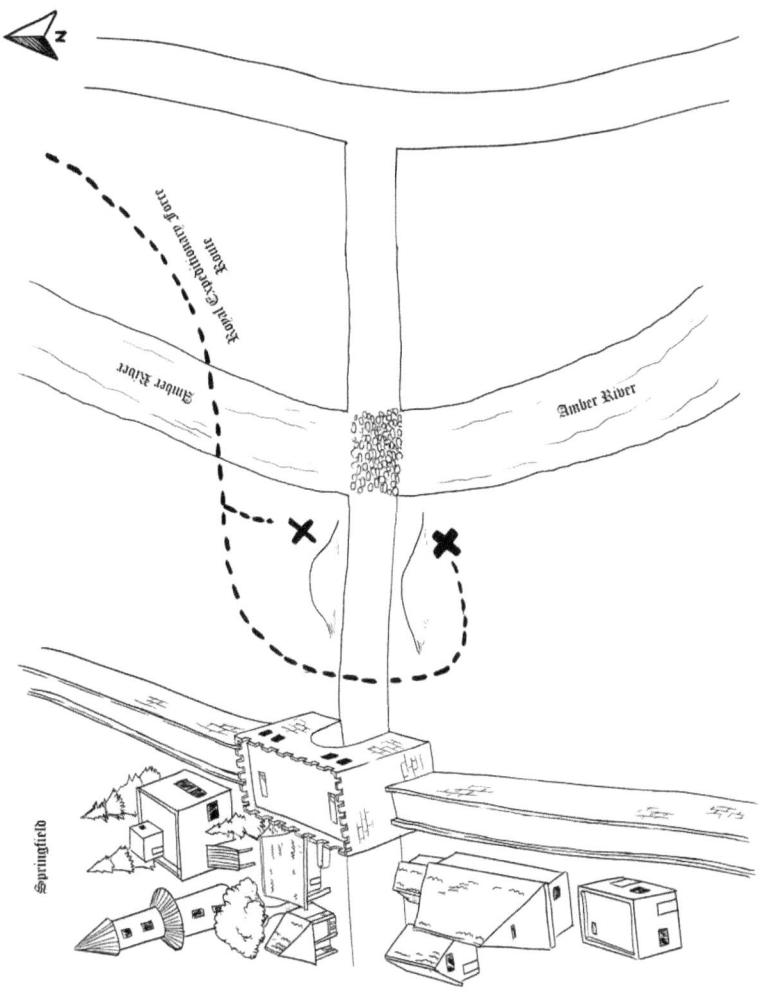

Ambush

Chapter Twenty-One:

AMBUSH!

"So, we trap them here?" asked the tall red-haired woman who called herself 'Fern.' "Yes," said Mage Arnold, "they will cross this ford here," he said, pointing to the map, "then proceed along the road between these two hills. Once they are in the middle of this pass, you swoop down with three Fire Dragons on each side and your best fighter blocking the center of the road. They will have nowhere to run. When you have destroyed the Royal Expeditionary Force, carry as many of their bodies as you can to Springfield, destroy the city, and leave the Franconian dead behind. Our agents will blame the attack on Franconia, and with the dead bodies of their elite Expeditionary Force littering the city, the King of Baize will have all the proof he needs to attack Franconia."

"Very well," said Fern, "how will we know when the Expeditionary Force approaches?" "I have been monitoring their progress from the sky, flying too high for them to see me. They have just reached Prarrieville. Tomorrow, your team will take over tracking them. I have other preparations to make." "How many magic-users are with the force?" asked Fern. "Only two. One newly-tested Wizard and a Sorcerer, seven Fire Dragons will be more than a match for them." "I just hope the other Clans are doing their part in this war," said Fern. "The Fire Dragon Clan better not be the only one fighting, or I will have words for the Dragon Council." "I understand that the Sea Dragons are attacking human ships from both countries, and the Stone Dragons had one of their Clan killed during their attack on Weaton. The Snow Dragons are supposed to attack the humans near the Snow Fields, but I have no news of them," said Mage Arnold.

"Very well, I will return to my Clan and make preparations to exterminate the Royal Expeditionary Force of Franconia," said Fern.

"Yes, there's an old smuggler's path that winds between Prarrieville and the ford that leads to Springfield," said the Eleventh Battalion Commander, Captain Brock. "It'll cut several days off your journey to Springfield, but it's a narrow trail, just barely wide enough for your wagons. Are you sure you don't want to go the long way around? It's longer but much easier," said Captain Brock. "You know the King," said Major Gerald tiredly, "he wants us there yesterday, and he doesn't care how narrow the path is." Captain Brock laughed, "I do indeed know how the King is, well, the best of luck to you. Teach those Baizians a lesson!"

Major Gerald just waved as the Royal Expeditionary Force pulled out of Prarrieville. The smuggler's path was not hard to find, and as predicted, it was very narrow. The Expeditionary

Force wove its way through the forest along the narrow trail. In three days, they had traversed the forest, and the path widened as it led down to the shallow ford across the Amber River. Before they left the cover of the forest, Edward asked Major Gerald to stop for the night, so they could discuss their next move.

"There's still a Fire dragon circling overhead," said Edward, "but I think he's having trouble tracking us in these woods. At least he's flying a lot lower than he was before." "So, have you thought up a plan?" asked Major Gerald. "I think so," said Edward. "I recommend that tomorrow, we break cover and head for the River Road. When we get to the ford, we camp, as if we're waiting for something. We light campfires and act like we're settling in for a couple of days. Under cover of night, we leave the wagons at the ford with Sorcerer Curtis, while the rest of the Force heads north along the River Road. When we find a likely spot, I'll find a way to get the Expeditionary Force across the river, and we'll cross into Baize under full concealment. I'll use the Seeing spell, like I used in Farmdale, to locate the dragon or dragons, and then we *quietly* move in behind them. Once we're in position, Curtis makes a Seeming of the Expeditionary Force and drives the three wagons across the ford, towards the pass. He stops just outside the pass." "How will he know when we're in position?" asked Gerald. "He knows how to do the Seeing spell," said Edward, "he can watch our progress."

"Then what?" asked Curtis. "Then you take the horses out of their tracers, so they have a chance to get away from what comes next," said Edward. "Which is?" asked Major Gerald. "We attack," said Edward. "Violently. We shoot enough crossbows into the dragons at close range so that they either die or flee." "That still leaves Sorcerer Curtis alone," said Gerald. "Once we're in position, Curtis, you take cover and put the strongest shield around you that you can. How long can you hold a shield?" asked Edward. "At least three hours," said Curtis, wryly.

"I wish there was some way we could make the wagons explode," mused Edward. "Explode?" asked Gerald. "Yes. If we could load the wagons with something flammable, like lamp oil, then set it off, it might kill a dragon or two and distract them from looking for Sorcerer Curtis. The dragons will know that *someone* drove the wagons, and they're likely going to be very angry." "How will I know when to take cover?" asked Curtis. Edward thought for a moment, then said, "Put a Tracer spell on this coin and give it to me. I'll dissolve your Tracer one minute before we open fire." "Got it," said Curtis.

"Let's be clear. Your first spell is a Seeming of fifty soldiers on horseback, moving into the valley. Your second spell is the Tracer. Once I dissolve the tracer, you take cover and erect your shield. Once you hear the commotion, you don't need the Seeming anymore, but be prepared to set fire to the wagons, once we figure out what to put in them that will cause the most damage to any dragons nearby." "What makes you think I can cast two spells at once?" asked Curtis, "I'm only a Sorcerer, after all."

Edward grinned, "I know that you were scheduled to take the Mage's Test next week. I have confidence that you can do this. Once you succeed, I will appoint you 'Mage Curtis.'" "You really are sneaky," said Curtis.

They camped in the wood line and discussed what they could load into the wagons that would cause the most damage to any dragons that approached them. As the cook brought them their dinner, he overheard their conversation and said, "Sir, have you considered using flour?" "Flour?" asked Edward in surprise. "Yes, Sir Wizard," said the cook, "flour is highly flammable. A good friend of mine was severely burned when some idiot put a new barrel of flour too close to the kitchen fire. When they opened the barrel, some of the flour billowed out and wafted into the fire, and then the whole barrel kind of *exploded* in a giant fireball. My friend barely escaped with his life, but he had second and third-degree burns," said the cook sadly.

"What's your name?" asked Edward. "Corporal Fry, sir," said the cook. "Well, Corporal Fry, when we get back to Kingston, I'm going to make up the strongest Healing Serum I can for burns and give it to your friend. If that's not enough to heal him, I'll try a Healing spell. I might not be able to totally heal him, but I'll bet I can make his life a lot easier." "THANK YOU, Sir Wizard!" said the cook. "No, thank *you*, Corporal Fry. You have just given me an idea of how to kill a dragon," said Edward. "How many barrels of flour do we have with us? Curtis, how are your Replicating skills?"

The ensign they designed was close to the one for the Royal Navy but dissimilar enough for the Admiral. The Royal Navy flag was navy blue with the initials RFN in gold, surrounded by a gold circle. The new commercial ensign was black, with FS in gold in a gold circle. It was hoped that from a distance, the flags would look close enough alike to deter Sea dragon attacks. Local tailors were overwhelmed with orders for the new flags as merchant ship Captains looked for anything to spare them from the dragon attacks.

As the HMS VALOR left port and headed back to Southport with six merchant ships in convoy, the sailors could only wait and hope the ploy would work. Two days out of port, the first dragons appeared. They circled the convoy, fired a few blasts of high-pressure water, then abandoned the effort, heading back out into deeper water. The first test was a resounding success.

Kathy entered the Admiralty building and headed straight for Admiral Vandall's office. The Admiral's receptionist asked if she had an appointment. Kathy put on her most menacing face and asked, "Since when does the Assistant Court Wizard need an appointment?" Completely cowed, Charolette, the secretary, hurried into the office and informed the Admiral that a 'pushy Mage' was outside, demanding to see him immediately. The Admiral sighed and told her to show the Mage in.

The office was impressive, with a large roll-top desk and floor-to-ceiling bookshelves containing ship's logbooks, atlases, and books on Naval History. One wall was a giant map of Baize and Franconia, and it had pins marking the current location of all Baizian and Franconian Navy ships. The map also indicated the location of all ports and Naval facilities in Baize. The Admiral put on a smiling face and said, "Mage Kathy! It's good to see you again. What can the Navy do for you today?"

Kathy said pleasantly, "Thank you for seeing me without an appointment, Admiral. I know your time is precious." "I'm never too busy for you, Kathy," said the elderly Admiral with a lecherous wink. "What's on your mind?" "Well, as you may have heard, I just returned from a scouting mission in Franconia. I returned to Baize on board the KBS GULFPORT, and her Captain informed me that his ship's magician was reassigned to Fleet Headquarters in Seaside over a month ago, and no replacement has been posted. I just wondered if you were aware of this."

The Admiral's jovial mood soured instantly. "Yes, I'm aware. In fact, there are very few of our ships that still have magicians assigned to them right now." "WHAT? How did that happen?" The Admiral replied angrily, "It wasn't my idea, I assure you. I received orders from the King to remove all magicians from our ships and post them to our port facilities! Something about using them as tariff inspectors to combat the increase in the Dream Dust trade, which is becoming a problem in the Kingdom. Now I've got Sorcerers and Mages inspecting cargo shipments instead of being deployed on our ships!"

Kathy was stunned. "May I see the order?" The Admiral opened his desk and extracted an official-looking document. It was on Royal letterhead and had the King's seal, but Kathy was suspicious. She murmured *"MAGNUS"* while steepling her fingers. The words on the page flashed briefly, then rearranged themselves. The order did, in fact, highlight the King's concern about the Dream Dust trade in the Kingdom and instructed the Admiral to order Navy ships to be on the look-out for Dream Dust smugglers, plying the coastal waters, but it did *not* direct the reassignment of Naval magical support.

Kathy handed the order back to the Admiral and said, "This order was altered by magic. Here is what it originally said." The Admiral took the order from Kathy's hand and read it quickly, his face reddening as he scanned the document. "Damn it! I knew I should have questioned this order! But Wizard Louis insisted that he came straight from the palace with it. His story was that some cousin of the King's had become addicted to Dream Dust, and so the King was determined to wipe out these drug dealers. Who could have altered the order?"

Kathy hesitated; she was not prepared to accuse the Court Wizard of such a high crime without additional proof. "It all depends on who handled the order after the King sealed it. It may have been altered before Wizard Louis received it, or..." "Or Wizard Louis has some reason for wanting our ships to lack magical support," finished the Admiral.

"I'll look into this, Admiral," said Kathy, "in the meantime—" "In the meantime, I'll see to getting our magicians back on their ships!" finished the Admiral. "Exactly," replied Kathy. "Well, it's been lovely to see you, but I know you have work to do. I'll show myself out, and Admiral—" "Yes?" "I would recommend putting those magicians back on their ships *quietly,* if you get my drift. Since the order was fraudulent, you don't need anyone's permission to move them back to their rightful place. I don't want whoever altered that message to get wind of what you're doing before I unmask them." "I understand completely, Mage Kathy. I'll see to it at once."

As Kathy headed for the door, the Admiral's secretary, who had been quietly listening at the door, hurriedly resumed her post at her desk. She would need to inform Wizard Louis of these developments during her lunch break.

It was late afternoon, and the commanders huddled to plan their operation. "Before we head out, I want to see what we're up against," said Edward. "Major, can I see your map please?" Major Gerald brought out his map while Edward retrieved his truncheon from the back of his wagon. Once the map was spread out on the table, Edward held the truncheon over the map and began looking for dragons. Almost immediately, six red snakes with wings appeared on the map, three on each hill, astride the road. Then, a seventh dragon symbol appeared over the road behind them. Major Gerald whistled. Edward marked the locations on the map with ink, so that when he released the Seeing spell, the locations would remain.

"This one," said Edward, pointing to the one that was behind the force, "is the one flying over us. I expect he'll take position in the middle of the road once we enter the pass. When we stop to confront the one in the road, the other six will attack from both sides. We'll need one company on each hill," said Edward, "that's one squad per dragon. Major Gerald, if you and the two Senior Specialists accompany me, we'll take the dragon that stops in the road." "One problem," said Curtis, "How will I track your progress? I have a map, but I don't have a truncheon yet." Edward smiled, "Simple, you may borrow mine."

The Royal Expeditionary Force left the forest and proceeded along the smuggler's path to the River Road and turned north, headed for the ford. Once they reached it, they halted and set up camp, making sure to light enough campfires to convince anyone watching that the force had settled in for the night. When it was fully dark, with just a sliver of a crescent moon, the force put on their concealment cloaks and quietly moved north along the river, leaving the three wagons and Sorcerer Curtis behind. "Remember to keep the Seeming in motion," Edward reminded

Curtis. "The dragon shadowing us from the sky will be watching. Hopefully, by daybreak, we'll be far enough upriver that the dragon will be focused on the Seeming and not detect us. We'll conceal ourselves during the day tomorrow, then cross the river at dusk and be well into Baize before sunrise the day after tomorrow. I hope to attack before noon the day after tomorrow."

The Expeditionary Force rode north at a fast pace for three hours as Edward scanned the river for a likely place for them to cross. When they came to a spot where the river widened and was much shallower, Edward called a halt. "We'll cross here, Major," said Edward. "That's a pretty wide span, Sir Wizard. How do you propose we get across?" asked Gerald. "I'm going to dig a deep trench just upriver, then create a sand bar across the river right here. We'll have to move quickly before the river washes away the sand, but I think it'll work," explained Edward. "I saw a large barn, a short way back along the road where we can take cover for the day and rest up. Once we cross this river, we need to move rapidly if we hope to catch the dragons by surprise."

"I like it," said Major Gerald, "Captain Fletcher, ride back and wake up the farmer. Inform him that we'll be spending the day in his barn. He'll be compensated for his trouble. Remember to take off your cloak before you speak to him. Hurry now, before the sun rises." Captain Fletcher moved off at a gallop, and the rest of the Expeditionary Force followed behind. They reached the barn just as the sun was cresting the eastern horizon.

As the troops were getting settled in the barn, Captain Fletcher introduced the farmer to Major Gerald. "Sir, this is Mister Rice, Mister Rice, Major Gerald." "Pleased ta meet cha," said Major Gerald. "I hope we aren't too much of an inconvenience." "No, at least not this time of year," said the farmer, "all the crops have already been taken in and shipped downriver to Weaton. Don't know what I'll be able to get for 'em, though. Terrible what happened." "Yes," said Gerald, "that's why the King sent us, to patrol the River Road between Colton and Weaton. We just need to rest here today, and we'll be off at dusk."

"Night patrols, eh?" asked the farmer. "That's when most of the thieves and smugglers are about," said Major Gerald. "I can't argue with that, Major. Now your Captain said something about compensation?" said the farmer hopefully. "Here," said Edward, handing over five gold coins, "and for that much, I expect some good, hot food for the men included."

The farmer gasped at the unexpected windfall. "Yes, Sir, I'll put on the kettles for some hot tea, and we'll cook up some ham and eggs for the troops. Be back in a jiffy!" The farmer raced off to the farmhouse to rouse the inhabitants and get them working on breakfast for the soldiers. "You didn't have to do that," said Gerald, "but the men will surely appreciate it."

For his part, the day was uneventful for Sorcerer Curtis. Maintaining a Seeming, even one this big, only took a manageable amount of power. He moved about the campsite, checking the horses and wagons, keeping the campfires burning, and watching the dragon circling high overhead. Around mid-day, he ducked inside Edward's wagon and scanned the map. He found the Expeditionary Force about three hours north along the River Road. The dragons had not moved from their previous positions. He wondered how Edward was planning to get the Expeditionary Force across the river. *I suppose he could dig a tunnel under the river, or maybe he could enlarge a fallen tree to span the gap,* thought Curtis. Either of those spells would take a lot of power and effort, and he doubted that Edward wanted to enter a battle with seven Fire dragons already fatigued. *I'll ask him later,* he thought.

As night fell, the Expeditionary Force left the cover of the barn and headed back to the spot on the river that Edward had identified earlier. Edward gathered the Officers and Squad Leaders and explained what was about to happen. "I'm going to go fifty yards upstream and dig a deep trench in the riverbed from this side of the river to the other side. I'm going to take the sand and silt from the trench and place it here," he said, pointing to the river right in front of them. "The river is going to flow into the trench rapidly, but the water on this side of the trench should be quite shallow, especially with all the sand I'm going to deposit here. When you see the sand stop rising, gallop across as fast as you can. The river will fill the trench and wash away the sand bar in a matter of minutes," explained Edward.

"How will you get across?" asked Gerald. "See that tree on the other side of the river? I'm going to put a tether on it, then jump into the river; the current will push me to the far side." "If you say so," said Major Gerald skeptically. "Trust me, I've done this before," Edward assured him. "Someone will need to lead my horse across and bring him to me when I reach the other side." "I'll handle it," said Corporal Fry. Edward nodded his thanks, dismounted, and handed the reins to the Corporal. He moved upriver and prepared himself.

"ENTRENCHO, SILICA" said Edward while making the scooping gesture, using his whole arm, and reaching as far as he could, then turning his hand upside down in the direction of the waiting soldiers. The river became a waterfall, as it poured into the newly-dug trench in the riverbed; the water on the other side lowered to a trickle and lapped against the side of the sandbar; the soldiers galloped across the temporarily blocked river. Just as the last trooper reached the other side, the trench filled, and the river resumed its course, washing away the sandbar as if it had never been there.

Wasting no time, Edward braced himself for the shock of the cold water, cast his Tether spell, and leaped into the river. Edward was buffeted and battered on his journey across the river, but he emerged on the far bank unscathed. He quickly dried himself with a warm Wind spell and was waiting calmly and dry, when Corporal Fry reached him with his mount.

Sorcerer Curtis sat back in amazement. One minute, the Expeditionary Force was on the east side of the Amber River. He got up to stir the embers of the campfire and looked back at the map, and suddenly, the entire Force was across the river and riding west at a rapid pace. *How in the world did he do that?* wondered Curtis. *I guess that's why he's a Wizard, and I'm just a Sorcerer.* Throughout the night, he tracked the progress of the Expeditionary Force and the dragons.

By dawn, the Expeditionary Force was closing on their attack positions behind the dragons. Curtis walked around the camp, extinguishing the campfires and making preparations to head for the ford. Once the sun was fully in the sky, Curtis connected the three wagons together with rope, removed the canvas covers from the wagons, took the lids off the barrels of flour, and headed towards the ford. Controlling a Seeming this large and complex, while moving was a challenge, and Curtis noted that occasionally, a simulated soldier rode through a tree or a bush; he hoped that the dragons didn't notice. Just before he entered the pass between the two rocky hills, he stopped, slipped out of the wagon, unhooked the horses from their traces, and looked around for a suitable place to seek cover. He found a cluster of boulders about thirty feet from the wagons that looked promising. He quickly positioned himself between the rocks.

When he checked the map, he found that the seventh dragon was now on the road just beyond the narrowest section of the pass. He had only been behind the boulders for a short time before his Tracer spell on the coin vanished. It was time.

As Kathy left the Admiralty building, she wondered if the Royal Guard had also received any altered orders recently. This conspiracy might involve more than just the Navy. She walked across the open parade ground and into the Army Headquarters building. Admiral Vandall's secretary watched her covertly from the window.

This time, Kathy was much more congenial as she approached Wizard James' office. His assistant, Mage Juliet, was sitting at her desk outside the door. "Good morning, Juliet. How are things today?" "As well as can be expected for a Firstday, I suppose," replied the attractive brunette. "What brings you by?" "If Wizard James has a minute, I need to discuss something with him," said Kathy.

Juliet checked the Chief of Army Wizardry's calendar, and said, "He has a meeting with the First Regimental Commander in about a glass, but he should be free now if you keep it brief."

"That would be wonderful! Thank you, Juliet," said Kathy, cheerfully. Juliet rose from her desk and knocked softly on the door, "Wizard James, Mage Kathy from the palace is here. She would like a brief word if you're available." Wizard James opened the door and said, "Kathy! It's good to see you. How was your mission to Franconia?"

"The mission was eventful, Sir. That's one of the things I wanted to talk to you about." "Come in, come in," said James, ushering her into the office. "Juliet, would you be a dear and bring us some tea? Thanks. So, Kathy, what's on your mind?"

Kathy related the results of her mission in Franconia and the troubling news she learned from the Admiral. "So, I was just wondering, Sir, has the Army received any questionable orders, directing the movement of our magicians?"

James looked troubled. "General Diaz and I were just discussing this very matter yesterday. It seems that he received an order last month directing our senior magicians to reinforce the magicians in Middleberg, Forkville, and Lakeshore. Something about stopping the drug trade. The General has been delaying the enforcement of those orders, but the King is most insistent that they be carried out immediately. Frankly, I don't understand it. Besides, any redeployment of magical support should have come through me, not the General."

"The order the Admiral received had been altered by magic. Have you had the opportunity to examine it yourself?" asked Kathy. "Now that you mention it, no. How about we hop over to the General's office and take a look?" Kathy was very relieved that Wizard James was taking her concerns seriously. Previously, he had been rather aloof and stand-offish. Just then, Juliet arrived with the tea. "Rats!" said James, "I forgot about the tea. Juliet, could you go ask General Diaz if he has a moment to join us? Ask him to bring that order we were discussing yesterday. Then fetch two more teacups, and you join us as well." Juliet rushed to do James' bidding.

"Juliet is a most effective secretary," said James. Not knowing the correct reply and not wanting to point out that using

341

a Mage as a secretary seemed to her to be a waste of magical ability, Kathy remained silent. A few minutes later, General Diaz entered, carrying a small valise with a sheaf of papers inside. Juliet arrived a moment later with the additional tea. The three magicians and the General moved to the conference table, and General Diaz handed James the Movement Order.

James scanned it briefly, then performed the Detect Magic spell that Kathy had used in the Admiralty. This order similarly flashed briefly before the words rearranged themselves. The order now instructed the General to advise the magicians assigned to the Army to be on the lookout for the contraband drug, 'Dream Dust,' among his troops. The order stated that this narcotic was extremely addictive, and its use was cause for immediate expulsion from the Royal Guard.

General Diaz reacted much the same way as Admiral Vandall had. "I'm really glad I never issued that order," he said. "Indeed. It seems as if someone is trying to remove the magical support from our armed forces," mused James. "To what end?" asked the General. "I suspect it has something to do with the dragon attacks," said Kathy, speaking for the first time. "No offense, General, but my investigation in Franconia revealed that ordinary soldiers, even the bravest, have little chance of defeating a dragon without magical support."

"You're probably right," said James. "It might be a good thing that we didn't have any troops in Riverside. They would most likely have been slaughtered just like the citizens." "So, what do you recommend?" asked General Diaz. "We should probably examine all of the recent orders from the palace, just to be sure that more of them have not been altered," said Mage Juliet. "An excellent idea, Juliet," said James, "General, have there been any other orders that you found strange lately?"

The General thought for a moment, then said, "Just the order moving the entire Regiment out of Springfield. I thought the King only wanted to move two Battalions, one to Westport and one to Colton, but the order moved everyone out of Springfield." "Do you have the order?" asked Kathy. "No," said the General. "I received instructions that the order was to be burned after I read it. Something about it being 'classified.'" "That's very suspicious," said James. "I agree, but at the time, I thought nothing of it. The order was sealed with the King's signet and witnessed by the Court Wizard.

"I think the Court Wizard has inserted himself into military matters far too much lately. I suggest we remove him from the distribution list of all military orders and communications until further notice," suggested James. "I concur," said the General.

"They have changed their flags," said Gek. "Now, every ship looks like a Navy vessel!" "Huh, I wonder why they did that," said Bruce. "That doesn't make any sense; Franconia has flown the same ensign for as long as I can remember. Merchant ships are prohibited from flying the Navy flag, and any ship caught doing so is confiscated by the crown."

Gek and Azure were back in Bruce's hut, commiserating on this unfortunate turn of events. "Is there any other way to tell Navy ships from traders?" Azure asked Bruce. "Let me think…Well, if you could get close enough, you could tell by the ship's *name*," he said. "I do not understand," said Gek. "How will a name tell us which ships have magic-users on board and which don't?" "Well," explained Bruce, "It's not so much the name of the ship; it's what's in front of it."

"In front of the ship?" asked Azure. "No. In front of the ship's name. You see, all Navy ships have 'HMS' in front of their name," said Bruce. "HMS?" asked Gek, confused. "It stands for His Majesty's Ship—HMS," said Bruce. "A merchant ship would have 'FS' for 'Franconian Ship' in front of its name." "What about ships from Baize?" asked Azure, "do they have 'BS' in front of their names?" Bruce laughed, "No, it's 'KBS' for 'Kingdom of Baize Ship'"

"That is very helpful," said Gek, "thank you." "Always glad to help a Sea dragon," said Bruce, "as long as it's just to help you avoid magicians. I wouldn't want to learn that you had any *nefarious* motives. You see, I used to have a lot of friends who were sailors. Well, I got to get supper goin.' You two make yourselves at home." Bruce went into the kitchen and started preparing the evening meal. "I really hope we do not have to kill Bruce," said Gek softly.

Curtis released the Seeming, and in seconds, what had appeared to be a bustling column of soldiers, resolved itself into three seemingly empty wagons and three horses, grazing by the side of the road. He raised the strongest shield he could and waited for the storm.

He didn't have long to wait; he was too far away to hear the twang of crossbows, but he heard the roar of dragons. From his position among the boulders, it seemed like four of the dragons had been killed outright, and the other three were badly wounded. One spun around on the mountain, spewing fire, looking for whoever had snuck up behind it and attacked. He just couldn't see anyone. A second volley of crossbow fire and the wounded dragon lay dead.

The other two dragons took flight, attempting to escape the deadly crossbow bolts; they both headed for the wagons, intent on exacting some vengeance on the humans. Curtis noted that both dragons were a brilliant scarlet red and that both had multiple crossbow bolts sticking out of their heads and torsos. As the dragons approached the wagons, Curtis sent a gust of wind towards the wagons, and a white cloud of flour, like fog, billowed out from all three wagons. Heedless of the fog, the two dragons launched flaming inferno at the wagons, freeing Curtis from having to ignite the flour with a Fire spell. When the flour ignited, the resulting fireball engulfed both dragons, searing their nostrils, burning their lungs, and charring their wings to ash. The dragons collided with one another, and both collapsed on top of the burning wagons. Curtis' shield barely deflected the enormous fireball; he was thrown to the ground, the ash and smoke choking him for an instant. When he arose, all that remained was three burning wagons and two dragon carcasses. *That's some serious flour power,* he thought.

Chapter Twenty-Two:
DIPLOMACY

Donovan lifted the boulder out of the roadway and tossed it into the canyon below. This was another one of those 'chores for the crown,' clearing the road of a rockslide. The Strength enhancement spell made the job much easier, as long as you didn't overdo it by trying to lift too heavy a boulder; and you had to remember to lift with your legs, not your back. As he threw the last few rocks over the side of the embankment, he saw Terry approaching, looking very serious. Donovan immediately worried for his father. He'd been gone a while now, and Donovan was sure that the Royal Expeditionary Force had not been sent out on a public relations tour.

Terry stopped in front of Donovan, pulled out a scroll, and read:

"Level Two Donovan Francis, you are hereby officially notified that on Endday morning, you will be tested for advancement to Level Three. You will present yourself at the Lecture Hall, one hour after the first bell." Signed, Noland, Headmaster, Franconia Wizards Academy.

"Easy, boy, you'll be fine," said Edward soothingly. *"SANNA,"* he murmured while holding his left hand over the wound. While Edward's horse, Enduro, had survived the explosion of the wagons, his left hind quarter had been burned in the conflagration. Unfortunately, the other two horses had not survived. Enduro quieted, and the burned patch faded away. The horse nosed Edward in appreciation.

His horse seen to; Edward turned his attention to Curtis. "So, Mage Curtis, are you injured?" "Are you serious?" asked Curtis. "About what?" asked Edward, confused. "*Mage*," said Curtis. "Do you have the authority to promote me to 'Mage'?"

"Well, *technically*, only the Headmaster of the Wizards Academy has the authority to promote a magician. However, I'm sure that Michael will endorse my recommendation without the need for any further testing of your skills. Moreover, as the senior *magical* commander of Wizard rank in a combat operation, I *do* have the authority to confer upon you a battlefield promotion. Therefore, Sorcerer Curtis Martin, for exceptional valor in combat against overwhelming enemy forces, I hereby promote you to Mage," said Edward solemnly. "Now I ask again, Mage Curtis, *are you injured*?"

"My ears are ringing, and all I can smell right now is fried dragon, but I am otherwise uninjured, Wizard Edward." "Good," said Edward, "because we've got to get to Springfield. You'll have to use my horse. Mind his left flank; it's probably still a little tender."

As they rode up the road through the pass to where the rest of the Royal Expeditionary Force was waiting. Edward explained how the attack had unfolded. "Each company of the Force took one hill. We dismounted and crept up as close as we dared behind the dragons. Would you believe they were sunning themselves on the rocks, like they didn't have a care in the world? When the dragon in charge landed on the road to block your path, the other dragons became a *little* more attentive, but not much. They were overconfident. Once Major Gerald, the two Specialists, and I got close enough behind the lead dragon, I dissolved the tracer spell on your coin. As soon as the Seeming faded, we opened fire. Four of the dragons died in the first volley of crossbows. I used a Blast spell to the back of the head of the one on the road. I'm not sure if it was the Blast spell or the three iron crossbow bolts that killed it, but it fell without a sound."

Edward continued, "Only three of the dragons survived the opening volley of crossbow bolts; two attacked the wagons, and one started flaming everything around it. We lost two soldiers from First Company, but the others were able to reload fast enough to get off a second volley and slay the dragon." As Edward concluded, they reached the waiting soldiers. "CONGRATULATIONS, MAGE CURTIS!" shouted the assembled soldiers. Curtis shook his head in embarrassment. "You told them?" "Of course!" said Edward. "Accomplishments should be celebrated!"

As they rode on toward Springfield, several of the soldiers came by to congratulate Curtis and thank him for his bravery in facing two dragons alone and emerging triumphant. When Major Gerald did the same, Curtis voiced his reservations about the legality of a battlefield promotion. "That's how I made Lieutenant," said Gerald, "and the last time we went out with Mage Edward and came back victorious, the King promoted every man in the Royal Expeditionary Force one grade. You know how often that happens?" "I have no idea," confessed Curtis. "Never. That's how often. I asked around, and no one could ever remember such a generous gesture from the King; *any* King," said Gerald. "Edward looks after the soldiers who risk their lives. You heard what he said to Corporal Fry?" "Yes," said Curtis, "it was certainly a very generous offer. A Healing Serum of that strength will likely cost him two golds." "The way I see it, that's one gold per dragon, and that's a bargain if you ask me."

As the Expeditionary Force approached Springfield, they spotted a lone figure in the center of the road, mounted on horseback, apparently waiting for them. "What do you think, Sir Wizard?" asked Gerald.

"He's a Wizard," said Edward, "I can sense that from here. What he wants is anybody's guess, but at least he isn't leading a regiment of Baizian soldiers. Let's go see what he has to say."

Edward, Gerald, and Curtis rode towards the Wizard. He made no aggressive moves, nor did he even conjure a shield. As they reined up before him, he said, "Gentlemen, I am Wizard Timothy, and I am here to surrender the city of Springfield to you."

Wizard Louis was enraged. That meddling Mage Kathy was becoming more than a mere annoyance. She was close to uncovering his involvement in the removal of magical support from the Baizian military, which he had carefully arranged to make the defeat of the humans easier for his kin. He looked at Admiral Vandal's secretary, a Fire Dragon Changed One, and said, "Char, I need you to eliminate Mage Kathy immediately. Go to her quarters this evening and tell her that you have an urgent message for her from the Admiral. When her guard is down, kill her."

"Do you want her death to appear to be accidental or a deliberate assassination?" asked Char. Wizard James considered the question. Both options had certain advantages. Finally, he said, "If you can make it look like an accident, that might be best as it will not arouse as much suspicion. A deliberate murder might cause the King to increase security in the palace, which is something we do not need." "Understood, Sir. Rest assured, she will be dead by morning."

Captain Matthews grinned as the HMS VALOR pulled up to the pier in Grotton. They had now escorted two convoys without incident, and both the merchants and the Navy were pleased. "So, Andrew," said the Captain, "it seems your suggestion is working splendidly." Andrew smiled, "Yes, Captain, at least so far." "What do you mean by that?" asked Captain Matthews.

"Sir, if the Sea dragons are really committed to attacking our shipping, they'll eventually find another way to tell Royal Navy ships from commercial vessels," said Andrew. "How could they do that?" asked the Captain. "I'm not sure. Maybe there's a difference when viewed from the air or underwater; maybe they'll learn to recognize Navy uniforms."

"I hope you're wrong," said the Captain as they disembarked and headed for the nearest tavern. As they walked along the wharf, a messenger rushed up to the Captain. "Captain Matthews?" The messenger asked. The Captain nodded, "Message from the Admiral, Sir. He wants to see you at once." "Any idea what it's about, son?" Captain Matthews asked the messenger. "If I had to guess, Sir, I'd say it's probably about the dragon attack on the port of Sundock."

Kathy was sitting in her easy chair by the open window of her tower bedroom. The evening breeze left much to be desired, and it was rather hot and stuffy in the chamber, so Kathy had availed herself of her newly acquired fan. As a magician, Kathy doubted that she would ever need to use the hidden blade in the handle, but the fan performed its customary function admirably. A knock on her door brought her to her feet, and she said, "Come in." Charolette, Admiral Vandal's secretary, hurried in, closing the door behind her. "I have an urgent message from the Admiral for you, Mage Kathy," she said.

Kathy beckoned Charolette to approach, moving to the open window in order to read the message by the light of the half-moon. Surprisingly, Charolette ran forward and attempted to push Kathy out of the open window. Shocked, Kathy held out her arms to ward off the charging secretary; her fan still clutched in her hand. As Charolette grappled with her, Kathy depressed the pearl button, and the concealed blade punched through Charolette's throat with little resistance.

Charolette crumpled to the floor, dying. Kathy leaned over her and asked, "Who sent you?" Surprisingly, Charolette merely smiled as she died.

Kathy considered her options, then said, *"DELERE,"* while flicking her right wrist at Charolette's body. The corpse instantly disappeared, leaving no evidence behind. Kathy sat down, her adrenaline still pumping. She carefully cleaned the blood off the fan blade and retracted it into the handle. *This was the best purchase I have ever made,* she thought.

"Just like that?" Asked Major Gerald, "No terms, just an unconditional surrender? Why?" The aged Wizard shook his head sadly, "Because we have been abandoned by the King," he said. "All of the soldiers were ordered out a few months ago, and I'm all that's left to defend the city from dragons and Franconians. I saw what you did to the Fire dragons that were ordered to ambush you. Any Force that can destroy seven Fire dragons in a single hour is too much for me. I only ask that you spare the city. The people are poor and hungry, and they have no hope left," said Wizard Timothy.

"We're certainly not going to slaughter unarmed civilians," said Major Gerald. "King Henry must be badly misinformed. He was told that the Kingdom of Baize was sending dragons against us, attacking our ships at sea, and was planning to invade Franconia." "We do not command the dragons," said Timothy, "the King sent all of our soldiers to other locations in the kingdom a few months ago because it was too expensive to support them so far from the Capitol."

"We had no idea," said Edward, "are things truly that desperate?" "We were never a prosperous nation," confessed Wizard Timothy, "you can't grow crops in the Great Salt Flats or the Western Desert. Without livestock for breeding and for food, we are a nation of vegetarians, who occasionally feast on fish caught in our rivers or shipped up from the coast."

They rode towards the city, the commander and the magicians followed closely by the rest of the Royal

Expeditionary Force. The city looked to have been prosperous once, with grand courtyards, and lush gardens, now overgrown with weeds. The citizens looked defeated; they rushed inside to avoid the soldiers and kept their eyes downcast. As they reined up before the City Hall, Wizard Timothy said, "Welcome to Springfield, where the only thing plentiful is despair."

"Who's in charge?" asked Edward. "The Mayor left with the last of the soldiers," said the old Wizard, "I guess I'm the only one in authority left in the city." "We need a place to stable our mounts and for our soldiers to rest. We've had a busy day," said Gerald. "Tomorrow, we'll survey the city and see what we can do to assist you."

"For conquerors, you're uncommonly kind," said Timothy, "Thank You."

Gek sat in the kitchen talking with Bruce; he really liked the old man and hated deceiving him about the intentions of the Dragon Council. Azure emerged from the back room, a strange and worried look on her face. "What is wrong?" asked Gek. "I think I am pregnant," said Azure softly.

THE END OF BOOK II

Please look for Book III, The Compassion of Enemies, *Forthcoming*

Prequel to The Compassion of Enemies

Donovan laughed as the fireball sped toward him. Assuming that this was just a Seeming, as had happened at the end of his Level One test, Donovan put only a minimal amount of power into his shield to counter the seemingly frightening but otherwise harmless illusion. The resulting blast hurled him to the ground and sent him skidding across the sandy soil of the Forces Training area. *They never made anything easy here, did they?* He rose, shaking his head, and reformed his shield for the next fireball, which was already speeding toward him.

His Level Three testing had been going on for hours, and he was nearly exhausted. It had begun with the Military History exam. Wizard Daniel had arrived at the Lecture Hall and presented Donovan with a terrain map. The map showed the area around an unidentified town. There were military symbols of an enemy force of battalion strength, arrayed to attack the town. "Donovan, I want you to depict on the map how you would deploy a Franconian Battalion to defend this town from the enemy depicted. Show where you would position our troops, the battalion commander, and the Sorcerer. When you are done with that, here is an identical map, with an enemy force positioned to defend the town. Show me how you would attack it with the same battalion," said Wizard Daniel. "You have one hour."

Donovan got right to work. Defending the town was simple. He arrayed archers on the flanks and positioned two squads of infantry in the center, with symbols indicating that they were to fall back, drawing the enemy into the area between the archers. The bottom of the 'kill box' was the remaining company of infantry, in fortified positions. Once the enemy was in the box, the Battalion's cavalry Troop would sweep around the back, completing the encirclement. The Battalion commander and the Sorcerer were positioned in the center, behind the infantry, with the Sorcerer acting as the Battalion's reserve force, ready to move to wherever he was needed.

Finished with the first map, Donovan moved to the second map; the enemy was arrayed in a three-up, one-back formation astride the road leading to the town. Three companies of infantry were positioned in a line across the road, with the cavalry company in reserve. There was no magician depicted with the enemy in either scenario. Donovan thought hard, then came up with a creative attack plan. When he was finished, he called Wizard Daniel over to grade his work.

"Your defense is a classic 'moving ambush,'" he said. How will you protect the archers from the enemy cavalry?" "The Sorcerer will use a Dig spell to create trenches in front of the archer's positions," explained Donovan. "Very good. This is a Passing answer."

"Your attack plan looks like a double envelopment, with two companies circling around to strike each enemy flank, but why is the Sorcerer alone in the middle of the road?" asked Daniel. "He is creating a Seeming of the attacking Battalion, sir," said Donovan. "If the enemy is focused on the Seeming—" "Then the real forces will be able to achieve surprise," said Daniel. "It might work, but it could cost the Sorcerer his or her life." "Sir, you told us that in war, some risks must be taken," replied Donovan. "So I did, and so they must," said Daniel. "Pass."

"Let's proceed to the Enhancements test," said Daniel. "We will start with the Sensing and Concealment spells. Please wait here for ten minutes while I head over to the Enhancements Training area, then come and find me." Wizard Daniel vanished, and the door to the Lecture Hall opened and closed. Donovan immediately began sensing where the Wizard was going. It appeared that he had stopped right outside the door of the Lecture Hall. When ten minutes was up, Donovan scooped up a pebble from the floor, walked out the door, and tossed the pebble at the concealed Wizard, saying, "Tag, you're it."

"I didn't think that was going to work," said Daniel with a smile. "Very well, now you head over to the Enhancements Training area and conceal yourself. I will give you ten minutes, then follow; if you can elude me for ten minutes, you will pass this part of the test." Donovan went immediately to the training area and considered where to hide under concealment. He finally decided to sit on the back porch of Wizard Noland's cottage. He didn't think the Headmaster would mind. He sat down, erected his concealment shield, and waited for Wizard Daniel.

A few minutes later, Daniel arrived. He roamed about the Enhancements Training area, blowing gusts of sand at various spots, trying to find Donovan. After ten minutes, he said, "All right, Donovan, you can come out now." Donovan dropped his concealment shield and walked further into the training area; Wizard Daniel shook his head at Donovan's audacity. Over the next hour, Wizard Daniel tested Donovan on his mastery of the Smell, Strength, Healing, and Stamina spells. When they were finished, Donovan asked, "How are you going to test my Secrecy spell?" Wizard Daniel smiled. "Terry, I need your assistance for this."

Sorcerer Terry, Donovan's Mentor, appeared at his side, dropping his concealment shield. "Now, Donovan, I want you to tell Terry something, then cast your Secrecy spell. I will ask Terry what you said. If he can give me the correct answer, your spell was ineffective." Donovan thought for a moment, then said, "We are having squid for lunch today." "I doubt it," Terry replied with a smile. Donovan then said, *"CONFIDO,"* and placed his right index finger against his lips. Donovan felt the power drain, so he knew the spell had been cast.

Daniel asked Terry, "What did Donovan say we are having for lunch today?" Terry replied, "I have no idea." "Pass," said Daniel, and Terry vanished again.

The next part of the testing was Serums. Donovan returned to the Lecture Hall and had to prepare Serums for Paralysis, Stamina, Truth, and Healing (major wounds) and test them all on himself (except the Healing Serum). While the test was difficult, Donovan was able to concoct all of the Serums within the required time limit. Next came the Seemings exam.

When Donovan arrived in the Seemings Training area, Wizard Mira, the very attractive Seemings and Changes instructor, said, "Donovan dear, can you please create a Seeming for me of a Royal Cavalryman, riding a white horse around the area?" This was the most difficult Seeming that Donovan had ever attempted. Creating moving Seemings was much more difficult than ones that were stationary. Creating a rider, no, a *soldier*, on horseback, moving, was challenging. Seemings usually took very little power to create because they weren't real, but this one was an exception to that general rule. When Donovan was finished, he called Wizard Mira over to inspect his work. She just smiled and told him to head over to the Forces Training area for his Martial Arts test. Donovan groaned.

As he entered the Forces Training area, Wizard Faith was waiting. "Donovan, you have already passed your Martial Arts testing, but this portion of the Level Three test is designed to tire you physically, before your Forces test. So, we can either spar for half an hour, or you can jog around the training area carrying your staff." Donovan said that he had enough practice running and that they might as well spar. "I was hoping you'd say that," said Faith, handing him his staff. "No magic," she said, indicating that this bout would not allow Seemings or other Force spells to be used. After thirty minutes of sparring with Wizard Faith, Donovan was seriously reconsidering his decision about not jogging. When the time ran out, Wizard Faith said, "That's enough, Donovan; Wizard Dylan is waiting. Good Luck."

Donovan turned and found Wizard Dylan, the Forces instructor, standing behind him. The Forces exam entailed Donovan performing the Tether, Reduce, Enlarge, Adhesive, and Sleep spells. Once all those were complete, Wizard Dylan said, "Now, it's time for me to test your protective shields, defend yourself!" Wizard Dylan began by blowing things at Donovan's shield: rocks, sand, cauldrons, and anything that wasn't nailed down in the Forces Training area was hurled at Donovan from the front, back, sides, and top. Donovan's shields held until the fireballs, which he assumed were Seemings, since the test for advancement to Level Two had culminated with Seemings of fireballs.

The first fireball had been a shock, the next two less so. Finally, three hard strikes came against his shield that Donovan never saw coming. Wizard Dylan smiled and said, "Congratulations Donovan, you have passed." "How did you cast a fireball?" asked Donovan. "I thought you told us that we could not cast fire, only ignite things at a distance." Wizard Dylan smiled and said, "I conjured a cloud of sawdust, blew it towards you with a Wind spell, and ignited it on the way." "What was that at the end?" asked Donovan, "I didn't see anything." "I cast a concealment spell over several rocks and blew them at you. I have found that a very effective technique against unprepared magicians."

Suddenly, all of Donovan's instructors and his Mentor appeared beside him. Wizard Noland unrolled a scroll and read, formally, "Level Two Donovan Francis, pending completion of your final task, you are hereby promoted to Level Three and will report to the appropriate instruction on Firstday morning. Congratulations." Wizard Nolan left as the other Wizards came forward to congratulate him.

"What do you mean, you think you are pregnant?" asked Gek. "Just what I said. I think I may be pregnant." Why?" asked Gek. Azure said, "I feel different, and something is stirring in here," she explained, rubbing her abdomen. "How could this have happened?" asked Gek, stupidly. "Gek," said Azure, "We have been rather *vigorous* in our mating, both in Dragon and human form."

"Is the baby Dragon or human?" asked Gek. "I do not know," said Azure with concern. "I have never been pregnant before. I do not know if conception occurred as Dragons or humans or if it even matters." "Who can we consult?" asked Gek. Both Azure and Gek looked at Bruce. "Don't look at me!" said Bruce. "I don't know nothin' about pregnant Changed Ones. Celeste and I were never blessed with children. It could be because we were different *species*, if you know what I mean. If it's human, you need to talk to a Midwife."

"What is a Midwife?" asked Azure. "A Midwife is someone who helps with the birthing process. She knows what to expect and has salves and potions to ease the pain. That sort of thing."

"Well, we clearly cannot ask a human Midwife for advice about a pregnant Dragon," said Gek. "What about other Changed Ones?" mused Azure. "Especially those that have had children. They must know something." "I suppose," said Gek, "Bruce, do you know any Sea Dragon Changed Ones we can ask?"

Bruce thought for a minute, then said, "Well, Celeste used to go down to Grotton every once and a while to visit a friend named Olive. I think I remember her saying that Olive and her husband were both Changed Ones, and they had two human children. She should be able to advise you," "How far away is Grotton?" asked Gek. "Well, it would take about two weeks walking, one day swimming as a Sea dragon, or a couple of hours flying," said Bruce. "It's the next big city along the coast; you can't miss it."

"I wonder if changing form is harmful to the baby," wondered Azure, "we know so little." "How about if we split up?" asked Gek. "I can fly down to Grotton, consult with Olive, and be back in a couple of days. If we both go, it will mean at least two transformations: into Dragons here, then back into humans in Grotton, then maybe back to Dragons to return."

"I do not think we should risk it," said Azure. "I hate splitting up, but it is certainly the safest thing to do." "I agree," said Gek. "So, Bruce, how do I find Olive?"

"So, how are we doing, Timothy?" asked Wizard Edward. "I would say that you're doing better than we could have hoped for," said Timothy, the elderly Baizian Wizard. "The healing clinic has been a huge success, and the people are very appreciative. Your soldiers have also restored law and order, and the merchants have actually started paying their taxes again."

"That's good to hear," said Edward, "because I'm not sure how much longer we can stay." "You're not leaving?" asked Tim, shocked. "Tim, King Henry sent us here to raid your treasury, rout any Baizian forces we encountered, then return. He did not envision us occupying the city and setting up a military government. Besides, what do you think is going to happen when King Donald of Baize learns of our presence?"

"He'll probably send the Army," said Tim, "but probably not here." "What?" asked Edward. "If I was the King, I'd send the Army to Westport. Springfield's too far away. Besides, all of our trade goods have to be shipped down the Amber River. It's too far to send them overland—too expensive. The traders would never make a profit. When do you think you'll have to leave?" "I'll talk to Major Gerald about it, but we can probably only stay about another week," said Edward. "I should probably head over and let what's left of the city council know, so we can start preparing for your departure," said Tim.

Edward left the vacant Mayor's office and walked over to the garrison commander's office that Major Gerald was using. He noted the guard outside the door. "Good morning, Major. How are things today?" "As well as can be expected," said Gerald, the commander of the Franconian Royal Expeditionary Force. "I was just wondering when you thought we'll have to be heading back to Kingston," said Edward. "I've been thinking about that m'self," replied Gerald. "We can't stay too much longer; the King'll be expectin' us back before too long. He's probably already wonderin' what's takin' us so long."

"I had the same thought," said Edward. "It's a shame, really; we just got this town back to some kind of order. However, I'm sure King Donald will be none too happy when he learns we're here." "You got that right!" said Gerald. "This city has some defenses, but we could never stand up against a large force for very long, even with a Wizard and a Battle Mage." "Tim thinks that the King will send his forces to Westport, rather than here," said Edward.

"He's probably right. There would be no point in sending the Baizian Army all the way out here. All the trade goods have to come from or be sent to Westport or Weaton along the river, and Weaton is still recoverin' from the dragon attack."

"I wish we could be of more help to these people," said Edward, "but you're right, we don't want to get into a fight with the Baizian Army," mused Edward. "You know, I wonder if that's the dragon's plan: provoke us into fighting each other, then attack when we are weakened." Gerald whistled. "That's a complicated plan, Sir Wizard. Are you sure that a bunch of ignorant beasts could come up with it?" "I'm sure that Victor could, and it sounds just like something he would do. Even though he's dead, they could still be following his plan, and I'm not so sure that dragons are as ignorant as you think they are. That ambush they set up for us was pretty slick."

"You're right about that. I'm just not sure what we can do." "What if Timothy and I went to King Donald and tried to convince him about the need for our two countries not to go to war?" asked Edward. "We would have to divulge what we know about dragons, and he may take some convincing, but I think it's worth the risk." "You may be right," said Gerald. "So, what do you recommend?"

"How about this: Wizard Timothy and I head to Baize; you leave First company here, with Mage Curtis, and take Second company back to Kingston and report to the King. It would leave you without any magical support, though." Major Gerald laughed, "Before I met you, we *never* had any magical support, and we frequently split the companies to perform multiple operations simultaneously. I like it." "I'll talk to Wizard Timothy and brief him about what we know about dragons." "OK," said Gerald, "I'll let Second Company know that we'll be leaving in about a week and have them start getting' ready."

Edward walked over and found Tim in the Mayor's office. "I just talked to Major Gerald, and we have a plan," Edward told Timothy about the dragons, how they could understand human speech, conjure magic spells, and transform into humans. He also told him about his belief that the dragon's plan was for

Baize and Franconia to fight each other, weakening both kingdoms before the dragons attacked. Timothy was shocked by the news but said, "You know, I'll bet the former Mayor was one of those 'Changed Ones' you mentioned. He made some damn stupid decisions over the last few years, some that no one could understand."

"You said he left with the last of the soldiers?" asked Edward. "Yes. Mayor Slate took off with the last battalion, probably taking most of the treasury with him. He claimed he was going to the King to ask him to reconsider removing all the forces from Springfield," said Tim. "Wait, the Mayor's last name was 'Slate'?" "That's right, Aldon Slate. Why is that significant?" asked Tim. "It could be," replied Edward, "All of the Stone dragons we discovered had last names that were types of rock. It could be just a coincidence, though."

"Stone dragons?"

"Yes. There are five kinds of dragons: Great dragons, which are gold in color; Sea dragons, which are blue or green; Stone dragons, which are gray or black; Snow Dragons, which are light grey or white; and Fire dragons, like the ones we fought in the pass, that are red." "I had no idea. I thought all dragons were red," said Tim. "According to our cooperating Changed Ones, there should only be Fire and Stone dragons on the west side of the Amber River, although, I expect the Snow dragons don't care much about river boundaries, since they live exclusively in the Snow Fields," said Edward.

"Well, this has been an interesting morning," said Tim, "I'd best go let the council know about the new plan and start getting ready for our journey." Just then, Major Gerald walked in. "Good morning, Wizard Timothy. I guess Wizard Edward has told you our plans?" "Yes, sir, and I appreciate your leaving some troops here along with Mage Curtis. Without me, there would be no one to offer healing to the citizens of Springfield," said Timothy.

"Is there anything else we can do before we leave?" "No, there is one thing I should mention," said Tim. "Several of our, let's just say, more *ruthless* merchants have all suffered fatal accidents in the last two weeks." "Really?" asked Edward, feigning concern. "Have you investigated? "I have. It seems that one fellow fell down a flight of steps and broke his neck, another drowned, two had heart attacks, and one was thrown and trampled by his horse."

"Are there usually so many accidents in Springfield?" asked Edward. "We have our share, but they usually happen to folks in the lower or middle-class. It's seldom that someone of wealth has such an accident," said Tim. "Would you like me to look into it?" asked Edward. "We certainly want Springfield to be safe." "No need, sir Edward, I just thought I'd mention it." Timothy left the office smiling slightly.

"Did we get them all?" Edward asked the seemingly empty corner of the room. Lance and Dirk both lowered the hoods of their concealment cloaks. "I think so, sir," said Lance, "there is one more person we're keeping an eye on. She's the owner of the Fielder's Choice Tavern. We think she is drugging the ales of her customers, then arranging for them to be robbed when they stagger out. We have *interrupted* several such attempts lately."

"Hmm," said Edward. "Here's what I want you to do. Both of you go visit her tonight, with your cloaks on. Once she is alone, drop your concealment and let her know your suspicions and what will happen to her if another customer gets anything *extra* in his or her ale. Then disappear again." Both Senior Specialists laughed, "That we can do, sir! With pleasure." The Specialists departed, and Edward addressed Major Gerald, "How are the troops doing with keeping the peace? I know they are not trained as Enforcers."

"They're good men, and they know right from wrong. Your idea about having some of the troops wear their concealment cloaks was genius. It saved a couple of 'em from bein' jumped. I think all the local crooks have learned not to mess with my troops," said Gerald with a smile. "I wonder," said Edward. "You have that look," said Gerald, "what now?" "I was just thinking how useful it would be if I had a Specialist along with me when Tim and I go to visit King Donald. If I need to sneak into his bed chamber to deliver my message, having Lance or Dirk with me could be very useful."

"If you want, you can take them both," said Gerald. "No," said Edward, "I'm already leaving you without any magical support; I'm not taking your Specialist, too. You may need him. If Dirk comes with me, then Corporal Knox, his apprentice, can remain here with First Company, and Specialist Lance can go with you and Second Company. Would that work?" "Certainly," said Gerald. "Let me just go and tell them." "No need," said Edward, speaking to the empty corner, "Corporal, go let Specialist Dirk know that he will be accompanying Wizard Timothy and me to Baize." Corporal Knox lowered the hood of his concealment cloak, grinned slyly, and headed out of the office.

"Those three are going to be the death of me," said Major Gerald. Edward laughed and said, "Before you go, I have another message for you to deliver to Wizard Noland for me."

"Of course," said Gerald. Edward handed over a piece of parchment that read:

<u>Serum Supplies</u>

Juniper

Anise

Sunflower seeds

Mint Leaves

Ivory

Nightshade

Eggplant

Oregano

Nutmeg

Yarrow

Xiao Mi La Pepper